A Ribbon of Sand

A Ribbon of Sand

a novel

Mike Shannon

Paperback First Edition   ISBN 13: 978-1-956872-15-6
AMIKA PRESS   466 Central AVE #23 Northfield IL 60093   847 920 8084
info@amikapress.com   Available for purchase on amikapress.com

Edited by Ruth Hull Chatlien and Jay Amberg. Cover art by Julie Shannon.

Designed & typeset by Sarah Koz. Set in Farnham, designed by Christian Schwartz in 2004. Titles in Zigarre, designed by Jim Rimmer in 2006. Thanks to Nathan Matteson.

To my parents,
Joe and Nancy Shannon—
we'll meet again

The girl was dying, and she knew it. Strange. Even with the grisly wounds inflicted on her, all she could feel was the warmth of the sun. Her eyes followed an osprey flying free in the darkening sky.

As far back as her memory stretched, she had daydreamed, and even as her breathing grew shallow, she fell into a reverie. All the cruelty and indignity the man she knew as her master had inflicted on her couldn't destroy her love for the island she had always called home. She could escape in her mind into the forest, gliding like a bird over the trees and ocean, far out of reach. It was where she was free to nourish her imagination, far from the relentless work and the brutality of her daily life.

The end was coming, like the onset of one of her daydreams. Yet, in her heart, she knew a part of her would remain as another aspect of the island she loved, the secret island that belonged to no one. A place that would long outlive the wickedness and hatred she knew so well.

She was gone.

1

Astride my twelve-speed Fuji, I headed to my friend Carlo's house by taking the back roads of Sheltered Harbour. Whenever possible, I avoided the direct route, utilizing a maze of concealed pathways as shortcuts between the residential cul-de-sacs and single-lane roads dotting the southern end of Leggatts, the island I called home. Flat and marshy, Leggatts is much like the other hundred-plus Sea Islands that line the coasts of South Carolina, Georgia, and Florida. Often referred to as the first line of defense against storms and hurricanes that regularly pound the region, they provide a buffer between the Atlantic and the mainland. This stretch of South Carolina is known as the Low Country.

The Sea Islands were first occupied, seasonally, by Native American tribes: the Chicora, Kiawah, Catawba, Cusabo, Creek, and Yamasee, among many others. These tribes hunted and fished the forests, lagoons, and shores until these islands became important to settlers from across the ocean. Industry and defense of this newly acquired territory became of paramount importance, leading to the assimilation or destruction of the native peoples. The bedrock of the new industry of labor-intensive cotton plantations was slaves. By the late 18th century, what is referred to as long-staple cotton was developed on these Sea Islands, and soon slaveholding planters had amassed fortunes on what pro-secessionists termed "King Cotton."

The Sunday morning mid-April breeze enveloped me in warmth

without the humidity that would join it by early afternoon. Never as free and wild as a Saturday breeze, the Sunday breeze felt threaded with mild caution, holding me back ever so slightly as if trying to lessen the impact of the coming school week. Monday lurked just a sunrise away.

My bike shot out from a hidden path between oleander bushes, tires spitting sand as I turned sharply onto Nighthawk Road, a newer street lined with houses that dwarfed the traditional one-story stucco homes. The families living there were recent island transplants, and with new residents also came new ideas that rubbed uneasily with "the old ways." Like the rest of Leggatts, fishing, shrimping, and farming had fueled Sheltered Harbour's economy for generations. Unlike the pragmatic mindset most long-time islanders held, not dissimilar to the tans that darkened their skin, this new blood brought in a love of golf, houses with huge decks, vast windows, and skylights, along with cars that cost more than most natives had in their life insurance policies.

Pedaling down Nighthawk, I glanced to my left out over Mungen Cove and the wide marsh surrounding it. Dark rain clouds were moving in fast. A few fat drops of rain splatted onto my forehead, and just when I had convinced myself that I could stay one step ahead, a wind-lashed thunderstorm engulfed me. Finally reaching the driveway in front of Carlo's house, I dismounted my bike, balancing on one pedal as I coasted up to the front door. His mom, watering the large potted plants in the foyer, saw me through the wide bay window.

"Come on in, Ash," Mrs. Spinetta chirped.

Carlo's mom always wore a smile. To have a classmate of her son's show up at their house wanting only his friendship seemed to make her truly happy. I had sensed this in her expression when I once caught her eyes settling warmly on Carlo as he and I were sipping Cokes, zoning out to a movie in the living room. Carlo was my best friend and, like me, had trouble fitting in at school.

I stood inside the door, quite soaked, as Carlo appeared at the top of the short staircase leading to the house's upper two levels. Chuckling, he threw his arms out before him. "Get a little wet?"

Shaking my head like a dog drying itself, I feigned an ashamed voice, "Naw, I just sweat too much. Why d'ya always have to bring up my embarrassing condition?"

It would have taken more than a bit of water to dampen my good spirits that day because Carlo and I were going over to the abandoned lighthouse on Declaration Island. The trip was far from ordinary because the island could be reached only by a land bridge at low tide. My discovery of the place had given me somewhere to escape, be alone, daydream, and do things I shouldn't be doing, like smoking cigarettes and a bit of grass. Declaration was avoided by most locals. Concerned parents insisted that their children avoid the dilapidated buildings, most prominent among them the lighthouse, at all costs. The skeletal framework tower of cast iron, ninety-five feet high, was an adult's nightmare. Parents imagined morbid scenarios in which the 112 steps leading to the cypress watch room were booby traps that led to everything from broken bones to death. If visitors reached the top, they found two rickety galleries to tumble from. I always found the galleries solid and completely stable, but adults hinted at other more mysterious reasons I had yet to uncover. While we waited for the showers to pass, Carlo led me into the living room, where we sat for a few minutes drinking Coke and watching a George Carlin stand-up special on HBO.

Our first stop was the General Store in Sheltered Harbour to pick up water and some chicken necks, as we hoped to do some crabbing. I had equipped the rear of my bike with a cargo rack that allowed me to attach a small styrofoam cooler for any crabs we might catch. Inside it, I had stored a couple of ring nets. By securing a chicken neck in the center of the circular net and letting it lay flat on the sea floor, we only needed to pull up the strings attached to the metal ring holding the net to trap any crabs feeding on the neck. Carlo wore an empty backpack for whatever we picked up at the store. Although his frame was stocky, Carlo's broad dimpled face made him look like a three-year-old kid whenever he smiled. I was always trying to coax him to laugh, to see that smile, so at odds with his tough-guy bearing.

We had become friends almost immediately when we met a year

and a half earlier. Our bond was aided by the T-shirts we were wear-ing. In the school cafeteria at lunchtime, one's chosen uniform spoke loudly of otherwise invisible boundaries and castes. The guys who wore football jerseys talked loudly in small groups and huddled close-ly over their lunch tables before leaning back in exaggerated open-mouthed laughter and a hail of high-fives as if they had mapped out a play. At nearby tables, other guys wore khaki pants and Polo or Izod shirts, differentiated only by color: yellow, pink, red, and green, col-lars upturned, and hair parted conservatively on the side and cut to such a precise length that I often wondered if there was a secret hair fairy who made the rounds on moonless nights, cutting each head of hair with magical machine-like precision.

In this atmosphere, it was easy for me to spot the new guy with shoulder-length hair and a Riot *Fire Down Under* T-shirt, the unmis-takable band mascot, a furry white harp seal with lightning bolts as pupils staring at me. It was a shirt I knew well, having one in my col-lection. Later, Carlo would tell me that the lanky guy wearing the Black Sabbath *Heaven and Hell* T-shirt clued him in but quick, like a flare fired over the assembled throng, to the strong possibility that he had found a friend in the sea of conformity that surrounded us.

Side by side, our arms hanging free, we rode into Sheltered Harbour. Still unincorporated in the early 1980s, the town was on the cusp of receiving its charter from the state. The community consisted main-ly of one-story and two-story buildings with brown, salmon, or burnt yellow stucco façades with a few older tin-roof clapboard houses and stores. Interspersed among this traditional island architecture were a few late-twentieth-century incursions, including strip malls, fast-food restaurants, and gas stations. Like the clashing architecture, the town's population comprised a strange amalgamation of fishermen and shrimpers whose families went back generations and newer res-idents tied to the incipient tourist-driven infrastructure and economy. As we whizzed past the rehabbed tin-roof house that served as the Sheltered Harbour Real Estate offices, Carlo waved at his dad, whose balding head we saw through the sash window, hunched over his desk, talking to a couple of prospective clients. Oblivious to the greeting, Mr.

Spinetta focused on pointing out something in a brochure he held out before him.

Carlo's dad had moved his family to Leggatts a year and a half earlier from New Jersey. He'd had something to do with a big stock brokerage firm up there, but while on vacation with his family, he became engrossed with the idea of getting in on the ground floor of the budding real estate market on the island. The ever-increasing influx of tourists that locals had to contend with had opened new opportunities for ambitious outsiders. After years of relative isolation, the island suddenly had a tourist season, commonly referred to by locals as the "Northern Invasion." When crowds from primarily northern states descended, they clogged the small island roads, acting as far as locals were concerned as if they had never driven a car before, seen traffic signs, or for that matter, encountered pedestrians. I don't know how often a car with a license plate from New York or Pennsylvania turned in front of me without a blinker, nearly running me over.

Carlo's dad was right, of course. He was perceptive in sensing that the island was on a trajectory that would radically shift the established fishing and farming economy into one based mainly on recreational tourism and leisure, with houses and condominiums constructed to take advantage of the ocean and golf course views. Hotels, condos, golf courses, and ostentatious houses sprang up like fleas on a dog's itchy back. Property, mainly oceanfront lots, went for staggering sums, and Carlo's dad was already making more money as a realtor than most people on Leggatts could even dream of. The "Northern Invasion" wasn't limited to just vacationers. Once Leggatts was deemed one of the premier commercial islands of the Low Country, wealthy, primarily white developers added exponentially to well-lined pockets with resorts and property—the new King Cotton.

Hands now firmly gripping the handlebars, I swiftly edged past Carlo, hanging a left onto Merganser Drive. I could easily leave Carlo in the dust on a twisting asphalt road like this with a twelve-speed bike made for just such surfaces. Glancing over my shoulder, I caught a glimpse of him, his long black hair billowing like a flag straight out behind him. Riding his fat-wheeled Schwinn King Sting put him at a disadvantage on this flat, smooth surface. I could waste him here. Both of us pedaled furiously, Carlo instantly picking up on the challenge.

In my cracking teenage voice, I half sang, half yelled the words to "Speed King" in a poor approximation of Deep Purple's Ian Gillan.

From far behind me, I could just make out Carlo laughing. "I blew my engine, man."

At the end of Merganser, with the harbor in full view, I balanced my weight on one pedal and dismounted the still-rolling bike. Several seconds later, red-faced, sweating but smiling, Carlo pulled up alongside me as I parked my bike in the bicycle rack at the side of The General Store. The General Store, sometimes called Jemcraw's after the owner, was a one-story mustard yellow building with a stucco façade. If a photo had been taken only of "Jemcraw's," one would never guess at the rather splendid view of a horizon full of masts and nets that lay just a few short yards beyond. Originally just a modified bay, the harbor had been dredged and expanded, with many docks added to accommodate not only commercial fishing and shrimp boats but also a growing demand by new residents for recreational boats and yachts. Always overhead were seagulls that wheeled, laughed, and cried, mixing with bells from boats and buoys. The sounds etched into my mind, along with the ever-present smell of fish, fresh and decayed, wafting in on the wind.

Laughing, Carlo and I rounded the store building, loudly discussing our contenders for the best song from Iron Maiden's newly released *The Number of the Beast*. We'd had a bit of concern in our circle before the album came out, as the former lead singer, Paul Di'Anno, had just been replaced with a guy who'd been the front man in Samson. In Carlo's and my estimation, Di'Anno was the singer of choice for Maiden, bringing with him a punkish attitude and swagger. That said, the two of us instantly accepted the new guy, Bruce Dickinson, with no qualms. Our conversation quickly transformed us into two impassioned politicians in debate. Carlo's arms shot up and down like he had decided to do jumping jacks without informing his legs as he blurted in rapid-fire, staccato, "The title track is definitely the best song on the album. Dickinson's scream is from another planet, man." Before I could say anything, he added, "That or 'Hallowed Be Thy Name'...or maybe 'Run to the Hills.'"

Nodding at his choices, I answered, "'The Prisoner' is my top pick. It's got everything you want in a Maiden song—Bruce screaming like a banshee, Adrian and Dave dueling it out, Burr pummeling the drums, and Steve Harris turning his bass into a galloping horse."

"'Children of the Damned' is great too," Carlo interrupted.

Like a young Abraham Lincoln, I stood my ground, tight-lipped and stoic. "So is '22 Acacia Avenue.'"

"They're all fucking great, though," Carlo concluded, a Stephen Douglas to my Lincoln.

"I think we can agree that the whole album will go down in metal history as the classic it is." Satisfied with our choices, we nodded at each other.

As the bell over the door jingled sharply, announcing our arrival, Carlo and I cast our eyes to the floor, hating the unasked-for attention. Nudging my arm, Carlo looked me squarely in the eyes. "I'll get some water; you pick up some necks." His voice, clipped and sober as if we were on a delicate mission that needed to be expedited with precision. Nodding in agreement, I set off down an aisle towards the back of the store. By unspoken understanding, we invariably aimed to complete our shopping as quickly as possible. Bottled water was necessary, as the island's tap water was always sour with sulfur.

Under thick brows and weighted eyelids, Jemcraw's eyes watched us suspiciously. Our long hair and heavy metal T-shirts presented an affront to his deeply ingrained idea of order. The domain of long hair was reserved for females, while males were supposed to have short hair (except, of course, for the one long-haired guy in The Oak Ridge Boys). The logic at play was just a few stops down the road from gauging superiority by the pigmentation in the skin. Jemcraw's creased, meaty forehead was a visible manifestation of gravity, pushing down on the two narrow slits that were his eyes, fighting a losing battle under the constant strain.

Usually talkative and ready with an opinion or anecdote with other locals, he was always withdrawn and reticent with Carlo and me, ringing up goods without acknowledgment of our presence, looking through us as if we were semitransparent or insubstantial—but always looking. Grabbing our money coarsely and grumbling was his recognition that we did indeed exist as something more than fleeting ghosts. On the days Jemcraw was absent, the younger employees stared after us wherever we moved, their eyes mocking with a young, fresh fire, more focused, alive, and threatening than the glare of the older man.

As we exited the store, Mr. Turnbull, who ran the bait and tackle shop a few doors down, brushed past us as if we were part of the doorway. Through the sound of the tinkling bell and the squeaking of the door's rusty hinges, as it swung closed, we heard robust laughter as Jemcraw said something unintelligible to Turnbull. At once, I felt a recurring sensation of being separated from the world, caught in a paralyzing light reserved just for me. Although this light kept me from seeing beyond it, I was sure that the key to a broader understanding I knew must exist was locked in a drawer behind the counter with Jemcraw. So how would Carlo and I ever know anything more?

Patting my friend's shoulder, I safely locked away that thought with an imaginary key of my own, far away from Jemcraw's drawer. I smiled to myself, seeing an opportunity to use a line from a John Wayne film I'd watched a couple of weeks earlier. Breaking into the stereotypical Wayne accent, I leaned toward Carlo as we approached our bikes. "Slap some bacon on a biscuit, and let's go; we're burnin' daylight."

His face lighting up, Carlo let out a sharp, loud laugh. "Lead the way, partner. I need a change of scenery."

We quickly rebounded from the shop's suffocating atmosphere, stowing the water in the backpack and the chicken necks in the cooler. Lifting his bike, Carlo swung it around and dropped it roughly, bouncing it on its fat tires. Settled on his seat, he squinted in the now-bright sunshine. "And you know exactly how to get there?"

Momentarily standing up off my seat as we started pedaling, I glanced at him. "Sure do, but it took me a while. It wasn't until my third trip there that I caught a glimpse of the light, but there are these interlocking lagoons towards the center of the island, and I was on one side of one of 'em, and it was on the other." I smiled, "So damn close, but so far. Finally, a few weeks later, Mike and I ran into this kid named Abe, who was coming across the land bridge that connects to Declaration. He pointed across the inlet at these two huge oaks and said that between 'em was a path, something I had never noticed before, and he said to follow it."

"And you finally found it, huh?"

"Yup. The damn forest is so thick that we didn't see it until it just loomed up over us when we rounded a turn in the road."

The path that Abe had pointed out ended at what was just discernible as the remains of a blacktop road threading its way through the green and amber hues of the forest. Decades earlier, before the government decommissioned the Declaration lighthouse in the early 1930s, this road connected the lighthouse compound to a long-vanished pier on the island's west end. A single-lane track of asphalt made up of crushed oyster shells had allowed for easy transport of provisions for the lightkeepers and lamp oil for the lighthouses because, at one time, there had been two.

Mike had been my best friend three years earlier when I was twelve. From my perspective, Mike and I were destined to be buddies for life. We'd go out into the woods surrounding our houses to explore and have make-believe adventures that seemed as real to us as anything else we experienced. We created imaginary characters so woven into our friendship that we could use mannerisms and phrases particular to them as shorthand, a coded language to convey thoughts in class when we were supposed to be acting more mature.

Like a lot of kids at that age, taboo diversions intrigued us: smoking cigarettes, sampling the hard alcohol from our parent's liquor cabinets, sneaking out to engage in some light vandalism, shoplifting candy bars and comics from the Piggly Wiggly, and if we were feeling cultured, stealing horror and pulp fiction novels from a local bookstore. The diversion that trumped all others, though, was stealing cigarettes, more for the thrill of taking them than for any immediate or long-term smoking purposes because, as our boldness grew, so did our technique, which exponentially increased the volume of our ill-gotten goods.

One day Mike announced a plan that would enable us to walk out with multiple cartons instead of just a pack or two. His idea was marvelously simple, which is why it worked. We would grab a paper bag from his kitchen pantry, throw in a few rocks to make it appear as if it was full of groceries, walk into the Piggly Wiggly, and beeline directly for the cigarette aisle. While one of us acted as a lookout, the other piled cigarette cartons into the bag, and then we walked out like we were following one of our moms. On one occasion, a bagger even asked if we needed help carrying the bag out. We told him we were fine, but thanks. Because we passed for two innocent kids, we stockpiled over twenty cartons of various cigarette brands without drawing attention to ourselves.

The thing is, we grew cocky. Even though we had enough cigarettes to open a small convenience store, we decided a quick "back to the roots" mission of shoving a couple of packs into our pockets would provide an excellent afternoon's entertainment and adrenaline rush. As luck would have it, though, we were caught red-handed. Once in the tobacco aisle, I ripped open a carton. Standing back to back, Mike faced the registers while I faced the meat counter, struggling to stuff a pack into my front pocket. Looking down momentarily to finish my task, I was stunned when my eyes returned to scan the end of the aisle.

Hunched slightly forward with one hand on the packaged meat cooler and the other gripping a meat cleaver, the butcher stood staring at me, his eyes like those of a giant owl, unblinkingly fixed on his prey. The man's furrowed brow and the thin strands of hair combed over his shining head presented a strangely riveting tableau that briefly mesmerized me. Before I could alert Mike, the butcher sprang over the cooler in one surprisingly fluid movement. I grabbed Mike's arm and took off in the opposite direction just as fluidly. Glancing over my shoulder, I saw the butcher's beet-red face as he yelled at us to stop before loudly alerting the cashiers and baggers of the two little thieves in their midst. With the exits blocked, we were quickly collared, the manager called the police to rattle us further, and the police summoned our parents. It was a heck of a production, and I couldn't help but feel like a ringmaster in a bleak little circus.

"Ladies and gentlemen, children of all ages! Welcome to the smallest, and for these two guys, most embarrassing show on Earth!"

It seemed an awful lot of attention for two packs of cigarettes, but I now realize that shaming us was the point. The butcher congratulated himself more than the employees did collectively. Seeing his chest puffed out like a peacock, I could imagine the fan of feathers ruffling up proudly behind his back. In the end, Piggly Wiggly did not press charges. The store called the police merely to remind us that crime doesn't pay, but being shamed in public, paying for the two opened cartons, and enduring the riot act recitation and grounding my parents gave me were enough to make me think. I wasn't concerned with rehabilitation so much as the location of future targets and improved planning.

The worst part of being caught was the end of my friendship with Mike. I never knew what he told his parents, but I suspect I was thrown under the bus. Mike called me the day after the event and said he'd been forbidden from seeing me for six months. For a kid of twelve, six months felt like a lifetime. Mike had already left our school a year earlier for a private academy off the island. That hadn't affected our friendship, but I suspect the six-month hiatus gave his mother enough time to poison his view of me with her repeated warnings about my character. Just a few weeks after Mike and I were finally allowed to hang out again, our get-togethers suddenly and unexpectedly stopped. A mutual acquaintance awkwardly told me that Mike wanted me to know our friendship was through.

In a fundamental sense, the close friends we have while growing up are interwoven with our first mature emotions. Although quite different, these friendships are as intense as adult relationships with a significant other. From an adult perspective, I can now see how his parents thought I was a bad influence and that Mike and I were like fire and gasoline together. I suppose, in many ways, we were—but Mike's easy acceptance of their judgment always rubbed me the wrong way and made me much more cautious about making new friends. Like family, I had never considered that a friend, particularly a best friend, could discard me and go on about their life. It had been a rude and jarring wake-up call. I became a bit less open, less free, less the butter-fly my mother always lovingly called me. That was the first time in my then-short life that I became a bit jaded. A bit of the sparkle the world had held out to me had been removed.

I know that shoplifting would bother most parents; it upset mine. The difference, though, is that Mike's mom had always seemed to have a problem with me. Mike had a younger brother named Jason, and his mom would say things like, "You and Ash have to leave. Ash is too ugly and will scare Jason's friend when he comes over." I looked just like any other kid except with shaggier hair. But in the mind of Mike's mom, I had always been a bad influence. So the shoplifting fiasco—as she put it, "the most humiliating experience of my life"—was the perfect opportunity for her to hit the reset button.

I wasn't aware of it then, but as a result, I held back in my friend-ship with Carlo before I felt confident he wouldn't lead me, like a will-o'-the-wisp, from a clear path only to disappear.

Now, pedaling at speed out of Sheltered Harbour, we transferred from Merganser to a bike path that led east to the ocean. Whenever possible, we used these paths that had begun popping up to accom-modate tourists because they provided a safe alternative to single-lane roads, which were always risky. Unfortunately, construction of the bike paths had been haphazard, and few had been completed, often ending in the middle of the woods. Luckily, our path led us to the Ad-venture Inn, the only hotel on the island's southern end.

The Adventure Inn, built around 1970, didn't live up to its name, hiding as it did behind high, protective sand dunes far from the crash-ing surf.

The hotel publicly welcomed anybody, but its visitors were almost all white. On the northern end of the island—the "black side," as white locals called it—stood a one-story motel used almost exclusively by an African-American clientele. This unwritten separation extended to grocery stores. The Piggly Wiggly on the southern end was where white locals shopped, while the north end had Glover's, an independent supermarket where seeing a white face was about as likely as spotting a Low Country cougar. Even into the 1980s, these patterns persisted, although segregation was theoretically a thing of the past. Whether I was shopping with my mom at the Piggly Wiggly or visiting vacationing white friends of my parents staying at the Adventure Inn, these patterns reinforced these unspoken codes.

Leaving the bike path, I hopped off my Fuji and walked onto the soft sand pathway leading from the rear of the hotel to the beach. Carlo sped past me laughing, his King Sting's fat tires finding no resistance on the shifting surface. Once on the shoreline's hard-packed sand, he dismounted to wait for me and smiled broadly. Fishing around in the front pocket of his jeans, he withdrew a partially crumpled pack of cigarettes and a lighter. Then, resting his bike on its side, he puffed away and gestured towards me. "Who has the upper hand now?"

Finally catching up, I shook my head. "You got me beat on this shit."

Carlo took the cigarette from his mouth and flailed his arms, exclaiming, "My bike's moto-cross and yours is more Formula One." No matter what he was describing, Carlo always accentuated his words with animated gestures. If he was describing an action scene from a movie, his arms became the explosions. If he was talking about a crab that escaped his net, he held his hands to the sky, imitating a riled blue crab's claws snapping at unseen fingers just out of reach.

Before us, the vast gray beach stretched into the distance like an enormous runway; Carlo and I rode like we were going to take off at any moment. A salty breeze buffeted us from behind, energizing and encouraging us. With the tide at its lowest ebb, we rode smoothly over hard-packed sand that would be covered by several feet of foamy churning waves in a few short hours. To our left, the sweeping dunes were dotted with tufts of sea oats and beachgrass. Where the dunes ended, the forest began. Cabbage palms were peppered about loblolly and longleaf pine, sand live oaks, wax myrtle, and yaupon holly.

Before us to our right, the beach fanned out, populated with sandpipers and piping plovers darting around like miniature Keystone Cops, while ruddy turnstones, true to their name, flipped stones with their beaks to uncover sea snails. The birds far outnumbered the few people sunbathing or swimming in the surf, another reason I always preferred riding to the lighthouse along the shore. For long stretches of the ride, there was nothing but salty air blowing hard on our faces, our eyes squinting to make out the long, thin tide pools crisscrossing the vast beige flatness, appearing like rivers must when viewed from the window of an airplane.

We could avoid the outside world for about four miles before having to turn back into the interior as we approached No Moon Creek. Crossing that wide tidal channel on bicycles was impossible, so Carlo and I had to trudge up a narrow beach access path that would take us, via several small residential streets, to Highway 241. This two-lane ribbon cut through the thick woods hunkered in their overgrown abundance on either side. To the south, 241 led to Sheltered Harbour, and to the north, it slowly turned westward toward the swing bridge that connected Leggatts to the mainland.

Riding single file, with me in the lead, we traveled the shoulder of the highway only for a few hundred yards before turning onto Barnwell Road, which a few decades earlier had been nothing more than a trail used by loggers to harvest the vast tracts of pristine island forests. No Moon Creek, which had forced Carlo and me inland, was a geographical line separating the island's southern "white end" from the "black side," which occupied most of the northern half. Of course, a small smattering of folks didn't neatly abide by this invisible line of demarcation. Still, this terminology was what most residents of Sheltered Harbour used to discuss island politics, give directions, or reference island history or geography.

As we rode past Mr. Garrison's house, a name I knew only because it had been carefully painted in yellow on the side of a crooked mailbox perched next to the street, Carlo directed my attention with a just perceptible nod.

"Hey, look at this guy." His voice was hushed and edged with apprehension. "See him?"

"Yeah, he's just trying to figure us out."

The land around Barnwell was open, with only a few trees serving as reminders of the primary forest stripped from this part of the island. Many long-standing African American residents utilized these clearings for farming. These families were among the oldest on the island and traced their histories back several generations to the cotton plantations covering the island before the Civil War.

I cast another furtive glance at the front yard where two old slump-backed horses were grazing, slapping flies off their backs with their tails. Further back was a small one-story house with a rusty tin roof, and standing on the sagging front porch that mirrored the curves of the horses' backs, was the presumed Mr. Garrison. Although probably seventy, he still stood at six-and-a-half feet with a solidly built frame, undoubtedly sculpted from years of working his farm. His deeply lined face glowered at us from under a soiled John Deere cap. His expression hovered between suspicion, bewilderment, and maybe even a touch of amusement.

I was friends with a kid named Abe, who lived within a stone's throw of Mr. Garrison's property. We had met on the Leggatts side of Mitchell Inlet—the body of water that separated Leggatts from Declaration—when I first began searching for the lighthouse, and Abe had given me the final clue to finding it. Because of this, Mr. Garrison should have been accustomed to me visiting the area, but he never seemed less than suspicious and surprised every time he saw me ride by. I imagined him thinking, *Where's this long-haired cracker boy and his equally shaggy friend headed to anyway?*

The humidity, which had been steadily increasing as the day progressed, always seemed to capture situations, faces, and things—both good and bad—and hold them in its grip. I have never been able to separate my images of the lighthouse from heat and humidity, and there too is Mr. Garrison's face, permanently frozen in an impenetrable scowl staring from his front porch, enclosed in the sticky invisible air, preserved as if in amber.

Not wanting Carlo to become preoccupied with our Barnwell Road reception, I stood up on my pedals, adding an extra burst of speed to power us past our audience of one. "Can't really blame him, I guess."

A cherubic smile filling his face, Carlo bellowed with zesty abandon the chorus from "Run to the Hills," a track from the new Iron Maiden album. Without missing a beat, I repeated the words as if Bruce Dickinson himself was in front of us on stage, thrusting out his microphone for us to sing along. Lost briefly in our "Up the Irons" fantasy, we pedaled to the end of Barnwell and onto a narrow sandy path that led to the low tide causeway that connected Leggatts to Declaration. This path took us out of Mr. Garrison's sight and into the deep shade of a thick forest. Overhead, oak, magnolia, loblolly, and slash pines effectively shut out much of the sun. We needed to dismount our bikes to push them carefully over the uneven, canopied pathway threaded with oak and magnolia tree roots. Lifting our bikes over a very knotted section, Carlo whispered his trademark, "This is a real clusterfuck, huh?"

It was a term he often employed for just about anything that annoyed him, particularly if a situation seemed in some way against him. As to why he whispered, well, there was something about that narrow dark road, with the trees pressing around us, that made a person want to be quiet. Although only about a quarter of a mile long, the winding track grew darker with each step. Besides the trees, only cicadas' rising and falling hum, an occasional crow, and the humid air accompanied us. It didn't take much to imagine a company of Confederate soldiers riding toward battle to confront their mortal enemy or a slaveholder's posse searching for runaways. The smothering, oppressive coastal heat added to the feeling that we had experienced a timeslip and were now making our way along a road during the "War of Northern Aggression," heading to a Confederate encampment with hot, tired, swearing soldiers at the end. Thick weeds cluttered the path; we had to keep brushing them out of our way.

I looked at Carlo and said, "Imagine trying to pull these things out; they're like little trees."

Wrapping both hands around a particularly monstrous example, like a knight trying to remove Excalibur from the stone, Carlo pulled with all his strength but managed only to strip off a couple of thick leaves. He shook out his sore hands and then shook his head. "It would take Arnold Schwarzenegger...or a backhoe."

"Or Arnold Schwarzenegger *on* a backhoe," I said. Carlo arched his eyebrows, clearly considering this possibility before we both just laughed.

Hesitating, Carlo looked up at the sliver of sunlight piercing the awning of trees that covered us, trying to catch its rays which seemed to dart and dance among the branches as if attempting an escape. Then, more to himself than to me, he said, "The roots are so deep it would be impossible to get all of them." There was a strange timbre to his voice, his face frozen in a half-smile, his gaze still fixed on the treetops over us—the expression of someone who wasn't sure if something was funny, scary, or somewhere deep in between. We shuffled and sidestepped as many weeds as possible, as though by unspoken agreement, they were better left untrod.

Emerging from the woods' claustrophobic closeness onto the dark gray sand of Leggatts northern end, I noticed a familiar figure approaching us from the west, skirting the dunes along the forest line.

"It's Abe," I blurted, scratching at a fresh mosquito bite behind my knee.

"Who's Abe?"

"The guy who told me how to get to the lighthouse," I reminded him. "He's a guy I bump into a lot here; he crabs along this stretch."

Tall and gangly, Abe wasn't copper brown like many islanders but matte black. In sunlight, his skin almost looked like it was infused with metallic blue. Sometimes I wondered if to him, I looked like a sentient bar of Ivory soap wearing a wig.

"Hey, Abe!" I called out.

His gaze, which had been focused on a red plastic bucket he held at his side, shot up as he craned his head forward, trying to make out who the two people were in his path. Then, suddenly, his hand flew up in a wave. "Hey man!" he yelled back, his steps quickening as I pushed my bike toward him.

Unsure of our unexpected company, Carlo dropped back behind me. The school Carlo and I attended in Sheltered Harbour was, in theory at least, "mixed" but was almost entirely white, while down by Bumelia Creek, a hamlet for many of the island's black residents, stood a school that was overwhelmingly full of black students. Unspoken though the taboos might have been, if you were a kid of the minority color going to the "wrong" school, you would be singled out as an aberration, or worse, "trash," by the majority of locals—and your family might be treated with a noticeable degree of unfriendliness.

I considered Abe a friend, but it probably would have been more accurate to call him an acquaintance. Soon after we met, I awkwardly discovered I wasn't allowed in his house. His mother warned him, as he repeated to me, "You hanging out with that boy'll only lead to trouble. You can bet he has no good on his mind." It was true that I often had no good on my mind, but not how I imagined his mother supposed. But, of course, her suspicions were just those of a watchful parent. Both Carlo's parents and my own, although not racists in my judgment, might have felt uneasy having a black kid over to one of their houses as it could potentially draw a hostile reaction from less open-minded locals. It might have been 1982, but Sheltered Harbour clung, however tenuously, to the specter of the segregated philosophy that had once been held in firm place by the Jim Crow laws. Although these laws had been officially abolished by the mid-1960s, unofficially, their influence held on like a bad-tempered snapping turtle unwilling to let go of the stick that it felt it had been prodded with.

Maybe I was more attuned to those vestigial racial barriers because of the ostracism I experienced. Even though I was white, and Carlo was of Spanish ancestry with a light olive complexion, going to the "right" school didn't afford us any sense of camaraderie with our fellow student body. We knew all too well what it felt like to be outcasts.

When Abe finally reached me, he was panting, putting both hands on his knees, breathing in large gulps of air.

"I think someone's been screwing with my traps 'cause there ain't even one pregnant blue so much as near 'em." We could quickly identify pregnant blue crabs by the bright orange egg sacks on their abdomens. This roe is delicious raw or in she-crab soup.

"It ain't us," I said, nodding towards Carlo while unfastening the bungee cords from my cooler to show Abe our nets and chicken necks. "Shit, are you putting those here in the inlet?"

"Yeah, I've been puttin' 'em here 'cause crabs been flocking lately to 'em like groups of hippies headin' to Woodstock," Abe chuckled, eyeing the shoulder-length hair Carlo and I wore.

"Yeah, yeah." I laughed. "Except you should know that rednecks are like poison to hippies, and where they're found, the hippie usually won't be." Carlo, no longer on alert, walked up beside me. "This is Carlo, by the way. Carlo, this is Abe."

They shook hands, and I could tell by Carlo's relaxed expression that any uncertainty he might have initially had was gone.

I looked out across Mitchell Inlet. "You should try Mash Creek on Declaration. Carlo and I are headed there now. I've been telling him about it and how I've been coming away with fifty crabs in under two hours. You can always be assured of peace over there, and there's nobody to mess with your traps."

"You're probably right, but I ain't seen no one around here today except you two mangy dudes." Abe grinned as he nodded his head forward, laughing his high-pitched, scratchy chortle from the back of his throat.

"Well, mangy or not, at least we'll have blues in the bucket," Carlo said.

We all laughed, and I patted Abe's shoulder. "You're one to talk, man; there wasn't a blue in the same zip code of your traps, if you remember." Then, glancing at Carlo sideways, I elbowed his arm. "You know, I think the crabs around here have finally seen the light and are joining the pilgrimage to Woodstock with us hippies."

"Maybe you got somethin' there," Abe said, looking us up and down in an exaggerated manner. Then, grimacing, he put his hands on his head and shook it in mock exasperation. "Just shows they ain't got no sense."

I smiled. "More like it shows they ain't afraid to be themselves."

Abe looked doubtful as I shifted my attention back to his immediate problem. "We'll keep our eyes peeled for any crab nappers, but if I were you, I'd put those traps over in Mash Creek."

Abe scanned the beach as if searching for clues. "If this bullshit keeps up, I think I'll do that. It's just so much closer for me to set 'em here." He turned back to face us, extending his hand. "Nice meetin' ya...Carlo, right?"

Carlo nodded. "Nice meetin' you, too."

"Well, I gotta get on home. I have a science test tomorrow, and I've barely looked at a book."

Seeing an opportunity to return his earlier jab, I smiled. "With your looks, you should be able to scare it into teaching you."

"You right there," he laughed, thrusting his hands out. "I'll lay some Kung-Fu on its ass if it gives me any trouble."

It was now my turn to shake my head as Abe waved his hand and began walking down the beach toward the path from which Carlo and I had emerged. "Later, y'all hippies," he shouted over his shoulder.

"Take it easy" and "See you around," Carlo and I responded.

Abe's figure slowly shrank as he retraced the footprints Carlo and I had made. He glanced back, and I wondered again what we looked like to him. Not too long before, the color of our skin had made us the center of attention. The previous winter, Carlo's parents had taken us on an overnight excursion to Savannah to see a concert. Initially discouraged to discover that Krokus and Def Leppard were bypassing the city on their current tours, we decided we'd have to be happy bathing in whatever decibels were available, so we bought tickets for Zapp and Roger, a funk band appearing at the Civic Center. Although it certainly wasn't our accustomed scene or musical genre, these two cracker boys agreed that the band's rhythm section satisfied our craving surprisingly well. Carlo's skin might have been more olive than white, but we stuck out like white marble statues in that mahogany crowd. Although everyone eyed us with suspicion at the start of the concert, by the time we were leaving, the two long-haired guys banging their heads had been accepted with smiles and some lighthearted laughter.

Recurring with the smell of salt on the breeze were other, more pungent odors of low tide: a sandy/muddy mixture comingling with clumps of rotting seaweed and scattered sea cucumbers dotting the beach. Then, caught by movement in the sky, Carlo and I looked up simultaneously. High above us, wings extended and locked, several turkey buzzards rode the thermals, their feathers shining silver as they caught the sun. The turkey part of their name was easy to figure out, as their feathers and red heads did bear a striking resemblance to wild turkey. I found myself staring at them, mesmerized. "Man, some people find 'em ugly up close, but they're something else gliding up there."

Carlo nodded. "They kinda look like X-Wing Starfighters, you know, when their wings are flat and not in attack position." He loved all things *Star Wars,* and even though the comparison was debatable, I said nothing. It didn't matter anyway, as something else caught Carlo's attention. Giving a little cough, he wrinkled up his nose and waved a hand in front of his pinched face. "I don't know about you, but low tide here smells like death warmed over."

"No doubt about..." I started before my words trailed off. A couple of dozen yards ahead of us appeared two men from behind a clump of saw palmettos and palms that concealed a bend in the shoreline. They had been walking from the south, so we hadn't seen them near the edge of the forest. Both looked to be in their mid-thirties, and they carried an old peach crate brimming with at least 200 agitated blue crabs. One had greasy shoulder-length hair, an unkempt horseshoe mustache, protruding lower lip packed with chaw, and a stained Budweiser T-shirt. The other guy was balding, squat, and unshaven, wearing cut-off jeans, work boots, and a far too small Marshall Tucker Band T-shirt. It was this guy who spoke in a slurred voice as they beelined towards us.

"Y'all know that nigger boy walkin' down a ways earlier?"

I exchanged glances with Carlo, and without hesitation, we responded "no" in unison. Carlo had just met Abe and had no history with him, but I felt an arrow of shame pierce me for how easily that word sprang from my mouth.

Scrutinizing us, the balding, squat man wiped the sweat from his forehead. "That better be true, 'cause if'n you girls whisper one word to him 'bout these crabs, we'll find ya, and no mistake, we'll stomp your motherfuckin' asses into the dirt."

His eyes flared like two red-veined marbles before he glanced at his partner and winked. His face contorted into a rosacea-compounded sneer as rivulets of sweat rolled down from the top of his shiny dome. "Comprende?"

The question, of course, was rhetorical.

Pulling his too-small shirt up, he wiped the sweat that poured from the top of his head like it was the source of a tiny river. "Then again, why would you know him? If'n you did, that would make you both niggers by 'sociation."

Letting out a high-pitched, wheezing guffaw, the thin guy fixed his bleary eyes on us. "You got that?" he shouted, causing his friend to flinch before spitting a long, stringy loogie of tobacco juice on the ground right between Carlo and me.

They moved in closer and stood staring for what seemed like hours due to the fact they both reeked of an unholy trifecta of alcohol, tobacco, and tooth decay. Horseshoe mustache man threw his head back, letting loose another wheezy laugh while patting his buddy's arm.

"I do believe they understand what we're sayin'."

The left eye of the squat guy twitched several times, and his face remained frozen in an open-mouthed grimace before he, too, broke into his high-pitched approximation of a laugh.

"You remember what he said 'bout squeelin' now," the short guy finally said, flashing a mouthful of yellow and brown teeth.

His thin mustachioed friend finally broke his gaze and half turned toward his companion. "Let's go cook up some sweet crab and polish off some cold 'uns."

As they started to move towards the path Carlo and I had recently used, he turned back. "And, uh, good luck tryin' to catch anything along this stretch; the crabs here really are partial to our company."

They set off laughing loudly, or at least the pot-bellied guy did. The other guy wheezed and hacked so much it was hard to tell if he was laughing or had swallowed his chew. Although the confrontation had rattled us, once they started walking away, we found ourselves giggling as they stumbled in the dry sand above the waterline, each guy gripping one side of the peach crate. With his out-of-place work boots, the Marshall Tucker fan was particularly amusing as he kept tripping and dropping his side of the crate, clutching at the skinny guy, who would sway and teeter, nearly falling over himself. Each time the squat guy dropped his side, crabs would spill out, raising their claws in agitated defense and pinching a groping hand more than once. Chuckling, without being able to help it, we continued on our way.

Although we could have easily ridden across the wet sand, we walked our bikes side by side. While my bike's thin tires were fine on the packed sand of the beach, they would be useless on the temporary causeway to Declaration Island. When crossing between the two islands, it was essential to keep moving, or one's feet would start sinking in the muddy sand that crept molasses-like over tire rims and feet. Freeing them took a surprising amount of energy.

Without saying anything, I stopped, laid my bike on its side, removed my shoes, tied the laces together, and slung them over my shoulder, and then rolled up the bottoms of my jeans. Following my lead, Carlo did the same. No matter the weather, jeans were always part of our attire; jeans and T-shirts publicizing all our favorite bands or Harley Davidson were an extension of us. I knew, of course, why our conversation had stopped, but instead of mentioning the drunken rednecks, I stood up and gazed across the inlet at Declaration. Walking over and standing next to me, Carlo stared at the island that was still a complete riddle to him. I patted his shoulder, faking a stereotypical pirate's inflection: "There lies the road to the unknown mysteries of Declaration. From here on in, we tread at our own risk, fellow traveler."

Placing his hands on his hips, Carlo arched his eyebrows in mock indignation. "Ah, he who speaks such things is the first to admit his fear. So, pray tell my friend, is it you who desires to halt *your* journey?"

I smiled broadly, little realizing that what he said foreshadowed future events. "Let us make haste, Carlo of Secaucus." For Carlo was, you see, originally from Secaucus, New Jersey.

I took the lead a few steps in front of him, setting the final leg of our journey in motion. To our left was Mitchell Inlet, and to our right, the scouring Atlantic Ocean glistening brightly: a thousand suns.

2

The path across the channel was only about a quarter-mile, and Carlo and I waded through the tide pools and little rivulets in silence. Declaration soon loomed over us, dark and green, the trees of the shore all rocking gently in the breeze, beckoning us like people on a pier watching a ship bring loved ones home from a long journey. Eons of pounding waves have continually reshaped the barrier islands, with hurricanes doing their bit to speed the unstoppable process. Erosion is perpetually shifting sand from the northern end of Declaration to its southern extremity. Not only is this erosion causing the southern end of the island to grow larger, but it is slowly filling in the mouth of Mitchell Inlet, creating the low-tide link Carlo and I used. Someday, this transitory isthmus will join the two islands as one.

In the early 1980s, even at high tide, the water wasn't more than four or five feet deep, but that was more than enough to put a person in the water at the mercy of dangerous rip tides and currents. Many people had drowned in the inlet, so locals repeated cautionary stories in the hope of averting future tragedies. One of the oldest tales, dating to the mid-nineteenth century, described a young boy visiting relatives who overheard the adults discussing the stone crabs that buried themselves in the banks of the inlet. Enticed, he snuck away with the idea of surprising everyone by bringing back a few for dinner. Finding a promising hole, he eagerly stuck his hand in only to have it grasped by a strong, unforgiving claw. With high tide moving in fast around him, the boy began screaming and crying, his pleas unanswered as he slowly drowned. The legend persisted that on dark moonless nights, people could still hear the boy's screams. Both black and white locals faithfully passed the stories on, and these folktales, with nuggets of truth sewn into them, hindered many from using the inlet for crabbing and kept many otherwise curious visitors from making their way across the narrow causeway to visit Declaration.

The stories conveyed much more than the dangers of a derelict lighthouse and long-abandoned hunting club. According to lore, things that were more intangible but no less dangerous grew in the shadows beneath ancient live oaks, things that exuded an atmosphere far removed from what passed as civilized. The abandoned island attracted me like a magnet for its lighthouse, solitude, and natural wonders —but what cemented the connection was its bewitching reputation. The rules that held sway in places like Leggatts didn't govern with the same authority on Declaration. The line between the normal and supernormal blurred somewhere during the passage across the thin ribbon of sand between Mitchell Inlet and the Atlantic, a ribbon that appeared and disappeared with the tides.

With Carlo close behind me, we left the causeway, pushing our bikes onto the hard sand of Declaration, then headed directly toward the forest that grew to the very edge of the beach. Above us towered a tangled wall of pine, magnolia, palm, and sweet gum, all seemingly held together by rope-like vines that dangled from crowded limbs and a thick understory of yaupon holly, wax myrtle, and seagrasses.

"Where are you going?" Carlo asked as we walked towards this apparent barrier.

I smiled as a thin, barely visible trail presented itself only as I began walking down it, like a magician's illusion revealed. "Down this path."

I maneuvered my bike into a narrow space several feet off the path between a cabbage palm and a saw palmetto bush, indicating Carlo should do the same.

"They'll be safe here."

Moving back onto the path, I pointed to where we had just been. "See?"

Carlo shook his head and laughed. "It's like the forest ate 'em."

Parched from our long ride, we retrieved a couple bottles of water and drained them in seconds. Then, repeating an action many people never outgrow, we tossed the bottles into the woods. Retrieving the styrofoam cooler from the back of my bike and carrying it pressed against my side, I led Carlo deeper into the island before stopping to look back down the path. Only a short distance away, we saw the beach, bursting with color and light, framed through a doorway created from vine and tree. We could still hear the euphoric chatter of seagulls, making it seem even more like an entrance to some secret garden. Lost for a moment in a reverie, far from the real world, I turned to restart our hike but noticed a conflicted look shadowing Carlo's face. Eyebrows arched, eyes fixed on someone not present, his lips slightly moving as if decisively answering this invisible person. At that moment, I knew he was reliving the encounter with the rednecks, and the realization sparked a twinge of guilt in me for telling those guys I didn't know Abe.

"Don't let those idiots get to you, man," I exclaimed. "Those dudes were loaded, and tusslin' with 'em would have been a mistake." Carlo looked at the ground, furrowing his brow. I had indeed hit on what had been vexing him.

"Nobody like that here, though, my man," I said, patting his shoulder before redirecting his attention to the path ahead. "Just ghosts."

Over time, I found not just one but three routes that led to the lighthouse. Today's path was the old, crushed oyster shell service road that once connected the light to a now long-vanished pier. I picked it for dramatic effect as it would allow us to emerge from thick undergrowth immediately in front of the rusting, imposing structure. Carlo knew as well as anyone else on Leggatts the stories and legends of the island with the strange name and mysterious lighthouse. But, far from being wary or cautious, like me, he was lured by the forbidden fruit.

After walking only a short distance, we found ourselves on the service road.

"Believe it or not, this is the road the lightkeepers used to use."

With an incredulous look, Carlo shook his head. "You can hardly tell it's a road at all."

Pleased with his reaction, I smiled and motioned with my head. "Yeah, I know; follow me down this way for a minute." I set off down an almost invisible trail that curved sharply, meandering through pines and Spanish-moss-festooned oaks before suddenly coming to a dead-end at a vast brackish lagoon, still and dark as a starless night. In places, the water appeared as rippling silver poured by shafts of light spilling from openings in the branches overhead. Several color-ful wood ducks floated on the water, the red-eyed males instantly identifiable.

Just over the treetops on the other side of the water, one could make out the old lighthouse's wooden watch and lantern rooms.

I pointed. "See her?"

"Wow, yeah, I see it! Is this the path you were on when you were first searching for it with Mike?"

I nodded. "This is it."

Swinging around, I returned to the main road. "It's funny too," I said, "because we were already on the road that would have led us right to her. I almost wanted to swim across, but..."

Carlo cut in, "The 'gators and water moccasins woulda been happy to have ya."

"Exactly. I thought of myself climbing up the bank on the other side, missing an arm and with two cottonmouths clamped onto my face, and decided I'd keep searching instead."

Carlo let loose one of his singularly infectious laughs as I mimicked my one-armed, moccasin-ridden self, shambling onwards while say-ing in a hoarse, shaky voice, "Lighthouse...must...find lighthouse... nothing will stand in way."

His eyes wide, arms folded across his chest, Carlo shook with child-like glee. "You'd be like the Black Knight in Monty Python and the Holy Grail!"

We both loved the Monty Python movies, so knowing it would give Carlo a maximum laugh, I added, "'Tis but a scratch."

As we started back down the neglected lane, I think Carlo could see why I hadn't believed it led anywhere. Toppled across it lay the trunk of a massive live oak. Climbing over this obstacle proved only that nature had obliterated any trace of human encroachment, completely reclaiming this section of the derelict road, which seemed simply to end. I felt a strange feeling of elation standing, small and hidden, amid the singing, swaying forest.

"Now what? Fly?" Carlo asked, only half-joking.

"That would be cooler, but we just need to get through this." I started ducking under low branches, weaving my way around an oleander bush. "As you see, the road magically reappears."

Our feet crunched over oyster shells as bird calls of all descriptions and the always-present rising and falling hum of cicadas surrounded us. Sounding like the narrator in a nature documentary, Carlo asked, "So what's the deal with this place? Why does nobody live here now?"

With that, I told him all I knew about the island's history with the certainty of a boy compensating for lack of confidence by presenting an abundance of it. Local history interested me greatly, so I explained that Declaration Island had sported several names throughout the years—often taken from the last names of Spanish, French, and English captains on exploratory expeditions to acquire new lands for their monarchs. One of the earliest was Isla de Gordillo, named by the Spanish explorer Francisco Gordillo in the 1520s. In a deferential move, he called the much larger island to the south Isla de Allyon after Lucas Vasquez Allyon, his superior.

Allyon created the first, if short-lived, European colony in North America. He was possibly the first European to use slave labor in the future United States. However, Gordillo was hardly a saint himself. With slave trader and sea captain Pedro de Quejo, he kidnapped natives from the Caribbean, sailing them up the Atlantic coast to sell as slaves. Together the two men captured at least sixty indigenous people near modern-day Leggatts and Declaration.

Slavery had been thriving for over 300 years on the Sea Islands when wealthy planter Pierce Gibbons purchased all of Declaration and a sizable chunk of Leggatts. He was one of the region's most outspoken advocates for seceding from the Union. Like many Southerners, Gibbons passionately believed that cotton was so integral to the prosperity of America that those who controlled it should also control the economic and political decisions of the country and indeed, the world. This belief became a Southern call to arms. In 1858, James Henry Hammond, a wealthy South Carolina planter, attorney, and politician, declared to the U.S. Senate, "In all social systems there must be a class to do menial duties, to perform the drudgery of life." By this, of course, he meant the slaves whose labor allowed cotton to reign supreme. Hammond also stated, "You dare not make war on cotton—no power on Earth dares make war upon it. Cotton is king." The term "King Cotton," born of this mentality, fueled pride in men like Pierce Gibbons.

In late December 1860, South Carolina became the first state to secede from the Union. Gibbon's conviction in favor of seceding turned fanatical at this time. He was staying at the "Big House" on the island, and to declare and memorialize his commitment to cotton, plantation life, and secession, he changed the name of his island, then known as Gibbons Island, to Declaration. As was common among Sea Island plantation owners, Gibbons resided on the island for three or so months annually. He lived in a sprawling mansion in Beaufort on nearby Port Royal Island for most of the year. In the war that followed, Gibbons would lose both of his sons. One was killed at Shiloh, while the other, wounded at Chancellorsville, died some months later of the dysentery that claimed so many soldiers' lives.

Instigated by General William T. Sherman and briefly sustained by the Freedman's Bureau, the government gave a large chunk of Gibbon's land to his freed slaves at the war's end. This arrangement didn't last long. General Rufus Saxton, inspector of settlements and planatations for the Freedman's Bureau, was removed from his post by President Andrew Johnson. This had dire repercussions for the new land owners, as it was Saxton who believed in redistributing confiscated Confederate lands to the people who had once toiled on them. Instead, Johnson pardoned many former slaveholders, including Pierce Gibbons, allowing them to reacquire their plantations. In an incredible twist of fate, Gibbons was able to sit on the wide veranda of his house once again, watching as his former slaves returned to work the fields for him.

To go from working the land one minute as property owners to toiling the same soil the next under their former masters must have been equal parts heartbreaking and bewildering to the recently freed slaves. A glimpse of light and hope was extinguished. To an outsider, it must have appeared as if Pierce Gibbons had picked up where he'd left off before the war, but his life was never the same again. He no longer had male heirs, and along with increasing age and illness, he also had to contend with hurricanes, then known as "line storms." But it was the loss of his sons that took the fight out of Gibbons. Finally, in the early 1890s, he left the island for good, returning to Beaufort, where he died.

Around this point, Carlo stopped walking and gazed up at the thick canopy of trees. "All that stuff is cool...and interesting, but—" He thrust his arms out in exasperation. "What about the lighthouse? Why are there so many weird stories and warnings to keep away? The Blue Lady's supposed to haunt the place, right? Is that why nobody lives here anymore?"

I shook my head, folding my arms in mock disgust. "I'm getting to all that. It's called suspense, brother!"

With a sinister smile, Carlo swung his hand down on my shoulder, gripping it in a nonverbal indication of impatience. "Well, then tell on!"

"It's better to peel an onion than to bite into it," I answered, oblivious to his frustration. Twenty years after the Civil War, Declaration was a lonely place. In 1880, Gibbons sold 150 acres to the U.S. Lighthouse Board to construct two range lighthouses, keeper's quarters, and outbuildings. The parcel of land extended from the ocean over a mile inland. When Gibbons lost interest in his Sea Island plantations, most of the freed people who had worked the Declaration fields moved to Leggatts, where a small but close-knit black community existed. The choice of Leggatts over Declaration had everything to do with accessibility to the mainland. Twice a week, a ferry plied the waters between Beaufort and Savannah, stopping at Hawkins Point on the western shore of Leggatts. On Declaration, in stark contrast, the only craft that visited were bateaux from Bluffton carrying small groups of hunters to a dock just north of the lighthouse pier and, much more infrequently, a Lighthouse Board supply boat that brought things like cans of oil needed to fuel the lighthouses' lamps. This was the extent of Declaration's traffic.

The lightkeepers were the only residents for many years, but this changed in 1919 when Pierce Gibbons' heirs sold the former plantation, long since reclaimed by the wilderness, to the Declaration Agricultural Society. Composed of wealthy Southern textile men, the Society purchased most of the island in hopes of bringing back the former glory that Sea Island cotton had bestowed on plantation owners of the previous century. Their dream of returning Declaration Island to a thriving cotton plantation ended before it could begin. In a classic case of bad timing, 1920 saw a boll weevil infestation devastate Sea Island cotton across the entire Low Country.

Finding themselves in possession of an island no longer suited for its intended purpose, the Agricultural Society members decided to turn it into a private hunting club. After all, under the wooded canopies and in the grassy clearings were an abundance of white-tailed deer, wild boar, turkey, pheasant, raccoon, squirrel, and even the occasional panther. For a change of pace, hunters could fish the pristine beaches for sea trout and redfish or the many brackish lagoons that dotted the island for largemouth bass. Not far from the lighthouse compound, the Agricultural Society built a hunting camp that included a pier separate from the one used by the lightkeepers.

The hunt club and lightkeepers shared the island's isolation for twelve years, but the hunting club had problems from the very start. It never seemed able to establish itself the way its founders had envisioned. Part of the trouble was the isolation that made it a sportsman's paradise. From the outset, hunt club members encountered difficulty finding the staff needed to run and maintain such an operation: a master of the hounds, deer drivers, guides, cooks, and a caretaker for the months the hunt club wasn't active. The hunt club tried to recruit those from among Leggatts Gullah population willing to relocate to the island, but this proved more difficult to achieve than expected. Declaration seemed woven into the local people's legends and superstitions, stretching back to when their relatives, some still living, had been enslaved under Pierce Gibbons. This shortage of workers made the hunt club an on-again-off-again proposition.

When the lighthouses were decommissioned, the hunt club became even less attractive, and the men who had invested so much money in the island slowly abandoned it. Clues to the reason were found in the whispered rumors that hunt club staff passed on to relatives. One story described hunters returning to camp after dark with their Gullah deer drivers and finding themselves engulfed suddenly in a strange, low-lying blue fog that descended upon them without warning. In the fog's shadowy heart, the figure of a woman in a blue dress glowered at them, arms outstretched, before disappearing into the night's shadows as they fled. Descendants of the original hunt club members would occasionally return and attempt to reestablish it on a smaller scale, but they rarely stayed for more than a night or two. By the early 1950s, the hunters stopped showing up, and the camp and its pier began the slow process of decay.

Picking a couple of stout sticks off the ground, I handed one to Carlo. Instantly a mischievous smile spread across his face. He set one foot slightly in front of the other, striking a stereotypical swordfighter's stance, thrusting the stick forward. In a voice full of delight, he cried, "On guard!"

A short, intense swordfight ensued until Carlo whacked my stick-holding hand, causing me to stumble forward, poking his leg. Brought back to reality by the sting of pain, I told him we needed to carry sticks for a reason beyond improving our swordplay. Swallowed whole on all sides by pressing pine and saw palmetto, we made our way slowly along the crumbling road. Ducking under low-hung, Spanish moss–draped boughs, I instructed him to keep an eye out for the giant banana spiders who constructed vast webs across just such spaces. With a body up to three inches long and a leg span of up to five, the spiders' bright yellow bodies and black and yellow banded legs at least made them easy to spot in the bright sunshine. A few steps further along the path, I demonstrated pushing aside a web with the stick I held out before me. Even with this caution, a couple of spiders nearly ended up on our faces when we encountered them within the most tangled, heavily shadowed parts of our walk.

After about half a mile, the thick woods opened onto a savanna of sweetgrass dotted with wax myrtles. The striking change didn't go unnoticed by Carlo. "It looks like someplace in Africa where you'd go on a safari."

"Yeah, doesn't it?"

I swept an arm forward. "It's all sweetgrass. You know, the stuff the Gullah people use to make baskets."

Descendants of slaves, the Gullah people had made baskets out of this grass for centuries, stretching back in history to their ancestral homeland on the west coast of Africa. Initially, they were "fanner" baskets used for winnowing rice. When the baskets transitioned from agricultural to household items, they became more elaborate and beautiful. The weaving technique was passed down from one generation to the next, and among the Gullah, this craft is considered a gift from God. Selling the beautifully woven baskets provides a source of income for them while keeping alive a rich part of their heritage and an unbroken link with their African ancestors.

Once I got started on a subject I was interested in, it was tough for me to stop, and as we hiked on, I continued to tell what I knew of the island—even as I wondered if the drone of my voice was annoying Carlo as much as my roundabout history lesson. This worry caused me to speak far too fast. With his expression turning from thoughtful to frustrated, Carlo repeated his earlier question, "What about the ghost?"

"What I'm getting at has everything to do with the ghost," I answered, dismissing his impatience while reminding myself to get to that part before we reached the lighthouse.

In 1881, the U.S. Lighthouse Board completed the construction of two lighthouses: a ninety-one-foot rear range light and a smaller beacon on the edge of the beach. When the two fixed red lights of the front and rear range were lined up one over another, ship captains knew it was time to begin their turn in to Sisson Sound and, after that, the

Lallawassie River. Unfortunately, the beach lighthouse didn't last long. Severe erosion on the island's north end kept altering the approach to the shipping channel, so a mobile light became necessary to allow for regular adjustments.

"So, what happened to the beach lighthouse? Is it still there?" Carlo asked.

"Naw, it's long gone. When the lighthouses were shut down in the early 1930s, the front light was swallowed up by the ocean in a hurricane."

I inched closer to answering the question that intrigued Carlo the most when I began to tell him what I'd uncovered about the specific lightkeepers who had lived on the island. His head snapped towards me like the hammer of a fired gun when he guessed those lightkeepers were directly linked to the island's resident ghost, the Blue Lady.

"FINALLY!" he yelled, flashing a sly smile.

Laughing at my long-winded ways, I continued at a more relaxed pace, knowing I had his full attention again. "The legend of The Blue Lady seems to have started with the Pauleys, who were the lightkeepers in 1893 when what's called the Sea Islands Hurricane passed directly over Declaration and Leggatts. Edward Pauley had been the keeper of the rear range light since the mid-1880s. His wife Margaret died unexpectedly in 1892 from a burst appendix, but they had one kid, a daughter named Charlotte, who was in her late teens when the hurricane hit."

Only seconds after I mentioned her name, Carlo burst out singing, and I joined in as a reflex. There was simply no way either of us could say the name Charlotte without hearing Iron Maiden's brutal exposé of a prostitute, "Charlotte the Harlot," in our heads.

"This Charlotte wasn't a harlot, though," I finally interjected once we had finished scratching the equivalent of a musical itch. "She was kind of a hero of the lighthouses."

After thinking for a couple of seconds, I added, "I guess she's continued to protect the island all these years because of her legend. You know, people are afraid of her, so they stay away."

I explained to Carlo that nobody expected the storm to be as devastating as it was, bringing with it a twelve-foot storm surge. Fighting courageously against wind and waves, Edward Pauley and the front range keeper, Edwin Tunbridge, struggled to keep the beacons lit. A portly man in his early sixties, Edward suffered a heart attack while carrying oil up the cast iron spiral staircase of the lighthouse.

In the logbook, Charlotte wrote that after enduring the storm at home alone for over an hour, she set out to find her father. Struggling against fierce wind, stinging rain, and knee-deep water, she managed to make it to the swinging door of the lighthouse. The entire frame of the building swayed and groaned in the ferocious wind. Charlotte frantically climbed the stairs, only to have her worst fear confirmed when she discovered her father's lifeless body sprawled across the first landing. Somehow, she managed to drag his body back to the house, heaving it up step by step to the second floor to keep it above the surging water that threatened to wash the house away even though it stood on the island's highest ground. At some point, Charlotte realized she was the only person left to tend the rear light until the storm passed, so she put aside her welfare to keep the oil lamp burning.

Sometime during the storm-lashed evening, the front lightkeeper, Edwin Tunbridge, drowned. People later conjectured that Tunbridge, aware that there was no foundation beneath the small mobile lighthouse, feared it would be swept to sea and, in a panic, attempted a retreat to the Pauley house, only to be overtaken by the rising water. Two days after the storm, rescuers arrived to find the rear range light still dimly burning and Edward Pauley's body wrapped in bedsheets on the house's second floor. After a short search, they found Tunbridge's body in a brackish lagoon about a quarter of a mile away. Charlotte Pauley, however, was missing. The only clue was a final notation in the logbook that was illegible except for "Tunbridge." This entry led to speculation that Charlotte had been swept to sea in her attempt to locate him. Unfortunately, Charlotte's body, unlike Edwin Tunbridge's, was never recovered.

Stopping to pull up his now-soaked Motörhead shirt to wipe his face, Carlo breathlessly said, "So I'm guessing Charlotte's the ghost. Why's she called the Blue Lady anyway?"

"Supposedly, when she was alive, she always wore something blue: a hat, flower, dress, pin, whatever. What's really freaky, though, and it's mentioned over and over again, is that whenever her ghost is going to appear, a weird, thick, low-lying fog comes out of nowhere. It's not a regular fog either. It glows from within with blue light, just like the hunt club dudes saw."

Finally satisfying his question, I grinned at Carlo.

"After the hurricane, the new lightkeepers living on the island started reporting unexplained occurrences and sightings of a bluish figure at night. The keepers here in the early 1930s were only too happy to leave after the light was decommissioned. So even though the hunt club members and staff had always whispered about a strange figure, it was only after the lighthouse was abandoned that reports of encounters with the figure really seemed to spike."

Something struck me. "Who knows, maybe they started seeing the ghost more because now they knew they were the only people on the island and couldn't explain it away as one of the lightkeepers. Or maybe the Blue Lady started appearing more because she was upset that the lighthouse and house where she'd lived with her dad were empty and no longer cared for."

Rounding a sharp bend, I stopped and dramatically announced, "And we're *here!*"

Poking out from the edge of the woods, looking like Dorothy Gale's house haphazardly dropped into Oz, stood the crumbling but still proud lightkeeper's house. Remnants of its original white paint, flecked and chipped, clung stubbornly to its clapboard façade. I led Carlo to the front, revealing a wide, sagging porch. Oleander and palmetto bushes pressed so thickly against the walls that it wasn't until we had passed the house that the beacon finally came into view across a sweetgrass field.

Each time I hiked to the light, I would have butterflies in my stomach, a nervous excitement that grew the closer I got. I felt a moment of elation when the tower appeared and then a release of the pent-up nervous energy of expectation, replaced with a sense of happiness.

From our vantage point fifty yards away, the light seemed to hide amid the heavy recesses of trees and foliage. Thickly vined live oak trees draped with Spanish moss encircled the beacon and seemed to join into one large mass, like a colossal banyan tree creating a fence to keep strangers out. However, as we walked closer, it quickly became apparent that the trees gave a wide berth to the lighthouse, even though the area had been growing wild for years. The wildlife seemed almost to defer to the tower, recognizing it as something special.

The Declaration light was a skeletal frame lighthouse as opposed to the more commonly portrayed brick lighthouses that appear in picture books and on postcards and jigsaw puzzles. The first thing that caught the eye was the skeletal frame, a sight to behold. Constructed of a hexagon of iron columns connected by a spider web of crossbeams and tie bars resting on concrete foundations, the frame supported a central cylinder enclosing the interior spiral staircase. Although the tower had once been painted white, only a few flecks still clung to it. Its façade was now mostly rust that bled heavily down its sides. Anyone unaware that the light once had a twin would undoubtedly wonder what it was doing in the middle of the woods.

Standing directly in front of the light was a massive live oak. Its thick moss-draped boughs extended from the trunk in snaking contortions, twice the distance of the sixty feet the tree rose into the sky. The oil house, camouflaged by the ocher Savannah brick that made up its sturdy walls, blended seamlessly into the forest that pressed against it. Its thick steel door was still firmly in place, as was its tin-plated roof. A massive cistern was made of the same brick and set just to the front and right of the lighthouse keeper's home. Peering through an opening at one end, one could just make out the surface of still, tar-black water. How many water moccasins called its inky depths home, I sometimes wondered.

Peppered all about the fringes of the sweetgrass field were red cedars. Closer scrutiny revealed cedar waxwings flitting from one branch to another, their high-pitched whistling calls filling the air. After stopping to take it all in, I headed for the lighthouse.

With each step, the shadow of the hulking frame gradually enveloped us. To me, the lighthouse was far from abandoned. Old, maybe, but not obsolete. I smiled, thinking the lighthouse directed me just as much as ships had once been. Since my first visit, I always identified the structure as a "she," and I sensed that she knew her form was still an attraction. The light she had once shown like a gleaming jewel was only ever a temporary adornment. She had served such a noble purpose, like a reassuring hand or guardian angel, guiding ships away from unseen dangers in storms, fog, and calm waters too —and allowing families to be reunited, supplies to be provided, and order to reign within its sight.

The rusted and decayed lighthouse harbored dark, whispered fears to many people. From its very barrenness grew many tales of unhappy spirits roaming the landscape and criminals and bootleggers who bided their time in the island's dark, concealed recesses. The Blue Lady was simply the story that had taken the strongest hold. I loved that, unlike the multitude of legends concerning blue and grey and white men and women who supposedly haunted lonely, desolate places, this Blue Lady was traceable to a real, well-documented person. A woman both terrible and inspiring. Inspiring because of her heroic efforts to keep the light burning on a tragic night and terrible because of the unhinged and vengeful spirit many had claimed she had become.

I suddenly realized Carlo wasn't next to me and looked back to see him standing where I'd been moments earlier. Swinging his head in slow circles, he took in the house, the live oaks, and the vast sweetgrass field before casting his eyes up to the centerpiece of the scene: the lighthouse. His expression mingled curiosity and enchantment. I would have been envious of what he was experiencing if I didn't feel the same way every time I visited. Having the lighthouse appear from the forest as magically as it did was akin to having a secret key to unlock a mysterious door whenever I chose.

"D'ya ever get that feeling you're being watched here?"

"Yeah, sometimes, kinda like something's watching and analyzing but not in a negative way. More out of curiosity, tryin' to figure out why you're here."

More often than not, though, I tried to convince myself that the feeling came from the proximity of the lighthouse, its hulking presence and black, empty windows creating the illusion of a sentient being, a Lemuel Gulliver keeping a wary eye on Lilliputians like Carlo and me.

Sharing that place with my best friend struck me as momentous. Overtaken by euphoria, I yelled, "Come on, man! Wait until you see the view from the top!"

Without looking back, I tossed the styrofoam cooler aside and charged through the doorway, taking two steps at a time up the cast-iron staircase.

Behind me, Carlo was laughing, out of breath. "I'm right behind you, man!"

I stopped by the narrow rectangular window when I reached the second, final landing before the watch room. The glass had vanished long ago, but the humid, still air surrounding me in that confined space felt like hot bottled breath.

Joining me, Carlo asked, "What's up?"

Smiling slyly, I just said, "Follow me." Then I climbed through the window, grabbing a tie bar and placing my foot on the steel beam that anchored the skeletal frame to the core. I then maneuvered myself to the outer tie bar and worked my way around the outside of the structure.

"Kind of a rite of passage," I lied to Carlo, not far behind me. "Hell of a view, huh?"

Birdsong competed with the buzzing of cicadas, filling our ears as a strong breeze tousled the upper branches of the trees surrounding us, causing them to roll like green waves. Overhead a blue sky held a blazing sun that smiled indifferently. Taking almost no notice of where I placed my feet, I soon climbed back in through the window. Then I watched as a sweating and smiling Carlo, one hand on a crossbeam, clutched the window frame and thrust a leg through the opening. The look on his face made me feel as if I were looking into a mirror. By his expression of excited wonder, I could tell that our exterior inspection had charged him up.

He laughed a satisfied laugh before asking earnestly, "So, did I pass the audition?"

"Yeah, you passed and are now hereby authorized to administer the ritual to any dude who makes it up here," I said with a flourish of my hand to make it official.

We then ascended the final few steps to the watch room. Unlike the exterior, the interior walls still held on to the white paint brushed on decades earlier. However, what really caught the eye were the names and dates that covered the walls and ceiling. Carved deeply into the timber planks were graffiti memorializing visits from hunt club members dating back to the 1930s, alongside those of adventuring teenagers from just a few years earlier. The messages were scrawled all over the interior of the lighthouse, the keeper's house, and the oil house. With so many people marking their visits, I felt amazed that I never saw another human being on that island unless accompanied by one. Funny how I just happened to bump into Abe across the inlet when I needed the final clue to discovering how to get to the lighthouse but then had never seen him on the island. I suppose the reason, as he had told Carlo and me earlier that day, was how much he preferred the convenience of the Leggatts side of Mitchell Inlet for crabbing.

Opening the sturdy door, I stepped out onto the gallery. Joining me, Carlo clutched the railing and said simply, "Wow." In the distance beyond, the treetops spread out over the silvery green of the vast sunspeckled Atlantic.

Turning, I headed back into the watch room, balanced myself on the empty window frame in the wall, then pulled myself up through the small opening that led to the lantern room. A ladder stood here when the lighthouse still operated, but it was now long gone. Once I was up, I poked my head down through the gap. "Come on up and check out the Blue Room."

With the awkwardness of doing something for the first time, Carlo managed to find the proper footing, hoisting himself into the small hexagonal room.

"So, why's it called the Blue Room anyway?"

"That's just what I call it." I walked out onto the much narrower gallery surrounding the lantern room. "You know, Blue Lady, Blue Room. Since this is where her dad was heading when he had a heart attack and where she had to keep coming to keep the light burning, it seemed like an appropriate name to give it. I also like, if you think about it, that it's the highest room there is from here to Savannah."

Carlo laughed. "And if you got high up here, you'd be the highest dude, in two ways, from here to Savannah."

"Damn right, man! We gotta do that here sometime."

Looking back through the permanently rusted-open door, Carlo seemed about to speak, but I answered his question before he could ask it. "They took the light out after they closed the place down."

Taking in the vast expanse of blue and green, the dazzling distant molten silver of the sea, my eyes followed a lone osprey as it flew overhead on its way to a nest on the eroded north shore of the island that I'd spied once while exploring. The bird seemed so close that if I only stood on my toes and stretched out my arms, I could brush its feathers.

A familiar feeling overtook me. Standing above the forest canopy, I felt insulated against the outside world that so often seemed to intrude. At that moment, I realized that I spent my life looking for exits without considering there were entrances too. Yet on Declaration, the need for an exit didn't seem to exist. It was the rarest of places—a world that, while I was there, eclipsed everywhere else, as if the glare of the sun forced my eyes not to look beyond its borders. A separate Earth conceived in the consciousness of an unseen being that I'd managed to connect with telepathically. Once enveloped by the green of the island, I felt I'd made the cut of a select list, granted entry to the only place I felt entirely accepted without doubts, questions, or admonitions.

While I fished in my pocket for my trusty pack of Camels, Carlo leaned against the iron railing, puffing away on a cigarette. With his free hand, he offered his lighter. Smoking intently, we leaned over the railing as I pointed out general directions to other sites of interest.

"Over that way, under a half mile, are the few buildings that remain from the old hunt club." Walking around to the other side of the gallery, with Carlo close behind, I pointed to a just discernible gap in the trees, which opened onto a wide marsh.

"Mash Creek is that way. There's a path to get there on the far side of the field in front of the light."

Snubbing out my cigarette, I carelessly tossed the butt over the side and watched it spiral to the ground, soon joined by Carlo's. "We better head over there if we want to get any crabbing done, my man."

With a too-serious look that made me smile, Carlo answered, "Let's get to it then!"

A few minutes into our trek down the narrow, heavily overgrown path, I quickened my pace, forcing Carlo to speed up until he had to wipe rivulets of sweat from his forehead. My acceleration ended as we emerged into another of my favorite spots on the island: a small, oval-shaped grove.

"These are persimmon trees. In fall, they have tons of fruit. They're damn tasty."

Inhaling deeply, Carlo seemed to absorb the spirit within the quiet, wild orchard.

"I'm familiar with these from hunting with my dad." He grabbed a branch, pulling his hand down over the leaves. "A grove like this is the perfect place to set up nearby if you're deer hunting. Once the persimmons start falling, deer come. They love 'em."

Moving slightly ahead, he looked over his shoulder. "You got a long wait for the fruit to ripen, though, man. It's not even summer yet."

"Yeah, that's all right. I don't mind waiting. I forget about 'em, and then one day I'll walk through here, and they'll be everywhere!"

"Well, right now, we don't have to wait for the things crawling on the bottom of the creek."

Carlo might've disputed it, but I could take a hint. Less than twenty minutes later, walking down what I believe had been one of the many paths the hunt club had cleared, we were on the muddy bank of Mash Creek. An unusually deep tidal creek, even during low tide, it was my favorite spot for crabbing on the island. Surrounded by an expansive tidal marsh, fingers of the forest here and there meandered right up to the deeply carved lip of the creek. Several oaks teetered precariously over the edge, giving the impression they could topple at any moment. Past victims of erosion were evident in the branches and tree trunks that protruded haphazardly from the dark water. The toppled trees provided the type of underwater cover where blue crabs most like to search for fiddler crabs, oysters, fish, and snails. The muddy creek bed was where the giant crabs, or "mudders," could be found. Catching a crab with a dirty underside meant it had been doing a lot of food scavenging in the thick mud on the calm creek bottom. Mudders were prized because they were almost always the biggest, meatiest crabs.

A massive toppled live oak straddled the meager width of the creek at its headwaters, and grabbing its many stout branches for balance, we picked our way out to the center. Once comfortably positioned amid the sun-bleached limbs, we tied the chicken necks to the center of the ring nets and tossed them into the dark rippling water. Pulling them up the first time after ten minutes showed four blues in Carlo's net and three in mine.

Teetering briefly before steadying himself on a branch, Carlo stood on the trunk. "Damn, you weren't kidding, man; this place rules!"

And rule it did. After only an hour, our cooler was full. The fifteen mudders we'd caught made our haul particularly memorable, so I had an extra spring in my step when we decided to head back home. Before leaving the island, we stopped by the lighthouse for a farewell smoke, sitting on the brick cistern. Carlo shook his head, taking in the rusting lighthouse and the dilapidated keeper's house.

"I know one thing for sure...I wouldn't want to be stuck here after dark."

"You got that right," I responded without thinking twice. As much as I loved Declaration and the beacon that lured me in the bright sunshine, the idea of being there as shadows drew together in the gathering darkness sent a real shiver down my spine. Local lore was full of stories of those who mocked the legend of The Blue Lady in daylight but quickly lost their nerve once the first fingers of twilight spread across the lighthouse and moss–draped live oaks, blending them into shapes of half-remembered nightmares. The mellifluous birdsong and buzzing cicadas of day transformed into chirping crickets, croaking frogs, hooting owls, and the lonely call of the whip-poor-will. Suddenly the stories told of the place were no longer fairy tales but lessons for the wise to heed, and all but the most foolhardy left the area without delay.

As we retreated, I related stories of the few who, on dares or bets, had attempted to spend the night—only to flee when an ominous knocking came from deep within the crumbling hulk of the lighthouse or keeper's house. The select few who managed to stay after sunset described an unnatural blue light seeping like liquid from the long-abandoned lantern room, followed immediately by a spectral woman wearing a dress from an earlier era emerging onto the gallery to stare at the person below with a twisted, unhinged smile and two black voids in her head instead of eyes. One particularly hair-raising tale detailed how the vengeful spirit would point and cackle from the gallery before disappearing into the tower. Immediately, the sound of her frenzied footfall descending the spiral staircase would become audible. I'd never heard of anyone sticking around to see what emerged from the door at the bottom.

Even more outlandish accounts detailed a hideous, deformed apparition darting mockingly among the foliage, scampering down gnarled oak boughs like a giant spider, its mouth a bent black hole emitting an unearthly howl. The most embroidered descriptions suggested the body was human, with the head of a wild boar or even that of a toad or reptile. Each retelling was embellished, growing more macabre with each passing year.

In many tales, sounds also accompanied the spirit: frantic breathing, mournful sighing, desperate sobbing, and rustling fabric. People might attempt to explain these away until they realized the noises weren't coming from insects or other nocturnal creatures but seemed layered on top of those natural sounds, like someone whispering into a tape recorder mere inches away. I often wondered which version of The Blue Lady, if she did indeed exist, was closer to the truth. Was she the terrifying hateful ghost most commonly described or something closer to the brave, loving daughter she'd been in life?

If these waking nightmares weren't enough to keep people away, rumor had it that the island also frequently harbored social outcasts:

murderers, wife beaters, and others living on the wrong side of the law. Locals theorized that these fugitives became so drunk in the night that they would never have known if they were followed or watched by the residents of that unholy ground—or maybe the outlaws swore an oath to the phantoms, sacrificing their souls in exchange for their lives. The consensus of the locals was that the island was just wrong. Desolate, dangerous, probably cursed, and better left alone.

As Carlo and I walked our bikes over the causeway to Leggatts, I smiled at him. "Thanks to all the legends about the place, we get it all to ourselves." I hesitated as a new thought assailed me. "Maybe someone catching a glimpse of us emerging from the forest will think we're ghosts or killers on the run."

The word "killers" acted as a switch, and in near unison, we both started half singing, half speaking a few lines from Paul Di'Anno's swan song of the same title. By altering the song's location from a "subway" to a "lighthouse" to fit the occasion, we placed ourselves at the center of the action.

Quickening our pace, we crossed the already narrowing land bridge. Growing waves were lapping within a couple of yards of our feet. It was a spring tide, so high tide would be at its supreme crest. The timing was everything when planning a trip to Declaration. Checking the tide chart in the local paper was essential before planning a journey between the islands.

With our backs to Declaration, the living sounds emitting from its tangled, green, secret places hushed into nothingness.

3

A mom's intuition often makes sense only in retrospect. The morning after I'd gone to Declaration Island with Carlo, I walked into the kitchen feeling the nervousness I always did at the start of a new school week. Putting her hands on my shoulders, my mom looked me straight in the eyes and said, "You're lean and handsome, and the girls will come around." At the time, it went in one ear and out the other without fueling my confidence.

"Okay...thanks, I'll make sure to let 'em know," I answered with dismissive sarcasm.

Only years later, as an adult, did I appreciate the gentle encouragement and love of those words.

My mom and dad were as loving and supportive as anyone could hope for their parents to be. But like most kids, I acted out of an unstable mixture of blind curiosity and a longing for dangerous adventure that flourishes so purely only in a child's mind. A mind unknowingly filtered by what appears so crystal clear at the time—naïveté. Driven by that curiosity, I ventured further out from what they would have allowed had they known what I was up to, but this trial and error is all part of the forward and backward steps of growing up.

While I sat eating scrambled eggs and bacon in the breakfast nook of our kitchen, my dad walked in and patted me lightly on the shoulder. "Morning, Ashey."

Instead of Ashley, he often called me Ashey, an affectionate take on my name. It was always Ashey in the morning or when he felt I was upset or frustrated. Otherwise, it was plain old Ash.

Just before I started third grade, Dad had moved our family to Leggatts from Columbia, South Carolina, to take a job as the head retail pharmacist at the Eckerd Drugs on the western end of Sheltered Harbour. My parents loved being near the ocean, so Dad jumped at the opportunity. He was always in my corner, going out of his way to give me freedoms he hadn't had when growing up in the wake of the Great Depression, and he refused to believe that pushing someone up against a wall necessarily made that person stronger. My uncles and aunts on his side of the family were equally encouraging with their kids but within much more traditional frameworks that didn't incorporate the quietly rebellious logic and particular brand of optimism my dad possessed.

The way he consciously rebelled against raising me in the rigid structure he had known meant a lot to me then and so much more now. He never told me to "cut my hair," "get with the program," or "toe the line," and on one occasion, he even broke into warm laughter when I told him the outcome of advice a school friend had given me. That friend had earnestly explained that I'd find a wider acceptance with my schoolmates if I started wearing Polo shirts. Following this suggestion, I wore a Polo shirt to school the following Monday but with a tiny alteration: I'd neatly cut out the horse and jockey emblem leaving a small hole that showed skin. "How clever!" was my dad's response, which spoke volumes about his distaste for homogeneity.

Like many a household, a weekday morning in ours was a study in contrasts. While my parents hustled, getting ready for work, I lumbered about like a bear shot with a tranquilizer dart, showering, dressing, and eating with eyes half open and shoulders sunk in defeat. Meanwhile, our two hopelessly optimistic family dogs scampered around the kitchen begging for a handout or, just as good, a piece of toast or bacon dropped on the floor. My parents had allowed me to name them: Geezer was a black lab, and Eddie was an Irish setter. I'd named Geezer after Black Sabbath's Geezer Butler, one of my favorite bassists. Eddie, common name aside, was christened in honor of the cadaverous, skeletal mascot of Iron Maiden.

Mom was a pharmacy assistant at the same drugstore where my dad worked. Her cheerful face was the first thing a person would see when walking into the store. She wore a smile more often and more sincerely than anyone else I knew, but her endless encouragement and support made me a mama's boy from day one.

Grabbing my backpack, I followed my parents out what we called the "back door," which was in front of the house, opening from the kitchen into a small, gated utility area that led to the driveway. Although the house was modest, the architect who had designed and briefly lived in it before us had included some eccentric touches. For example, a whimsical triangular window at one end of the vaulted ceiling in our living room served as a frame to capture the changeable mood of the sky.

Not as straightforward were the two odd windows in my parent's bathroom. One was only a foot wide but ran horizontally for five feet along the length of the tub at eye level for a person of average height. The other was a rectangular window that gave a nice view of the entire bathroom for any passing perv. Mom and Dad felt we were set far enough in the woods on our quiet cul-de-sac to not worry about the shower window and that the thin, semitransparent curtain that hung about halfway down the other window was more than enough for privacy.

A fireplace in the living room was flanked by large sliding glass doors that opened onto a wooden deck, but similar sliding doors in the two bedrooms opened directly onto the thick woods that still surrounded the house. Only two other homes stood on our street at that time, with still-empty lots predominating, allowing the forest to swallow our small, cozy home. Of course, having a sliding door open from my room directly onto a concealing forest was either a bad or great feature, depending on whether you were a concerned parent or a restless kid. As a kid, it was a dream come true, and I slipped out on weekend nights to engage in nefarious little adventures more times than I care to remember. Either the architect who designed the place, who had two children of his own, was the most naïve guy in the world, or he had encased himself in a self-constructed amniotic sac composed of blind trust and no circumspection. Or maybe his kids were not ones for nocturnal naughtiness.

Architects like the one who created my family's house were part of the new breed of islander. His timing couldn't have been better, dovetailing as it did so perfectly with the influx of recent transplants to the island. His eccentric touches drew a wealthy clientele who craved aesthetic embellishments. Although longtime residents didn't understand the trend so clearly at the time, the balance had begun shifting away from the hardworking, pragmatic fishermen and farmers who had been the island's bedrock for generations. Most old island families lived in small clapboard or stucco houses that were emblematic of this pragmatism. Now, they had to contend with the lawyers, doctors, and developers who insisted on houses that visibly characterized their perceived positions in the world.

As I hopped on my bike, my parents climbed into the family Oldsmobile Delta 88 and slowly backed out of our short gravel driveway. I shot past them briefly, but as the car overtook me, I glanced at them and gave a small wave, nodding my head. Mom's lips were easy to read: "Have a great day at school." Then she blew me an exaggerated kiss. Mothers often perceive their teenage children as babies, and I guess my mom thought I was a baby who just happened to have long hair and wore Black Sabbath T-shirts and jeans as swaddling clothes.

Snaking down a short, hidden pathway of crushed pine needles, I emerged onto Merganser. From there, I transferred onto a golf cart path of a recently completed eighteen-hole course. Then with the precision of a surgeon—at least in my mind—I cut a path between two brightly attired golfers returning to their cart.

"Goddamn punk, watch out!" one of them yelled.

A one-fingered wave from me resulted in unexpected pursuit from them; I'd underestimated the power my middle finger wielded. This conflict changed my usual plan of using the course's cart paths to get to school, so I maneuvered back onto Merganser. A quick check over my shoulder found the chase terminated at the edge of the road. Two red faces shouted unintelligible words, and raised arms shook fists as I rounded a turn in the road. My heart was pounding with adrenaline, but I couldn't help but laugh and wonder if I'd thrown them off their games. Kids have their versions of the boogeyman, and maybe I was instead a bogey man or bogey boy for those golfers that day. Perhaps even a double-bogey boy—if I'd rattled them enough.

As I got closer to school, the recurring sour feeling in the pit of my stomach, always most pronounced on Monday mornings, grew along with dryness in my mouth. Once the first single-story, lime-green-stucco buildings came into view, my legs began to feel as if small weights were tied to them, becoming heavier and more wobbly with each yard I pedaled. Soon the two central buildings that made up Leggatts School spread out before me. The building containing the first through sixth grades was referred to as "the Lower School," while the other, reserved for the seventh through twelfth grades, was naturally dubbed "the Upper School." Clustered around the back of the Upper School were three beige, pressboard double-wide trailers that contained several more classrooms—a necessary stopgap measure to accommodate the expanding school population. Like the rest of the island, the school had recently experienced accelerated growth beyond what the original buildings could comfortably hold.

My destination was the Upper School. To use the dean's and principal's quaint phrase, I'd been "held back" in the fifth and sixth grades, so instead of this year being my third one in that building, it was my second. Every day I saw kids who had been my classmates in the Lower School, but now they acted as if they'd never known me.

Jumping off my bike, I parked it in the first slot at the end of one of several bike racks that sat between the side of the building and the parking lot used by staff and those upper-class students who had cars. Before I could turn around, I heard my friend and bandmate Scott's unmistakable, stoned Californian inflection.

"I'm goin' off the rails on a crazy train!" he yelled, beelining at full speed straight for me, shaking his handlebars as if they were coming loose.

He was my only friend in tenth grade, music erasing boundaries that so effectively kept others at a distance. Stopping inches from me with a self-satisfied laugh, he smiled. It was impossible not to notice that Scott combed his sandy blonde hair in a unique style. From a part that started almost halfway down the side of his head, he raked his hair forward so that it covered his entire forehead, creating a shelf over his permanently smiling face. If I didn't know otherwise, I might have assumed he was desperately attempting to conceal some incredibly early-onset balding.

Wearing a salmon Polo shirt with an upturned collar, he was a master tightrope walker, straddling the line between the preppy and burnout cliques. A fine line maneuvered by having slightly bushy but parted hair cut at a still acceptable length, the obligatory Polo shirt, and an attitude that the majority read as laid-back instead of stoned. This balancing act allowed him to exist just outside the radar range of the jocks and others looking to challenge anyone beyond the invisible lines of the "acceptable."

That his smile found inspiration in the most potent redbud grass known in the Northern Hemisphere never seemed to cross anyone's mind. Neither did the bottle of Visine he was always dispensing into his eyes. I knew he was a pretty good guitarist, that his dad was a builder who'd moved his family down from Illinois (Scott's apparent California accent notwithstanding), and that neither Scott's dad nor mom paid him much attention except to provide a sizable allowance that Scott used to buy and generously share a seemingly endless supply of pot.

The movie *Fast Times at Ridgemont High* wouldn't hit the theaters for another five months, but in front of me was a kid who could have inspired perpetual stoner Jeff Spicoli. I could never get enough of Scott's infectious stoned laugh, which punctuated his rambling jokes, told with regular interruptions of "Wait, did I tell this part already?" or "Oh man, I forgot how it's supposed to end," or "I think I just combined two different jokes." Every punchline was accompanied by that semi-dopey stoned laugh, drooping eyelids, and some of the reddest eyes this side of the beastie that adorned the new Uriah Heep album *Abominog*. Conveniently, I was wearing my *Abominog* T-shirt that day, so I could confirm it firsthand.

"Only way to kick the week off is with some Planty and Pagey," Scott said, smiling. Then, adjusting his Sony Walkman's orange foam ear pads, he obliviously started singing "Dazed and Confused" just slightly too loud.

It was Led Zeppelin or nothing for Scott. His praise was offerings left on a sacred altar. How there was no guitarist better than Jimmy Page, Robert Plant was the best singer that ever was or will be, John Bonham was a better drummer without a pulse than any drummer with one, and John Paul Jones was born with a bass in his hands.

"Sounds like a painful birth for his momma," I'd responded to that comment a few weeks prior when we were jamming in his garage.

Scott laughed but quickly, as if Jones could somehow hear him, put on as grave a face as he could muster and said, "Well, right after they slapped his ass." Then he laughed again as I joined in, laughing at his laughter.

All around, the clamor of kids making their way towards the glass front doors of the Upper School grew in intensity as the 8 A.M. start of classes loomed. A cacophony of laughter, greetings, and shouts of acknowledgment merged into one, creating a knot in the pit of my stomach. The posse was congregating, the angry villagers closing in on the castle, and the lynch mob storming the jail. As Scott and I joined the throng, I adjusted my headphones, put my Walkman snugly into the front pocket of my track jacket, and pushed "play." Instantly the voices around me were erased as Thin Lizzy's "Bad Reputation" gave me a much-needed audial hypodermic of heavy aggressiveness. Phil Lynott's rumbling bass locked in tandem with Scott Gorham's unrepentant bold chords and Brian Downey's ferociously propulsive drumming gave me a euphoric boost to start the day. The commotion and expressions on faces around me seemed to synchronize with the relentless groove. Two seniors on the football team held an animated discussion, their arms rising and falling in sync with the drums filling my ears, and two girls laughed, mouths wide open, seeming to sing the words that pulsed through my head.

With the doors unlocked, the assembled student body slowly filed through them. Nodding my head in time to my music, I glanced over at Scott. Eyes closed, he was singing along to his tape, blissfully unaware of the two girls next to him, chuckling at his obliviousness. True, he wasn't exactly circumspect. His expression seemed more appropriate for a guy singing in the shower. As we began to move forward, I glanced behind me to see the perennially just-under-the-wire Carlo approaching, his own Walkman in place, lips faintly moving, silently singing along to his music. We nodded at each other as he joined the snaking line of people slowly squeezing through the doors, the striking head and serpentine body of the canebrake rattlesnake preceding the rattle of Scott, Carlo, and me.

For Carlo and me, the music we immersed ourselves in contained a duality essential to our mental survival. One half was the need for an escape from the monotony and conformity that school represented, which pushed up against the other aspect—specifically, the direct transmission of a visceral, powerful otherness pulsing into our DNA, muscularly flexing against obedience, regimentation, and uniformed order, the heavier and louder the music, the better.

On another, equally important level, listening to music stimulated our imaginations. When Scott would blast Zeppelin's "The Ocean," I could hear waves created from drums, guitar, and bass crashing on a shore while feeling a strong, salty breeze on my face. The song "Misty Mountain Hop" evoked crisp air and mist brushing my face, while before me, for whatever reason, some old settler was dancing a jig. When Carlo and I would crank Rainbow's "Man on the Silver Mountain," I was looking up at that miraculous mountain, marveling at the equally silver dude standing there. When we played Uriah Heep's epic "The Magician's Birthday," I was mingling among the Orchid Orchestra in the middle of a mystical forest glistening with dew at the break of day. What's important is that the images didn't necessarily need to align with the lyrics or the writer's vision of the song.

The seeds that sprouted in my mind were tangible extensions of the songs, every bit as intense and integral as the music itself. This freedom added another layer of escape. The right to interpret what I heard however I pleased was power too, and another wrist-twisted dagger to the heart of neat and tidy classification. Counterintuitively, the barrage of sensory stimulation provided by music cultivated a centering stillness more potent than anything I experienced in a classroom. Even if I could not yet define it, the stillness imparted by the audial turbulence and tumult was more vital to me than being repeatedly told that education was essential.

Once inside the building, Carlo and Scott veered left as I headed down the central hallway to my locker. Keeping my eyes mainly on the green-and-white tile flooring, I walked slump-shouldered, lost in the sounds pounding in my ears, the kids and teachers around me momentarily forgotten. Avoidance of the inevitable, though, could only last so long, and the wait was unusually short that day. Only when I was in front of my locker did I raise my head to glance about me.

To my left, I noticed Brice, one of my antagonists, standing with his back against his locker a few yards away. A tight end on the football team, he had skin so deeply tanned a dark reddish-orange that he looked as if he had emerged from the bottom of a creek bed, a creature wholly comprised of Southern red clay. A particularly severe case of acne made his face even redder, an epidermal manifestation of *Exorcist* proportions that physically revealed his domineering, aggressive personality. I'd often seen him working on his dad's shrimp boat in Sheltered Harbour. His dad was usually yelling at him. Once when Brice was staring off into the distance, his dad walked up behind him, clipped his ear with the back of his hand, and yelled in his lethargic drawl, "Godamnit Brice, stop actin' like a lazy nigger and sort them fish."

In school, Brice was chatting animatedly with Otto, a linebacker, and when Brice caught sight of me, he nudged his teammate's arm to alert him I was in the vicinity. They looked at each other, snickering, before heading towards me. Pulling my headphones down around my neck, I braced for the inevitable.

Most people at school expressed their dislike of Carlo and me by simply not talking to us or laughing in hushed tones when we were near. However, several guys on the football team were particularly vitriolic in their attacks, which could become physical if their repetitive words didn't trigger the response they were seeking.

"Oh man, Otto, something *really* stinks around here...you smell it?" drawled Brice.

"Yeah, it's coming from...." Otto craned his neck out towards me. "Right about here."

"Phew-wee, you're right."

With a smirk, Brice moved in close and turned sharply, slamming his shoulder into mine. "The janitor needs to take out this rotting garbage before it stinks up the whole building."

As part of the same motion, he swung around and walked away with Otto in tow. The two returned to talking as if nothing had just happened.

It hadn't always been like this. My family had moved to the island when I was in third grade, and at that age, cliques and the general lines of friendship weren't yet clearly delineated. The boys and girls in the classroom and playground accepted me equally. My friend Mike and I even devised a game that became a popular recess activity. It was a steal-the-flag type game: one team's territory had at its center a geometric dome climber, or Jungle Jim as we called it, and the other was a picnic table directly across the playground. Mike and I were delighted when our game became all the rage with several girls. Especially as we were, at least until a couple of other guys caught on, the only two boys participating. As the game involved lots of running after each other, tagging, and getting close to the other sex for the first time, it was much more exciting than the simple description of trying to get the "enemy's" flag might suggest. Often, when a girl would catch either Mike or me, she'd wrap her arms around us and giggle. Such bashful flirting was an enthralling, invigorating, miraculous confidence booster.

However, within just three years, nascent cliques bloomed into fully formed alliances, allowing a definite hierarchy to develop. Being held back twice in a row blocked my entrance into a suddenly rigid structure. The ranks quickly closed, and I found myself on the outside looking in. Sensing this new rigidity regarding friendships as an unwillingness to bend, I decided I wouldn't change to have these one-time friends accept me. Our differences became invisible walls none of us were willing to remove, preventing us from seeing the substance of the person right on the other side.

When the school administration held me back the second time, their supposed remedy actually fed the monster they had hoped to tame. Math was a significant stumbling block for me, but it wasn't the real problem; the teachers, the dean, and even the principal didn't know what to make of me. "Holding me back" was supposed to shake me out of an assumed mental lethargy, but in practice, it was a form of humiliation, especially in such a small school. As all classes were made up of no more than twenty-five people, the first few days of a new school year were anxiety-ridden marathons where I felt under microscopic observation.

"Hey, you're in the wrong room; our class is over here," someone would say. When I responded that I was where I was supposed to be, the kid would nudge another, nodding towards me to share the news.

By lunchtime, several kids were whispering to other kids across the lunch tables, and for the first time, I experienced the lonely force of isolation. Sometimes the rejection was subtle, but often it wasn't. Small groups of my former classmates would pass, look at me, and laugh. If I didn't fit in before, now I felt like the latest acquisition in a zoo, naked and trapped.

Acting out became my only way of making contact with my new classmates, who generally regarded me as the "dumb kid" who had failed a grade. The class clown would be an affectionate term, but I was more akin to those most bothersome of Low Country critters, the chigger, clamping onto the skin of one teacher after another, causing a persistent, sometimes maddening itch. My "bite" was interrupting the teacher with a smart-ass comment, pointing out an insignificant part of a lecture I found humorous, or spotlighting an unfortunate choice of clothing. My observations and interruptions brought me scant attention and a few laughs from the kids who otherwise disregarded me or, in some cases, derided me in public. To me, behaving badly also felt like revenge on those who wielded power: "If you're going to make a fool out of me, well, I can return the slight in kind."

In short order, the teachers just wanted me out of their hair and for me to cut mine. My grades didn't improve, but the administration finally allowed me to move forward. I have no doubt I often appeared to teachers and students as unfriendly and antisocial, but this wasn't who I was. I had wings on my back that wanted to unfurl, but without understanding how to impartially analyze the actions and reactions that solidly embedded ideas of inferiority in my head, not only would those wings not rise, they stopped growing. Not until I was an adult could I finally perceive the protective shell I had constructed around myself. I would almost always avert my eyes if someone made contact with them. Because of these feelings of inadequacy, being two years older and taller than my classmates, I unconsciously slumped my shoulders and cast my head downward. This posture had the effect of deterring others from interacting with me. Although my T-shirts and hair suggested it, I had no desire to be an outsider. At least, not at first. I wasn't yet able to realize that the hard image I presented just reinforced the wall of isolation I so keenly felt but which ran counter to many of the other feelings I kept locked inside: the longing to look as I chose and to pursue my interests, yet be accepted as an equal. Unable to understand how to reveal those feelings to others or to integrate them into the person I sensed was within me, I constantly projected a wall that was stage dressing, a moveable prop.

What increased my frustration each time the school held me back was that I'd initially been trying to succeed. My parents assured me all I needed to do was study harder, to apply myself until the blur of each lecture resolved into a clear focus. However, if the lecture had to do with math, I understood about as much as if I'd tried to read a book tossed out a high-rise window as it sailed past my floor. Late nights of my parents tutoring me led only to sleepiness in the classroom. Several years passed before a diagnosis of ADHD made sense of my learning difficulties. Until then, teachers, deans, and principals all insisted I was not paying proper attention and was being lazy or purposefully obtuse. Everyone told me all I needed was discipline— to clear my head of extraneous impulses and cultivate a work ethic.

I've never been able to wrap my head around the idea that holding someone back will help them progress. I needed a more interactive strategy. Maybe the authorities thought forcing me into a distinctly awkward situation would finally make me realize the error of my ways (whatever they were) and set me in line to walk the straight and narrow. Unfortunately, the only thing that was straight and narrow was their strategy—which only compounded the malady, turning the proverbial cold into something much more chronic.

The truth, of course, is that answers are not always simple. I was already something of an outsider due to my long hair and my T-shirts, and it seemed abundantly clear to me, even then, that the administration was using me as a cautionary example of what could happen to a student who deviated from inflexible academic and athletic parameters. The way the kids around me focused diligently on building CVs to clear a path into top-tier colleges and high-paying jobs amazed me.

For a brief period in the fifth grade, I befriended a new kid named Nathan, who had just moved to the island from Aiken. As a newcomer, he hadn't yet grasped the rules of who he should be friends with to be accepted into popular circles. Nevertheless, in the spirit of friendship, he told me several times that all I needed to do to be "accepted" was cut my hair, wear Izods and Polos, and try to act like everyone else. Then, like magic, the ostracism would stop. He meant well, but we drifted permanently apart when I took part of his advice, showing up in that Polo shirt with the logo neatly cut out (the brainstorm my dad had found so clever).

Unlike most other students, Nate remained friendly but surrendered to the allure of the proverbial bag of gold dangled before him. Specifically, he became one of those boys who pursued tennis and golf and avoided all stumbling blocks on the road to acceptance, with the predictable benefit of having equally well-coifed, disciplined girls take notice of him. Of course, I wanted girls to take note of me, too, but not at the price of giving up who I was.

I could have cut my hair and worn the clothes that Nate suggested. Except that the way I looked was part of who I was. If I had tried to force myself into someone else's prefabricated idea of what would make me acceptable, it would have been like waving a white flag, surrendering to a force bent on assimilation. The thought reminded me of a movie Carlo and I had seen on cable TV, the remake of *Invasion of the Body Snatchers*. If everyone gave in to the expectations of others, like the characters in the film, we would fall asleep only to have replicas of ourselves emerge from pods, numbingly going about our circumscribed business. Carlo and I had joked about what a Kiss concert would be like in the Body Snatcher's world. All the pyrotechnics, dry ice, make-up, songs about cold gin, gods of thunder, love guns, and rockin' and rollin' all night would be in place, but pod-Kiss would sing the words without emotion or any of the overly enthusiastic physical embellishments of the human performers. The audience, in return, would stand there in their *Destroyer* or *Rock and Roll Over* T-shirts with their DIY Gene Simmons grease paint staring blankly at the stage. Going through the mechanical motions of the rock concert experience without any individuality or fun.

After Brice and Otto wandered away from me that Monday, I put my headphones back on and turned up the volume as Thin Lizzy's "Southbound" began, perfectly matching my mood. Phil Lynott's voice, plaintive and impassioned, rode the crest of a slowly breaking wave. The words he sang created a bridge directly from him to me. He was an Irish poet who meant as much to me as Dylan Thomas must have to others.

Out of habit, I deposited books in my locker, grabbing my math and geography textbooks and a notebook, which was a perfect canvas to draw the stylized logos for my favorite bands, including one for the band I was in with Carlo and Scott. Math was my first class, and drawing helped me appear engaged in the lecture while also fending off the ennui that sapped the very essence of my spirit.

As I turned, resigned, toward class, there she was.

Ally. Ally Sherrin.

As far as I was concerned, she was the quintessential girl, the object of my desire and conductor of my raging hormones. She was in ninth grade, one year ahead of me, although one year younger. In the one year we were classmates before the administration held me back the second time, she'd captivated me from the moment she first appeared at our classroom door. She often wore an expression planted somewhere between faint amusement and vague but intoxicating disapproval. It was lovely. Her lower lip usually puckered in a slight pout. She reminded me of Nicolette Larson. They shared the same long, wavy, dark blonde hair cascading down her shoulders and back, which she habitually brushed back with her hands. I never tired of watching her, especially in gym class, the only class we shared. When we'd been classmates in sixth grade, Nicolette Larson's "Lotta Love" was all over the radio as if preordained by a mysterious force.

Sadly, not even the power of a theme song had been enough to advance my interest beyond a longing from afar. Within one school year, we were in different grades and, for all intents and purposes, different worlds. That damned song, though, had become a leitmotif I couldn't shake no matter how ridiculous and oversentimental the connection between reality and fantasy was. Every time I saw Ally, that song rang in my head.

She seemed so relaxed standing there with her friends that she might as well have been at a party, anywhere but school. That carefree, nonchalant demeanor was equally attractive and irritating to me. My conflicting feelings about the ease with which she conducted herself in school and the way she brightened otherwise drab hallways only made my crush take on an awkward adolescence of its own. I didn't possess the confidence Ally exuded, and I was socially stunted—especially around cute girls. My crush wouldn't be contained, though, and would have to trip over its shoelaces in the same awkward way I attracted all kinds of unwanted attention while making my way from class to class.

The kids around me all seemed to be maturing much faster than I was, but when I thought about it, I wasn't that bothered. Sometimes, as I watched other kids in my class, it struck me that they emphasized acting mature—or what passed as mature. Guys and girls seemed to alternately instigate and respond to secret cues. Their casual nods and winks suggested sexual tension, which I heard several had satisfied. If I wasn't particularly bothered that I wasn't maturing as fast as the kids around me, I wasn't thrilled about it either. The confidence everyone else displayed in abundance made me feel even more disconnected, thinning the few tenuous similarities I shared with my classmates. At that point, the extent of my physical contact consisted of being hugged by my parents or bumped into by some dude in gym class. I was spinning, constantly spinning in an orbit that seemed to take me farther away from the pull most other students were locked into. This feeling of always moving farther away from those who stayed in such close proximity threaded its way through many of my thoughts.

Ally had dated a couple of guys on the football team, popular guys who reinforced her position as a popular girl in the small, elite clique of kids who, from my perspective, seemed bent on creating a facsimile of adulthood. Her status didn't suffer even when one of the guys she dated had a temper problem that his frequent use of alcohol and drugs exacerbated. That is until he created increasingly embarrassing scenes that fueled school gossip. The situation culminated at a weekend party when he found Ally too inattentive because she was talking to friends. Underestimating how drunk he was, he'd grabbed her for a kiss and torn her blouse open, scattering buttons across the floor. That humiliation was the final straw for that relationship. The façade was paramount, its maintenance an ongoing work of vigilance that bordered on obsession.

Through dogged persistence and the ability to pick ourselves up after rejection, Carlo and I managed to finagle invites to a couple of huge parties at seniors' houses when their respective parents were out of town. Maybe we provided a bit of background color. Who knows? Composed primarily of juniors and seniors, these parties were striking from our perspective as spectators, watching how these kids, only a bit older than we were, interacted. They broke into pairs, scattered about the house, and chatted to each other with a poise highlighted by the snippets of conversation Carlo and I overheard. Their uninhibited talk of the wildest places they had had sex—accompanied by equally casual caresses, chuckles, and knowing affirmations—made it clear that they were merely amateur understudies who could repeat the lines they heard without fully understanding them, no matter how detailed the impersonation.

Sitting on the periphery at these parties, sipping a few beers with

Carlo, I realized I just plain liked being a kid and was puzzled by this simulated maturity around us. More specifically, I felt it was my right and duty to be a kid and nothing else. I even unironically smoked and drank like a kid. In the end, Carlo and I agreed that the general vibe of those gatherings was just off. Parties and alcohol were fun, but to my fifteen-year-old mind, cranking out Judas Priest on a boombox while passing around a doobie with my buddies was a better fit than the saucy high-society cocktail parties those high schoolers seemed so bent on emulating.

Since I was labeled an outsider by most kids and staff, I would steadfastly be an outsider. Considering all I saw around me, I had no more desire to be an insider within school walls than at parties. The school was vigilant in keeping guys like Carlo and me out of sight. Our pictures were taken just like everyone else for the class pages of the yearbook, but a person would need a keen eye and a magnifying glass to see hints of us elsewhere in that book; we were specks on the periphery of images of day-to-day school life. Humiliation and ostracism certainly influenced Carlo and me to become class clowns. Attention felt good, particularly when cute girls in the class giggled or even laughed aloud at our antics. We often went too far in that attention-seeking direction at the expense of many teachers' sense of class control and decorum, but we were at least recognizably kids. Annoying, certainly, but kids most definitely.

Math passed as expected. I made a good bit of progress in my notebook on rendering a mascot for the band I was in, Steaming Broth. Carlo, Scott, and I had come up with the band name one day out in the woods behind Scott's house while smoking a doobie.

"Our band should have a word like steaming in it," Scott had suggested, "because, you know, our music is steaming."

"Like soup," Carlo blurted.

"Yeah, right, Carlo," Scott sneered. "Maybe we can have Campbell's sponsor us!"

"That would be a big-ass backer," Carlo snapped, clearly annoyed.

To diffuse a potential argument, I said, "No, but broth could work: think about it, a big-ass cauldron of foul-looking, steaming broth being slurped up by some creepy intimidating dude."

"Yeah, like Swamp Thing!" Carlo shouted as if hit with a vision. The movie version of the DC Comics character Swamp Thing, part plant, part humanoid creature, had played at the island's one-screen movie theater a few weeks earlier. They filmed the movie north of Leggatts in Charleston and on Johns Island. Having a Hollywood movie shot so close to us made us all feel like we'd almost been a part of it. Influenced by the potent redbud we were smoking, we suddenly felt that Steaming Broth and Brothman were meant to be.

During the first period, the feeling of claustrophobia that visited me regularly returned, and the classroom seemed to become tighter and more congested. However, when I stepped back out into the bustle of the hallway, I became aware of a slight sense of anticipation. Two things buoyed this feeling: my next class was geography, taught by Mr. Box, my favorite teacher, and my friend Tab was walking towards me with his two most characteristic traits on full display—namely, an exceptionally infectious, near-permanent grin and tousled hair that sat on his head like a wild bramble on a cliff edge, shaped by the persistent action of the wind.

Tab had a full face with eyes that grew into bright flashing saucers when something excited him, which was often. A bit stout, he had a gait that reminded me of a nimble penguin as his sneakers, topped by uneven socks, always pointed slightly outward. Or maybe he was more an energetic Teddy Roosevelt, bustling through the halls of the White House between equally pressing engagements. Still, several yards away, he began to talk animatedly.

"Ash! I ahd a denist appoinant this orning," he called, his voice slurred from Novocain, "but made it inh tie fuh secun period." Light perspiration dappled his forehead, and a couple of sweat beads broke free, rolling down his face.

"Well, you picked the right time to get here. I worked on the band mascot and want you to do the final drawing." Flipping through my notebook, I handed over my art. Once Carlo, Scott, and I named our band Steaming Broth, we took inspiration from Iron Maiden's murderous skeletal mascot, Eddie, in deciding we needed one too. Carlo and I instantly started throwing out ideas; Scott was more than happy to let us take the reins in creating "Brothman," a hulking, muscular figure seen as a dark shadow with steam rising off his body.

Tab's eyes lit up, and he laughed his belly-laugh stamp of approval.

"I luh it! Yeah, I can woor on it o'er the we'end." Surveying the preliminary drawing, he commented on the squiggly vertical lines emanating from Brothman's body. Pointing at them, he let out another belly laugh. "They loo ike stench lines. You know, like when a car'oon charac'er is supposed to stink, and there are lines represen'ing how bad eh smell."

"Well, they're supposed to represent steam," I answered earnestly.

"I can see 'em as dat ooh," Tab chuckled and then put on his best business face.

Satisfied enough with Tab's approval, I followed him to his locker, where he deposited a pile of books and grabbed a candy bar that he ate almost instantly.

"Bet your dentist loves you, man."

Mouth full of Mars bar, Tab nodded effusively. "He does!"

"Oh, yeah." I fished in the front pocket of my jeans and withdrew a wad of crumpled fives and singles, money that Carlo, Scott, and I had pulled together for whatever supplies Tab would need for the project. It was forty dollars, a sizable chunk of change for three young dudes.

Tab was a guy whose placement in the school hierarchy was a bit blurred—like Scott but for entirely different reasons. Tab was always focused and at ease in a classroom, seeming to suck in knowledge as if by osmosis. He was also a great friend. His life and take on the world gave me a distinctly different perspective than either Carlo or Scott. He wasn't remotely into heavy metal except for the illustrated fantasy magazine of the same name. Devo and Thomas Dolby were more his speed, and he loved Doctor Who and Dr. Demento equally. I had to think outside my normal parameters in his presence. This fresh perspective was both eye-opening and fun, making it seem utterly reasonable that anything could happen at any moment. As a kid, that sense of the completely unexpected lying in wait to pounce out of even the most mundane situation made me feel like I was acting in an adventure comedy movie.

Tab had moved to the island from California a year earlier with his dad. When we first met, he told me seriously, "I wasn't named after Tab Hunter, so don't even ask."

Even though I had no idea who that was, I exclaimed, "Damn, that was gonna be my next question."

Giving me a wary look, he preempted the natural follow-up question: "And no, not the soda pop either."

Tab's dad was an original, too, an artist who painted mainly watercolors that found an eager market with tourists. Often Tab's dad would be the one to open the door when I stopped by. He always told me to call him Charlie, but I could never call him anything other than Mr. Keating. Usually shirtless, he stood there, his thin arms incongruously offset by a protruding belly, which looked like he'd just swallowed a bowling ball. "Ashley"—he always called me Ashley—"come on in and see what I'm painting." In one hand, he almost always clutched a bistro glass of red wine. Whenever I recall his face, my brain summons up Ravel's *Bolero* blasting from his stereo, although he played jazz too —stuff like Shirley Horn and Dakota Staton. Gesturing me into the sunny living room with its sliding door wide open to let in the salty breeze off the inlet on which their condo perched, he'd nod towards his canvas, on which might be a marshy landscape at twilight or an egret on a Spanish moss-covered branch.

"What do you think?" he would ask, cocking his head to the side, looking at me as if I was now the subject.

"I really like it," would be my stock answer, and invariably I did.

"Not too bad for some tourist from Cincinnati to take home, huh?"

As a broad smile broke across his face, he reminded me of a boho *Wizard of Oz* scarecrow gone slightly to seed. The feeling of anything being possible I got from Tab pervaded that household, nourishing Tab's curiosity and creativity. For starters, he drew and painted ambitious sci-fi pictures, including an ongoing comic inspired by a Ralph Bakshi film called *Wizards,* which was one of his favorites. Even more thrilling were the sensitively rendered latex masks he made. They were by turns startling, gruesome, and menacing but, like magic, revealed various aspects of his restless mind. Everything he created spoke loudly of who he was as if the contents of his brain had partially spilled onto the walls and bookshelves of his room. Similarly, the records and posters of Black Sabbath, AC/DC, and Iron Maiden splattered haphazardly about my room were manifestations of my own brain.

As Tab and I began walking towards our next classes, Carlo, who had disappeared after math to get to his locker, scrambled up behind us in a half jog, a broad smile on his face.

Catching his breath, he greeted Tab. "Hey, what's up?"

"Not ooh much, had rhee' avities filled," he answered as if admitting to being part of the James-Younger Gang. Or maybe as just a guy with a big sweet tooth looking for the bad boy potential in that fact. Carlo's answering nod came from experience, and he added to the subtle outlaw vibe by cocking his head, placing his hands on his hips, and looking severe and dour, channeling the soul of Lee Van Cleef.

"I hear ya," he said in a just audible monotone. "Been down that road before, my friend."

Entering Mr. Box's classroom, Tab instinctively sat at a desk in the front row while Carlo and I, default setting switched on, made our way to the back. With a serious look, Mr. Box, arms crossed, approached us.

"All right, gentlemen, I know I usually ask you after class, but I thought I'd ask before it today. Who was the first guitarist for Fleetwood Mac way back when they were a blues band, and Stevie Nicks was nowhere in sight?"

Looking at each other, then back at Mr. Box, Carlo and I shrugged.

More to himself, Carlo said, "They were a blues band?"

I opined, "Fleetwood Mac without Stevie Nicks sounds like a whole lotta ugly."

Mr. Box shook his head, chuckling, and waved his hand over our heads.

"Well, you guys have your homework for extra credit."

One day out of the blue, Mr. Box started giving us questions about rock music, often stuff just a little before our time. Of course, like any question given in a class, we often didn't have a clue, but it stirred our curiosity. If we didn't know the answer immediately, we usually would the following day.

Mr. Box had a thick, slightly unkempt beard and a shaggy friar fringe surrounding a great bald patch, accompanied by an informal manner of speech peppered liberally with dated words like "man," "cat," and "groovy." I liked to imagine him in the thick of the 1960s counterculture and the alternative lifestyles that culminated in the Summer of Love. Without a doubt, these aspects already set him apart from the rest of the school staff, but what put him right over the top was that he shared a surname with Mick Box, guitarist and wah-wah peddle master of one of our favorite bands, Uriah Heep. Though Uriah Heep was bashed mercilessly by magazines like *Rolling Stone* and eclipsed in the music press by groups like Led Zeppelin, Black Sabbath, and Deep Purple, Carlo and I championed the band with a zeal bordering on fanaticism.

The Uriah Heep *Abominog* shirt I was sporting that day was a personal trophy. The band's latest album was released in the U.K. in March, but it would not see an American release for another six months. I had acquired it half a year before the rest of America by ordering an import copy from the Record Bar in Savannah and the T-shirt through a new magazine called *Kerrang!* The shirt became an instant favorite of mine. The "Abominog" was a sharp-toothed red beastie with equally sharp little horns and a giant maw, agape and salivating. It seemed to catch the eye of everyone I passed. For me, that was a sign of a T-shirt doing what it should. I suppose I felt endeared to that creature because I thought that was how most people in school saw me.

Getting a big smile and an encouraging "Right on, guys" from Mr. Box compelled Carlo and me to focus on the lectures and assignments in his class. Little did we realize that, as a result, we'd soon be treading into previously unexplored territory. That day, everyone in the class was handed a paper printed with the outline of Africa, lines marking the borders of all its nations, and little stars signifying the capitals. The goal of the test was to name each country, capital, and river correctly. With two weeks' notice, Mr. Box had set the test for

Monday to give everyone an extra weekend to study. By the bits of conversation, I could pick up around us, much of the class lacked confidence in the undertaking. For once, however, Carlo and I were ready. We had studied independently and quizzed each other until we were thoroughly prepared and utterly confident. We turned our papers in first while others glanced nervously and repeatedly at the clock. Then, indulging in the rare sensation of academic accomplishment, Carlo and I leaned back in our chairs, placed our hands behind our heads, and smiled. At the front of the room, Mr. Box gave us a quick thumbs-up with a little grin.

Our apparent self-assurance, which might have struck some as arrogant, turned out to be justified, and it felt damned good. We wouldn't receive the test back until the following day, but I knew I'd correctly named every country, capital, and river. I'd even included the names of the Atlantic and Pacific oceans, the Mediterranean and Red seas, and the Gulf of Suez. As it turned out, Carlo and I, along with two girls who were among the brightest students in our grade, received the highest scores. Sarah and Jean both got 98%, but as Mr. Box proclaimed the following day, "I was proud of all of you on this test. There was a lot to remember, but Ash and Carlo, our rearguard, are our Africa champions. They both hung loose and were the only cats to get a perfect 100%. Really proud of you guys. Groovy!"

As Carlo and I made our exit at the end of class, Mr. Box stopped us.

"Hey, you guys both finished the test faster than everyone else, and you did so with notable confidence. I really dig seein' that, guys, and on that note, I brought in something I thought you'd both really appreciate and dig seein' yourselves."

He opened the top drawer of his desk and removed a manila envelope. Opening it, he handed us several photos. "I think you'll know who these cats are."

Standing shoulder to shoulder, we took the pictures, and our expressions instantly transformed from curiosity to delight.

"No way!" Carlo blurted.

"You were front row for Blue Öyster Cult?!" I exclaimed, my voice rising in pitch and cracking when I got to the last word.

"Thought you guys would really dig these photos. Yeah, a few years back, I was a freelance photographer for magazines like *Creem* and *Circus.*"

Each new picture was more amazing than the last, and for Carlo and me, it was akin to looking at the first images relayed to NASA after the Viking lander set down on Mars. The first shot showed Mr. Box backstage with singer Eric Bloom and guitarist Buck Dharma! Another picture was of him and the Bouchard brothers, drummer Albert and bassist Joe, with keyboardist Allan Lanier poking his head in while Mr. Box and the brothers hoisted Heinekens! Not to mention an iconic shot from the front row of the whole band in a line, playing guitars. Their famous five-guitar attack! Mr. Box had now risen from the coolest teacher at our school to an all-around major dude.

Speaking too fast from excitement, I blurted out, *"Secret Treaties* is their best as far as I'm concerned, and 'Astronomy' is their best song." Before Mr. Box could respond, I added, "But 'The Red and the Black' from *Tyranny and Mutation* is sometimes my favorite."

Just as Mr. Box opened his mouth, Carlo picked up the baton: *"On Your Feet Or On Your Knees* is my number one, and '7 Screaming Diz-Busters' takes gold as their best song in my book."

Mr. Box said something that went in one ear and out the other. The teenage mind can take in only so much mind-blowing at one time, and we'd just had some major league mind-blowing. Walking out into the hallway, we looked at each other, shook our heads, and laughed. The day had just turned a lot groovier and a hell of a lot heavier, to use Mr. Box's lingo.

The third period every Monday was gym. Carlo and I hated wearing the school's sanctioned gym outfits, so we rarely did. By the time we strolled into the gym, most of the mixed seventh to twelve graders had already changed and were shooting baskets. As soon as we appeared, Ms. Burns, the no-nonsense, somewhat haggard gym teacher, beelined towards us.

"Will you guys *please* dress out today?"

It was a valid question, for which our stock answer was almost always "no," but for whatever reason—maybe the buzz we had just received from Mr. Box and the fact that we liked basketball—we answered simultaneously, "Sure" and "Why not."

Of course, seeing Ally exiting the girl's locker room provided me with the best incentive of all. Quickly dressed, Carlo and I found ourselves on the basketball court. Instead of using the whole court for one game, Ms. Burns had two half-court "mini-games" played simultaneously, one by the boys and one by the girls. As everyone couldn't play at once, Ms. Burns would rotate the players to ensure everyone got some playing time. Those not on the court sat on the bleachers and watched. My good luck continued when Carlo, Scott, and I were all chosen to play on the same team. Once in a while, you're just "on," doing whatever you're doing, and that was one of those fine days. I quickly drained three baskets and nearly had a fourth where the ball spiraled around the rim until deciding it wasn't going to drop.

On the far end of the gymnasium sat Ally and her friend Andrea facing the girl's half-court game. Occasionally, they glanced casually at the boy's game. Maybe that was why I overextended myself at one point and dove to keep the basketball inbounds. Realizing I would hit the court hard, I twisted to break my landing and knocked the wind out of myself. My effort had been successful, though, as I had managed to keep the ball in play. It ended up in the hands of Sean, who was able to make a layup and draw a foul.

Carlo and Scott dutifully sauntered over to check on me. With a look of concern, Carlo shook his head and said, "What a clusterfuck."

Scott, half-smile plastered on his perpetually stoned countenance, thrust his arm out. "Were you trying to impersonate Superman? The flying part looked good, but you need to work on the landing."

Taking his extended hand, I couldn't help but smile. "Yeah, thanks, man. I'll keep that in mind."

By this time, Ms. Burns had walked over from the girl's game and barked hoarsely, "Go take a breather in the locker room, Ash. Class is almost over."

Boykin, one of Ms. Burns' two gym aides and a senior on the basketball team, flashed her a quick smile that seemed to be one of relief. To have an outcast playing as competitively as anyone else on the court didn't fit into the neatly ordered school castes. Now, if I had been Duncan or Bruce, the two junior varsity players on the court at the time, Ms. Burns and Boykin would almost certainly have come to push me, speaking in bright, hearty tones, "Come on, get up and get back in there! It's all about teamwork—no pain, no gain!"

Circling from the far side of the gym to the locker rooms, I had to pass directly by Ally and Andrea, who were both watching me as I approached. As I neared them, I indulged in a little game I liked to play. I would say Ally's name in a just audible pitch as if we were a couple, or at least friends, always with the assumption that she wouldn't hear me. Or maybe with the hope she would. Either way, it gave me a little vicarious thrill to speak her name aloud in public, surrounded by so many people, like I was one of them. Maybe I liked saying her name with her nearby so I could pretend I was greeting her at my front door. Oh, the mystery and havoc of raging hormones.

I uttered, "Ally," at a volume barely above a faint whisper, so weak that I was dissatisfied with myself. Deep within my daydream, I hardly realized I was passing directly beside the two girls as they sat chatting on the bleachers, their eyes lazily following me. I repeated her name, raising my voice in what I still considered an inaudible range. "Alll-eeee."

However, my voice was clearer and stronger than I had imagined, and both girls stared incredulously up at me. Whatever topic they had been discussing was temporarily forgotten. In an aloof tone, Ally asked, "What did you say?"

"Uh, Nothing," I spluttered.

Taking a few more steps, I hesitated, then turned down the short hall that led to the boy's locker room before feeling compelled to look back. Andrea had returned her gaze to the court and was laughing, probably at me, but I caught Ally quickly lowering her face and staring at the floor.

She had been looking at me!

Sweeping the sticky hair away from my eyes, I looked back towards the bleachers again. Maybe I had been so winded from the game and my fall that I hadn't seen clearly. This time, for only an instant, she looked directly at me with a curious expression...and a shy smile. Two almond-shaped eyes were meeting mine with all defenses down.

Then I realized I was smiling too. I felt an intense, almost painful elation but also strange loneliness like an inmate looking at the warden's wife—two completely different worlds with space between that seemed impossible to span. Did that really happen?

What would I say if I spoke to her anyway? Mixed feelings spiraled around my head like the ball I shot earlier that swept around the rim before falling away from the basket.

A strange new elation wrestled into my mind and mingled with my typical daily emotions. Thus distracted, I entered English class.

Speaking in a loud whisper, Carlo waved his arm to alert me. "Over here, man." Entirely lost in thought, I'd started sitting at a desk near the middle of the classroom.

"Zoning out, can you blame me? Today's topic is metaphor in fiction."

"Very good, Ash! I'll have to mark it down that you actually heard something I said in class," Mrs. Honse interjected.

With class underway, Mrs. Honse, a stout woman who I used to tell Carlo the term "big-boned" must have been invented for, spoke passionately, her face reddening as she discoursed about *Moby Dick*. Her eyes scanned the class until they suddenly rested on me, apparently remembering my earlier response to Carlo about the topic of that day's lesson.

"So, in the novel *Moby Dick*, in the sections I asked you to read for today's class, what does the great white whale represent?"

Seeing an opportunity that begged to be seized, I paused briefly, met Mrs. Honse's expectant gaze for dramatic impact, then asked, "A big dick?"

The explosion of laughter at my crude yet well-placed wisecrack was precisely the reaction I desired. Julie, a cute girl one row in front of me, even looked at me while laughing. Shaking her head, Mrs. Honse raised her hands to settle the class down.

"Not the answer I was looking for. You'd better watch your mouth, or it will be another trip to the dean's office."

"I'm sure he might have some questions for you about the pornography you're teaching a bunch of innocent kids," was my insolent reply. More chuckles followed, but they were more muted. I was pressing my luck.

"Well, why don't I march you down to Mr. Knight's office right now, and we can discuss your rudeness and continued desire to disrupt my class."

Used to the routine, I slumped out of my chair, whispering to Carlo, "See ya on the other side." Then, as Mrs. Honse escorted me from the room, I had to push it way too far.

"So what's the metaphor for a great white whale dragging me out of class?"

Oh, that one went over well. Exclamations of shock and surprise escaped the door closing behind me.

In the office, a wholly exasperated and red-faced Mrs. Honse explained my latest insolence while Mr. Knight, his gaunt face accentuated by round wire-rimmed glasses, admonished me with an equally red face. The veins bulging in his neck and from his left temple suggested the guy whose head exploded in *Scanners,* a movie Carlo and I had enjoyed on HBO a few weeks earlier. After Mr. Knight and Mrs. Honse finished reading me the same riot act I regularly heard, I was allowed to return to class after giving the assurance that I would keep my ears open and mouth shut. The administration reserved punishment for larger productions.

The rest of the school day passed like any other day, but even with the usual minor setbacks, I felt like I was floating just off the ground. I couldn't get Ally out of my mind. She had looked right at me—and smiled. At me! In my reverie, rounding a corner of the sidewalk on my way to my bike, I almost bumped into Carlo, who I hadn't seen since English. He told me he'd lost a few dollars that were in his jeans and thought they might have fallen out when he had changed into his gym clothes earlier.

"Another reason not to dress out for gym. Now I'm losin' money because of it." Carlo shrugged his shoulders, then his eyes lit up with another thought. "Man, you had the whole class laughing and talking the entire time you and Honse were gone. 'What's the metaphor for this great white whale dragging me out of class?'" He broke into a short belly laugh. "I kept picturing Ms. Honse's head on a whale's body every time she said 'metaphor' for the rest of the class." Then Carlo's eyes grew wide. "Wait, that can't be a metaphor. Her head *is* attached to a whale's body!" He convulsed in childlike glee, and I couldn't help but join in. Before he caught his breath, he changed the subject. "Video arcade at four, right?"

As we set plans to meet later at the arcade, I broke into a brisk walk, patting Carlo's shoulder to do the same. This action occurred unconsciously; I always tried to pass the gym immediately after school before the football players headed into the weight room.

"Tab can't make it. He has to run some errands for his dad or somethin'," Carlo said as we approached the bike rack. Rubbing his hands together, he affected an intimidating tone, raising an eyebrow with mock menace. "Be ready to lose that top score of yours at *Red Baron* 'cause it ends today." *Red Baron* was our favorite game, as shooting down World War I biplanes was fun and seemed more "metal" than *Pac-Man, Donkey Kong,* or even *Joust,* which was Tab's game of choice. My exceptionally short attention span made games like *Joust* too damn frustrating.

"Your gonna wish you had that money you lost if you hope to steal my crown," I joked, "'cuz you're gonna need a lot of practice." My bold proclamation manifested out of the confidence produced by the memory of Ally's smile. Those eyes that had looked right at me were oval and brown like perfect almonds. As I made the connection, an obscure fact that Mrs. Hennessey had rattled off in natural science class popped into my mind. The almond is the center of the fruit of a tree that belongs to the rose family. How marvelously appropriate, I thought, that even Ally's eyes hinted, however obscurely, at the rose's sweet fragrance and delicate beauty. I guess all it took for me to retain information was a super pretty girl to highlight the example.

My daydream ended when I saw Carlo's face flush, his eyes widened in panicked concern. Before I could react, a forearm slammed into my shoulder blades. In the same instant, Carlo was violently shoved, then quickly swung around into a full nelson. At that exact moment,

I felt my arms forced into the same configuration as Carlo's. We were both hustled around the side of the building that faced an area that was always quite empty after school. Once we rounded the corner, our attackers slammed us against the stucco wall facing each other, the left side of my face and the right side of Carlo's pressed hard against the sharp surface.

Otto was a linebacker on the football team, but it took him and Trey, another linebacker, to hold Carlo, a big guy in his own right. Someone pressed my face against an exceptionally sharp edge that cut into my cheek. Carlo shot me a look of helplessness mixed with fear and anger, and I'm sure my expression matched his closely. Then Brice's drawl told me who my tormentor was.

"What are you two long-haired fairies up to hanging around the gym, huh?"

Snorting with excitement, Trey and Otto seemed to draw energy from Brice's words. Otto answered, "Prolly settin' up a date with each other."

Trey laughed loudly, a sort of verbal high-five. "I think you're right, Otto."

Brice's hot breath blew in my ear as he picked up this theme: "I bet they're past the hand-holdin' stage and are fixin' to move onto the next base."

While Otto and Trey redoubled their efforts to contain Carlo, Trey grabbed the back of his head, shoving it directly in front of mine.

"Go on and kiss. You know ya wanna."

"Yeah, go on and kiss faggots." Brice spoke so close to my ear that it seemed like he was the one getting set to do some kissing.

"You know guys," he continued, "my daddy says these two come from a long line of fairies, and he knows what he's talkin' about." Pressing his chest against my back forced my face to dig deeper into the wall. "My granddaddy used to run your kind outta town. Too bad the law around here so fuckin' backwards now 'cause you should both get a cross burned in your yards. You two a couple of white niggers."

Brice had moved in so close I felt his lips against my earlobe. He whispered hoarsely, his words pulsing with excitement: "What you think of that, stinkin' faggot?"

Brice's racism seemed as deeply ingrained as his tanned skin or his shrimper dad's wrinkles—and was accepted by his friends just as naturally. Otto and Trey both laughed in an exaggerated fashion. In an attempt to distract myself from the pain, I imagined their gaping mouths like huge empty caves from which bats could fly out at any second.

With great relief, I heard the voices of adults approaching from around the corner, and I felt the grip on me release. Raising my hand, I dabbed a drop of blood I felt dripping down my cheek and turned toward the unintended rescue party, made up of Dean Knight and James, the head custodian.

"There a problem here, boys?" Dean Knight asked, eying the strange group before him.

"No sir, just talking about football," Brice assured him.

Mr. Knight smiled, nodding approvingly. "Fine, fine—a healthy topic, boys—but don't forget to focus on your studies." He scanned the three footballers and added, "That's of equal importance." Smiling flatly and evenly, he scanned the odd group again, confident that his inane and simple remark could lead to success and happiness.

"Hope you're all going to the pep rally this Friday, Brice, Otto, Trey—" His eyes narrowed as they fell on Carlo and me. "Uh,...boys."

Turning, he walked off, resuming his instructions to the custodian.

Smiling broadly, Brice sent us a limp-wristed wave. "Tootles, love-birds."

"Yeah, remember to wear rubbers... Oh yeah, it don't matter with fags. Never mind," came Otto's voice from over his shoulder as the group departed.

After brushing back his hair with both hands, Carlo rubbed his face and voiced his frustration, looking like he'd just been dropped onto a strange new planet. "Fucking assholes."

"If you think about it for a second," I said, "it doesn't take too much imagination to see that they're the ones who secretly want to stick each other. I mean, those remarks came out of nowhere—unless they already think that way but don't want to admit it."

This comment seemed to reinvigorate him and made me feel better too. It brought us a little much-needed confidence after yet another degrading confrontation. No doubt about it, the interactions we had to endure with Brice's brigade had just taken a turn for the weirder.

Straightening up, Carlo put on a brave face, "So, still on for four, right man?"

"Hell yes, hombre, and prepare to lose."

As Carlo turned and walked a little ahead of me, I heard him mutter, "I hope not," in a way that I knew had nothing to do with video games and everything to do with our precarious position in the school.

I've heard that the experience of military conflict is so overwhelming that people in battle experience something known as the *fog of war*. This term encapsulates the doubt that seizes combatants—doubt about what they are capable of, what their adversaries are capable of, and what those adversaries' intent is in the conflict. Confusion and uncertainty can metastasize like cancer within one's mind, bringing paralysis and atrophy to the rest of the body.

Similarly, the unexpected and the new are part of the very fiber of a young life. We engage with the world around us using only the isolated, fragmentary bits of advice and intuition we glean through our interactions. Opening our minds and hearts willingly to the world around us, we are often baffled and stunned by our experiences and left with profound but submerged scars that often don't reveal their full toll until years later. I call this the *fog of youth,* and I was fumbling in it headlong.

4

When Ally and I locked eyes, it had been a glorious lightning strike moment that had illuminated a smile directed at me exclusively. I was convinced the moment preordained that something *big*— no, *earth-shattering*—would inevitably follow. Our relationship would bloom like a million bluebells in spring, with star showers and rainbows adorning the sky, and every eye in school would watch us in awe and envy. Instead came the great resounding crash of *nothing*. Monday led to Tuesday, and the final bell sounded on Friday before I could figure anything out.

All the best moments are alchemy. One element mysteriously transforms what was common on its own into part of something greater, more beautiful, when comingled. But, I guess one could say that ingredient remained elusive. The magic was still dormant, off somewhere in the wings.

Saturday was my favorite word when I was fifteen. Topping a long list of reasons for making Saturday sacrosanct was that it was band practice day. We irregularly rotated whose house would suffer, leaving those within earshot wishing Thomas Edison had dropped his notion of electricity. Firmly within the range of our Fender and Peavey amps for the second week in a row were Scott's parents and neighbors. Unlike my family's house, constructed on a concrete slab at ground level, Scott's house was built after new flood zone regulations were enacted, which required it to be twelve feet above the ground, leaving an oversized garage and storage space beneath the house proper. In other words, a practice area that was big enough, with a bit of imagination and the help of some California redbud, to make us feel like we were Led Zeppelin or Deep Purple in their private studio.

Opening the case that held my Danelectro Longhorn bass for the fourth time, I rechecked that all my necessities were in place: black cowhide guitar strap, extra flatwound strings, and coiled Fender guitar cord. Then I grabbed a secret weapon—my Boss Bass Overdrive pedal. Besides its ability to slather the world in black sludge, it helped me approximate the fabled Geezer Butler tone, making it a necessity in my arsenal, mainly when we played Black Sabbath's call to weed anthem, "Sweet Leaf." An additional benefit was the pedal's ability to mask the inevitable flubbed note in a quaking wall of fuzz.

"Are you ready yet, Ash?" my mom yelled for the third time from the end of the hall. "If you need a ride, we have to go now because I have to go shopping."

I appeared with guitar case in one hand and bass pedal in the other as if it'd been her holding me up instead of the other way around. We headed out to my mom's station wagon, where I put my gear in the back seat, and we were off. When we pulled into Scott's driveway, I could hear his guitar blaring from the garage in a mighty but failed attempt to nail the opening chords of "Heartbreaker." Like Carlo's dad, Scott's father was one of the island's wealthy new breed. He'd surprised Scott with a beautiful cherry sunburst Gibson Les Paul for his birthday a year earlier. To Scott, no other model would do. After all, it was Jimmy Page's guitar of choice.

"I'll be back just after four to pick you up," my mom said as I grabbed my bass. Then as I passed the open front passenger-side window, she added, "Hopefully, you won't be deaf by then."

With a sudden thunder crash of Carlo's drums joining Scott's racket, it struck me that she might have a point, even though it was moot. The smile that plastered itself across my face was the visible manifestation of the adrenaline that coursed through my body, siphoning the sound from that garage into fuel for my young brain.

After playing Ritchie Blackmore's iconic opening riff, Scott half sang, half spoke into the microphone some impromptu lyrics set to Deep Purple's "Smoke on the Water." His voice echoed from the speakers, "Ash came out to Scott's place, near a Leggatts Island shoreline... to practice songs for a talent show; we didn't have much time...."

"We have to finally decide which two songs we're gonna do," Carlo interjected with a tinge of exasperation. I plugged my bass into my Peavey TNT amp that I'd left behind at Scott's the previous week and plucked out the repeated motif of Rick James's "Super Freak."

"I was thinking about gettin' funky."

"I don't think so," Carlo said with a laugh that only partially concealed his frustration. With just three weeks before the annual school talent show, we still hadn't decided what songs to perform. Technically we were allowed only one, so we'd cunningly chose to create an "epic." Admittedly, it would be an epic comprised of two entirely distinct parts because they would be two completely different songs. What all three of us liked most about the idea was its subversive aspect. If we immediately slammed into the second song without a break, the judges and audience would be none the wiser—and how rock and roll is that? "Stairway to Heaven" had two parts, so we were just creating a new combo. Lighting a cigarette, Scott grabbed the mic. He half-heartedly coughed into it in a weak impersonation of guitarist Tony Iommi's tape-looped cough, famously triggered by a big hit off a doobie, which serves as the intro to "Sweet Leaf," Sabbath's famous ode to pot. Through feedback and wafting cigarette smoke, Scott kicked into the sludgy opening riff as I plugged into my Overdrive pedal, joining in with Carlo as we all instantly transformed. We were all pretty good players, but combined, we created a mighty, fuzzed-out din that transported us from a humid garage in South Carolina to the stage of the Cal Jam, where we were playing in front of 400,000 transfixed fans. Another typical Saturday practice session was properly underway. For some, it was meditation. For others, yoga. For others still, a fishing rod and a quiet pier. For us, the recipe mainly called for an abundance of decibels.

Scott and I took turns at lead vocals, alternating individual verses and regularly adding our trademark Ozzy Osbourne "We love you all" or alternately "God bless you all" in tandem for our adoring, invisible audience. When we finished, all three of us agreed that "Sweet Leaf" should be one of the songs we would perform. However, neither Scott nor I was particularly enamored of our singing ability or that of the other, so we decided on the spot that sticking to instrumental versions would be the best bet. The idea of one of us transforming into the frontman and being the center of attention was just one step too far. "You can't go wrong with an instrumental." Carlo nodded from behind his kit. "Adding vocals would be a real clusterfuck."

For the second song, we'd narrowed it down to three possibilities: "Swords and Tequila" by Riot, "Running Free" by the one and only Iron Maiden, and Ozzy Osbourne's "Over the Mountain" from his *Diary of a Madman* album released the previous November. Already in heavy rotation within our circle, that album had earned an unexpected level of adulation after the shocking death of Randy Rhoads in a bizarre airplane crash in March. On the other hand, Iron Maiden was a band we'd played a lot in practice, particularly the Paul Di'Anno stuff. We felt this suited us well because, much like early Maiden, we had a definite punk attitude. More succinctly, our raw ambition exceeded our ability, but how punk was that?

In our naïve estimation, we were perfecting a punk/metal hybrid. Our enthusiasm had a mind of its own: untamed, overly carbonated music that, in a perfect world, would be played while Mongol warriors swept en masse down mountainsides on horseback. With that in mind, we discarded "Running Free" and went for "Over the Mountain," the most ambitious song of the three. Tackling his drums like a steroid-enraged linebacker, Carlo pounded out his approximation (most of what we did was approximation) of Lee Kerslake's rolling drum triplet that served as the song's intro.

Swinging off my bass, I rested it against my amp. "Not bad...let me have a go." This tug of war was a long-standing issue between Carlo and me. We both loved the drums and bass in nearly equal measure, the whole rhythm section thing, but we weren't equally adept at both.

Handing the drumsticks over, Carlo smirked. "Knock yourself out."

Taking my place behind the Ludwig kit (if his son was going to play the drums, Carlo's dad wanted him to have the best), I threw myself into what I assumed was the very spirit and soul of the song. The jagged, discordant thumping that rebounded and ricocheted off the walls and ears of all assembled sounded like a body being thrown on top of the kit as both fell down a long staircase. The music press commonly referred to Lee Kerslake as a "body drummer," but I knew the sound I'd created wasn't what that description meant.

The loud laughter that followed my attempt was nearly as thunderous as the sound I had made beating the skins, and I simply responded, "This time, it's bass for me." Several false starts and two complete run-throughs later, we were confident we had nailed "Over the Mountain." Scott wasn't exactly Randy Rhodes, but by streamlining the solos and focusing more on the aggression of our interpretation, we were pretty satisfied. Even though we didn't say it aloud, I think we felt it necessary to play an Ozzy song as a tribute to Randy Rhodes. We all idolized him and had agreed he could rightfully take his place as the fourth face on the Mount Rushmore of rock guitarists, which already included Jimmy Page, Ritchie Blackmore, and Jimi Hendrix.

One thing we could be sure of when we practiced at Scott's place was that his parents, who were rarely home anyway, would never check on us. Because I had such loving parents who were interested in my life, I had difficulty imagining the isolation that Scott and his brother and sister felt in that house. That thought always disappeared from my mind, though, as soon as Scott produced his ceramic water bong in the shape of a wizened wizard. Packing the bowl with a generous amount of redbud, he lit up and inhaled for what seemed a small eternity before exhaling the most ungodly and hilarious amount of smoke this side of a Cheech and Chong movie. Then the coughing started. Deeply baritone and explosive, it rebounded off the walls as my drumming had just minutes earlier; all the while, his face grew redder and redder, his sandy-colored hair accentuating the crimson mask it framed.

Between ragged coughs, Scott handed the bong to me, his voice guttural and hoarse like a guy who had just crawled from a burning house to collapse on his lawn. "Here you go, man...be careful. It's hitting really well."

"Are you sure?" I joked, taking the wizard who'd seen us through many a jam session and creative block.

After Mr. Wizard had made a couple of rounds, we were all well-fried. The conversation then took a natural turn to our other favorite subject: girls.

With his eyelids drooping more than he probably imagined, Carlo leaned back against the wall on his drum stool, hands shooting out before him like he was grabbing something.

"I think Peggy Welch is the hottest chick in school. It's like not even a contest." I realized then that his hands were caressing an invisible outline of Peggy.

Hair disheveled and falling over profoundly red eyes, Scott let out a guffaw. "Like what kind of contest would that be? Line up all the chicks in school before the talent show and have all the guys grade 'em?" He shook his head. "Man, that's really stupid!"

A short pause followed before his eyes and mouth opened wide as if he'd stepped on a tack. "Wait, Carlo, that's actually the best fucking idea I've heard in a long time!"

We burst out in the kind of laughter that comes from strong grass.

"So, I'm guessing Ally's your winner, right?" Carlo asked.

He, Scott, and Tab were the only people who knew about my infatuation. Before I could answer, Scott added, "Yeah, is it Ally who still makes your choad explode? Gets your dickie sticky? Has your dong switched from a limp Liberace to a little Elvis?"

A prolonged bout of laughter ensued as I hit one of those stoned moments when I couldn't stop for a couple of minutes, the laughter making me laugh more. When I could finally wrangle the wild laughter stallion, I nodded. "Yup...."

"Hell, man," Carlo interjected. "Even your names seem custom-made for each other. Ash, Ally. You're like a couple from a romance novel."

Seeing an opportunity he couldn't let pass by, Scott declared, "Well, you'd know since you've read so many of 'em."

"Fuck you," Carlo answered, leaning forward over his drums.

"No, fuck you."

This exchange went on for half a minute until Carlo administered the coup d'état.

"Fuck you more!"

Another round of laughter erupted, but it was more muted than earlier. Tension always simmered between the two. Each guy seemed to feel he was superior to the other. This simmering contest of strength began when they met and seemed to grow from each guy thinking the other was subtly, or not so subtly, making fun of him—which was true. Carlo thought he was brighter because he was a drummer and wasn't stoned as often, while Scott considered himself superior because he was a guitarist and wasn't stocky.

Steering back to the original topic, I said, "There's something about that girl. It's been on my mind since it happened, and, well, she smiled at me last Monday."

Noticing a distinct lack of comprehension on my friends' faces of the gravity of my words, I added, "Like a sexy smile, not a smart-ass smile."

Scott eyed me, "She's cute for sure, but like most chicks at school, it's all about how she looks with a dude." He lit up a cigarette and exhaled. "And you ain't that dude, dude."

I could absorb that bullet because our conversations were an open season, all topics considered fair game. We spoke as if the invisible barriers that surrounded us in nearly every aspect of our daily lives simply didn't exist. When we were together, choice alone was our only consideration. Naïveté, which could and did get me into a lot of trouble at that age, also served as a protective buffer, particularly when having a crush on a girl who was supposed to be in a different league than I was. So, with no hurt feelings on my part and the lingering tension between Scott and Carlo in temporary abeyance, we decided to run through our songs again a couple of times to perfect what was, at least to our ears, damn near perfection already.

On Sunday morning, around ten, some news I was waiting on came through.

"Ash, Tab's on the phone," my mom said, popping her head around my bedroom door.

When I picked up the receiver, Tab's excited voice acted as an electrical current sending a charge through me. "If you want to see what I've done with your logo, stop by any time today."

After calling Carlo and Scott, I biked to Tab's place. Scott hadn't been home, but Carlo said he'd be there as soon as he could. Thinking we'd hit the pool, I put my swimming trunks on under my jeans and attached my boombox to my bike's cargo rack, securing it with bungee cords. In under fifteen minutes, I was knocking on Tab's door to be greeted by his perennially shirtless dad, clutching his perennial glass of wine—no matter that it was 10:30 in the morning.

"Ashley, good to see you. Tab's out by the pool."

Tab and his dad lived in Fiddler Creek Villas, one of the first in an ever-expanding number of complexes springing up all over the island. This one comprised forty or so three-story units built near one of the tidal creeks that emptied into Chicasee Sound. In the center of the complex was a huge swimming pool intended for the exclusive use of villa residents and their guests, which had become one of the favorite hangouts for Tab, Carlo, Scott, and me. It was a sanctuary, all of us needing a central place where we could hang out and be ourselves, away from judging eyes. In one of my daydreams, I'd decided it had been created by the Metal gods exclusively for our amusement because no matter how hot and humid the day, the pool was almost always empty.

We rarely had to deal with interlopers. One such occasion involved three college guys visiting the island on spring break. As Warlord's "Deliver Us From Evil" blasted from my boombox, they wandered through the gate, said, "How's it going," "What's up," and "Hey," then proceeded to strip naked and jump into the pool. After splashing around in obvious alcohol-fueled glee for a few minutes, they got out, dressed, said, "Take care," "Cool music," and "Y'all have a good 'un," and left. As we all stared at the still agitated water, I said, "Somewhere in the universe, dice were rolled, and we got that instead of Cheryl Ladd and two of her friends."

After unfastening that same boombox, I made my way stealthily to the pool. I could just see the top of Tab's wiry hair over the low stucco wall and oleander bushes surrounding three sides of the pool. The fourth side consisted of the bathrooms and changing rooms. Tab was reclining on a lounge chair, his head buried in a comic, oblivious to the world around him. Clearly, he hadn't heard me approach on the gravel path that ran along the perimeter of the pool wall, so I silently pushed open the metal swing gate and crept up behind him. I turned the volume knob all the way down on the cassette player and pressed play. Then, when I was standing right over him, I turned the volume up to maximum.

Comic flying, Tab leaped out of his chair with a strangled gasp, all to the strains of Accept's musical uppercut "Breaker." The unmistakable larynx-scouring voice of Udo Dirkschneider acted on Tab like a lightning strike.

His face a mask of bewilderment, Tab spun around, clutching a hand to his chest.

"Holy shit Ash, I didn't know you were there...I think I had a minor heart attack!"

Patting Tab on the back, I laughed. "Only minor, huh?"

"I didn't think you'd be over for a while. Let me just go grab the drawing."

While he ran back to his condo, I doffed pants and shirt and dove into the welcoming glass-smooth water. During my breakneck bike ride, humidity enveloped me like an invisible syrup, and the relief was instantaneous. By the time I surfaced for a second time, Tab was standing at the pool's edge.

"Here it is. I think you're gonna like what I did with your idea." He threw a towel at me.

I dried off, and just as I was sitting down, Carlo came with a purposeful stride through the swing gate.

"Perfect timing, my man. We were just about to look at the drawing."

With the authority of General Patton barking at his troops, Carlo

—who loved to add a touch of drama whenever it seemed warranted— yelled "Wait!" He thrust a hand into his pocket and withdrew a pack of cigarettes. After taking one out and lighting it, he nodded at us. "Okay, we can now proceed."

Tab's work gave real definition to Brothman's mountainous muscles and gave his face a sinister, domineering expression. As we examined his work, Tab said, "When I was doing my drawing based on your sketch, I kept thinking how the lines coming off of Brothman looked like they could be stench lines, so I added a couple of flies too." Carlo hadn't heard this before, and a quizzical look crossed his face. Tab elaborated, "You know, like when a character stinks in a cartoon, there'll be wavy lines coming off him."

Feeling déjà vu, I protested, "It was meant to be steam."

Carlo added, "It looks like steam...except for the flies."

I smiled wryly. "Even though Brothman probably does stink a bit, the lines I drew were meant to be steam."

His forehead creasing in concern, Tab asked, "So you do like it? Do you think it needs changes?"

Holding the drawing a few inches from my face, I scrutinized it closely for a few moments, then broke into a smile. "No, I think it's brilliant," I said slowly before adding, "But when you do the full-size version, just leave out the flies."

Carlo's cherubic face lit up like a kid on Christmas morning. "Besides the flies, I love it!"

Beaming, Tab let out an exuberant chuckle. "Well, I'll get started on the backdrop right away then."

In just three weeks, we would use the backdrop for our fast-approaching school talent show performance. Every year towards the end of May, a talent show held in the gymnasium featured acts like comedy sketches, dance routines, maybe someone singing a favorite popular song, and someone else playing an original composition on the school's upright piano. This year, the assembled student body and staff would be introduced to a band with several imaginary albums under its belt: *Brothman Ariseth,* which was, naturally, their first album; *Brothstein,* which was a concept album with our hero Brothman depicted on the imaginary album cover vaguely resembling Franken-stein but with more trademark "steam lines" coming off him, and the obligatory double live album; *Brothissimo: Live in Italy.*

There was no doubt about it: nothing would ever be the same af-ter Steaming Broth descended upon the unsuspecting victims of Leg-gatts School.

5

As a boy, my days felt long and multifaceted, even picaresque if I imagined myself in that misunderstood hero role. I constantly took in a barrage of new information, unfiltered by experience, and acted upon it through an often awkward trial and error rather than analysis. At school, my unanalyzed routine continued. I stepped lightly around those I registered as threats, and in the classroom, I verbally barged in and then lapped up the shallow bowls of acknowledgment that came my way: a threadbare, tightrope existence in many ways but only in school. Once out in the warm air, hanging out poolside, jamming with "The Broth," or best of all, immersed wholly in the wonders of Declaration Island, I was a more at ease and complete human being. Bridging these two extremes seemed as conceivable as *Dawn of the Dead*-like zombies overrunning the school and eating everyone.

In the weeks that followed our brief exchange, I'd glanced at Ally many times during gym, but I always found her occupied, talking to friends or engaged in whatever activity Ms. Burns had on tap for the day, with one exciting exception. On a rare, treasured "fun day" when the class could vote on our activity, we almost unanimously chose capture the flag. Being the fastest kid in our gym class, I swooped in, seeing myself as a bird of prey, towards several members of my team who'd been captured. Keeping just ahead of my pursuers, I tagged Ally's outstretched hand, freeing her and four other players from the chain in, if I do say so myself, a perfectly executed jailbreak.

She giggled. "You're a fast boy, aren't you?"

Without breaking stride, I smiled and said, "You inspired me." I kept my eyes on the ground as I circled back towards the safety of our team's side, hardly believing the words had come from my mouth.

"Kinda confident too," I heard her say as I led my liberated teammates back to safety. When I turned to look back at Ally, Ms. Burns was blowing her whistle, shouting gym was over and we should head back to the locker rooms.

Ally was walking several yards ahead of me, flanked by two friends, all lost in gossip. Just as well, I thought, because the confidence Ally had mentioned was something I was in short supply of outside of capture the flag or playing bass. The little confidence I could muster came from focusing on other things: running or getting lost in a song or sitting at the top of the Declaration lighthouse, feet dangling over the edge of the gallery like a king surveying his green kingdom of whispering trees. As for Ally, I hadn't even been able to look at her when I'd spoken. I felt as if a light and fragile thread would be forever severed if I did.

Mirroring the jailbreak in capture the flag, I had recently taken a big step towards increasing what I perceived as freedom. Many of the kids in the Upper School had replaced their bikes with mopeds, enticing me with promises of distance tamed and time saved. The mopeds were all the colors of the rainbow—red, blue, yellow, orange, and purple —and their names were also enticing: Raleigh, Puch, Honda, Motobecane, Peugeot, Garelli, and Sachs. A local ordinance banned motorcycles and scooters in Sheltered Harbour. They were too noisy, spoiling the peaceful, natural idyll. Mopeds, though, were legal, and suddenly Declaration Island could be a mere hop, skip, and a jump from my door instead of an all-day undertaking.

Working after school doing yardwork around Sheltered Harbour for the past three summers had paid off, and on one thrilling Saturday, my parents drove me to Savannah so I could buy the moped of my dreams. Some dreams, it turns out, *can* be purchased. After a whole lot of research, I had settled on a brand still absent from the motorized symbols of freedom parked on the side of the school: Vespa, which meant *wasp* in Italian. Best known for their iconic scooters, Vespa also made mopeds. I didn't care that they came from Tuscany because, with the motto "Not just a scooter, a way of life," to me it was just Harley Davidson by another name. The feel of the wind and the right to choose whatever road I wanted to (or at least more than I could have on my bike) appealed to me greatly, so I bought a silver Vespa Grande.

The top of the Vespa moped line, the Grande had a sleek tubular style frame incorporating the fuel tank, which was far more streamlined than any other moped at school. Integral to its design was an extra-long double seat, mag wheels, chrome footrest, and retractable rear foot pegs. For my money, it was the flat-out coolest and most aesthetically pleasing moped ever made. As it was too far for me to ride back to Leggatts, my parents had to spring for a carrier attached to the fender of my dad's Delta 88. Only two weeks after I bought mine, Carlo had his own, having converted to the church of Vespa after taking mine for a forty-mile-an-hour spin. He didn't choose the Grande but rather a model called the Si. He picked it for the reason that made perfect sense to him: his favorite color was black, and as the Grande didn't come in that color and the Si did—it was a no-brainer.

Soon Carlo and I had slightly altered an old biker saying to fit our needs: "I don't ride a Vespa to add days to my life. I ride to add life to my days." Riding side by side on our badass Vespas after school down the arteries that spun out from Sheltered Harbour made another biker credo solidify in our minds: "Brothers not of kin but brothers of the wind."

The tangible internal buzzing of youth now had two mighty and fast-flowing rivers to deal with in the minds of Carlo and me. One was our shiny new "Iron Horses," and the other was the growing power and confidence in the music we were making. Steaming Broth had taken on a life of its own, and all three of us in the band spoke of it as a living, sentient thing. "The Broth will let us know what it wants." "You join the conquering Broth or get run over by it." "Brothman is a force of nature. He'll dine with the gents and sleep with their wives. Like nature itself, he's neither for nor against those who listen, but when he rumbles into town, he does it with the force of a hurricane."

We felt part of an unseen power, and we all loved it. On occasion, the Broth would speak through us like the Oracle at Delphi. A mere two weeks before the fast-approaching talent show, he chose to speak through me. After finishing a run-through of "Sweet Leaf," I brushed the hair out of my face, glanced at Scott and then Carlo, and found words pouring from me. Carlo later reported that I wore an expression of grim determination, my voice somber and steady as I blurted, "We need to get in and not let up with our set at the talent show."

Scott laughed, breaking the suddenly serious atmosphere, "What's wrong, puddin' pop?"

"It's not what's wrong, Musketeer; it's what could be more right," I said cryptically. During an earlier jam session and bong round table some months before, we had decided that if the three of us had to be a candy bar, it would have to be the 3 Musketeers. Cannabis could often make otherwise frivolous topics take on a real gravitas. Carlo had suggested Milk Duds and then Chunky with Raisins, the latter of which he saw as a name for our band.

Scott, though, had shot it down in flames straight off. "That name won't fly," he protested, looking at Carlo, "you'd get top billing as Chunky...and I don't want to be a fuckin' raisin."

As we were ensconced in Scott's garage, I lit up the ceramic wizard bong resting on my bass amp, inhaled deeply, and passed it to Scott. After he and Carlo had imbibed, I continued loudly, full of a solemnity that even I realized was too much. "We should open with 'Outlaw' instead of 'Sweet Leaf.' If we hit the audience with 'Outlaw' and lead right into "Over the Mountain," the full undiluted power of the Broth's sound will come through like a Panzer division. We'll catch everyone off guard, and they'll become our innocent victims!"

My pitch had risen steadily as I spoke, and I was sure I was getting a taste of what Winston Churchill must have felt when he gave a rousing speech. "You know, the element of surprise...like an air raid. By the time we're done, everyone will be looking at each other like, 'Are we dreaming, or did that just really happen?'"

"Outlaw" was a ferocious track from Riot's watershed album *Fire Down Under*, a song, band, and album that were all our favorites, but

"Outlaw" had never even come up in earlier discussions. Before either could respond, I continued, "We all know "Sweet Leaf" kicks ass, but "Outlaw" will be more like a jab before the uppercut. Its pure adrenaline will catch the audience completely by surprise. 'They'll fall to their knees...'"

"'And repent if you please,'" Carlo yelled, completing a line from the Judas Priest song "Exciter." We understood the words as direct encouragement to the band, passed on miasma-like from Brothman himself.

Scott seemed to pick up this unseen force, agreeing without protest. "Well, we better get to work then!"

And that's what we did. All the pieces fell into place like a preordained thing. After we finished our sixth run-through, Carlo stood up from behind his kit, threw his sticks in the air, and proclaimed, "Brothman has spoken!"

On Monday, when Carlo and I entered Mrs. Adlai's music class, we were given great news. As the kids filed in, she motioned us over to her at the front of the room.

"Oh, boys, I wanted to tell you that anyone performing musical numbers in the talent show can use this room after school this week and next. It will be on a first-come, first-served basis." With that bit of information, things suddenly became more real. It was momentous when I could focus on something important and see the pieces fall into place. Steaming Broth was now moving from the bedroom and garage, with an audience composed of Eddie, Geezer, and on occasion, a kid named Paul, to 500 people held in rapt attention (if we had any say). This clarity, however, wasn't reserved only for the positive in my mind. Any glimmer of hope I sensed had to have its perfect dark counterpoint—a reminder to be extra wary, to cheer up only so much before that cheer would somehow be inverted, sliding down unseen tracks greased with doubt the instant I'd processed the thought our band was finally coming of age.

After school, I decided to leave without stopping by my locker. I was riding a high I didn't want to come down from yet. With just my notebook, science book, and Walkman, I exited by a little-used back entrance, hoping its isolation would enable me to avoid any potential run-ins with my antagonists, who often appeared ghostlike out of the blue with alarming and increasing frequency. To my right, closely bordering the school, were the thick woods of a forest preserve. Ahead of me to my left was the parking lot that I beelined for, a journey of a mere thirty yards. Just around the corner, my Vespa was waiting to carry me away. As usual, my mind wandered, imagining a colossal light show blazing above Steaming Broth on a massive stage as the three of us kicked into "Outlaw" to rapturous applause. Putting my headphones snugly onto my ears, I pushed play, having already queued up that same song to keep myself soaring as free as an osprey heading for its perch out of reach on Declaration. Powerful and intense, Guy Speranza sang of an impending showdown, and little could I know how prescient his words were.

Mouthing the lyrics, gripping the Walkman in the front pocket of my jacket, I closed my eyes for a couple of seconds and turned my head skyward to catch the warmth of the sun. When I opened them, I almost walked directly into Brice and Trey, rounding the corner to the parking lot. The parking lot where my moped, a stallion to freedom, awaited me to fire it up and hit the road, leaving that damn school in the dust. A shove to the chest knocked me back several steps, and my headphones fell back around my neck. The notebook and textbook tumbled to the ground.

"Look who we have here," Brice bellowed. "Looks like you dropped something. That was clumsy." Swooping in behind me, Trey thumped his chest against my back, pushing me towards Brice.

"No one around to interrupt us this time, huh, Pot-Ash?" Pot-Ash was the least offensive barb in their limited arsenal.

Straightening my back, I looked my nemesis in the eye to see if I could detect any sliver of commonality, the slightest hint of shared common ground. If it was there, I wasn't seeing it.

"He doesn't have much to say, does he," Trey roared directly behind me. "Kinda rude."

"Yeah, it *is* rude!" Brice grabbed the Walkman from my pocket. "Listening to..." Opening the Walkman, he pulled out the cassette and read aloud, "Riot, *Fire Down Under.*" Then, bursting into an exaggerated laugh, he returned his attention to me. "From under where, your balls?" In an instant, I'd gone from Riot in stereo to Brice and Trey laughing in full surround sound.

"Let's make sure you're not so rude again, don't ya think?" Lifting the cassette high over his head, he yanked the tape out with his other hand, letting it collect on the ground in a shimmering pile. He tossed the cassette on the sidewalk and crushed it under his Adidas high tops to add an exclamation point. Funny, the things you remember in a situation where every second feels like minutes, but his big-ass Adidas remain etched in my brain next to a pile of unspooled tape.

"Listen up, faggot, don't litter on school property. Dean Knight wouldn't like that at'tall."

Automatically, I stooped to pick it up, and when I stood up again, Brice, who was standing so close to me I instantly knew he had no clue about proper oral hygiene, said something that didn't initially make any sense to me. "Man, Trey, this dirtbag's smokin' so much weed he can't keep his balance."

He made a hand gesture I didn't understand, then shoved me backward again. Been there, done that, I thought, but this time I tumbled over Trey, who had positioned himself on all fours behind me. I tripped, falling hard onto my shoulders and head, knocking the wind out of me and covering my back in pine needles and dirt. Laughter pierced through the ringing in my ears, and I just caught the end of another verbal volley from Brice.

"A lesson to watch your step when you're stoned!"

He then scoured up all the mucous he could find in his throat, quite a reserve, it turned out, spitting a massive loogie at my head, which I just managed to avoid by rolling onto my side.

"Seems he can move when under fire," Trey offered, as both of them broke off into a deafening round of laughter before stomping off through the door from which I had just emerged. And so, another day at Leggatts School came to a close.

After classes finished on Tuesday, I entered the music room with a sway to my step. That morning, I'd dropped off my bass and amp for our first on-school property practice session. It felt subversive. Carlo was already there assembling his drum kit. At the same time, Scott, oh so delicately and precisely, adjusted one of his tuning pegs, scrutinizing his beloved electric guitar tuner like a surgeon performing delicate brain surgery.

Without looking up, Scott jokingly said, "Bassists are *always* the last to show up."

Removing my bass from its case, I attached the strap, swung it around my shoulders, and sniffed. "Just the great ones."

Within ten minutes, we'd kicked into our two-song set, and I could tell that Scott and Carlo were feeling the same weird sense of power I was. The thought that *our* music was penetrating every crevice of each classroom, rushing over every desk, reverberating off chalkboards, rattling each pane of glass had given us all a sense of empowerment. We were captains guiding our unstoppable destroyers into the harbor, while on the beach, natives stood awestruck at what they beheld. During our second run-through of "Outlaw," with all three of us locked into a mighty groove, I glanced up. Around the half-opened door poked Brice's head; then he and Otto sauntered in. They flopped into chairs in the back row, turning the ones in front of them around and propping up their feet. As this unexpected audience scrutinized us, we took it up another notch. The sounds we made had a life of their own, taking any negativity or intimidation in stride. Then a strange thing happened. Glancing again at the two lounging figures, I noticed that each was tapping a foot in time with our music.

Surprisingly, this wasn't a feel-good moment for me, and I took a few seconds to register why. We would receive a brief reprieve as long as we were providing entertainment, specifically music—something acceptable for long-haired guys to do. But, like cold water seeping over me, came the sense that we were playing exclusively for their diversion. The unconscious half-smiles plastered on their faces made them look like a couple of yahoos enjoying a minstrel show. That impression erased anything positive I could've taken from entertaining two of my tormentors.

After practicing, I passed Mr. Box's classroom, and seeing that he was still grading papers, I darted in. He had lent me the first two Fleetwood Mac albums a few days earlier, which I had recorded onto cassette tapes, and I wanted to let him know I'd return them the following day. His asking Carlo and me a few weeks earlier if we could name Fleetwood Mac's first guitarist had made us genuinely curious about the band's early blues-based albums and their family tree. By the time the door clicked shut behind me after my chat with Mr. Box, a smile spread across my face. I felt extra cool because I'd answered an unexpected "extra credit" question, instantly spouting out the name of future Rolling Stone Mick Taylor as Peter Green's replacement in John Mayall's Bluesbreakers. As this little triumph swam in my head, Trey—the member of the trio who'd been missing from our earlier practice session—suddenly appeared. As he passed me, heading in the opposite direction, he bumped my shoulder hard. My smile disappeared as a huge one spread across his broad face. He turned to me with his chin up in the air. "Watch where you're goin', faggot."

Although the trio's repertoire was limited in action and words, it was effective through repetition. I wanted to believe these encounters rolled off my back, but they took up residence in my subconscious. Their effect wasn't apparent to me in my day-to-day life, but they had burrowed into me, altering the feng shui I had carefully tended in such a way that it took some time for me to recognize the alterations —things like the slight deviations of my routes in and around school, the way I would catch my reflection in the school doors and see my shoulders sunken. I'd always quickly straighten up, but it didn't register at the time that slouching was my default setting. Patterns I discarded as little quirks were broken shards of excavated pottery that would slowly need to be reconstructed into what they had been and might become again.

When Saturday rolled around, a giant imaginary clock in my mind began to tick away the hours until the following Friday when Steaming Broth would unleash hell on the public at large. None of us was nervous because we didn't really have anything to lose. For most participating students, I assumed that their dance routine, violin solo, standup comedy act, or dramatic reading from Tennessee Williams could add only a little extra luster to their experience at Leggatts School—a nice photo in the yearbook with a witty caption to add a little cherry to the cake.

For both Carlo and me, it was cathartic. A hand grenade tossed to explode in the center of the gym, announcing who we were via the music we loved—loud, heavy, unapologetic. The thrill of knowing that the whole school had to listen to the blood and iron of our symbolic voices expressed through music almost entirely alien to them was akin to what an athlete must feel when the endorphins kick in. We felt caught up in a headlong, inexorable rush, all of us far too inexperienced to sense any nervousness beyond the desire to play to the best of our abilities.

That Saturday, practice was at my house. To avoid the inconvenience of deconstructing and reconstructing his drumkit multiple times, Carlo had left it at school. For similar reasons, Scott and I left our larger amps there too. With the talent show just a few days away and the majority of our gear at school, our only option was to make do with what we had. So Carlo came over that day with a beat-up snare drum and high hat retained from his first set. A few minutes later, Scott walked in with his guitar case in one hand and his tiny five-watt Harmony Power Pal practice amp in the other. Like a police dog locked onto a perpetrator, Geezer excitedly sniffed and pawed at Scott—a perennial canine favorite in my house, with all the exciting herbal scents emanating from his jacket pocket.

"Well, look who's here, a wannabe Jimmy Page," I said in a specific high-pitched warble.

Carlo, Scott, and I all "gave voice" to Geezer and Eddie to make jokey observations and convey things we just wouldn't come out and say as ourselves. The voice usually sounded a bit like an inebriated and opinionated Mickey Mouse.

"*Gonna be*, Geezer," Scott corrected.

Still in Geezer's voice, I said, "What a black lab? Welcome to the club, man! Licking your balls will soon be your new favorite hobby!"

He set down his equipment, fished out his Visine, and put a few drops in each eye. Then Scott put his fingers to his mouth to indicate smoking a doobie and whispered, "Can we?"

"Yeah, but we have to wait for my mom to leave, and she's only going to the post office, so the sooner we start practicing, the sooner that's gonna happen."

We plugged into our woefully inadequate amps, and all three of us sat on chairs I'd grabbed from the dining room. My available amp was a Pignose five-watt. It was a cool-looking little thing, but it provided only one guarantee: for one weekend, my neighbors could enjoy the natural ambient sounds of a barrier island instead of three exuberant kids honing their next-generation metal/punk majesty.

Within minutes of my mom leaving, we packed a bowl and passed it around as we stood by my half-open sliding door, blowing all the smoke outside. We then ran through a few laughably tinny, feeble renditions of our setlist, which we did more out of a sense of obligation than from hopes of gaining anything valuable.

Once it became clear that Carlo's snare drum had been reduced to a glorified metronome, overwhelming the collective ten watts Scott and I were pumping out, we set our instruments aside. Carlo had arrived that day with an album he'd just bought and couldn't stop talking about, and seeing his opportunity, he removed it from its sleeve and thrust it at me. With an eye-gouging cover that made me look at forks in a new light, the record was *Blackout,* the latest by the Scorpions. Putting it on, I turned up the volume. What then occurred was an often sought but too rarely attained perfect confluence: Scott's prime redbud and brand-new music playing on my brand-new turntable, not just any turntable, but a Technics SL-10, the birthday present to end all birthday presents.

I liked to imagine that the future, everything that could be, was somehow bundled into that one small object in my room. Turning the volume up just as Scott started saying something about how he wished he could get a guitar sound like Matthias Jabs, I suddenly found myself far away, lost in the words of the album's power ballad, "No One Like You." Before me, Ally's face was framed, like a close-up in a video, with that half-smile/half-pout on her lips, her hair bigger than in real life. She was looking at me provocatively, indicating I should follow her through all the dry ice smoke that had magically appeared. From somewhere unseen, the Scorpions lead singer Klaus Meine started singing imploringly, giving voice to my hormonal wishes.

"Hellllooo? Hey Ash, you still with us?" Scott leaned forward on his chair, waving a hand in front of my eyes, an amused, stoned look plastered on his face.

"Yeah, I'm here. I was just thinkin'...."

"Let me guess. Ally, right?" He grinned, leaning back in his chair. "You gotta face it, dude, shit like her smilin' at you don't matter; she ain't never gonna do anything beyond that with you. She can't. She's a fucking prissy chick who has her reputation at school, and that's all that matters to her, man."

Having sauntered over to me a few moments earlier, Geezer rested his head on my leg, seeking head rubs.

Taking on the silly Geezer voice, Carlo said, "He's right, man, best to keep your mind on the band...and the talent show." Knowing "his" voice, Geezer's ears sprang up, and he looked at me as if on cue.

I changed the subject by pointing out the window at my mom's station wagon, pulling back into the driveway, so we all decided to run through the songs a couple more times. Just as we finished, we heard the three customary taps on my door. Opening it, my mom greeted me with the friendliest smile imaginable and held out a plate of sandwiches. The smile drew attention away from her eyes, which were scanning the scene for any tell-tale "red flags" like cigarettes or the odd joint. Trusting me too much created a blind spot in my mom's perception, often causing her to edit otherwise strong circumstantial evidence, like our red eyes. Once she deemed all was fine, she set the plate on my dresser.

"Thought you boys might be hungry with all the practicing," she said, scanning our faces. My mom always made the rounds to check up on me when I had friends in the house, particularly when my door was closed. If her visits annoyed me a bit, her sandwiches were welcome, but the way Carlo and Scott attacked them seemed like a giveaway to me. To my amazement, instead of yelling, "Your voracious munchies prove you were all smoking pot when I was gone," Mom smiled and said, "Dig in, guys. I can make more if you want."

His mouth full, Carlo mumbled, "These are delicious, Mrs. Howe."

Equally stuffed with corned beef, crumbs spilling from the corner of his mouth, Scott insisted, "I'm already full, but thanks. This really hits the spot."

After polishing off the sandwiches, the guys seemed to pick up on a vibe I was trying to mask. The pot we'd smoked, that damn Scorpions song, and Scott's cold assessment had shone a spotlight on things I usually kept in the dark. Although I was far from knowing how to analyze my feelings, I'd become introspective and quiet. I barely noticed when Carlo left the room to phone his mom to pick up Scott and him. Things I'd managed to keep under wraps now nagged at the back of my mind: the seemingly endless rounds of abuse at the hands of Brice and his friends was one thing, but the weird blank space where I wanted Ally to be was something else altogether. Without knowing why, I settled under what felt like the lead vest they had me wear when I was getting X-rays at the dentist. Except this one covered me completely.

Carlo patted me on the back. "See you tomorrow, man, right?"

His words reminded me I was supposed to ride my Vespa to his place to watch movies the following day. "Oh yeah, I'll be there."

My voice was as upbeat as I could muster, but even I could tell I didn't sound enthusiastic, so I added, "I'm feeling a little out of it today, but I'll be cool tomorrow."

"You're not cool now, so how are you going to be tomorrow?" came Geezer's voice from Scott, always the consummate smart-ass.

"By chillin' today," I feebly replied.

When they had left, and I was heading back to my room, my mom stopped me in the hall, put her hands on my shoulders, and looked straight into my eyes. "Is everything okay in your world? At school? Is someone giving you a hard time?"

How moms, the good ones, can sense these things never ceases to amaze me. No, no, and yes were the answers to her questions, but I simply wasn't any good at communicating my feelings yet. I loved her and appreciated her concern, but I certainly wasn't ready to spill my guts. I didn't really know how.

"Yeah, everything's great. Just thinking about the talent show and stuff. I'm fine." I could tell from how she continued looking into my eyes that she knew I was holding things back but also that I didn't feel capable of expressing my concerns.

Kissing my forehead, she pressed my head against hers. "Okay, Ashey, just know that your dad and I are always here for you."

"Thanks, Mom, I know."

Knowing is one thing. Understanding another.

On Sunday, around nine in the morning, I received a most welcome call from Tab. The backdrop for Steaming Broth's talent show performance was ready! None of us, not even Tab, had thought he'd be able to finish the thing until the following week. After making some quick phone calls, I agreed to act as the emissary to view and either approve or reject the final piece as worthy of backing the Broth. If rejected, I figured Mr. Keating could use it as a tarp when painting. After I showered, I put on my jeans and Black Sabbath *Mob Rules* T-shirt and made it to Tab's place in record time. He had told me to meet him by the pool, where he said he'd string up the backdrop on the outside wall of the changing rooms. I instantly knew that Tab had hit the proverbial ball out of the park. Brothman was a shadowy, hulking, menacing figure. The steam rising off his imposing form, with its massive arms, outstretched over a bubbling cauldron, was everything I had envisaged and more.

"*Oh my God!*" I half yelled. Tab's beaming face showed he was hugely pleased. "You've outdone yourself, you talented bastard!"

An elderly, cadaverously white guest wading in the pool's shallow end let out an audible gasp. He then exited the pool; wrapped a towel around his gaunt form; looked over me, Tab, and the backdrop; sniffed loudly; and left. Yup, Brothman was already proving effective!

Tab stretched his arms skyward. "I felt Brothman guiding my hands. Like a telepathic bond." He paused for effect. "He told me to do it right, or he'd kill me."

"I think he would," I laughed, then spontaneously hugged him. The guy was such a real and true friend, willing to go above and beyond because that's just how he was wired. "Thanks, Tab. This is gonna put us over the top. It's a masterpiece."

His eyes momentarily became saucers; then he broke into a huge smile.

"I almost forgot...." Rummaging through the front pocket of his cargo shorts, he handed me back twenty dollars. "Your change." He looked at me sincerely. "My dad had a lot of the stuff I needed on hand, and when I told him what I was doing, he told me to help myself."

I was going to tell Tab to thank his dad but then quickly said I wanted to thank him personally. When I did, his enthusiasm fed my growing excitement even further.

"Ashley, it was a pleasure. I've always been a patron of the arts, and you boys are the next generation's standard bearers."

Tab's dad would drive him to school on Monday to store the backdrop in the music room. Tab was also our unofficial stage crew member, as he would be the guy to figure out how to hang the damn thing behind us.

Every day after school the following week found the Broth in the music room, honing our sound like a master bladesmith perfecting his blade between hammer and anvil. I thought of the band as a knife, able to cut through the invisible barriers that sometimes felt all too solid. On Tuesday, we arrived a bit late, so we had to wait our turn, sitting at the back of the room watching a girl practice a piano solo, followed by a choreographed dance routine that included two of Ally's friends. On Thursday, we were just beaten to the room by another band composed of juniors and seniors with the rarest of creatures: a lead singer. They had chosen to perform Rick Springfield's "Jessie's Girl" and honed their version to a reasonable facsimile of the massive hit, but Carlo, Scott, and I found their choice to be bland and safe. We all agreed their song was probably the hot ticket to win the show because of those two factors and the fact that the guys were all clean-cut, active in sports, and generally popular.

When Friday came, it caught me off guard. Rolling onto my back, I slowly opened my eyes and rubbed them before running my fingers through my hair as if I didn't have a care in the world. Like a crash of thunder, though, the realization hit me. That afternoon I would be on stage introducing to the collected eardrums of the entire student body and faculty how heavy metal music should, or maybe more appropriately, could sound.

▬▬▬ As we grow older, the misguided sense we are in control of time lessens, and the loosening of this imagined force allows the inexorable to sweep us up in its current. This imagined capability subsequently outlines those days of naïve certainty and determination in a much bolder frame than we ever could have considered while experiencing them. Such was the case with the talent show.

The talent show took place in the middle of the school day—a special two-hour break from routine. Out of twelve acts, we were to be the fifth. Scheduled before us were two seniors, a guy and a girl, who would show off the latest dance moves that would stand out in a New York nightclub. We'd be followed by "The Working Class Dogs," the upperclassmen performing their note-perfect version of "Jessie's Girl." They had taken their name from the album *Working Class Dog*, which features that song. Their backdrop was a blown-up version of the shirt-and-tie-wearing dog of the album cover with photos of the four band members sticking out of the shirt's chest pocket instead of old Rick. I had to admit it looked great and was quite funny.

While the acts that had yet to perform loitered behind the temporary stage constructed for the occasion, I noticed that Duncan, the guitarist for the Working Class Dogs, was eying me. Moments earlier, he had been huddled with his band, reviewing their pending performance in minute detail. Then he broke away and approached me. Part of the "preppy" contingent, he wore a pink Polo with collar upturned, his usually carefully parted hair tousled to portray a rocker. A junior, he was comfortably embraced by the popular contingent of the school, and although we had only ever said a few words to each other, he'd never given me a hard time. I always assumed this stemmed from our shared interest in music. Now, as he neared me, I could tell he was distracted. I was sitting on stacked-up tumbling mats against the back wall, joking around with Carlo, when he walked up and asked incredulously, "Aren't you nervous at all?"

His tension was so palpable that it made me consider what he was asking. The truth was that, although Scott was edgy, neither Carlo nor I was the slightest bit nervous. Maybe we just had less to lose. I was excited, but that was it.

"No, not at all. It's just fun, man, no big deal."

He shook his head, looking at the large curtain that formed the back of the stage. "I'm nervous as hell," he muttered before walking away.

Just moments later came the announcement that had assumed an almost mythical place in my mind, like an echo from a dream I'd had over and over again. As the school's two disco superstars exited stage left, Mrs. Adlai walked in front of the microphone on the right side of the stage. She spoke in her clipped, precise manner: "And now everybody, we switch from the world of modern dance (I glanced at Carlo and chuckled) to the world of modern music. Although heavier and louder than many of you might be accustomed to, I think you will enjoy the melodies and enthusiasm of..." She looked at an index card in her hand. "The Steaming Broth."

I didn't notice that she had taken it upon herself to add "The" to our band name until a few days later when I heard a tape of our performance that Duncan had captured on his boombox. Also, on that tape, right after our introduction and very close to the recorder, the voice of Mr. Box repeated our band's name with a playful gravitas, emphasizing the word "Broth." Our guitars slung over our shoulders, Scott and I trotted onto the stage while Carlo followed a few steps behind, clutching his drumsticks tightly. Our backdrop unfurled behind us on perfect cue the moment we were in position, revealing Brothman in all his steaming glory. Only the top of Tab's head was visible as he stood on a ladder, timing the drop to perfection.

Scott and I plugged into our amps, and after a fast "One, two. One, two, three, four" from Carlo, we kicked into "Outlaw." Adrenaline rushed through me so intensely that I visualized myself as a coffee percolator with my head as the top about to pop. Hair flying free, banging my head in time to the thick waves of sound blasting from our amps, in one sweeping glance, I took in the seemingly vast audience; Scott's smiling face, his head thrust back, eyes closed, looking like

Jimmy Page; and then Carlo pounding his drums as if Iron Maiden's Clive Burr had possessed his body. Our performance was a glorious and beautiful high; during it, I cared about nothing except how we sounded so together, so alive, like one undulating mind, telepathically linked. All our hours of practice were paying off, and I could tell we were in the zone, having a blast.

As planned, without a break, we segued into Ozzy's "Over The Mountain," the rolling drum salvo that starts the song almost certainly sounding to our uninitiated audience like a brief rhythmic interlude instead of a new song. Here we took things to yet another level. We blasted off into the stratosphere on sound waves bent to our will. The unsung words of dreams coming true and riding shooting stars ran boldly through my head.

Then our set was over, and as I stood there feeling as happy as I could remember, the loudest applause I had ever heard erupted! People were whistling, shouting, clapping, and even stomping their feet. I unplugged from my amp, and all three of us took a collective bow, then ran off the stage into the hall that led to the weight room, where all performers completing their act were to exit. James, the head janitor, a tall, lanky African American from the island's northern end, met us at the doorway. He was more than just some guy who cleaned the school. He was someone all three of us chatted with regularly, often slipping into the storage room where we'd commiserate with clandestine smokes accompanied by crude jokes threaded with every bad word yet invented. These were acts of rebellion on all our parts, seeking the thrill of walking the razor's edge—which, in retrospect, could have gotten us, as kids, a lot of detention and after-school toilet scrubbing but could have cost James his job.

"Man, all right!" he shouted enthusiastically, high-fiving and patting each of us on the back. "You boys were goin' for it...you were burnin'!"

Pure elation is what I felt, and the smiles and pride on Carlo's and Scott's faces told me they had traveled to the same place I'd just journeyed. These were my friends, and I wouldn't have traded them in for any other dudes in the world.

6

A funny thing: all that cheering and applause made me feel, briefly, like a conquering hero returning to my homeland from some faraway battle. A land I'd never really felt connected to before. That enchantment, however, extended only as far as the threshold of the gymnasium because once I walked into English class immediately after the talent show, no one made a single comment to me, positive or negative, about the performance. Just like any other day, multiple conversations wrestled for prominence before class started, blending into one loud but indistinct murmuring punctuated by occasional clear words and laughter.

As it turned out, The Working Class Dogs won the talent show, as I suspected they would. Surprisingly, I was happy for them and congratulated Duncan when he walked into the hallway after their performance. Out of breath, a broad smile plastered on his face, he thanked me exuberantly, adding without hesitation that he'd really liked our performance too. Only one winner was announced, no runners-up, but every other act was thanked. Just to have performed was a triumph for Steaming Broth, and truth be told, our pride in each other was enough.

Another funny thing: sometimes, just knowing that Declaration Island was there, out of sight but always waiting, was enough to give me a boost, to keep me going. I could draw energy from the mere thought of its wild, untouched lands nestling like a secret, hidden but close.

This boost was only a short-term solution, though, and after two or three weeks, I would have to trek back to its shores to set back the proverbial horizon. Allowing my senses to recharge. Pushing back the horizon freed me from the confining cage of anxiety, allowing the wonder to find its way to the center stage it should always occupy in a young mind.

━━━ The Monday after Steaming Broth had unveiled its might, I spent an extra hour on latrine duty assigned to me and a kid named Billy, who sometimes joined in my razzing of a teacher. This recent offense was a particularly obnoxious verbal assault on my math teacher, Ms. Zeitz. While lecturing, she took a few steps from the chalkboard to the front of the class when she accidentally bumped a chair next to her lectern, creating a noise that sounded unmistakably like something else.

"Sounds like someone had too many beans with their lunch today," I suggested.

Thin and wiry, her straight black hair cut into a bob, Ms. Zeitz turned towards me with a beet-red face. Before she could even hope to respond, my hanger-on Billy chimed in, "Wow, that sounded like it hurt."

"And might've left a mark," I helpfully added.

The classroom erupted into deafening laughter, and poor Ms. Zeitz's face became even redder, her expression a mix of embarrassment, anger, and frustration. She knew she couldn't fight a fart joke in a room full of kids. Instead, she ensured Billy and I were given an hour to clean the boy's bathroom after school. James, the custodian, laughed while passing me a cigarette, showing us where the mops and toilet scrubbers were.

"For when you're done and heading home," he chuckled again as he left us to our chores.

Finishing up, I bid Billy farewell and headed out the front entrance, less concerned about running into my tormentors as the school was nearly empty except for the drama club. As I walked along the sidewalk that ran the length of the gym toward the parking lot designated for mopeds, a side door burst open just after I had passed it. Three girls were exiting the drama club meeting. One was Ally. Once I reached my moped, I could make out the girls' voices as they faded into the distance. Then unexpectedly, the sound of hurried footsteps approached me. Always half expecting a confrontation, I glanced over my shoulder, prepared for the worst. But, instead, standing right in front of me, slightly out of breath, with an infectious and quite adorable smile, was Ally.

"I just wanted to tell you that you sounded totally awesome last Friday." She cocked her head back. "You should have seen the look on some of the teachers' faces when you started playing!"

I didn't answer because I initially didn't register that she was speaking to me.

"You look totally different without a guitar."

Caught off guard by the whole situation, I blurted, "It's a bass."

She wrinkled her nose, and her face pinched. "Isn't that a guitar?"

"Yeah, a bass guitar...a bass," I answered unimaginatively, smiling and looking into her eyes before shifting my gaze onto my moped.

"Okay, have it your way, a bass." Her expression shifted into amusement and something else I couldn't put a finger on. Certainly, not the faint disapproval I used to think I'd detected.

"Whatever you call it, you sounded totally awesome in the talent show."

"Oh, thanks.... Well, I mean, you've seen me before without it." I tried to calm down and act like the in-control guy of my daydreams. "We're in gym class together." My face flushed. "I mean, we're usually broken up into different groups, so..." My suave banter petered out. Not seeming to notice this faltering confidence, her face lit up with glee.

"The things you and your friend say to Ms. Burns makes me laugh so hard sometimes."

"Carlo," I blurted without thinking.

"What?"

"Oh, uh, Carlo's the name of my friend." Speaking to Ally unexpectedly was overloading my mind, and I had the disorienting feeling that I was someone who had just flickered in from another dimension, my reality not synching with that of this world. "If I can't think of a good comeback, Carlo's always there to pick up the slack."

My brain might have been under serious bombardment, but one thought rose to the top: Steaming Broth's music and some smart-ass comments I'd made had stuck in the memory of that ridiculously cute head. A shy but resolute smile crossed my face, and I glanced into her eyes before looking at the ground. "Sometimes I'll just say somethin' 'cause I'm bored, I guess."

Lightly bumping my shoulder with hers, she looked at me with mock admonishment.

"Well, you could dress out more often than you do."

Again, just briefly, my eyes locked with hers. "I'll keep that in mind in case I can't come up with anything to say."

"I'm just messin' with you, you know."

Her words had barely registered when a weird tingling ran over my face, and I looked up at the sky as if something extraordinary had appeared. "Do you like exploring strange places?"

"What?"

A curious inflection in her voice drew my attention back to her, and I was startled to discover her steady gaze meeting mine. Then I noticed how much prettier she was close up.

"Well, I was wondering if maybe you might want to check out the old Declaration lighthouse sometime. It's beautiful over there."

A conflicted look clouded her face. "I've heard about it, but I've never been there. My dad told me once that it's dangerous to cross over because of the tides or something."

"It is if you don't time it right when you go." I almost felt that some-one was tempting the words out of me, as if a course had been plotted and I was merely following. "I just thought you might want to see it."

I could hardly believe that, in a roundabout way, I had asked her out. As soon as I'd made the suggestion, though, came an overwhelm-ing feeling that she would dodge the idea and it would die in infancy. Much to my delight that negative scenario vaporized in the next moment.

Ally looked around as if someone might be listening, and her front teeth pressed down on her lower lip. Then she looked me right in the eyes and said, "Yeah, I'd love to," leaving me stunned. Again, she quickly scanned the parking lot and the door to the gym before adding, "I just won't tell my dad."

She cupped her hand against my ear and whispered, "Let's keep all this our secret." Feeling the warmth of her breath, knowing that her lips were so close to me, was intoxicating. Without completely taking in what she was saying, I smiled obliviously, caught up in the thrilling electricity of the moment, akin to the first high of a drug that quickly turns to addiction.

"Of course," I think I said.

A minute later, I was speeding away from school as fast as my two wheels could carry me, looking for the fourth time at the number she had written in blue ink on my palm. Her number on my hand! That Saturday, we were going to go to Declaration Island. Together.

I let out a short victorious whoop to the sky, heavy metal, the Blue Lady, miracles, and magic: *Vive la resistance* and all that.

Excitement and joy can hide what should stand out in sharp relief —a red flag against an otherwise white background. In my euphoria, the invitation to journey to the gloriously isolated lighthouse couldn't have suggested the seed of a problem without an easy solution. If I had instead suggested to Ally that we meet at the arcade in Sheltered Harbour, her reaction might have revealed the unseen currents that were at play just beneath the otherwise bright, shimmering water. Yet, whether I knew it or not, I had been moved into a position where those same currents could carry me forward. To show me things my boy's eyes needed to see. So I played my part and said the words, blissfully unaware. Over the following week, I saw Ally in the school hallways and gym, but it was as if our conversation on Monday afternoon had been nothing more than a fever dream. She offered me no eye contact, much less a covert smile. Yet, I had her number, and the mere thought of her holding my hand and writing that number on my palm made my heartbeat increase and made me feel light-headed in a way akin to the sensation I experienced when inhaling nitrous oxide before the dentist gave me a filling.

In the immediate days after my exciting encounter, I called Carlo, which presented two sides of a shiny new coin that caught the light and dazzled for entirely different reasons. One side was purely self-ish, to brag, but the other was borne out of friendship, a simple urge to share my astounding news. He said he was happy for me, but he paused before adding with foresight I was then incapable of, "Just be careful, man, and watch yourself." Only much later, from a detached perspective, could I understand why his voice was edged with caution. The spectator in the stands can often see the other team's strategy un-fold before the player on the field does. At the time, my adrenaline was too great to understand what he was saying or why.

Even so, I didn't just discard his sentiment. I could tell the concern was genuine, reaffirming why he was my friend, so I stored the cau-tion away. That hint of care added to my growing sense of self, contrib-uting to a reserve of strength I could call on when needed.

I held off calling Ally until Thursday. Whenever I thought of mak-ing the call, my lack of confidence felt like a swarm of Luna moths in my stomach. When I finally psyched myself up, her dad answered. Before I could say more than, "Hi, is Ally home," she had picked up another line.

"It's all right, Dad; it's a guy from my drama club." That I wasn't a guy from her drama club didn't seem important at the time. Simply making the call had made my heart race and my mouth go dry as it did when Carlo, Scott, and I took an herb break while practicing.

"Umm, it's Ash, uh, I was calling to see if you still wanted to check the lighthouse out on Declaration Island this Saturday?" After hesi-tating to let my thoughts catch up with my mouth, I added, "I thought we could ride mopeds over. I think you have one, right?"

"Of course, I wanna go over there with you, and of course, I have a moped, silly." She spoke with freshness and the same hint of flirtation that made me high on Monday. All my doubts instantly disappeared. "Come over around ten. Is that an okay time to go with the tides?"

"Uh, yeah, ten's great."

"Well then, get your butt over here, and I'll meet you at the end of my driveway. That way, we can just get going. I live at 16 Briarwood.

Know how to get here?" I told her I'd figure it out, but I already had weeks earlier out of curiosity.

Two things struck me: I was blown away that she really wanted to go to Declaration with me, and I felt a zing through my entire body when she said, "your butt."

My mind raced a mile a second with the million things I needed to consider. Serious thought would have to go into which T-shirt to wear. I'd need to bring my boombox and some cassettes for music once we hit the island—and my backpack to carry the boombox. I should make a cassette with some songs she'd like mixed in with my metal favorites. Washing and shining up my moped seemed like a good idea too. I wanted my Vespa, the equivalent of my noble steed, to sparkle to prove that I was a worthy knight.

Was I dreaming? I lightly slapped my face, bringing me to the quick conclusion that I'd stepped into a waking dream. Out loud, I exclaimed, "Calm down, Ash," but how it sounded surprised me. The words came out with the same tinge of excitement I'd felt when Ally first approached me. Apparently, I wasn't good at concealing elation, even from myself.

After school on Friday, I made a couple of customized mixtapes to bring on the excursion with Ally. She liked what was popular on the radio, but I'd been able to get more specific by catching fragments of conversation between her and her friends and snatches of songs she sang to herself between classes. I even managed to borrow the single of Adam Ant's "Goody Two Shoes" from my bathroom-cleaning buddy Billy who "borrowed" it from his little sister.

Fueling my excitement was the knowledge that the prettiest damn girl in school was going with me to my favorite place, my secret place; the gravity of that hit me like a tidal wave. Not in a million and one years would I have considered that I'd be riding mopeds to Declaration alone with Ally after I'd asked her out—and she accepted! I found it hard to believe any of this was real. But, then again, I had been drawn to the story of the Blue Lady without too much-added embroidery, so this unexpected door opening should be something I could accept without clinging too stubbornly to reality.

I could have chosen any of my many T-shirts for my day out with Ally, but only one seemed suitable for such a momentous occasion. After much deliberation, I decided on the T-shirt that depicted the cover of Blue Öyster Cult's most recent album, *Fire of Unknown Origin*. The drawing of austere-robed figures clutching their blue oyster shells under a starlit sky seemed to capture somehow both the mystery and the mystical such an unforeseen day promised. It was classier and more refined than one of my Black Sabbath, Iron Maiden, or Uriah Heep T-shirts, which were more suitable for hanging out with my buds. With some effort, I wedged my boombox into my little-used school backpack, along with a couple of bottles of water. The last thing I wanted was a pretty girl wishing she had water when I showed her Declaration's untamed beauty.

I brushed off my mom's question of where I was headed for the day with a vague, "Just hanging out with a friend." She answered my vagueness with a specific: "Well, be careful and wear your helmet, so you don't end up with a fractured skull if someone hits you." Mom's reminder was a wise one and something I would usually heed, but I still managed to "accidentally" leave it behind. Although the island had a helmet law, the police rarely enforced it. More critical than helmet laws or motherly concern was my desire to have the windblown rebel look, not squashed "helmet hair," for my date with Ally.

In a minute, I was on Merganser and had pushed my Vespa to her limit. Town regulation stipulated that mopeds in Sheltered Harbour were supposed to have only a top speed of 30 miles an hour, but my Vespa, being the free spirit it was, could often get up to 45. That glorious day, my automatic variable transmission seemed to be telepathically linked to my exhilaration and adrenaline, and it edged me deliriously towards that big 5-0.

A more beautiful day would've been difficult to imagine. The humidity was milder than we usually experienced in late May, and the temperature was more warm than hot. Above stretched a deep blue sky hiding and revealing multiple hues within its depths. Without slowing down, I veered off from Merganser when the road forked onto Jessamine and then hung another, this time sharp, left onto Briarwood

Court, at the end of which was Ally's house. As I rode up, I saw her sitting on her moped at the end of her driveway. She wore a Clemson University T-shirt, white shorts, and her hair in a long French braid. Her helmet rested on her lap. I had never seen her dressed so casually before, and my heart skipped a beat. She watched me approach with the biggest, prettiest smile on her face. Something was fundamentally different about her that I couldn't initially put a finger on until she opened her mouth. Crossing her arms, she scrutinized me, exuding a freedom she didn't betray in school.

"On time, cute, hair ready for a Pert commercial." That she'd mentioned my hair instantly confirmed my decision to leave my helmet behind. And did she say I was cute?

"Well, you're the last two as well," I replied awkwardly. "And I suppose you're also on time as you're clearly ready to go."

Dismounting her moped, she looked at me and shook her head. She then turned and ran back up her driveway towards the open garage door, telling me over her shoulder, "If I'm gonna wear a helmet, you have to as well."

In a moment, she was back, thrusting a black helmet at me. "It's my brother's, but he's away at college." She grabbed the bottom of her shirt with both hands, lightly stretching it out to emphasize which college exactly. Then, without letting me catch my breath, she was back on her moped, putting her helmet on.

She said with the slightest hint of urgency in her voice, "Let's get going. I'll follow you."

"Yeah, uh, okay," came my not-so-witty reply. "I brought along my boombox and some water."

A look seemed to descend on her face, suggesting that something weighed on her mind.

"Is everything okay?"

"Oh yeah, I'm just really excited about seeing the island."

Although the clipped tone of her voice hinted that something was agitating her, there was no way I was going to press it, so I put on the helmet and sped off. Glancing behind to make sure she was with me, I began the route I'd planned over the previous two days. Mopeds weren't allowed on the beaches on the island's southern end, so I had figured out a way to use residential streets that paralleled the beach, a few golf cart paths to connect to other residential streets, and the dreaded Highway 241. Unfortunately, we couldn't avoid using the highway for about a mile along the island's north end. The more direct route I used when riding my bike, which included the pathway just past Mr. Garrison's house, was impractical because the tree roots that littered it would be impossible to pass with mopeds. Instead, I planned to head past Barnwell Road, following the highway as it turned west, before exiting onto Cogginsville Road. From there, we'd head north to the Oyster Hall boat launch, where we could transfer onto the beach along Mitchell Inlet, then ride east to the causeway.

I wasn't a fan of using more public thoroughfares to get to my beloved island, but since the introduction of a moped into my life, I had to adjust to taking a busier route. The fit was imperfect, but switching from a bike to a moped had advantages. Speed was the main one, allowing me to spend more time on the island and at the lighthouse while expending less energy on the journey. Although the day wasn't unusually muggy, the temperature was steadily rising. Luckily, I'd had the foresight to realize I didn't want to be some sweat-soaked stinky dude once we got to our destination, a more important consideration than it had ever been with Mike or Carlo. Going the extra mile that morning, I had even slapped on some of my dad's Old Spice.

Making our way back up Merganser, I kept glancing over my shoulder because I was still in a daze that I was with Ally—and because she seemed to be holding a good distance behind me. Far enough behind that it felt like we weren't riding together. When we finally turned onto Painted Bunting, a meandering, winding, sparsely populated residential road, I stopped and waited for her to catch up.

"Am I going too fast?"

"Oh no, I just want to make sure I don't miss which way you're going."

If her answer didn't make much sense, I wasn't about to let on. "That's cool. It gets a little tricky coming up as we have to get on a golf cart path." I took her in with a sweeping glance before dropping my gaze to the ground. "Let's just say golfers and I don't always see eye to eye."

"You're full of surprises, Ash," she said with mock exasperation. "Even golfers aren't safe when you're around."

"Well," I straightened myself into a fully upright position on my seat. "At least we can outrun golf carts."

Luckily, the fairway we ran parallel to was bereft of golfers that day. I hadn't wanted my first outing with Ally to be sidetracked by a confrontation with an angry out-of-towner slicing a tee shot or missing a crucial putt because of my intrusive shortcut. Only twenty minutes later, we were riding single file, anxiously navigating the short section of highway we couldn't avoid. Ally was still hanging back more than seemed necessary, and with cars and trucks whizzing past just a couple of arm lengths away, I sighed with relief when we made the turn onto Cogginsville Road.

Thinking she was still some distance back, I looked over my shoulder and was happily surprised to see her right behind me. I gave her a thumbs-up and yelled, "We survived!"

Riding up next to me for the first time that day, eyes wide and full of light, she shouted, "That was crazy but fun!" Any tension I'd sensed in her earlier when we met in front of her house was completely gone.

Glancing between her and the road ahead, I said, "That's nothin'; just wait until you see the island." When I looked back at her again, I was surprised to see her looking at me, which sent an electrical zing ricocheting through my body. "It's beautiful," I added, thinking more of her than our destination.

Cogginsville Road ended next to an empty concrete boat launch, which jutted either out onto the beach or into the water, depending on the tide. From there, we switched to the wide, low-tide beach bordering Mitchell Inlet. The waves were barely discernible ripples lapping the shore in the distance, and as they had retreated, they thoroughly scoured and smoothed the sand until it resembled a fresh sheet pulled tight across a bed. A path constantly renewed. Behind us, side by side, snaked the thin tracks of our tires, occasionally weaving and crisscrossing but constantly pushing forward.

As we approached the low tide causeway, I stopped to look at Ally. The butterflies that usually preceded my visits had returned to my stomach, now joined by a few new friends. The sun beaming across Ally's face illuminated her features, which seemed less circumspect than in school. I saw no trace of the expression that initially attracted me to her: that mixture of amusement and mild disapproval. In its place was a young girl, pretty as a peach, wearing a smile painted with delight, undiluted and pure. It breathed life into me, and my exuberance came out in words: "You look really pretty."

Surprised at the freeness of my proclamation—and not wanting to give Ally time to digest what I had said—I flung my arm out towards the narrow land bridge. "Just wait till you see the island. I've never ridden my moped over the causeway, but when walking my bike across I have to keep up a good pace, to keep from sinking into the sand, so punch it when we head across."

As if I needed a second opinion, the sound of blood pumping in my ears confirmed my excitement. Not wanting to say something stupid that would spoil the momentum I felt was building, I simply asked, "Ready?"

Nodding, she said, "Yup."

The wind blew in strongly off the Atlantic as, riding side by side at speed, we crossed the thin ribbon of sand that unwound before us. Oystercatchers, sandpipers, and terns fanned out, taking short flight or merely trotting away in spindly-legged double time as our motors announced our approach. From the ocean, three pelicans flew directly over us, headed towards the quieter recesses of Mitchell Inlet while seagulls swooped and glided above the distant waves. Ally's head swung left and right, taking in the sun glistening off the water and the green, swaying hues of Declaration, which drew ever nearer. Her focus landed on me as I happened to be glancing at her. Her expression was something to behold: eyes squinting in the face of the wind, a mischievous smile spread across her face. For a few seconds, I felt we were Bonnie and Clyde keeping just one step ahead of the law. Joy built within me, threatening to overflow. In such a circumstance, only one outlet could provide release—music! Half singing, half talking, I burst into Queen's "Crazy Little Thing Called Love."

When I reached the part of the song where I sang how I was ready, a voice as pretty as the face it came from joined in the refrain, "ready, Freddie." The sky instantly turned a deeper blue, and the sun swelled to twice its normal size as we sang the song's title in unison. Rolling onto the beach at Declaration, I stopped near the edge of the forest, removing my helmet as Ally pulled up next to me, beaming. "Oh my God, that song has always been one of my favorites!"

"Me too."

She tilted her head back, rolled her eyes up, and put the back of her hand to her forehead, "It's like a sign!" Then, removing her helmet, she undid her braid and shook her head vigorously while simultaneously running her fingers through her hair. Realizing that my hair, so perfect when I'd set out earlier that day, was now certainly a flat, compressed mass, I followed Ally's procedure exactly but then removed a comb I always kept in my back pocket—being permanently pressed between my tight jeans and butt molded every comb I carried to a distinct curve. After shaking my head to dry out and fluff my hair simultaneously, I ran the comb through it, surreptitiously taking in my handiwork in the rear-view mirror. I smiled. If there was a god whose sole purpose was to make sure a dude's hair looked as windswept and rugged as possible, well, he'd made sure my hair was perfect. As perfect as the werewolf drinking a pina colada at Trader Vic's in Warren Zevon's song "Werewolves of London."

Ally thrust her hand out. "Can I borrow your comb?"

To say her request caught me off guard would have been an understatement. Wasn't borrowing a guy's comb supposed to mean something? Wasn't it a subtle way of letting a guy know you dug him? It seemed loaded with innuendo, coded meaning and—

"Do you mind?"

One of the butterflies fluttering about my stomach broke free and tickled my throat. "Uh, yeah, sure, here you go."

Of course, I'd seen her combing and brushing her hair in school after gym class, but she was using *my* comb this time. Bending her head down, she flipped her long hair forward, carefully combing her thick curvy locks. When she flipped her head back up, she looked as stunning as I'd ever seen her. Grabbing the rubber band she'd placed on the seat of her moped moments earlier, she put her hair up into a simple ponytail. Alice Cooper was known to go through several costume changes during his concerts, but right before me, in under two hours, I had seen three different hairstyles from Ally, all for an audience of one. So let the rabble have Cooper. Right now, I felt like privileged royalty.

"Thanks." She smiled as she returned my comb. Then leaning over her handlebars, she said, "I like your custom curve."

"It conforms perfectly to my head, but I'm not sure what that means," I answered, feeling equal parts silly and giddy.

"Mine too." Straightening up, she added provocatively, "It's an awesome curve."

My face flushed as an image of a blushing bride flashed through my head, and I let out a laugh I intended to sound suave but which came out like a five-year-old at his birthday party.

To extricate myself, I said, "Let's park these things."

Incredulously, Ally followed me as I pushed my moped onto a nearly invisible pathway, and we were swallowed by the swaying green of the pine, palm, and magnolia.

Resting her moped on the other side of the cabbage palm I had leaned mine against, she showed another smile I had never seen from her—one that she directed at nothing but me. "I didn't even know where you were going. It's like you created an entrance by just wishing it was there." I smiled back because her sentiment expressed a feeling I hadn't ever been able to define.

The salt air blowing in off the ocean stirred the forest from sleep. Above us, sunlight broke through the leaves and fronds like pieces of a mirror that had been shattered across a bed of green. Holding out my hand, I helped Ally step over a freshly fallen oak bough. "There are so many things about this place that feel like they were created by wishes." Once she was over, I quickly retracted my hand. "Sometimes I swear I wish to see, I don't know, a whooping crane, and then in the next minute, I see one. It's like the island taps into your mind if you let it."

Pointing ahead to a sweetgrass field bordering a curve in the path,

Ally excitedly whispered, "Look!" Scattered about the clearing milled a herd of twelve or so white-tailed deer comprising does, fawn, and two bucks with velvet-covered antlers. All quietly munched away. "Oh my God, the fawns are so adorable. I've never seen so many together at one time."

"That's because there's nothing here to scare 'em. You know, no cars or people either."

Her expression changed to one of enchantment. In much the way she was taken with the slowly moving group of deer, I was taken with her. She squinted to focus on them. "Most of those are does, huh?"

Seeing an opportunity to impress, I pointed to two of the deer closest to us, a mere twenty yards away. "Only some of 'em. See those two? Those are what are called button bucks."

"What's that?"

"See those little stubs at the top of their heads?"

"Umm." Ally put her hands above her eyes to shield the sun as she looked to see what I was describing. "Oh yeah, I see. What are they?"

"They're antlers just beginning to poke through," I answered, feeling like Marlin Perkins with a sidekick a lot cuter than Jim Fowler.

Ally pointed to the patch of perfect blue that seemed cut out over the field and called again, "Look!" Soaring majestically over us was a solitary osprey, one I knew well, having discovered its nest a few months earlier. It flapped its wings just once.

Without embarrassment or needing to explain, I said, "That's a friend of mine." We watched until the bird disappeared. "I'll show you where her nest is some time. It's a beautiful spot."

Ally had moved right next to me. She looked down the path, then up at me, where her eyes lingered. "I'm sure it is."

Her closeness and attention were welcome, but I was still trying to find my footing in unfamiliar territory. When she asked, "So where to now?" I set off, relieved to have broken from her gaze

Pointing to our right, I answered, "Well, this way."

Despite my excitement, I feared an unwanted awkwardness could engulf me at any moment. Impulsively I decided to take a different path to the lighthouse than I'd planned, and we soon joined up with the same path Carlo and I had used to reach Mash Creek a few weeks earlier, winding our way around the great marsh that cut deep into the island. It was a meandering, barely used segment, mere inches across in places, where sky, tidal creek, patches of salt grass, and lone trees draped with Spanish moss made me feel I had stepped back in time to a place far removed from anything to do with life on Leggatts in the twentieth century.

Scanning the quiet, open space before us as a gentle salt wind brushed our faces, Ally dreamily said, "It's like Egypt, and we're the king and queen walking along the Nile."

I moved toward a striking late-blooming pink camellia amidst azaleas and cardinal flowers being visited by a couple of hummingbirds. Ally was too mesmerized by the tiny birds zigzagging from blossom to blossom to notice.

Stepping just off the path into the forest that ran along the marsh's edge, I picked the flower and held it behind my back. As I sidled up to Ally, she was still transfixed on the hummingbirds that seemed suspended on invisible strings.

She slowly turned back from the birds and said, "I love this spot."

I swung my hand out from behind my back. "If you're going to be the queen of the island, you need this."

Delighted, she lightly twirled the pink flower back and forth by its stem and then said just above a whisper, "It's beautiful, Ash." She placed it behind her ear. "I'll wear it like a queen should."

"Well, it's definitely more beautiful now," I caught myself saying before an idea struck me, sending me running ahead thirty or so yards.

Behind me, I heard her yell, "Where are you going?" As I came to a point where the path forked, I stopped, knowing which way we had to take. Half jogging, Ally caught up to me, slightly out of breath. "If you're trying to ditch me, you failed, boy."

"Oh yeah, sorry," I answered, only half listening.

"You're fast. Have you ever thought about joining the track team?"

The question had floated through my head before, if only fleetingly, and I answered, "I don't like the whole school team spirit thingy."

Ally gave me a sarcastic look, her voice mirroring it as she asked, "No?"

"That," I continued, "and I like my hair the way it is and don't want to cut it."

Her sarcastic expression melted into a shy smile. "I like your hair, too." Her hesitant look caught me off guard. It seemed counter to the confident demeanor she usually projected, but it also introduced a magnificent tingling sensation that spiraled through my body.

"You put that speed of yours to good use when you rescued me from jail, remember?"

I did but was stunned that she not only remembered playing capture the flag in gym class but also seemed to recall it as something special. "Yeah, well, that was something to run for, a damsel in distress and all."

We looked to scan each other's reactions and laughed.

"You and Carlo cracked me up a couple of weeks ago. Ms. Burns got all angry and called you guys communists because you weren't wearing gym clothes like everyone else, and you told her that not dressing out was the opposite of being a communist as you were expressing your individuality." She laughed. "Then you said *she* was a communist for wanting everyone dressing exactly the same and doing exactly the same things."

Again, I was stunned that she remembered and enjoyed something I'd done, even if it was only me acting up to gain some recognition.

"I just had a thought." I pointed to our left. "This path goes right through an old hunt club that used to be here, and then another path leads to the most incredible beach you've ever seen."

Staring at me, she waited for more detail, so I added dramatically, "It's a skeleton beach."

A quizzical look furrowed her brow. "What in the heck is a skeleton beach?" When I didn't answer—too busy daydreaming about her expression—she persisted, "Like bones lying scattered all over the place?"

"It's where erosion made part of the forest become part of the beach. Hundreds of trees just sprout out of the sand. They're all bleached by the sun and kinda look like skeletons."

Her look had now changed to that of curiosity.

"And if we're lucky, the Marsh Tackies will be there to meet us."

A huge smile filled Ally's face. Many girls at our school were fascinated with horses and took riding lessons at a stable outside Sheltered Harbour. Only a few Marsh Tackies were found on Leggatts, and those were mainly used to herd cattle by residents on the north end of the island, who could trace their lineage back to the days of slavery. So very few natives of Leggatts had ever seen a wild Marsh Tacky, and I knew it would delight her.

A petite, beautiful horse, the Marsh Tacky was, and remains, endangered because of the overdevelopment of its already limited habitat along the coast of South Carolina, particularly the Sea Islands. Originally introduced to the region by Spanish explorers in the Sixteenth Century, Marsh Tackies thrived on the islands as workhorses particularly favored by the Gullah people. The small herd that remained on Declaration dates back to the antebellum period, and in later years, the hunt club used them for hunting and rounding up game. After the hunt club closed, the horses roamed free.

Plunging into deep woods, we had to closely follow the remnants of an old game trail so overgrown with shrubs and trees that getting lost was a real possibility. On more than one occasion, I'd found myself completely turned around and even surprised to realize I was on another part of the island. Leaves, needles, and fronds crowded around Ally and me, slowing our progress but delivering an unexpected benefit. Forced to walk single file, Ally kept close behind me, regularly clasping the back of my shirt and, even better, clutching my arm. This closeness made me feel quite strong while all around us, the buzzing of cicadas crescendoed and fell in the now thick humidity of midday. After a few obstacles, including an enormous banana spider that scared Ally almost senseless until I gently moved the spider and her web out of the way with a stick, we broke out of the woods and into the overgrown clearing of the old, long-abandoned hunt club.

The compound centered around the clubhouse, a long one-story building where the hunters used to stay. One side of the building had been the bunk room; the other comprised the dining room, living room, kitchen, and showers. A few white paint flecks remained, but the collapsed roof, empty windowpanes, and sagging front porch, which had given way to several trees growing through its floorboards, spoke of abandonment and decay. Just behind the clubhouse, only partially visible from our vantage point, stood the remains of the tool house. Its roof was completely gone, and several small trees grew unhindered through its rotted wood plank floor.

As we rounded the main building, other structures revealed themselves. First was the cookhouse; two of its walls collapsed, next to which stood the remarkably well-preserved brick generator building, its steel roof still perfectly intact. Inset into the wall just above its thick steel doors, a concrete plaque read "Power Plant." All traces of the dog pen were gone, and evidence of the meat house where the Gullah cook would've hung the butchered meat was limited to several concrete pilings.

Standing on the clubhouse porch peering through one of the empty windowpanes, Ally said in a loud whisper, "This place is really creepy."

"That's just because abandoned places are always spooky," I said. "They say the hunters who used this place abandoned it because they kept catching glimpses of the Blue Lady, the ghost who's supposed to haunt the island."

Turning from the window, Ally looked at me, nonverbally asking for more information.

"I don't know. Seems to me the hunters probably just scared each other telling ghost stories in the middle of the night on an isolated island." As I had intended, this answer seemed to satisfy Ally, and I added, "Follow me; you're gonna love the beach."

She ran ahead of me before suddenly stopping. Swinging around, she laughed. "Wait, I don't know where I'm going!" Her arms swept out before her. "C'mon boy, lead the way!"

Winding through a field strewn with purple coneflowers, persimmon, and magnolia, we soon entered a thin finger of deep forest that slowly changed from live oak and pine to wax myrtle, red cedar, and cabbage palms as we approached the ocean. We could just hear the surf over the foredunes, and then, as if plunged into a waking dream, we emerged onto the beach. Protruding helter-skelter from the sand, spreading out to the north and south, were hundreds of sun-bleached tree trunks and boughs that looked like skeletons of whales, Kraken, and plesiosaurs. The bone-white relics seemed to scratch the deep blue sky, while the far-off sea looked like gray shale, the sand like smooth marble.

Running forward with her arms outstretched as if about to take flight, Ally shouted with glee, "This is incredible!"

I joined her running among the skeletons, darting under boughs and jumping over trunks until something caught my eye. Kneeling, I called out, "Hey Ally, check 'em out." Several mating horseshoe crabs grouped together near the water, the males clinging to the backs of the females.

"What are they doing?" Ally asked.

"It's love time." I chuckled. "You know, dim the lights and guess the rest." Then, absorbed by an image of Bryan Ferry singing "Love Is the Drug" to mating horseshoe crabs, I chuckled again.

"Let's leave 'em alone. I feel like a crab voyeur," Ally said, shaking her head.

Making the stereotypical "Wakka Wakka" guitar sound from porn flicks that everyone knew, even if, like me, they hadn't yet seen one, I joked, "Debbie the horseshoe crab was a love machine. One horse-shoe male was never enough for her lustful cravings."

Rolling her eyes, Ally pushed me. "Crab porn, huh? Is that what it's come to?" Then she exclaimed, "Look, Ash!" She pointed at four Marsh Tackies trotting about fifty yards to the north of us. Two were chestnut, and the others were a roan and a grullo. The roan and one of the chestnuts were frolicking, nudging each other's necks, buck-ing up and down.

Once again, the island seemed to read my mind. "Oh yeah, they're beauties, aren't they? I was hoping they'd be here today."

I looked at Ally, who was transfixed by their wild grace. Unexpect-edly, she wrapped her arms around one of mine. It seemed an uncon-scious act on her part, but it sure felt good from where I was stand-ing. Her eyes told me she was far away, lost in following the hooves clomping up and down. The nickering and blowing from the horses' nostrils could take one's breath away if that person were willing to give themselves entirely to the moment. Ally clearly was. She spoke as if from a place of deep peace. "Just look how happy they are...they're majestic."

I had always loved the Marsh Tackies, and that day, their outward happiness mirrored what I felt inside. Along with the rare beauty and grace the Tackies brought to the wild lands of Declaration, I could now add the memory of Ally cuddling up to me to the list of reasons to protect the endangered creatures. Time was flying, though, and I had to keep high tide in mind. So I told Ally, "I saved the best for last. Let's head up to the lighthouse!"

Turning from the Marsh Tackies, who had become aware of our presence and trotted further up the beach away from us, Ally fell in quickly beside me. I could see her out of my peripheral vision, glancing up at me.

"There used to be two lights that were lined up." I motioned to a spot that would be covered by high tide. "Somewhere around there was where the front light used to be."

Clearing the dunes, we worked our way up to the crumbling section of the road that had connected the two lights. The rear light was now entirely obscured by the slash pines and live oak surrounding her. Stopping momentarily, I took off my backpack to get out some water. Preoccupied with my present company, I had forgotten I was wearing it until that moment. I gave a bottle to Ally and opened another for myself.

"Sorry, they're warm."

"I didn't even realize how thirsty I was until you handed it to me."

We drank greedily and only checked ourselves when our thirst was satisfied.

Sweat rolled down my forehead, and I wiped it away with my forearm before taking the empty plastic bottle from Ally and putting it into my backpack along with mine. Trying to impress her with my circumspection, I didn't toss the bottles as usual. Then, hoisting my backpack on, I turned and started walking again. "Now you get to see the old girl."

A curious look crossed Ally's face. "Well, there's a girl next to you, in case you didn't notice. Who's this other girl?"

"Sorry, I always think of the old lighthouse as a girl."

Arms crossed, Ally furrowed her brow and exaggeratedly pouted her lips. "At least you don't refer to me as the 'old girl.'" She jokingly punched my arm. "You better not!"

Feeling suddenly awkward, I glanced at my feet, laughing in that way one does when hoping a laugh is appropriate. Not for the first time, Declaration came to my rescue. As we passed one of the several brackish lagoons that partially encircled the lighthouse compound, a grey heron waded on the far bank, hunting for bream and insects. Upon hearing our approach, it spread its huge blue-grey wings, rising elegantly from the water in flight, spindly legs jutting out straight behind it, circling the lagoon twice before flying off towards the west. We watched in wordless awe, then trekked on, soon breaking from the wooded cover into the sweetgrass field that let me know we had arrived. I grabbed Ally's hand to lead her but quickly released it.

"Uh, sorry, follow me this way." She smiled, but I continued until we stood before the broad, glorious live oak that seemed to guard the lighthouse. Behind it, partially concealed, rose the rusting beacon. I could swear it seemed to be smiling as if it were happy to see me again.

Running onto the porch of the lightkeeper's house, I told Ally about Charlotte Pauley before disappearing through the front door into the stillness of the close, humid air saturated with the smell of mildew and rot that the interior held. Following, Ally looked up to where I stood halfway up the rickety staircase.

"Charlotte lived in this house." Motioning to the stairs, I continued, "She dragged her dead father's body up these very stairs as the hurricane raged outside. Somehow she kept the light going but went missing and was never seen again."

"Like what happened to her? Didn't someone come to rescue her?"

"Rescuers did come, but by the time they got here, she was gone. It's thought that she went to the front light to get help from the keeper there, but like him, was swept out to sea."

Ally's face looked like she was back in time, hearing the wind and rain thrashing the house. "It's so sad but romantic. She loved it here, fought for it, and never left."

"Well, she wasn't seen again as a person, but supposedly her ghost is."

"Have you ever seen her?"

"No."

I descended the stairs and walked outside towards the lighthouse. "But a lot of people have, like the hunters who used to come to the island and stayed in that old camp we walked through." Kneeling, I took off my backpack to remove my boombox.

Ally's face glowed in the splintered sepia sunlight filtering through the leaves and moss of the live oak. "Wow, you thought of everything."

"Music makes everything better," I responded instinctively.

"So, what did the hunters see?" she asked.

"Not just the hunters but other lighthouse keepers and just people like us, visiting," I elaborated as I fumbled with the boombox, rewinding the cassette. "Except they'd see stuff at night, not in daylight. There are all kinds of stories about The Blue Lady; that she seems insane, is part animal, and even has black holes where her eyes should be." Ally hung on my every word, eliciting feelings similar to those I'd experienced standing on stage, except with a new sensation of intimacy reserved for a rapt audience of one. For a reason I couldn't identify, I pulled back on the embellishments I'd reveled in when telling Carlo about the island's past. "Like all ghost stories, people try to make everything scarier by adding more outrageous details until by the time they pass it on, it's twice as bizarre and terrifying."

I must have had a particular look on my face or hesitated a bit longer than usual because Ally asked, "What is it?"

"One thing pops up over and over again in every version, though: before the ghost of the Blue Lady appears, there's always this weird, liquidy, low-lying, bluish fog that comes out of nowhere, before she does, I guess to let you know she's near. It's always mentioned that it seems to give off its own light, like it's lit from within."

Not wanting to linger too long in the world of the dead, I switched on the tape and instantly drowned out the natural sounds around us. Blasting into the thick air was "Magic Power," a euphoric song by

Triumph, perfectly distilling both the desperate hope of youth and the power of music to dramatize those feelings, making them even more real. I'd carefully chosen the song, thinking it would be melodic enough to appeal to Ally's taste but still hard rockin' enough for me to hold my head high. Keeping in mind that I was on a date, I adjusted the volume to keep it below the "everything louder than everything else" level Carlo and I preferred.

Moving to the front of the lighthouse, I set the boombox on the cast-iron steps that led inside. Emboldened by the music, I spread my arms out wide. "So, d'ya think you could be into a guy who loves places like this?"

Hands-on hips, Ally stepped back to scrutinize me, a mischievous, unguarded smile on her face. "I think I could learn to."

I grabbed the boombox and half-shouted, "Follow me," as I shot up the spiral staircase. Each step was fueled by the girl whose footsteps sounded behind me, along with the words Rik Emmett sang about the power of being young, wild, and free.

When I reached the watch room, I glanced back at Ally before stepping onto the gallery, where a strong breeze greeted me. The words blasting from my speakers perfectly matched my emotions. Setting the boombox down, I surveyed the endless panorama of green and blue encircling us just as Ally's bright, breathless voice swept over me.

"I looove this music. It's like it was written just for us being here right now....Who is it?"

Taken aback by how pretty she was, I straightened to my full height. "Triumph. They're Canadian dudes," I answered as nonchalantly as possible. An excited nervousness pulsed through my veins, and I didn't want it to end. As I turned my attention back to the wild world that seemed to be swallowing the solitary perch that held us, Ally's eyes followed my lead. Fishing around in the front pocket of my jeans, I removed a partially crushed pack of cigarettes, flicked one halfway out as coolly as possible, pulling it out between my clenched lips.

"I won't kiss you if you smoke that." She smiled broadly and tilted her head to the side.

Not needing to think twice, I tossed the unlit cigarette over the edge. Then, without hesitation, as I wanted to since the first time I ever saw her, I cradled a hand around the back of her head, fingers lost in the softness of her hair, gently pulled her towards me, and kissed her. Ally's arms wrapped tightly around me, pulling our bodies even closer together, making me feel happier than I'd known was possible. It wasn't just a kiss: it validated that I was more than just the class clown, or a member of a band, or a part of the forest and sea of Declaration. Ally was a spectacular kisser, and, at that moment, I revolved around nothing but her. Oblivious. Elated. Human. I had not only recaptured the initial euphoric rush of our first proper meeting but had eclipsed it.

Time was temporarily malleable; a pause button beyond my experience had been pressed. When we finally rejoined the sunny, birdsong-filled day, our foreheads were pressed together, and we were looking down through the wooden slats of the gallery at the green forest beneath us. Simultaneously, we both began giggling, our eyes looking anywhere but at each other. The sound around us started up again slowly as though someone turned up the volume on the wilderness until I realized there was music too—music that was like nothing my boombox was accustomed to. Adam Ant's hit "Goody Two Shoes" pulsed out of the unsuspecting speakers, throwing all my metal cred out the window.

I had put the song on the tape as a surprise for Ally, and its effect was precisely what I'd hoped. Playfully jabbing a finger at my chest and bobbing her head in time with the beat, she started dancing and singing along. Then she wrapped her arms around my shoulders, pulling herself right up against me, all the while swaying to the music.

"Didn't know you were an Adam Ant fan. You're full of surprises."

"I thought you'd dig it," I said before deciding to appear a bit more cultured. "Or, I mean, appreciate it."

She erased my correction by exclaiming, "I do *dig* it!"

Pulling up tight against me, she sniffed my cheek. "We're out in the middle of nowhere, and you smell good." She nuzzled her nose against my neck. "So suave." Her voice was playful but also warm and genuine, all barriers down. I was assailed by one of my silly thoughts: me high-fiving a giant bottle of my dad's Old Spice.

Then the impending return of high tide chased that silly thought from my mind. All too soon, Ally and I were heading back to our mopeds on the old road I had recently taken with Carlo. We walked along, lost in the disorienting world of awakenings. After a moment, I realized we were holding hands, making me feel as wild and free as the Marsh Tackies we'd seen on the beach.

Squeezing my hand, Ally excitedly whispered, "I think someone's watching us!"

Peering around the trunk of an old magnolia was a squirrel merrily chirping away at our approach. When I mimicked his greeting by drawing air in between my pursed lips, he craned his neck forward inquisitively, his two eyes like small black marbles staring at me. First, he chirped, then I chirped. Then, to get a closer look at the strange giant squirrel passing by, he climbed down the tree trunk a couple more feet, chirping all the while, his bushy tail waving and shivering as he steadily inched down farther. The little creature looked equal parts confused and fascinated. Ally watched until the squirrel was no more than two feet away from my face, giving every indication that he might actually jump onto me.

"Watch out; they're cheeky here," I said.

Tugging on my shirt, Ally grinned, "Y'all sure are."

When we're young, we have almost no recognition of danger or real threat. We're elastic. We're not versed in the pitfalls and traps that lie hidden, surrounding us on all sides. That blindness is, however, the secret to the euphoria that can strike with such impossibly magnetic force when we're young, enveloping our body and soul. That elasticity and resilience allow daily abuses to be shed soon after they've assailed us, but there's a tradeoff. Youth is not wasted on the young as some say: youth needs innocence and ignorance just as much as lungs need air. However, it doesn't take long for head-on impacts with previously unseen obstacles to chip away at the blind spot we had once used so successfully as a shield.

Lost in laughter and the thrill of discovering each other, we pulled into Ally's driveway. As she got off her moped and removed her helmet, her dad rushed out of the open garage door. His expression conveyed anger, bewilderment, and disappointment. "Get away from that boy, Ally! What the hell are you doing?" Brushing past her, he rushed up to me. "And *you!*" he screamed, the veins in his neck bulging. "Get the hell outta here!" The pointing finger at the end of his outstretched arm suggested which way I should go.

Like a bear protecting its cub, he swung around with his arms out defensively to keep Ally separated from me. "Get in the house, girl! Right now!"

I didn't need any further encouragement. Seconds later, I was whizzing away from Ally's house, the whole scene more jarring because of the protected bubble I'd been in since kissing her.

Our first date had officially concluded.

7

Riding at speed away from Ally's seething dad made me feel like one of the protagonists from *Easy Rider*, trying to escape taunts of close-minded, small-town locals in a rural outpost. Come to think of it, I *was* doing that, except on a Vespa instead of a Harley chopper.

A couple of hours after I returned home, my mom was doing dishes when the wall phone rang. When she answered, I glanced up from the magazine I was reading in the living room. Mom turned, beckoning me with her free hand. As I entered the kitchen, she covered the mouthpiece. "It's for you, Ash. It's a girl!" Her voice held a detectable edge of excitement.

In a voice not much above a whisper, Ally said her dad didn't like guys with long hair but that she would love to come over to my house whenever we met up next. To tell the truth, I'd never even thought of her dad before—but the memory of our kiss softened the blow of being yelled at. Taking everything into consideration, I figured it had been the best day of my life up until that point, eclipsing my previous high a couple of weeks earlier when Steaming Broth had set the world to rights. Adverse events notwithstanding, I felt pretty damn good. Dealing with negative reactions to my appearance was nothing new. As I didn't want to date Ally's dad, the powerful memory of that kiss suspended high above the forest on Declaration was enough to push his disapproval from my concerns. Ally at least made it seem like no big deal.

"So, I was thinkin' I could come over to your house next weekend, like on Sunday."

At her suggestion, another revelation overwhelmed me—a riptide I was blissfully powerless against. Next weekend was the first weekend of summer! Suddenly, I had a girlfriend and the wide-open untouched canvas of a whole summer to venture into unknown territory. Consciously struggling to maintain my composure, I said, "Next Sunday sounds perfect—"

"Great! And I know where you live, Ashley Howe."

"You do?"

"Mmm-hmm. Know how I figured it out?"

"Uh, asked someone?"

"No, silly, I looked up your last name in the phonebook. There's only one Howe listed, so I figured Robert Howe was your dad."

"You're like a cute Sherlock Holmes," I answered and quickly added, "if he was a girl."

"Sheryl Holmes." She giggled. "Hey, since my dad is being so unreasonable, I was thinking we should keep our thing a secret." When I didn't respond, she said, "You know, not tell anyone. I mean, there's totally no reason to tell our friends right now. Or let on at school."

"Yeah, sure, that makes sense," I answered obliviously, floating as I was far up in the sky on a fluffy white cloud. Since Ally would come over the following weekend, I assumed my mom and dad were exempt from this edict.

When I hung up the phone, my mom, who was puttering around the kitchen trying to catch what she could of my conversation, asked, "So, who was that?"

"Just a girl from school."

"And?" my mom persisted.

"And that's it." I turned and walked to my room, where I sat in the chair in front of my stereo, put on headphones, and blasted AC/DC's *Powerage* at maximum volume. Not telling my mom about Ally had nothing to do with keeping a secret. It didn't occur to me to open up to her about this remarkable, even mind-blowing, turn of events. As I scrutinized the album cover, thinking my hair was almost as long as Malcolm Young's, my mom appeared at my bedroom door. I could see her mouth moving, but by the time I'd removed the headphones, she was fed up.

"Never mind, just trying to have a conversation."

As she walked away, I shook my head and thought, *Moms.* Then I put my headphones back on to focus on the hypnotic groove of "Down Payment Blues." As Bon Scott sang in his inimitable growl about how not doing much meant a lot to him, I realized I was in an opposite predicament. For a guy who'd never thought of himself as someone big on planning things, I'd suddenly become rather plan-driven, starting with the talent show. Plans for meeting with Ally now topped my list, but another scheme was underway. In a couple of weeks leading up to summer break, Carlo, Scott, Tab, and I had devised an elaborate prank to play on Paul Geiger, a hanger-on to our little group of misfits. Paul would occasionally show up to watch Steaming Broth practice, awkwardly cough his way through a proffered cigarette, and pass on smoking grass as nonchalantly as possible when offered. His sartorial choices—colorful Izod or Polo shirt, khaki pants or shorts, and aspiring junior executive haircut—placed him firmly in what could be termed the classic preppy set.

His hair and demeanor reminded me of a character named Rick Wright in the once wildly popular TV show *Magnum P.I.* We tolerated Paul but stopped far short of granting him full membership into our ingrown circle. His tentativeness made it clear to us that he wanted to dip his toes into the world of the "bad boy" but not take it too far, rather merely experience what lay on the other side of the fence, almost like we were an interactive, living history museum. Instead of mingling with our country's forbears at Colonial Williamsburg, Paul was listening to the strange loud music of bands with exotic names like Tygers of Pan Tang, Cirith Ungol, and Witchfinder General in a smoke-filled garage where talk of Brothman was conducted in laughing fits that varied in intensity depending on the amount and potency of the weed.

Tentativeness, however, wasn't what Carlo, Scott, or I were about. Tab fit in because of his oddball tastes in hobbies, his left-field imagination, and his knowledge of horror and obscure animated films, which were never less than diverting, especially when high. We embraced him because he focused mainly on things outside our primary purview but which still interested us. His eccentricities dovetailed nicely with our sense of ourselves as outsiders.

Ally wouldn't come to my house for a whole week, but the current Sunday promised other pleasures. When morning rolled around, I woke with a strange but not unfamiliar mixture of conflicting thoughts that seemed to be running in several directions at once. I felt elation—thanks to the bright addition of a girl taking a central position among my usual preoccupations—but also the regular unanalyzed brew of confusion, anger, hopelessness, and, indeed, hope. Imaginative diversions usually quelled my ADHD admirably; the more elaborate they were, the better. Luckily, the prank we intended to play on Paul gave me a doozy to tide me over until I met up with Ally again.

Three Saturdays earlier, while lounging poolside, Tab and I devised a plan to see if we could construct a legend and then figure out how to slot it into the real world as seamlessly and believably as possible. Once we'd agreed it could work, the next step was determining the perfect victim. Almost simultaneously, we both laughed, shouting, "Paul!"

Our basic storyline involved a curse placed on Declaration Island by the Blue Lady. To this end, Tab excitedly told me he knew a way to make paper look old, which would enable us to create what were supposed to be pages torn from a lightkeeper's diary that we would, by sheer luck, "find" concealed in a crack in the plaster walls of the lightkeeper's house. These pages would outline in dramatic prose the lighthouse keeper's fearful conclusions concerning a curse placed on the island by the spirit of Charlotte Pauley, aka the Lady in Blue. We could leave no room for doubt that this curse was explicitly focused on the lighthouse and the keeper's house. We first described how Charlotte had been swept out to sea following the deaths of her father and the second lightkeeper. Then we detailed how the later lightkeeper came to believe that the spirit of Charlotte, driven mad by her ordeal, remained insane in death—and could, by force of will, possess any unlucky person who set foot on the island as a warning that it was her domain.

The pages would further reveal that the diary's author, one Peter Byford, had witnessed the possession of his assistant Paul Geiser, a name picked specifically because of its similarity to Paul Geiger. Byford described how Geiser's face seemed to "change" one night after returning from tending to the light, as if something had entered his consciousness, driving him mad and causing him to attack Byford, who was forced to kill him in self-defense with an ax. The pages would further reveal that Byford believed the Blue Lady considered herself the island's protector. Byford felt the possession took several attempts before taking hold, first manifesting as a brief flickering across Geiser's face, over which another face seemed superimposed. Byford asserted this was the first sign that his assistant had been marked for possession.

Tab's talents came to the fore as he magically aged several sheets of his dad's stationery. First, he crumpled them up, creating random small rips and tears, then soaked them in coffee before baking the sheets for several minutes in the oven. Next, he rubbed some dirt into the sheets, carefully burned some of the edges, and browned other select spots with a lighter. These efforts really made the pages look like authentic parchment torn from an old leather-bound diary.

As Scott and Tab had never been to Declaration before, we planned to ride over with Carlo later that morning. The plan was to show them how to get there and figure out where to conceal the diary pages and what everyone's precise positions for the prank would be. I had written out detailed instructions, noting landmarks to look out for so they could still find their way if we got separated. We all had mopeds except for Tab, who'd borrowed one from an arcade buddy. After showering, I popped on my headphones and sat by my window to watch for arrivals. Carlo was the first to show up, and before I could say much more than "how's it going," Carlo threw his hands out before him.

"So, c'mon, details! What happened with Ally?"

"I don't know. We just like rode around on our mopeds for a while and hung out."

It's not as if I were lying. I was just being a bit vague. I had no intention of telling him I'd taken her to the lighthouse when it had taken me months to feel confident enough in his friendship to take him there. My improvised plan was to keep things as unspecific as possible, but because Carlo was my best friend, I couldn't help but break my promise to Ally by revealing that I had kissed her, and it had been phenomenal.

His eyes widened in genuine surprise, and a broad smile spread over his face. "All right!" he exclaimed as I reciprocated an unexpected high-five.

Saved from further questioning by the sound of Scott's battered Puch pulling into the driveway, I glanced out the window. He had been in so many accidents that I was surprised the thing was running at all. Bent pedals, a shattered rearview mirror, and various scratches and dings spoke of many encounters where gravity and asphalt had won. Both my parents were at the pharmacy that morning, but even though Scott couldn't be sure, he immediately pulled out his trusty pot pipe from his denim jacket and brazenly lit it as he walked to the front door. When I opened the door, he gave a huge, stoned smile and exhaled a massive billowing cloud of pungent smoke.

Then he broke into a guffaw. "Your parents aren't home," he said through a cough, and when I didn't initially answer, his face flushed. "Are they?"

"No, man, they're at work, but you're pushin' it."

His stoned smile quickly returned. "That's how I am, my man. I like to live on the edge."

His actions spoke of his devil-may-care nature, and I hoped he wouldn't be the weak link in our rather elaborate prank. Finally, a loud sputtering motor signaled that Tab had arrived on his borrowed green and silver Sachs. Sauntering up to the front door, he appeared as he always did, wearing clothes that seemed to be an afterthought: baggy cargo shorts, untied sneakers, and a rumpled orange Izod that looked like it had been pulled from the bottom of a hamper. When I gestured them into my room, Scott removed his jacket, unnecessary except as a place to conceal his grass and Visine, and revealed one of his prized

T-shirts bearing the logo of Led Zeppelin's record label, Swan Song. Geezer and Eddie followed closely behind us, with Eddie excitedly sniffing at Scott's jacket, which he tossed on top of my dresser.

"Man, you shoulda named your dogs Cheech and Chong. They're always after my grass."

Giving his T-shirt a once over, I chuckled as that Swan Song emblem, consisting of a naked, winged man floating in the sky, always struck me as off. Based on a nineteenth-century painting by William Rimmer, as my older self could've told my younger self, it was notable for excluding a vital part of the male anatomy. A subtle suggestion that the music of Led Zeppelin was somehow neutered. That clearly wasn't the case, so the guy's disability never sat well with me, and I let Geezer do the talking. "Look, guys, he's wearing the shirt with the Ken doll who borrowed one of Barbie's wigs."

Carlo let out a sharp laugh. "Imagine a chick going back to his house, and when she's about to go down on him, she finds he doesn't have a love gun."

"Fuuuuck you," was Scott's reply. "It's the coolest logo of all time, man."

"Okay, okay," I said, putting my hands up. Tilting my head to the side, I concluded, "I still think it would be a lot cooler if it were a super-hot chick with wings and huge knockers floating through the sky."

Scott squeezed a few drops of Visine into his eyes, weighing my argument before flashing a sly smile, "Well, I'll give you that one."

Suddenly remembering something important, I went to my dresser to retrieve the directions I'd written out a couple nights before. The task had proven more difficult than I'd initially thought. When I sat down to write, I quickly realized that instructions like "once you pass the big live oak that is fallen across the road" and "when you pass the sweetgrass field with the wax myrtles" would have to replace road names and landmarks like gas stations, churches, and houses. Handing out the sheets of notebook paper, I told my only half-listening friends to follow me closely when we hit the road and to hug the shoulder of the highway when we had to ride on it briefly. Not that it mattered to us, but riding on that shoulder was illegal.

As far as journeys go, it was mercifully uneventful, except for the impromptu sing-along Carlo and I instigated as we navigated Highway 241 to serve as a helpful distraction from the cars and the one eighteen-wheeler that tore past us blaring its horn. Carlo rode up next to me and, with a quick nod, caught my eye and started half singing, half shouting the Judas Priest road anthem, "Heading Out to the Highway."

Without missing a beat, I joined in, my voice competing gallantly with the traffic noise. Wherever in the world Judas Priest's Rob Halford was at that moment, he could rest assured that no usurpers rode that stretch of highway, just a couple of Hells Angels out looking for trouble.

Once that dicey bit of our ride was over, the rest was smooth sailing, and we soon arrived on the overgrown and wild shore of Declaration. The only unusual aspect of our trek by foot to the lighthouse was when we came across the first of the several path-straddling webs of banana spiders. Carlo pulled out a can of aerosol deodorant from his backpack. With a flick of his lighter, flame and spray joined, creating a mini version of a flame thrower, scorching the webs and the poor, unsuspecting spiders into oblivion. Scott then commandeered the spray can, playing judge, jury, and executioner, commencing an ongoing tug of war over who would fry the next spider, which raged between the two until we arrived at the compound.

When the lighthouse rose before us, Tab broke into a big smile. "This place is unreal!"

"Looks like a place Jason would stalk to kill some kids like us," Scott blurted, looking in turn at Carlo, Tab, and me and then letting out a self-satisfied laugh. The idea had never struck me before, but it didn't take too much to imagine the hooded killer of the sequel to the *Friday the 13th* film creeping around the place.

I led the three to the lightkeeper's house, which I felt would offer the best hiding places for Tab's diary pages. After a short search, we found an ideal spot in a crack in the plaster above the fireplace. We widened it a bit to allow a hand to easily reach in to conceal the pages from anyone who might enter the house before we next did, but once secure, we all agreed it was perfect. As Tab and Scott would precede us to the island, we showed Tab where to hide under the house, which was raised on pilings. We broke into excited laughter as Paul's terror played out in our imaginations, and we agreed it would be great fun and worth the effort. Then Carlo, Scott, and I smoked celebratory cigarettes and a well-packed bowl of redbud as Tab ventured off to figure out his escape route after completing his contribution to the prank. Scott flashed a knowing smile, and Carlo and I gave almost imperceptible nods, sure that Tab was extricating himself from the pressure of partaking. At least, that's what I initially thought, but as I headed off after we'd finished smoking, I found him in the sweetgrass field, staring at the lighthouse and beyond, lost in deep thought. Silently I chastised myself, realizing I never should have second-guessed him.

It truly was an experience getting high at the lighthouse for the first time, and with Tab back with the group, we climbed to the top to take in the view, stopping on the final landing to show Scott where his position would be and exactly what he should do. The day was partly cloudy, and sunlight appeared sporadically through the long-vanished window frames, stretching out shadows that appeared and disappeared on the twisting iron steps. When we stepped out onto the gallery, the whipping wind instantly dispelled the thick atmosphere of the confined central cylinder, and we all sat at the edge, arms resting on the iron crossbars of the railing, dangling our feet over, laughing at everything and nothing, basking in our utter freedom. Just a short distance below us, the green of the treetops swayed, rustling in unison. Glancing up, I could visualize Ally and me kissing just behind where I was sitting. Another thought suddenly superseded this near-perfect memory. I smacked my head and stood up.

"Oh man, I almost forgot!"

"What, how stoned you are?" Scott broke into a laugh, turning his pale complexion beet red in moments.

I shook my head. "No, you two," I said, pointing to Scott and then Tab, who again seemed mesmerized, taking in the strange beauty of the place, no doubt imagining a plot for some outlandish movie utilizing such a location, "have to pass...."

"The initiation!" Carlo finished, hands shooting up over his head, proud that he had already passed it.

High he might have been, but hesitant he wasn't, and Scott was out the window of the landing below the watch room before I could even finish telling him what he needed to do. As sober as the pope, Tab erred on the side of caution, declaring in his laughing, disarming way that he wouldn't climb around the lighthouse in this life or the next. "If I go out there, that next life's gonna be here a lot sooner than I want it to be," he concluded.

Such was his personality and our affection for him—well, at least Carlo and I—that we didn't press the point.

Just before we headed down, Carlo's quite stoned, cherubic face lit up like the lighthouse had been reactivated. Assuming the authority of Richard Burton portraying Hamlet, he raised his arm. "Wait! Dude, we have to do something!"

"What?" I answered, having no idea what he was talking about.

"Pack one more bowl, Scott. If you don't mind, there's something we have to do."

Once the bowl was packed and passed around, Carlo looked at me, gesturing to the room above us. "You first, sir."

Once all four of us had made our way into the small hexagonal lantern room—always the Blue Room in my mind—Carlo thundered, "Ash, my man, you or maybe three of us, are officially the highest people in two ways all the way from here to Savannah!"

Carlo and I burst into the laughter that comes only after smoking good grass, laughing longer than we should have. At the same time, a befuddled but happily high Scott looked on, repeatedly saying, "I don't get it," as a confused but abstaining Tab just shook his wiry-haired head, grinning a bewildered but sincere smile.

On that momentous day, sitting there in The Blue Room with all my friends, I felt we'd reached the end of a pilgrimage; the warm breeze and light spilled over us in that temple, offering communion, granting each one of us an escape, an emancipation of sorts. Not only was I at the epicenter of my favorite place in the world, but under the influence of some very heady grass, I could almost forget that another world awaited me just across a narrow channel. Looking around at my friend's laughing faces, I realized that the pressure I keenly sensed in that other world was too intrusive in my everyday life. In contrast, high above a separate, abandoned, and wild world, the sound of the cicadas and wind through the trees held sway over the Marsh Tackies, trees, and surf that were its denizens. And maybe a ghost.

That the next day was Monday didn't even bother me. After all, we had only one week of school before the mundane transformed into the sublime. The anticipation felt like a mixture of my birthday and Christmas morning, but instead of looking forward to a single day, what I anticipated would last weeks on end. Appearing in my mind's eye as an enormous parade float made of gargantuan letters colored in sparkles and outlined in flashing multi-colored lights was the two-word message I'd waited all school year for—*summer break!*

▬▬▬ That Monday, I entered school with a strange, dangerous confidence, like the Hindenburg drifting leisurely over Lakehurst, waiting for a mere spark to blow. Usually, I arrived as the doors were unlocked, but that day I'd stopped by a lagoon near the Lower School to smoke a cigarette before making my way into school and heading straight for Mrs. Honse's English class without so much as a pencil. *Pretense be damned,* I thought. We'd reached the smoldering end of another school year, and I had plenty of other things on my mind. All heads turned toward me when I entered the classroom. Everyone was already seated, and Mrs. Honse was fully immersed in her lesson. Several junior varsity athletes sitting near the front of the class smirked, and Mrs. Honse turned, hands on hips, and eyed me warily.

"Ashley, please take a seat. You do know that class started ten minutes ago, don't you?"

Instead of answering, I smiled.

Noticing my lack of a textbook or notebook, she shook her head in exasperation. "I see you have come prepared today and ready to take notes and participate."

As she turned back to the class, I rushed to the chalkboard and scratched from top to bottom, watching the pained expressions and listening to the groans that rolled across the room like a wave.

Mrs. Honse's face turned red. "That's *not* the participation I was hoping for, Ash." She pointed at my waiting desk next to Carlo. "Sit down!"

I could feel her staring at me as I made my way to the back of the room, and my intuition was confirmed when I reached my seat. With her arms folded, she clearly wasn't quite done.

"I certainly won't be missing your little interjections this summer."

I met her gaze. "If I wasn't here to keep you on your toes, you'd lose your edge."

"My edge, Ash, is plenty sharp. Now keep your ears open and your mouth shut!"

I could see Carlo in my peripheral vision shaking his head "no." He probably felt that there was no real sport in making waves with summer break so near, but the hydrogen of confidence keeping me afloat was getting ever closer to that spark.

"But without tin cans like me to test yourself on, you won't be able to prove you can still cut a tomato neatly in half."

Sporadic, hushed laughter broke out in small pockets about the room.

The red that colored her face was now joined by what could only be described as storm clouds. "Any more smart alec comments, Ash, and you are going to see the principal."

Shrugging my shoulders, I slumped forward, rested my chin in my hands, and smiled at Carlo. He shook his head and whispered, "Let it go," before smiling. I could see his position, but I could tell he could also see mine.

The spark met the hydrogen and ignited, propelling a last comment toward Mrs. Honse. "Guess you're just gonna have to squash that tomato with that big fat butt of yours instead."

True to her word, I was soon sitting before Mr. Broadbent as a flustered Mrs. Honse described my latest offense. Slumping in my chair, looking sullenly at the floor, I partially listened, raising my eyes now and again only when one of the adult voices hit a sharp peak. During one of these moments, I discovered I'd be painting shelves in the library for the rest of the week and into the summer until I finished. But before I could dip a brush in a can of paint, my mom and dad would be informed of my latest insolence. Fear shot through me that my punishment might threaten my planned activities for the following weekend. However, I convinced myself I could probably get off without too much collateral damage by offering to do extra things around the house, like sweeping the pine needles off the roof and doing yard work.

With a far clearer picture than I had, my parents knew that my often rude, immature behavior was an attempt to be acknowledged, a reaction to the predicament I found myself in. They both sympathized with me and understood better than I did the adverse, long-term repercussions of having to contend with powers at school who held strings that could be used to bind me. The most extreme form of this control had been exercised on the two occasions I'd been held back. From my bound position, it was nothing more than punishment and far from the beneficial measure they presented it as. In practice, the remedy of holding me back to allow me "more time to learn" served only to humiliate me. My dad's suggestion that I be tutored after school in the classes I had difficulty in was rejected as logistically unworkable. That refusal brought into sharp focus that I needed more of what my classmates didn't—and therefore was as far removed from a remedy as possible. When I fought against my predicament, it was perceived as acting out for its own sake, making my struggle as effective as a horse kicking in his stall.

Naturally, my mom was upset with this latest offense, which she made clear by leaving the pharmacy early to meet me when I got home. But her words were easy to tune out. I might've appeared to be listening, but I was off again via my free-roaming ADHD: I first replayed an Anvil concert I'd seen in Savannah a few months earlier; then I retraced my weekend climb up the spiral staircase of my rusted lighthouse. Nods and "I'm sorries" only partially quelled the frustration we both felt.

When my mom left to pick up Dad from work, I grabbed the latest issue of *Kerrang!* magazine and flopped on the living room couch. I was reading when I heard my parents pull up, car doors closing, their voices slowly clarifying as they walked up to the house and entered through the kitchen door. After walking into the living room, my dad sat next to me and patted my knee. Still wearing his white pharmacist coat, he had a funny, conflicted-looking smile.

"Ash." There was no Ashey in this situation. "I heard you got in trouble today at school. Your mom told me she got a call from Mr. Broadbent saying you insulted Mrs. Honse again."

Before I could respond, he warmly put his hand on my shoulder. "Look, I know this has been another really tough year. Your grades are actually worse than last year."

His eyes seemed to stare past me and looked watery. "They're not talking about holding you back, which is a good thing; my guess is that they're now just trying to push you through." He exhaled a humorless laugh. "Try to keep your comments to yourself and do the best you can. You know I'm always here to help you with any questions you have about math or science, and your mom can help you with English and history."

I stared blankly at the open magazine on my lap, specifically at a full-page ad for Krokus's new album *One Vice at a Time.*

Aware of my tendency to drift away when being spoken to about topics that bored me or made me uncomfortable, my dad squeezed my shoulder. "Okay?"

I caught his eye for a second. "Yeah, okay."

"So, your mom tells me a girl called you, huh?" He squeezed my shoulder again, "What's that all about?"

I gave a slight shrug. "Just a girl from school. We hang out."

Again, the cover of the Krokus album drew my attention. An image of a steel gate, as one might find in a castle's dungeon with mist floating out through it, which seemed to conceal more than it revealed. Yet that unknown element was what kept drawing my attention. I had no doubt the album would soon be in my collection. Glancing back at my dad, I added, almost as an afterthought, "She's coming over on Sunday."

If frustration clouded my cluttered mind, Ally was the main contributor. On Saturday, we shared what was, as far as I was concerned, the single best day of my life. How completely fitting that our first kiss had been on an island called Declaration because, for me, it was a declaration of the first order: Ally and I were a couple. However, back at school that week, everything between us seemed like nothing more than a vivid but fading dream. There Ally was in gym class, talking and joking around with her friends but without acknowledging me in any way whatsoever. Except once when she flashed a quick, surreptitious smile when nobody was looking as the class returned to the gym after playing soccer. I felt sure that Carlo thought I'd manufactured the whole story of kissing Ally to save my pride after an unsuccessful date.

Then Wednesday afternoon, between classes, I saw her walking towards me with a hurried step as I was grabbing a notebook out of my locker. Swallowed in the chaos of those few in between moments, she must've felt she could briefly approach me without anyone noticing. She clutched a folded piece of paper, which I realized was a note she wanted to give me. Just as she extended her hand, a fidgety kid named Chip bumped her arm, causing the note to fall onto the floor. Completely oblivious, Chip continued on his way. For a second, I could see the tangible shock that shot through Ally's body. If anyone besides one of us picked it up, our secret would be revealed to the school and destroy her reputation. Just as she bent down, another hand grabbed it. The hand belonged to Clem, a running back on the football team. Ally's face literally went ashen white. If Clem read the note, he could publicly shame the traitor in their midst. I could almost hear the excuses running through her mind: "It's just a joke," "It's dialogue for a character I'm rehearsing for a play..."

Instead, he handed it to her. "Here, Ally, I think you dropped this."

"Thanks! People really should watch where they're going," she said, rolling her eyes. Giving her a confident smile and a wink, Clem hurried off to his next class. With a just detectable shake of her head, signaling the transfer was off, she stuffed the note in her front pocket, smiled at one of her approaching friends, and disappeared down the hallway. Her attitude towards me in public was confounding, but I also found it kind of sexy to be her special secret.

The rest of the week was the same, differentiated only by green paint after school and shelves that seemed to multiply as I painted them. The monotony was broken only by illicit smoke breaks with James in the storage room at the back of the gym. He often faintly smelled of alcohol, but I imagined I would too if I had to deal with a school full of loud-mouthed kids every day. Although Friday was a half-day, I still had to paint after school. Arriving early for Mr. Box's geography class, the very last class of the school year, Carlo and I made good use of our time, commandeering the colored chalk and executing our Sistine Chapel ceiling on the blackboard. It was a collaborative effort of Brothman raising his arms menacingly with a summer vacation message inspired by Alice Cooper: above his outstretched hands, the words "School's out" were written, and beneath his imposing form was the word, "FOREVER."

Walking into the classroom, Mr. Box showed mock surprise as he flung his arms above his head. "I see Brothman was here and left all of us a message."

He paused briefly, then said, "As this is the last class, I think it would be risky to ignore Brothman's sentiment. School's out, kiddos, have a great summer, don't get into too much trouble." His eyes fell on Carlo and me as he uttered these last words and winked.

8

Carlo, Paul, and I trudged through the cicada-buzzing forest with humidity so thick it felt like walking through a steam room. I led the way with Paul behind me and Carlo at the rear. In defiance of the heat and humidity, Carlo and I were wearing our stock jeans and black T-shirts, making us sweat about twice as much as Paul, who was wearing a muted pink Polo shirt, white tennis shorts, and shoes so white they almost made me squint. The sky was heavily overcast, threatening rain—a perfect day to play our prank. All around us, shadows gathered in the gaps between the imposing live oak, magnolia, and pine trees. Sounding somber and serious, Carlo spoke up. "This whole island is supposed to be cursed. You've probably heard the legends of the Blue Lady?"

Paul nodded. "Yeah, everyone's heard those."

"Well, the lightkeepers and the hunting club members that used to come here knew about them too, but they never went into any detail about how the curse worked." Carlo paused for effect, adding with an emphasis I thought was almost too dramatic, "But there's no doubt people *died* here because of the curse, and it scared off those who remained. That's why after the club and lighthouse were abandoned, nobody ever returned here to live." His voice now booming, a dash of Orson Welles threading his trademark Richard Burton gravitas, he gestured forward with tightly clenched hands. "The very *ground* we walk on *knows* we're here. Everything is connected, and the Blue Lady is never far away."

Paul's face pinched like he'd just bitten into a lemon. He scanned the thick woods and treetops as if something were watching us. Stopping suddenly with sweat rolling freely down his forehead, he swatted at a mosquito on the back of his leg. Then he wiped away the sweat that fell into his eyes with a terrycloth tennis wristband and squinted as if trying to make out something ahead of us. "It does kinda feel like we're being watched."

I mused that it would be handy to have one of those wristbands at that moment, but it was way too far removed from a spiked Bruce Dickinson, Iron Maiden gauntlet and too close to a Mike Reno of Loverboy accouterment for me.

Stone-faced, Carlo sidled up next to Paul. "Yeah, there's no doubt it's a real clusterfuck." He turned his head slowly, eyeing our surroundings as if sensing something before looking back at Paul. "A real clusterfuck run amok." I noticed a small, satisfied smirk cross Carlo's face and knew that this catchphrase addition would become another staple of his vocabulary.

As Paul again scanned the forest around us, the steady rise and fall of the cicada's hum seemed to dramatically underline everything that had been said. Then Carlo jerked his head forward. "Did you guys hear that?"

Attempting to sound serious yet inquisitive, I craned my head forward. "Yeah, it sorta sounded like a voice calling."

His forehead wrinkling in concern, Paul followed our gaze to the random spot in the woods where Carlo and I were staring. "I'm not sure I heard anything, but there are so many weird noises...." Cutting Paul off, Carlo turned to face him and exploded with alarm, causing Paul to stumble backward. Carlo's eyes looked as if they would pop from his head. Paul, stunned, half shouted, "What is it?" and stared imploringly at Carlo, then at me.

Carlo stared back at Paul, furiously rubbing his eyes while breathlessly shaking his head as if someone had just thrown a cold bucket of water on him. "Y-Your face."

"What about it?"

"It changed, like shimmered...for a second, it looked like another face was there like it melted into another face!"

153 —

"It must have been sweat in your eyes," Paul said, looking to me for support.

I shrugged but thought it was an excellent time to take the attention from Carlo, who was getting too into his performance. "I wasn't looking at you when it happened, but it wouldn't surprise me."

"Like what d'ya mean?"

"Weird things happen here all the time. You know, all the people who've seen the Blue Lady over the years. She was a lightkeeper's daughter and was swept out to sea after a hurricane." I gazed into the woods. "Some say she haunts the island because she died here. It's the only place she ever really knew, and now she thinks of herself as the island's protector."

Turning my head from Carlo, who had started cracking a smile, I stared into Paul's eyes. "She went insane, they said, before she went missing. Her dad died while trying to keep the light burning. She took over for him, but it was too much. After that, she lost her mind, so who knows why she does what she does...or to who."

"For a couple seconds, *your* face changed," Carlo reiterated, sounding like he was still trying to convince himself.

"This place is freaking me out," Paul blurted, all pretenses down.

Putting an arm around his shoulders, I reminded him why we were there. "You said you wanted to see the lighthouse." I took the cigarettes out of the front pocket of my jeans and lit one. "You wouldn't want it getting around that you chickened out once you got here and ran away like a little girl." I took a long drag, let my point settle in, then exhaled. "Well, would you?"

"No, but—" He shifted his weight from foot to foot. "It's just freaky to hear that your face changed into someone else's."

"Well, it did, and it was *weird!*" Carlo said.

Looking him straight in the face, I gave a frustrated sigh. "Don't be a pussy, Paul."

Paul glanced first at Carlo, whose folded arms accentuated the expression of disgust he wore, and then at me as I casually puffed away on the cigarette. I shook my head and looked at Carlo. "Well, I guess we could turn back, but it seems pretty lame."

"No, no, I'm cool," Paul said halfheartedly. "Let's see this place."

"Atta boy." I snubbed out my smoke on a pine tree. A few yards on, I glanced over my shoulder. Paul wore a look of grim determination but managed a wan smile. Just behind him, Carlo had a massive rictus grin plastered across his face, almost making me laugh out loud, so I spoke instead. "We're just about there."

Since we had gone through a lot of effort to set up the whole charade, I crossed my imaginary fingers that, first and foremost, both Tab and Scott were at the lighthouse compound and where they were supposed to be. Second, I hoped that Scott wouldn't blow the whole thing by tumbling out of the lighthouse door in a cloud of pot smoke, laughing before the prank had run its course. I'd told them that I would speak loudly as we approached so they'd know to get into their designated positions and to keep quiet, and that's precisely what I did. "Just around this last curve, and we're here!"

The mood of any place is affected by weather and lighting. That day the sky had slowly darkened as the clouds thickened, and with the muggy, heavy air stirred only fitfully by the occasional breeze, it felt like someone was walking nearby, just out of sight. Adding exponentially to this oppressive atmosphere was the lighthouse. With several derelict buildings huddling closely beneath her, the structure gave off an imposing, desolate, and haunted vibe. The empty windowpanes of the lighthouse and the lightkeeper's house were black, sightless eyes. I had hoped it wouldn't be sunny, but the dark, churning sky, and the rising wind had exceeded my hopes. Running ahead, I jumped onto the front porch of the keeper's house in one bound. The rotting planks creaked loudly.

"This is where Charlotte Pauley lived."

Climbing the steps, Paul joined me with a quizzical look. "Charlotte Pauley?"

"The Blue Lady," Carlo answered, ascending the steps himself. "Come on; you can see the steps that she dragged her dad's body up after he dropped dead of a heart attack lugging oil up the lighthouse."

Once inside, we moved from room to room, Carlo and I speaking quietly to emphasize the tragedy that had occurred there and to magnify the creepiness as if we didn't want to draw any unwanted attention from whatever might still occupy the place. Our house tour ended in what had once been the front parlor, where years of humidity had caused the oak floors to sag precariously as we carefully shifted around the periphery of the room, making our way to the fireplace.

"This would've been where the lightkeepers wrote and read after doing their chores." I rested my arm on the mantelpiece. "You can almost hear their voices if you listen closely enough...."

Paul scanned the shadows that seemed to grow from the corners of the room, joining in the center of the thick plank flooring. The light entering through the windows formed three thin strips that were quickly absorbed by the darkness that lay all around us.

Carlo's eyes fixed on something above the fireplace. "What's that?"

We followed his gaze, and Paul spoke first. "What's what?"

"What are you looking at, man?" I asked.

"Up in that crack in the plaster, it looks like there's something in there."

Turning to face what Carlo was pointing at, I reached my hand in. "Yeah, you're right."

Acting like I was struggling to dislodge something, I finally pulled my hand out, clutching several pages of what looked like old paper from a diary.

"Whoa, what's that?" Paul asked as he and Carlo crowded in to get a better look.

Walking to one of the windows, I excitedly exclaimed, "There's writing on it!"

"Read it out loud," Carlo urged.

Squinting as if I found the writing difficult to decipher, I said, "It seems to be part of a diary from some lightkeeper named Peter Byford." It was a name I'd chosen because Peter Byford, better known to the world as Bif, was the lead singer of heavy metal legends Saxon, and I knew Carlo would get a kick out of it. "There's a lot missing, but this Byford guy seems like he was worried about his assistant keeper, some dude named Paul Geiser. He writes here, 'My assistant Paul, who was appointed to this station two years ago, had always been such a trustworthy, reliable, and hardworking fellow, but recently, in the wake of an incident that has made me question reality, he hasn't acted like the person I have come to know.'"

Huddling close against me in the oppressively hot, sticky air of the parlor, Paul shifted uneasily, continually looking over his shoulder back at the staircase in the front hall.

"Listen to this shit," I stammered excitedly, "'I passed Geiser around eleven that evening as he emerged from the lighthouse at the end of his shift. Greeting him in my normal manner, I was flabbergasted,'" —Carlo chuckled at my choice of word—"'and utterly taken aback when instead of returning my salutation, Geiser glowered at me. His face seemed to suddenly present what I can only describe as a flickering, and for an instant, I would swear on a Bible, his face changed into someone else's.'"

"WHAT!" Paul stepped back towards the hall. "It doesn't say that."

I handed him the beautifully rendered faux moldering page. "See for yourself."

Carlo boomed, his voice ricocheting off the flaking walls, "That's exactly what I saw!" Turning to face Paul, he added, "It's super weird and kinda creepy that your name and this assistant keeper's name are so similar too."

Paul shook his head in disbelief, scrutinizing the frayed, dark paper and exclaiming, "Oh maaan, it says here that this Byford guy"— I made sure not to look at Carlo—"thinks the flickering he saw was part of some curse."

Wanting to retake control of the story, I grabbed the page back. "Let me see...yeah, it says here—" I scrunched my eyes up, finding Tab had done his job a bit too well. "The lightkeeper believes there's a curse associated with the lighthouse. He doesn't go into detail, but it seems like he must have in one of the pages of the diary these were a part of." I fanned them in the air. "But he writes that this curse, whatever it is, only seems to strike every ten years, focusing specifically on one particular person as a sort of warning to others."

Paul seemed truly uncomfortable, looking back and forth pleadingly between Carlo and me. "But what would this curse want with me?"

"Well," I continued, "I don't know exactly why, but Byford believed the face he saw for a moment in place of Geiser's was the first indication that Geiser had been marked for possession as part of that warning to whoever else might find themselves on the island."

"A warning from who? The Blue Lady? Or what?" Paul's voice held a genuine note of alarm.

Glancing at him grimly, I returned to the pages in my hand. "He writes here, 'After that incident, I convinced myself that I was merely tired, that it had been the shadows and darkness playing a trick on my eyes. In consideration of events soon afterward, however, it now seems clear that something was trying to take control of him. A week or so after that initial incident, I remember calling him one morning from the lantern room gallery to help me clean the lenses. Far below me, in the shadow of the lighthouse, he stood frozen in mid-chore. It was as if a statue had replaced the man who stood there moments earlier. In his curled arms, he carried firewood but seemed as motionless as the trees of the surrounding forest. It was a completely still day, but yell as I might, he didn't move. I descended the lighthouse and walked up behind him, placing my arm on his shoulder. Much to my consternation, at that moment, he reacted as if woken from a dream. He dropped his burden'"—a great contribution from Tab that really captured a period feel—"'and spun around as if he momentarily knew neither where nor even who he was. I have no doubt, with what I now know, that if I had laid eyes upon his countenance'"—kudos again to Tab—"'it wouldn't have been his own.'"

Falling silent, I feverishly scanned the tattered pages, seeming unable to take in what I was reading.

Paul couldn't conceal his agitation. "Well, what does it say?"

Clutching the pages, I smacked my forehead with my free hand. "Oh, my God!"

"What?" Paul pleaded.

"Some more pages are missing, but shit got really fucked up here, man! Apparently, Geiser just started acting completely unlike himself. The assistant had once been a friendly, happy guy who loved telling jokes and playing checkers with the keeper, but it says here, quite suddenly he became irascible and misanthropic."

"What do those words mean?" Paul asked.

Remembering how, with much laughter, Tab and I had poured over his dad's Roget's Thesaurus, searching for the most antiquated-sounding words we could find to bring our narrative to life, I looked up. "I think it pretty much means he became an asshole."

Then I continued, "But listen to this. One night the head keeper was reading in this room and heard what sounded like someone on the front porch." My eyes scanned the porch through the gaping window frame before returning to the page. "He says here, 'Upon opening the door, I was confronted with a person inhabiting the skin of someone I'd called friend. He wore this skin like you or I might put on a change of clothes. I cannot overstate this fact: the person before me wore Geiser's Lighthouse Board-issued overalls and flat-top cap, but in place of the hardworking, affable man I'd known now stood something demented, dare I say evil. Most importantly, the face he wore was that of someone or something else.'" The way to construct a "curse," Tab and I had decided, was to keep things a little ambiguous.

"'In his left hand, and I feel it necessary to stress this as Geiser was right-handed, he held the ax we used to chop the firewood, while his expression held a burning rage. Before I could ask what he was doing, he proceeded to raise the ax high above his head, bringing it down with force, missing my fleeing form by mere inches, and burying the blade in the doorframe, which bought me a precious few seconds. In a state of panic, I ran to the parlor and grabbed my rifle, which by the hand of providence was leaning against the wall near the fireplace, loaded, as I'd had it in mind to shoot at the raccoons who had of late been getting into our larder in the overnight hours. I scarcely had time to retrieve it, for as I turned around, Geiser was again upon me raising his tool-turned-weapon. Without a moment to spare, I fired, hitting him square in the face.'"

I stopped to let the words settle in before adding, "Then Byford states how he had to write an official account for the Lighthouse Board log but felt it important to explain what he felt really happened. Stuff that would've gotten him fired from his job and probably put away if he'd told anyone else. As he'd been repairing a crack in the plaster above the fireplace, it proved a perfect spot to conceal his diary."

Paul looked at me and then Carlo imploringly. "But what does it all mean?"

More to myself than to Carlo and Paul, I said, "I wonder." Then I reached my hand back into the gap in the plaster. I played up that I was fishing around. "Got something!" I excitedly yelled, removing three more pages of the mysterious diary.

Hastily scanning them, I looked up with deep concern.

"Man, this explains a lot. Byford writes he decided to look over the logbooks from previous keepers to see if he could find any clues to what was happening. Thanks to the detailed log entries, he found that weird stuff happened like every nine or ten years after the big hurricane in 1893. Byford had to kind of read between the lines 'cause like him, these other dudes couldn't just come out and say something supernatural was happening. So, apparently, every nine or ten years, unexplained and violent shit would suddenly happen." (Tab and I were vague about the timeline, as 1982 didn't line up with the hurricane of 1893, and we couldn't be sure Paul didn't know about it.)

"That's really freaky shit," Carlo interjected, looking gravely at Paul, "Real freaky and scary shit!"

Paul looked to me for some glimmer of light. "Does this Byford guy say what he thinks was going on?"

"He does. Apparently, in the logbook, there were entries every nine or ten years recording the death of a head keeper, an assistant, or—" I paused for a few seconds to build up the tension.

"Or what?" Paul and Carlo screamed in unison.

"Or a visitor!" I finally revealed.

The color drained from Paul's face. His expression reminded me of someone from a movie slowly sinking into quicksand.

"In 1902," I continued breathlessly, "a keeper fell from the lantern gallery for no apparent reason. Then in 1913, a woman named Charlotte Harlette"—I emphasized the second syllable of that last name, a nod to a favorite Iron Maiden song, "Charlotte the Harlot," but why I set up so many obstacles in our fabricated story I can't say, except like most kids, the risk was all the fun— "was visiting a sister who was married to the head keeper when she became obsessed with the rear range lighthouse. The keeper had to ban her from entering the tower because she kept interfering with its functioning. While carrying oil up to the lamps, the keeper and his assistant constantly encountered Charlotte on the narrow staircase, making passing difficult."

Paul hung on every word. When I dared a glance at Carlo, he lip-synched the name "Charlotte Harlette," clearly teetering on the verge of prank-ending laughter.

"Byford states the official log noted that Charlotte became delirious from some undiagnosed illness and tried to attack her sister violent-ly with a straight razor, but the keeper and his assistant managed to subdue her. She died later that day, but Byford thought the details were oddly vague, suggesting that her death wasn't natural."

Again, I read in silence as Carlo walked to the window. "Did you guys hear something?"

Paul followed and looked out apprehensively. "I don't think so."

I remained silent, seemingly riveted to the diary pages.

"I thought I heard someone laugh or something." Carlo waved his arm and turned his attention back to me, but Paul scanned the over-grown compound with great intensity.

"Maybe I heard something too," he said distractedly.

"Holy shit!" I yelled, startling Paul, who grabbed his chest as he spun around.

"What? What is it?"

"In 1932, the year the lighthouse was decommissioned, the young son of the new assistant keeper came running out of the lighthouse in great distress. He was shirtless and screaming incoherently. He refused to talk about what happened and was overcome with what's described in the log as a great and terrifying fever that affected his mind until he was transformed from an innocent, happy boy into..." I paused, slowly looking up. "Something deranged, bestial, and pro-fane. He needed to be tied to his bed, where he died screaming."

Turning with an awkward jerky motion, Paul fumbled towards the house's front door. His voice betrayed a growing fear as he cried, "Why would I be picked for this curse?"

"I don't know, but I'd be nervous if I were you." Carlo sniffed. "I mean, this diary seems to make it really clear that a person is chosen every few years to serve as an example or whatever you want to call it, and it's been a lot longer than usual since the Blue Lady has been able to set an example." Carlo's voice rose dramatically. "It's also super weird that I saw your face change before we found these pages."

Trying to ratchet up the urgency without being too theatrical, I called out, "There's one more thing." Before Paul could respond, I frantically gestured for him to rejoin Carlo and me in the parlor. Emboldened at how the power of my words had pulled him back into the room, I continued to apply pressure. "Biff, uh, I mean Byford"— I struggled to suppress a laugh—"says after the two deaths he witnessed, he heard strange knocks from underneath the house. Byford believed they were made by the same spirit that had possessed Paul Geiser, as well as the others he read about. He feels it was the deranged ghost of Charlotte Pauley—the Blue Lady—letting visitors know that the island is hers and that should never be forgotten."

Wiping his pale face with his wristband, Paul seemed very agitated. "Well, I mean, we came here, we saw the place, and I didn't chicken out. I mean, I don't think we really need to hang out...you know?"

Setting into motion Tab's contribution, I smiled reassuringly. "Don't freak out, man. We haven't heard any knocking sounds or seen any blue mist." I explained that people often saw a blue mist before seeing the Blue Lady. "You wouldn't miss someone knocking on these floors," I said loudly, stomping my foot to drive home my point. Recognizing his cue, Tab produced three loud knocks from beneath the sitting room, which adjoined the parlor.

Wearing an expression of sheer terror, Paul ran to the front door and onto the sagging porch. Clearly going with the flight aspect of the fight or flight reaction, he forgot the four steps leading up to the porch and tumbled face-first onto the pine needle-covered sandy soil, breaking his fall with his hands but scraping a knee in the process.

Carlo and I ran out and helped Paul to his feet. While I grabbed one arm, Carlo grabbed the other and, at that exact moment, broke into laughter, savoring every second of Paul's suffering. Luckily, Paul seemed so genuinely disoriented that he didn't notice, or maybe he thought Carlo was laughing at his up-close-and-personal meeting with the ground.

"Take it easy, Paul," I said, putting a reassuring arm around his shoulder and motioning under the house. "It was just a sound. It did come at a weirdly appropriate moment, but look, there's nothing under there."

Bewildered, Paul fell to his knees to look under the house, cringing like a person expecting to be slapped. The clouds seemed to clear a bit from his mind, and he smiled weakly. Tab, of course, had immediately escaped to a hiding place behind the oil house.

"Sorry, guys. I don't know, the stuff you were reading, the curse, the knocking...." He slowly rose, taking his wristband off and pressing it against his knee. "And Carlo saying he saw my face change. I guess I just lost it."

"Well, there's only one more thing to do, and then we can head home," I said.

"What's that?" Paul asked, knowing the answer but hoping for a miracle change of plan.

With a little too much gusto, Carlo patted him on the back. "The top of the lighthouse, my man!"

The lighthouse looked unusually foreboding under thick, dark passing clouds. The rust dominating its façade appeared like a fresh spattering of arterial blood left from a slashing blade. Because I was riding an adrenaline high, that's exactly how my eyes perceived it. Paul stared up as we approached with a look of anxiety mixed with morbid curiosity. I reminded him of the little boy who'd run from the building decades earlier, shirtless and possessed.

"According to that diary, nobody ever knew what the poor kid saw, but he definitely saw something and didn't live long after he did."

With that, I urged Paul to take the lead up the spiraling staircase, which had room only for single file. Carlo and I built upon Paul's palpable sense of unease as we slowly completed our upward clocklike rotations.

"Weird that the little kid was shirtless," Carlo said as if to himself.

"Yeah, and completely out of his mind," I added. "It would be terrifying to encounter something in here. I mean, we're confined.... trapped, really. We could only run down these stairs if anything happened."

"Yeah, and if it was the Blue Lady, there really isn't an escape." Carlo paused to let that sink in. "Is there?"

When we stopped on the first of the two landings, I peered out the narrow sash window at the unsettled grey day. The breeze scraped the branches of nearby trees against the skeletal supporting columns and beams as if they were bristles on a giant hairbrush. Cicadas within those branches rode out the rising wind with a noticeable edge of agitation to their buzzing song, rising and falling, increasing then receding endlessly. It was like a crescendo of waves collapsing on a storm-tossed beach, made suddenly forlorn, transforming them into the sizzling foam pulled back, only to be pulverized and then supplanted by the next upsurge.

Paul and Carlo seemed as transfixed as I was by the gray light that filtered through the swaying branches. The competing duo of wind and cicada tymbals seemed to oppress and exhilarate in equal measure, keeping an invisible barrier between us and the nature we had no control over—a force that was neither for nor against us.

Through the window, a gust of wind brought with it several fat raindrops. "Looks like we're gonna get some rain." I turned to them, looking as grim as possible. "We better get this done with."

With that, I gestured to the next segment of the staircase that disappeared as it curved up to the second and final landing before the watch room. With a glance, first at me and then at Carlo, Paul flashed a weak smile. He looked, I imagined, like a soldier in the moments before storming the beach at Normandy. Nodding, he turned, gripping one hand on the thin hand railing.

A couple of steps behind Paul, like a prison chaplain accompanying a soon-to-be-executed convict, Carlo said, "God only knows what that little kid saw when he climbed up here, but at least he didn't suffer too long."

Paul slowly took each step with what seemed like helpless resignation. He wasn't going to say he was afraid, though. Once he had taken a firm hold of the line we'd offered, he knew it was all or nothing. This was a rite of passage. The alternative was a shame that would follow him, one he would be incapable of living down. Sliding up the railing, his hand pulled his body forward while his feet, uncertain but resolute, lifted, then landed on each step as if weighted with lead. I heard short scuffling sounds as the soles of his shoes scraped the cast iron.

Even on sunny days, the darkest sections of the lighthouse were between the landings. A few more steps and the welcoming light from the next landing's window should have flooded the staircase. But, instead, it grew darker as we plunged into an abyss as black as ink.

"That's weird," I spoke through the impenetrable blackness that swallowed us as if somehow, instead of climbing into the sky, we had descended into a cavern that had never known light. "We should be seeing daylight from the next landing."

With his voice amplified by the darkness, Carlo shouted, "Something's wrong!"

"Here," I said, fishing the lighter from my pocket and lighting it. Its weak orange flame picked out our three faces and a circle of the vertical, peeling wooden planks that made up the interior walls. "It should be as bright here as the last landing...." My voice slowly trailed off.

"Listen, I heard something," Carlo whispered loudly. "Someone, or something, is here."

Paul was on the final step before the landing, Carlo and I just behind him. Hesitating, Paul's right foot returned to the step it had just vacated. "I'm scared."

A groaning creak from the stairs on the far side of the landing came without warning, seemingly responding to his fear. Paul let forth an audible gasp as we were thrust into the maelstrom of a banshee's wail.

"Ahhhhiiieeee!"

Clearly, this was the voice of a spiteful, vengeful spirit swarming around us from above. Then, with another metallic squeak on the staircase just beyond our vision, a figure suddenly jumped onto the small cast iron platform. In the flickering flame of my lighter appeared a screaming, shirtless Scott, hair combed forward, wearing nothing but tennis shorts.

Paul let out one of the most terrified, blood-curdling screams I've ever heard and flew past me in a panic. Yards ahead of the signals from his brain, his feet flew out from beneath him—his ankles, then his backside thumped down the steep, twisting stairs. His right hand managed to clutch the railing, which prevented an even worse fall. Before he could get up, the gray light of day flooded the lighthouse's interior.

An unbridled, raucous belly laugh exploded in the confined space and seemed to tremble the iron stairs. In one hand, Scott was holding the cardboard we had told him to put over the window. His other hand rested on his knee as he bent over and roared with laughter in that way only he could: face beet red, contorted with mirth, tears streaming down his cheeks from squinting eyes.

Fighting for gasps of air while lording over the sprawled Paul several steps below, Scott stood shaking his head. "Oh...man...haaa, haaaa, you looked like you shit your pants."

With that, Carlo and I joined in until the central cylinder of that old skeleton-framed lighthouse gave off a sound that could have rivaled a foghorn had the light still been active. Our laughter alone would have been capable of guiding ships from fifteen miles out at sea.

Stretched out prone on the stairs, his hand still gripping the railing, Paul looked up at us blankly, eyes wide open, mouth agape—the human equivalent of a blue crab minding his business feeding on a chicken neck before being hoisted up into the harsh sunlight in a net.

Hearing our thunderous laughter and knowing that the prank had been played to its conclusion, Tab came up the stairs. Within seconds, he joined us, looking at Paul. Still lying awkwardly on his back, he remained motionless, except for his eyes which darted from Scott, Carlo, and me to the new arrival who stood just beneath him on the stairwell. By far the least afraid of all of us to show kindness, Tab offered his hand, which Paul took.

Shaking his head, he slowly stood up, voice flat and dazed. "It was just a joke, huh?"

"No, it was real, and you're cursed," Scott answered, pulling a shirt on and then combing his hair into its singularly peculiar shape.

"Well, you got me."

"That's an understatement," Carlo laughed, a tinge of cruelty slipping through. "Like sayin' Hitler was just kind of a dick."

"Or that Hurricane David was just a light summer breeze," I added.

Suddenly, as if a light had been switched on, Paul's face lit up. Something approaching pride filled his expression as if he had passed a test and was now part of our ranks. That thought was the furthest thing from our minds, though, and the four of us laughed long and loudly. We mimicked Paul's reactions to every stage of the prank as we recounted it in minute detail: Carlo reenacting Paul's expression when he said his face had morphed into that of another, Scott impersonating his terrified scream, Tab joining in with a chuckle over Paul's frantic flight from the house after his resounding knocks, and me recounting how pale, solemn, and petrified he looked just before we entered the lighthouse. Paul even timidly joined in, laughing as if the joke hadn't been centered exclusively on him or entirely at his expense. Just like any group at school, ours could close ranks with amazing speed and the same prejudice as those groups that abused us. Most friends are peripheral, chosen to occupy spaces that beg to be filled. Paul was peripheral to each of us for different reasons, providing a diversion and outlet for pent-up frustrations.

Except for Carlo, none of us had ever been outwardly antagonistic towards Paul in the way the school jocks commonly were to Carlo and me. But Paul always seemed tentative with us, unsure how far he wanted to step into our world—and that tentativeness rankled. The prank was simply a laugh at Paul's expense, nothing more, nothing less. Harmless fun, we all assumed. I suppose that, to an extent, Paul had indeed passed a test, but even before the following school year, he left the murky waters of our wake and moved back to terra firma. Carlo and I saw him hanging out in Sheltered Harbour with members of the school's tennis team. When school began again, it was no surprise that he'd joined the team himself.

We would nod at him, and he'd nod at us, but both sides had discarded the experiment of friendship. Were some, or all of us, to blame for not meeting the other person on the foundation of a solid middle ground? Yes, but at the time, we just thought the prank had drained the allure of our group from Paul's system. From my perspective, the gag had concluded successfully with the feeling that it had done little harm. Innocent fun at Paul's expense was how Carlo and I filed it away, laughing about it when it would occasionally come up in conversation. As an adult, I find it hard to believe this is how I rationalized it at fifteen because the carefully planned cruelty very well might have had the same effect on Paul as my lingering memories of my tormentors had on me.

9

Considering the amount of energy, planning, coordination, and timing we'd put into our prank, the school authorities might conclude that I was prevaricating or lazy when I said I had trouble focusing on activities that adults deemed mandatory. The difference was that the prank had been an activity that captured my imagination. On Leggatts in the early 1980s, kids had to create their diversions, and once we'd agreed upon the plan, Carlo, Tab, Scott, and I were committed to our prank's successful execution, and for reasons I wasn't yet willing or capable of analyzing, successes had begun neatly stacking up for me one on top of another. In my ignorance, I could see no reason for this enchantment ever to abandon me again.

I awoke on Sunday, noting the return of the butterflies that used my stomach as a regular stopping-off point on their migratory journey. Although the nervousness was like the one I always felt approaching the lighthouse, this feeling was much more pronounced. A fragile uncertainty made up the framework of my relationship with Ally, yet it felt like steel and concrete when she was near me. When she smiled at me, I could add rebar to that analogy, and when she kissed me, I became not only strong but something that could ignore gravity completely: a boy transfigured into a B-17 Flying Fortress.

When the phone rang just after nine, I knew it was Ally. Outfitted only in PJ bottoms, I ran into the kitchen and grabbed the receiver as my mom reached for it.

"Excuse *me!*" she exclaimed, recoiling exaggeratedly.

Wearing the blinders of youthful exuberance, I stared ahead as if she wasn't there. "Hello?"

"Hi Ash, it's Ally. I hope you're not too much of a sleepyhead 'cause I was thinkin' about coming over in like an hour."

Behind me, my mom grumbled, "It would be wonderful if you could show half that much energy on school day mornings...."

"Yeah, yeah, an hour's great. D'ya know how to get here?"

"I will after you give me directions, silly boy."

After doing that, I hung up, struck by an intense emotion bordering on mania!

"Let me guess." My mom put her hands on her hips. "I've never seen you sprint like Bruce Jenner to answer the phone before, so that must have been the mystery girl."

"She's no mystery," I answered as I tried to decide everything from what music to play to what T-shirt to wear. "It's Ally, a girl from school. She's coming over in an hour."

Mom's tone changed instantly. "Well, a little notice would've been appreciated, but what a nice surprise!" She gave me a warm, loving hug and kissed the side of my downturned head. "Oh, Ashey, you'd better get ready, then."

I'd already decided to wash *and* blow-dry my hair to maximize the essential feathering effect. After styling my hair to perfection courtesy of Mom's blow dryer, I chose my Riot: *Fire Down Under* T-shirt. Its furry baby seal mascot occupied the perfect middle ground between entertaining a cute girl and advertising a much-underrated band. I had quickly decided that the back deck would be the best place to hang out; it had options that covered all possible bases: chairs, a table on which to set my boombox, a hammock slung between two oaks that the deck was built around, and most impressively, on the other side of the deck, a recently purchased trampoline that provided much entertainment for the whole family, including Eddie and Geezer.

With much the same speed I exhibited earlier when answering the phone, I sprinted down the hallway when the doorbell rang a few minutes past ten. It wasn't an Olympic gold medal performance, though, as my mom was already opening the door when I got there.

"Well, hello, you must be Ash's friend...." She let the question dangle.

"Ally, I'm Ally."

"I'm Ash's mom. Please come in." She stepped aside and smiled. "What a nice name Ally is."

Not for the first time, I was utterly floored by how pretty she was. The open front door framed her like a portrait. Her hair was again in a French braid, and she wore beige shorts that extended to just above her knees—more conservative than I would have preferred—along with a red and white striped tank top.

Geezer and Eddie excitedly jumped to meet the visitor, and Ally bent down to greet them. "Aren't you just the cutest guys?" she cooed, scratching Eddie behind the ears while simultaneously petting Geezer's belly as he made himself instantly comfortable with her.

"So nice to meet you, Mrs. Howe," she said, looking up before glancing at me, smiling a smile that put thoughts into my fertile brain that had nothing to do with dogs or moms.

I directed Ally with a quick wave of my arm. My mom leaned in towards me and whispered as Ally briefly walked ahead, "I told you they would come around." I flashed her an appreciative smile, realizing moms are often right, even if the self-consumed teenage mind doesn't usually recognize it. This girl had certainly come around, and there wasn't another one in the world I would have chosen over her.

"Follow me out back." I beelined through our living room, pointing out the dining room and kitchen on our way. "Thought you might want to check out our trampoline."

"Totally!" she gushed.

My boombox was already pumping out The Police's latest album, *Ghost in The Machine.* I loved it but kept that fact from Carlo and Scott, only sharing it with Tab, who said he liked it too. The song that filled the summer day as we headed for the trampoline was, in a bit of beautiful universal alignment: "Every Little Thing She Does Is Magic." Instantly throwing her arms out at her sides, Ally started snapping her fingers and swaying her hips. Sting, Andy Summers, and Stuart Copeland were my new soulmates. Without any hesitation or formalities, we began jumping and laughing on the trampoline.

"You have the nicest hair," Ally surprised me by saying.

"Well," I said between enthusiastic jumps that bounced Ally ever higher, "you have the nicest everything."

Realizing the unintended forwardness of blurting out my private thoughts, I quickly added, "I mean, you look fantastic." My face must have turned red because Ally flashed me another smile that spoke of things my lower half was interested in without caring if my mind kept up—dangerous ground by any assessment.

"You keep me on my toes with your surprises," she said between breathy, jiggling bounces. "I never would have thought you were a Police fan."

"Well, yeah, the band, at least," I joked. "Sting's a great bassist."

"Is he?" she chuckled.

I was hardly paying attention to what I was saying. I'd heard that some people were susceptible to hypnotism, and I had just discovered a form that was truly effective on my pubescent brain. With jigglings and gyrations in very specific areas, Ally's developing body had me under a spell I had no chance of escaping. As if possessing a telepathic link to my recklessly progressing thoughts, my mom appeared. Carrying a tray with sandwiches and iced tea, with Geezer and Eddie in joyful pursuit, she was like a physical non sequitur to conclusions I thought only I was drawing.

Waiting for us to sit down and start eating, my mom looked at Ally, then me, flashing a smile that conveyed she was happy for me.

As she headed for the door, Mom spun around as if she were a teenager herself. "There's plenty more of everything," she said unnecessarily, turning down the volume on my boombox in that absent-minded, second-nature way moms have.

With enough sandwiches to feed Carlo, Scott, and Tab if they suddenly appeared and a full pitcher of iced tea, neither Ally nor I was in danger of starving—unless, of course, the dogs managed to make off with our food in a moment of distraction.

"Thank you so much, Mrs. Howe. Everything looks delicious."

"Oh, it's just some sandwiches." My mom smiled. "With all that exercise, you need to eat."

"Your mom is sooo nice," Ally said.

Chuckling, I kept my head bent towards my sandwich but lifted my eyes to look at her, thinking I had detected something more than a simple statement. I flashed a cheeky smile. "Yeah, she's nice." I took a sip of iced tea, then put forth my deduction. "I know, no Motörhead T-shirt, all her teeth, and not a tattoo in sight."

Ally broke into the laugh I'd heard from her at school when she was joking around with her friends. "Well, not all of those."

"No, my mom and dad have nothing to do with how I turned out. At least as far as my taste in music and hair goes." I leaned back and looked deeply into her eyes. "I just gotta be me."

Meeting my gaze, Ally smiled a smile that spoke of things that were awakening in me but of which I had no experience. "I wouldn't want you to be anyone but who you are."

The feeling that had assailed me at the lighthouse a week earlier possessed me completely. I wanted to kiss her badly, and I must have made a motion to do that because my mom appeared at the door with a watering can in hand.

"Don't mind me," she said nonchalantly, looking everywhere but at us. "Just need to water the ferns."

As she busied herself with the hanging plants on the porch, I leaned in conspiratorially to Ally.

"I'm really glad you came over, but as you've probably figured out, privacy isn't easy to come by around here."

My mom began distractedly singing "America" by Neil Diamond, who was one of her favorites. As was typical for her, she had mangled the lyrics from immigrants setting out for America into a strange, nonsensical ode to goats, grains, and hay. I lowered my voice just a little more. "Next time we get together, we should go out somewhere."

Ally blinked and gave me a flat smile.

"Are those goats on the train, that's our country America...," my mom sang.

"You know, so we don't have my mom watering plants and singing over us."

"Oh yeah." Ally glanced absently at my mom. "I mean, your mom's sweet, but that's a good idea."

Mom's voice rose as if she were now on a stage backed by a full band. *"Home, where we need to bale hay..."*

"Well, maybe on Tuesday, we could head over to the theater in town. They're showing *Poltergeist.*"

"Oh, we're planting rice today..."

Ally's eyes darted down to the corned beef sandwich she was holding, which she pulled in closer when she saw Eddie had turned into a salivating, wet-nosed sandwich torpedo honing onto a target. "I'm like totally not into horror movies."

"In the ear of the corn..."

"How about going to the arcade instead?"

Lost in her duet with Neil, my mom let loose with extra gusto, *"In the ear of the corn!"*

Then, freezing with the watering can still held up to a fern, she smiled self-consciously at Ally and me, called the two dogs, headed toward the door, glanced back once, then disappeared into the house.

"I've never been into video games at all."

"I guess there's always the new youth center," I suggested halfheartedly. Located just outside Sheltered Harbour, it offered pool and ping-pong tables, foosball, and dartboards, all in what was supposed to be a safe, non-judgmental environment. The one time I ventured in, the crowd, which seemed composed of every jock from school, immediately turned me off. An overly competitive intensity pulsed from every activity in the room, with the guys showing off for each other and especially for the few girls there.

Ally's answer to this suggestion was one I could get behind. "That place is always sooo crowded. I always want to leave the second I get there."

Feeling like I was racing through options shot down as fast as clay pigeons at a gun club, I threw out one last suggestion. "I know, let's go to the beach down by the Adventure Inn."

"Oh, the beach sounds like fun," Ally answered, much to my relief. "But let's not go to the beach by the hotel but that *beautiful* skeleton beach on your island."

Probably because the lighthouse was always the center of my Declaration activities, it had never crossed my mind to go swimming there, but the thought of having a beach—and Ally—all to myself washed over me like a warm wave. I smacked my hand down on the table. "That sounds like a blast!"

At that moment, my mom opened the sliding door to let out the always enthusiastic Geezer and Eddie. Taking their arrival as a cue, I stood up and, digestion be damned, flung myself off the balcony onto the trampoline with both dogs in excited pursuit. The magical combination of wagging tails and happy barking was all the enticement Ally needed, and soon all four of us were bouncing or being bounced with wild abandon. In no time, we were all lying on the trampoline, fully winded. I had little doubt that my mom had let the dogs back out to provide fuzzy physical barriers between Ally and me. With Eddie curled up against me and Geezer against Ally, we stared at the trees and sky. Turning, Ally rested her elbow on the canvas, cradling her head in her hand.

"I love how you just do what you want and don't care what anybody thinks."

I turned to look at her a moment before answering. "Not everything I want to do." Propping my head up like Ally, I smiled, "If I did everything I wanted to, I wouldn't have waited so long to talk to you."

Her expression became far away, eyes squinting like she'd sipped something bitter. "Well, I'm glad we're talking now...and that I know you."

Sensing the conversation getting more serious than I was ready for, I stood up and jumped off the trampoline.

"Hey!" Ally laughed, sitting up and swinging her legs over the edge.

I could tell she was going to ask a question, so I got there first. "What is it?"

"I was gonna ask if I could see your guitar?" She scrunched up her nose. "I mean bass."

Empowered by the recent victory I'd shared with that bass, I grabbed Ally by her waist and hoisted her onto the ground. Feeling a familiar awkwardness threaten my budding confidence, I walked across the deck, calling over my shoulder, "Yeah, follow me."

As I marched through the living room, my mom popped her head through the breakfast nook. "Keep the door open, Ashey."

Although I was aware that Ally was watching me closely, my confidence with music made me feel at ease as I thumbed through my albums until I found Cirith Ungol's *Frost and Fire*. Carefully removing the album from its sleeve, I put it on my record player, swung the guitar strap over my shoulders, turned on the amp, set the needle onto the opening groove, and began playing along with the title track. I'd chosen the song because it would give me ample opportunity to not only play an unusually funky bassline for such a heavy song but also to show off a dramatic mid-song slap bass technique: three big, fat, plucked *"bwamp, bwamp, bwamps."*

Watching me, Ally folded her arms. "Can you show me how to play something?"

Swinging the bass over my head, I carefully placed it on her, adjusting the strap to rest more comfortably. I felt like a golf pro giving a private lesson to a receptive housewife. Standing behind her, I directed her right hand over the pickup closest to the neck, and her left onto the fretboard, pressing myself intoxicatingly close against her so I could demonstrate. Within a few minutes, Ally was playing the opening riff of Rick James's "Super Freak," the bane of Steaming Broth jam sessions. After that, we moved on to the rattling bass intro of Iron Maiden's "Running Free." While Ally was getting the hang of that, I was getting the hang of her. Then my dad, who had just returned from a jog, peered into the room.

Unlike Mom, who would almost certainly have been uncomfortable about my up-close-and-personal teaching technique, my dad smiled. "Hi Ash, just wanted to meet your friend." Standing in my doorway, sweating from his run, he rested his hands on his hips. "Getting a guitar lesson?" He looked at Ally.

"Ash is a good teacher, but I don't think it's sounding like it should."

Then realizing she hadn't introduced herself, she added, "I'm Ally, Mr. Howe."

"Ally, it's really nice to meet you. I'd shake your hand, but I'm a bit of a sweaty mess." He returned his glance to me. "I'll let you guys get back to your lesson." Then, almost as an afterthought, said, "Try to keep it down a little bit, though, huh? It sets your mom on edge."

"Will do," I said, returning my dad's smile, which seemed infused with reassurance and a hint of pride.

When Ally left an hour later, I followed her outside to her moped. By a twist of fate, she had parked in front of the shed, which concealed us from the house.

Ally looked at me mischievously. "I think this is the first time we've really been alone today."

"Yeah, my parents were kinda all over the place." I glanced over my shoulder.

"Your parents are nice," Ally said, wrapping her arms around me.

I pulled her in even closer and bent my head down, pressing my forehead against hers. "Yeah, they're nice, but you're beautiful, and I've been wanting to kiss you all day."

"Then what are you waiting for, boy?"

The answer was a kiss that made me feel like I was caught deep in a fever dream—one I wanted to linger in indefinitely. My pulse raced, a scout ill-prepared to evaluate incoming information the instant our bodies pressed against each other and her tongue started mingling with mine. The only information I obtained was that the storied French kiss was more than just an abstract term bandied about by seniors at school or an album by Bob Welch. It officially confirmed to my often-skeptical mind that our earlier kiss had really happened, and now I had the luxury of savoring where before I'd had to contend with surprise.

In Ally's company, my comprehension of the mundane was, at best, sketchy. So, I was a bit rattled to realize we couldn't make our trek to the beach on Declaration for another week and a half. When making plans, I'd failed to consider all the lawns I had to mow, weeds

I had to pull, and pine needle-strewn roofs I had to sweep as part of my one-person lawn care sideline, not forgetting the shelves stretching to infinity I had to paint as my school punishment. If, in the past, I'd primarily needed money for records, T-shirts, and gas for my moped, now I had the added expenditure a girlfriend incurred. At least, I assumed it would at some point. For the present, we didn't need money for any of the activities we managed to fit in between my yardwork and shelf painting and Ally's part-time job at Zippy's ice cream parlor. We met at my house or the forest preserve that lay halfway between our houses. Spending all that time alone in the woods had benefits, allowing us to focus on nothing else but each other.

As I sped across Leggatts to the boat launch at Mitchell Inlet, two competing thoughts wrestled for my attention. The first, taking control like the Masked Superstar utilizing his patented Cobra Clutch, was the craving for new music, nearing a fever pitch with the knowledge that Carlo's mom would drive us to Oglethorpe Mall in Savannah the following weekend. Once there, Carlo and I would beeline for the Record Bar, where I would spend a sizable chunk of my lawn work money fattening my pocket. I also optimistically considered all the fun places I would take Ally to spend the rest of that cash. By the time I was riding the shoulder of the highway, however, the focus of my thoughts had shifted exclusively to Ally. She had called me the night before and said that it would make more sense to meet at the boat launch instead of running the risk of her dad seeing us riding our mopeds together. Although I didn't like the idea of her riding alone on the highway, I'd agreed to her request, feeling that I was the only one jumping through several hoops of fire to make time for the date.

Scott had tried in vain to get me to his house to jam three times during the week, including that Sunday, but I had spent almost all my free time away from my chores with Ally. In keeping with my vow of secrecy, I came up with several excuses that seemed weak even to me, including a broken bass string with no spare and a summertime cold. My reason for that Sunday was that my dad wanted me to help him move some things to a storage locker that he rented off the island in Bluffton. "Whatever," came Scott's annoyed reply.

In preparation for swimming on Declaration and anticipating seeing Ally in her swimsuit, I made a new mixtape incorporating a bewildering gumbo of heavy metal mayhem with the latest from The Go Go's, Hall and Oates, and Duran Duran. In my quest to include music I thought Ally would want to hear, I inundated my fellow classroom instigator Billy with requests to pilfer Billboard top 100 singles from his sister's collection. At least my moped expedited the process. "Wouldn't have ever guessed you were a Duran Duran fan, Ash," Billy told me as he handed over a new batch of singles from his oblivious sister, who thought Billy was borrowing her records to annoy her.

"Music man, expanding my horizons... You know me."

"I do. That's what I don't get," Billy had answered.

I had set out with a backpack loaded with a boombox, water, and a couple of bottles of Yoo-hoo. Ally said she would make us some sandwiches, which was good because my short attention span contributed to an impatient, sloppy sandwich-making technique that often led frustratingly to what resembled innocent wedges of bread attacked while peacefully minding their own business, jelly, and peanut butter oozing from their injured sides. Even the squashing effect of a backpack couldn't have covered up this fact.

A pang of doubt gripped me as I approached the boat launch at the end of Cogginsville Road and saw it was deserted except for a parked pickup truck with an empty boat trailer. I needed to remind myself that, in my permanent state of impatience, I had arrived extra early. Removing the backpack, I walked over to a wooden bench and sat, pulling out a flattened cigarette from the mashed pack in the front pocket of my tight jeans. Lighting up, I inhaled deeply, languidly eying a couple of pelicans sunning themselves on the two remaining posts of a pier that had washed away after Hurricane David blew through in 1979. It would be my only chance to smoke before Ally arrived. Ten minutes later, as a speck coming down Cogginsville Road grew, I made out Ally riding her moped, her braided hair flying out behind her. Like me, she had chosen not to wear a helmet. Standing up, I quickly mashed the cigarette into the soft, dry sand and retrieved a crushed chunk of Hubba Bubba from my overstressed pocket. While watching her now audible moped zipping towards me, I chewed the gum vigorously to dispel any scent of smoke that Ally was so good at detecting.

By the time she pulled up, she was beaming. Several cascading strands of hair had broken free from their braid, and they focused my attention on her face, freshly rose-tinted from the wind and sun of her ride. Her eyes sparkled with a spirited exuberance that spoke of spontaneity and independence. She was boldly going against her father's wishes and exuded a carefree spirit I felt I could almost breathe like the air.

"Well, I wasn't run over by a truck or hit like a deer, and I think all of me is here," she said in a voice threaded with adrenaline.

I took her in slowly from the feet up in a playful manner, feeling like John Travolta's character Danny in the movie *Grease* as he checked out leather-clad, cigarette-smoking Olivia Newton-John. Fanning my face with the back of my hand, I could only concur with her conclusion. "Yeah, you're all there, all right."

She rolled her eyes and grabbed my T-shirt, pulling me in for a kiss. I quickly took the gum out of my mouth and tossed it on the ground. The strong current she imparted recharged me entirely.

Ally pulled away, shaking her head. "Nice try, boy, but you taste like bubble gum and cigarettes—unless that's a new flavor."

I shrugged my shoulders, looked at the ground, and smiled.

Changing the subject, she casually motioned to the metal basket on the side of her moped. "I have sandwiches in here." Then putting one hand on her hip and the other on the front of her Zippy's T-shirt, she said, "And my swimsuit's under here."

Temporarily mesmerized, I stood there with a dumb smile on my face.

She waved a hand in front of my eyes. "Helllooo. Is there anybody in there?"

"Uh, yeah," came my witty reply. "I have music, water, and Yoo-hoos."

"Oooh, Yoo-hoos. You sure do know how to romance a girl," she said.

"Never fails." I smiled.

Her playful sarcasm wasn't misplaced. How to treat a girl was uncharted territory for me, but besides a few faux pas and awkwardness, things seemed to be going pretty well.

"Oh," I added, placing a hand unthinkingly over my crotch, "and my swimsuit's under here."

"Is that what's under there?" She had a way of saying things that made me feel simultaneously silly, self-conscious, and enticed. It kept me off-balance, but I kind of loved it.

"Well, let's hit it," I said, extricating myself from the feeling that a spotlight had just picked me out on a stage. Within seconds we were zooming along the low-tide beach of Mitchell Inlet. Above was a azure sky without a cloud in sight. The ever-present ruddy turnstones, plovers, oystercatchers, and sandpipers skittered or took short hopping flights out of our way as we made fast time on the hard sand. Just off to our left, appearing as an ever-growing patch of green, was Declaration Island. When the thin ribbon of sand between the two islands was beneath us, I couldn't help but feel that Declaration had arranged a greeting. Greens of every shade billowed and swayed in a warm, inviting welcome.

Once we arrived on the deserted beach, the breeze swept away the muggy air that had encased us on Leggatts. As we parked our mopeds in their usual hidden spot, a veritable explosion of the citrus-honey scent from thousands of magnolias in their late June bloom bombarded our senses. The wind swirled the bouquet around us, making it seem like the forest had been freshly laundered for our visit. The look of wonderment on Ally's face let me know that she was as intoxicated by it all as I was. If an island could be said to smile, then this was it.

Flowers lined the pathway and speckled the forest: oleanders with pink flowers; azaleas in yellow, violet, white, and pink; yuccas with towering spires of white flowers; white daisies and purple coneflowers; cardinal flowers of deep red; tiny gold bearded beggarsticks; and long-stalked musk thistle with red-purple disk flowers. We walked in silence, dazzled by the rainbow of colors and the thickly scented breeze. Above us, the bright sun pierced a blue-sky, intent on showing off each petal in all its glory.

Ally spun around with her hands stretched out. "Oh my God, I've never seen so many flowers blooming at once in my entire life."

Watching her disappear momentarily into the kaleidoscope of color, I could only agree, "I called ahead that you were coming and asked the spirits of the island to bring some flowers."

In my wildest imaginings, I couldn't have summoned the blooms surrounding us. They filled our spirits with a bright wordless song, reassuring us we were safe, equally encouraging us to catch and cup the wondrous new emotions welling up within. Those were flowers, too, ready to embrace the sun, concerned only with the moment, the present footstep.

We walked without words for a few yards before Ally turned to me with a curious look. "I can almost believe that you did, Ashley Howe."

We reached to find each other's hand and walked on. So taken were we with this face of the island that even a sizable indigo snake, its scales shining a blackish-purple in the bright sunshine, didn't faze Ally. She merely stopped, clasping her arms around one of mine, and smiled in surprise, her eyes sparkling and alive. When we approached the skeleton beach, two sharp "yewks" drew our attention to the sky as an osprey swooped down onto the upper branch of one of the bone-white trees.

"That's the male osprey of the island."

Glancing back and forth between the bird and me, Ally smiled. "There's only one?"

"Well, there's a female too."

"How can you tell them apart?"

It was just the question I wanted her to ask as I'd read everything I could find on them at the public library after watching them in wonder on previous visits.

"See how his neck is mostly white?"

"Uh-huh."

"Well, females have more dark streaks on theirs." After being momentarily lost in the bird's wild beauty, I told her something else I had learned. "Ospreys have one partner for life."

Looking up at me, she grabbed my arm again with both of hers. "That's so romantic."

Her eyes moved back to the bird. "He must have come to greet us."

"I think he did. Remember what I said about the island tapping into your thoughts?"

"Yeah,...why?"

"I swear I was just thinking how great it would be if one of the ospreys would be here, and well, there he is."

"There's one thought the island doesn't need to help me with." Ally let go of me and ran toward the surf. "Swimming!"

Shaking off her flip-flops, she stopped next to a fallen tree, where she took off her T-shirt and shorts, hanging them on a bleached branch. Ally wore a one-piece turquoise swimsuit, and she was so beautiful it almost overwhelmed me.

Not needing any extra encouragement, I was out of my pants and shirt in a flash, running into the water to join the laughing, splashing girl.

To my surprise, I saw she was giving me a quick once-over. "You have really nice legs."

Although I was thrilled to receive such an unexpected compliment, I immediately turned the attention back to her. "Yours are *much* nicer."

Ally darted under the waves only to pop up behind me, playfully splashing when I turned around, her expression so relaxed and joyous that her already pretty face almost seemed to radiate light. We were soon transformed into otters, diving beneath the dark green water, circling and brushing against each other before breaking the surface under the pretense of surprise. Since we couldn't open our eyes in the salt water, we had to reach out blindly for the other person. This necessity provided a tacit excuse, conveniently allowing us to discard barriers to get closer to each other. Our hands boldly touched thighs, stomachs, arms, and hips. The freedom our game allowed was liberating and intoxicating, making me feel as if I'd stepped out of my physical body to view the awakening of part of my consciousness.

Like a newborn, emerging into a world where colors, light, and touch intimated the coming of a new reality.

The tide was at its lowest, the waves so small and the water so smooth that, in time, we both ended up floating on our backs, looking up at the endless expanse of sky, broken only periodically by a gull, tern, or pelican. Lulled by the slight roll of water beneath our bodies, we would occasionally catch the other's eye, then languidly look back up at the blue that spoke of infinity.

I looked over at her once when she wasn't aware of it. She was traveling somewhere far away in her mind. Her eyes were closed, and her face wore the most contented expression I'd ever seen. Almost without realizing it, I found myself smiling before movement on the shoreline diverted my attention. Several Marsh Tackies stood only a hundred yards away: three grullos, a couple of chestnuts, a roan yearling, and a striking black, its coat shining brightly in the sun. They were peacefully foraging near the edge of the forest, having just made their way over the dunes onto the dry sand above the high-water mark.

"Look, Ally," I whispered. "The horses heard you were here too and came to say hello."

Her expression remained unchanged as she slowly opened her eyes and gazed languidly at the shore. A smile then painted her face. We stood in unison, our feet sinking slightly in the soft sand beneath the rippling waves that came up just above our waists.

"They're so beautiful, Ash." She took my arm. "Look at the black one. He's stunning."

Though taken with the horses, it was Ally's touch that had my undivided attention, and I wrapped my arm around her. She responded by encircling me with her arms, joining her hands at the side of my waist. We stared mesmerized at the horses that acted as if we weren't even there, then shifted our gaze into each other's eyes. Laughing softly, we looked away before staring back into each other's eyes. The salt breeze swept around our bodies, drawing us closer. We embraced without words and lost ourselves in a long, deep kiss. When we finally pulled back, we were no longer smiling, and I detected in her expression the same unspoken something welling up within me.

It was a vast surface of which I could neither discern the horizon as an edge nor the start of a curve suggesting a whole unknown world. I could only conceive of it as an enigmatic affection that, if formed into words, would resolve into inscrutables along the lines of timeless, immovable, and passion in all its extravagance—stark monoliths all, standing alone. There was beauty concealing a core of confusion. An intractable shell that would not yet yield to pressure exerted on it. Although I didn't understand the meaning of the words then, beyond their literal definitions, there was a hint of some foreboding with the softest whisper of melancholy.

My eyes landed on the osprey perched high above us. His steely eyes looked down on us as if peering into our souls. My limited experience with girls hadn't prepared me to analyze the strange signals I sensed from Ally, and it wasn't too difficult to ignore them in favor of the purely physical sensations we were both feeling as we kissed and embraced again. Maybe clinging to each other was nearer the truth. We were holding onto this thing we had discovered in each other, a thing making both of us unwilling to let go.

As another breeze buffeted us, Ally shivered lightly, and I realized I was chilly too. Unfortunately, neither one of us had brought towels. This oversight made us laugh, and with no other option, we decided to lie on the soft, dry sand until we dried off. It was amazing to consider that I'd gone from dreaming about Ally to kissing her on a windswept beach in just a few short weeks—a dramatic contrast that could have been expressed musically by spinning a wholesome *Up with People* record followed by Black Sabbath's crushing *Sabotage*. It was dramatic and heady stuff for a boy who was still trying to find his footing in the world just the other side of Mitchell Inlet. Funny, I thought, that usually whenever I glimpsed my reflection at school or in town, I was slouching, but walking with Ally on Declaration, I felt straight and tall.

After eating our lunch of sandwiches and lukewarm Yoo-hoos, we redressed and quietly made our way down the beach to another pathway. Upon picking up my backpack, it hit me that I'd never brought out my boombox. We'd had so much to take in around and within us, it never crossed my mind, but I couldn't remember the last time music hadn't provided a background when I was hanging out. Today, I had fully engaged my attention elsewhere.

Walking to the beach, I'd wanted to skirt around the lighthouse, so I had chosen a secondary path that the hunting club had most likely used at one time. When planning our day, I'd decided to save the lighthouse for last to ensure that each segment of our trek led somewhere extra special. Yet, I was as surprised as Ally when starting down the new path, we found ourselves in the middle of an enchanted persimmon tree grove—another surprise planted by the island. Persimmons weren't supposed to bear fruit until late fall, yet here was a grove full of trees bearing plump dark orange fruit.

Ally trotted ahead, dropping the tote bag she'd insisted on using to hike out the remains of our lunch—no polluting on her watch. She stood in the center of the grove and spun around, swinging her arms. "You never know what you're going to see next here!"

Reaching out to a heavily fruit-laden bough, I picked one, handing it to Ally. She cupped it in her hands and gave me a quizzical look, unsure what it was. Left undisturbed on Declaration, persimmon trees were much more common there than on Leggatts.

"It's a persimmon fruit," I told her.

She brought it up to her nose. "It doesn't smell like anything."

Taking the fruit from her, I grabbed a small pocket knife from my back pocket, cut off a wedge, and took a little bite to make sure it was ripe. It was.

"It's what it tastes like that's special, Ally," I said, handing her the yellow-orange slice.

She bit into it tentatively, but her expression quickly changed from uncertainty to delight as a smile broke across her face. "Yum, this is really good. It tastes a bit like honey."

I raised an eyebrow as if imparting a great secret to her. "Its charms are hidden, kinda like mine."

I was joking, but she put her free hand on my face. Her voice quiet, like we were conspiring, she said, "I've discovered two hidden secrets now."

"There aren't any secrets here, Ally."

She bent her head slightly forward, eyes darting back and forth as if she was fretting over something. Her demeanor made me kiss her forehead. Then, she raised her head and looked at me with an intensity matched by softness that almost knocked the wind out of me.

"I love you, Ash."

The words seemed to hang there momentarily, a light flashing across them before slowly fading into a fine bright mist in the sun. The forest became distinctly greener, the abundant flowers turned their thousands of petals to reflect their singing colors upon us, and the song of a Carolina wren on a low branch revealed a secret voice of the forest I'd never before detected. At the same time, the ever-present cicadas emphasized what she'd said with an exuberant crescendo.

I answered in words that felt liberating but inadequate. "I love you too, Ally."

As we wrapped our arms around each other tightly, I immediately understood what it meant not to want to let go of someone. The moment pushed time aside, and we stood that way for what could have been seconds or hours before we resolved the moment in a kiss. Then, hand in hand, we walked on in silence as the lighthouse rose before us like a castle spire: proud, solid, welcoming us to the realm she stood quiet vigil over. After we'd spiraled our way to the top, Ally and I stood holding each other as a strong, perfumed breeze embraced us too. The tops of the trees below us rolled and swayed, and far off the blue-green ocean sparkled radiantly. Neither of us said a word, yet I could tell Ally felt as much a part of the island as I did. The girl in my arms was the queen of Declaration, and I was its king. We surveyed the beauty that seemed to celebrate the declaration we had just revealed to each other.

Our herald, the osprey who had stayed with us on the beach, flew above the ancient live oak guarding the light, then over the open sweet-grass field in front of the lighthouse towards his perch on Buck Point, the easternmost tip of the island. He let out several sharp cries to announce our happy news to the world below. Our kingdom was at peace and was rejoicing. The life pulsing below us swooned in warm-hearted indulgence and joy. Only later did I realize, with some surprise, how few words we'd spoken on that visit. Instead, we'd followed an unbroken path from the saltwater lapping the sand, through the dunes and trees, up through the wild profusion of flowers, into the sun shining off the horses, and through the music from birds and cicadas; the energy from all that life now ran through my arms and lips and into Ally, completing a circuit that continually renewed itself. When we'd finally made our way back to the causeway, we took a little bit of everything that island was with us, knowing that we were a part of something with magic in it.

10

During a rare moment of introspection, in that vague yet vast way kids often think of things, I felt that what Ally and I told each other should have been a lot to take in, but it wasn't. It seemed natural and right. She loved me, and I loved her. It was simple. Except, of course, it wasn't. With an entire summer to immerse ourselves in, I felt no reason to think of any bigger picture. Her words filled my head, echoing in a repeating loop: "I love you, Ash."

Before Ally, I had loved only my parents and my dogs. From my friendship with Carlo, I felt a brotherly love, but this was altogether different. When I thought about Ally, I felt like I couldn't get enough oxygen. My head would spin, and I'd see stars as though I'd fallen, knocking the wind out of my lungs. A few years earlier, the band Sweet had a hit single titled "Love Is Like Oxygen" that warned that too much oxygen would get you high—but not enough, and you'd die. Maybe because that Sunday had seemed so perfect, like a dream, Ally and I had parted, saying only that we would see each other again really soon. We needed to rest, take in everything, and bask in it all. With this mindset, I finally called Scott and Carlo to get together to jam.

Hoisting my bass and amp out of the back of my mom's station wagon, I could already tell that Scott was in a cranky mood. He criticized Carlo's intro to Led Zeppelin's "Rock and Roll."

"You're playing it too fucking slow, man. Pick it up!"

"If I pick it up anymore, I'll be airborne," came Carlo's annoyed but sheepish answer.

"Yeah, but you should be in an F-16, not a hot air balloon, you doof."

"Is the old couple fighting again?" I said, entering Scott's garage.

Swinging around, Scott turned his smoking barrels on me. "Well, look who finally decided to put in an appearance." His voice held no playfulness.

As I plugged in my amp and took my bass out of its case, Scott continued his outburst, directing it over his shoulder at Carlo. "Guess who I saw holding hands and getting all kissy?"

Surprised, I turned and looked at him, momentarily lost for words.

"Yeah, that's right, Ash, you and...what's that bitch's name? Ally?"

"What?"

"Yeah, you and Ally walking in the forest preserve when you told me you were fucking sick." He shook his head. "Liar."

"What, were you following me?"

"No, man, I was on my way to the arcade that you never go to anymore and thought I'd catch a buzz first and ducked into the woods and guess who I saw together." He looked at Carlo. "Bet you didn't know Ash here's somehow managed to get a girlfriend."

My expression must have still registered surprise as Scott went in for the kill. Bending forward, craning his neck, he sneered, face red from the summer sun, making his expression even more dramatic.

"Did you get the whole football team's sloppy seconds from the skank?"

Something I didn't know I had snapped inside me. I lunged at him, pushing him back several feet until we tumbled over his amp. A cacophony of screeching strings and feedback filled the garage from the guitar that hung across Scott's chest. Our scuffle escalated when I grabbed the collar of his shirt and slammed his back several times against the floor. Kneeling on top of him, I pressed my hands on his guitar to push myself back up. I stood, looking down at my victim. Like a teapot taken off a flame, the tension immediately simmered down. Sitting up, Scott brought his guitar to his face, closely scrutinizing it to make sure it was undamaged. Once he was satisfied, his expression instantly softened.

"Sorry, man, I was just mad and thought I'd say something to really piss you off." His trademark smile returned. "And I guess we could agree it worked."

With the tension dissipating, we laughed as I extended my hand to help him up. "Look, man, sorry I didn't tell you anything." I glanced over at Carlo. "He knew, but Ally's dad doesn't want me hanging out with her, so she had me promise to keep our relationship secret."

Scott nodded. "I'm happy you're seein' the chick you always had a hard-on for." He gave me one of his big goofy smiles. "And I really gotta say I'm impressed because she doesn't date dudes like you." Then, shaking his head, he corrected himself. "That is until now."

Removing the little bottle of Visine from his pocket, he leaned his head back and put a couple of drops in each eye. "I think you're missing something, though."

"Whad'ya mean," I asked, slinging my bass around my neck.

Scott pulled a sheet off the giant elephant that had been in front of me all along. "Dude, she wants to keep it secret so her friends don't find out. It would ruin her reputation."

So hopelessly caught up in the strange, exciting world of having a girlfriend, I had missed signs that now seemed written in flashing neon, like never meeting anywhere in public where her friends or members of her clique at school could see us.

Scott could tell I hadn't realized this and tried his best to soften the blow. "Don't get me wrong, I mean, the fact that she's taking all the risks she is shows she's totally into you, so you should be proud of yourself." He pulled out a bowl, lit it up, inhaled, and let out a massive cloud of smoke. The look on his face made it clear he was feeling philosophical. "I mean, if I didn't see it with my own eyes, I'd have said the chances of you dating Ally Sherrin would have been about as likely as Ozzy Osbourne building a rocket and being the first dude to land on Mars."

I gave him a sarcastic look. "Thanks a lot, man." However, seeing an excellent opportunity to return his verbal jab, I added, "Or your boyfriend shooting a missile right into Uranus."

"Fuck you," he replied, laughing as I joined in. Considering the rocky start to our practice session, we did quite a bit of laughing that day.

After attempting to master the tempo of Zep's "Rock and Roll," which proved impossible due to Scott's exacting standards when it came to his favorite band, we moved on to Deep Purple's "Space Truckin'." We didn't fare much better with this choice, as Scott unadvisedly tried to spiritually channel Ritchie Blackmore's guitar and Jon Lord's Hammond through his Gibson, only proving he was far from a psychic medium. Realizing that song was also dead on arrival, we switched to "Hard Lovin' Man," where Scott's attempt to match Blackmore's outro turned into a clattering, tuneless dissonance. Carlo and I watched in open-mouthed awe, coming perilously close to bursting into laughter when we caught our mirror images. That laughter easily could've led to the second physical altercation of the day.

Switching gears, we somehow managed a good run-through of "A Thousand Days in Sodom" by a band called Venom, which had taken us by storm when their debut album, *Welcome to Hell*, was released a year earlier. Much like Steaming Broth, they were sloppy, fast, and aggressive. Covering a band that understood the beauty of imperfection allowed our typical sloppiness to become an asset, assisting in a masterful, if abbreviated, run-through that boosted our confidence. That positive momentum, however, came to a screeching halt when we attempted to tackle Black Sabbath's chunky, riff-laden "Supernaut." In this case, Carlo let Scott know that he was a million miles away from emulating Tony Iommi's monster riff, which was the soul of the song. If Scott's untouchable band was Zeppelin, Black Sabbath was Carlo's.

After taking a cigarette break to cool down, we tried to get our practice back on track by tackling Iron Maiden's "Running Free," a song we used as a default setting, having played it dozens of times together. Scott and Carlo might have been in the zone, but now I became the weakest link. I was daydreaming, replaying the day I'd taught Ally the song's bass line.

Our practice session proved we were rusty, but something more contributed to our lack of chemistry that day. Even though we got stoned and laughed like we always used to, I sensed that I had put a chink in the armor of Steaming Broth. It had always been just the three of us against conformity at school, expressed through music. Now I had lied because a girl, an outsider, influenced me. I'd taken a bite out of the metaphorical Three Musketeers we'd be if we were a candy bar, and I did it behind their backs. I found out that day that keeping major things from friends who cared about me undermined our bond. I took the lesson to heart. Not that I would have shared these insights with Carlo and Scott. The last thing I needed was Scott saying in his slow-stoned drawl, "Don't be such a fag."

▬▬▬ Although I was now keenly aware that Ally had organized all of our woodland walks to decrease the chance of bumping into anyone from school, the knowledge didn't detract from all the fun we had spending time together. With no dramas involving other friends, and no gatherings with all the distractions they bring, we had gotten to know each other on a much more intimate level than we would have in a more traditional dating scenario. Two days after my buddies and I reestablished our bond in the Broth, I again found myself with Ally on a remote path in the forest preserve just outside Sheltered Harbour. Hand in hand, we perched on a low-slung live oak bough overlooking a brackish lagoon. On the far bank, no more than thirty yards away, basked a twelve-foot alligator, taking in the day just as we were. We had become so used to his presence that we'd nicknamed him Boss Hogg after the chubby, shady character from the TV show *The Dukes of Hazzard*.

All native islanders knew how many untended dogs and cats were eaten by the gators that populated the island's many lagoons—something that came as a most unwelcome surprise to new residents and tourists. As developers continued to build houses and golf courses incorporating the scenic possibilities of these lagoons, the number of pets ending up as lunch increased exponentially. Of course, Ally and I kept a safe distance, but we loved watching the alligator swimming and sunbathing at what we had come to consider "our" lagoon.

Our frequent meetings in the concealing woods had cultivated a sense of security and complacency that allowed me to discard my typically circumspect nature, devoting myself to the magnetic pull of Ally's almond eyes. I found myself telling greatly embellished stories to watch her nose crinkle or her eyes open wide in astonishment. Or, even better, so I could bask in a manner quite different from our alligator friend, in the forming of a soft smile on lips I wanted to kiss all the time. The summer had been particularly kind to Ally, tanning her skin a light bronze, which drew my attention to her smile and dark brown eyes even more than usual. Thinking of a legend I knew that would elicit one of her enticing facial expressions, I jumped off the tree, grabbed her by the waist, and set her on the ground. Then we started again down the narrow, overgrown path snaking back into deeper woods.

"You ever heard of Boo Hags, Ally?" I began

She furrowed her brow. "Boo Hags? What in the world is a Boo Hag?"

"They're kinda like vampires, except instead of sucking your blood, they 'ride' their victims when they're sleeping. The Gullah people say they can sneak in through even the smallest crack in your house, and they straddle ya, suckin' the breath outta ya, which is what sustains 'em."

"Where'd you hear about these things?" she asked incredulously.

"I know this black kid on the north end of the island, named Abe. He has a great-aunt who lives over on Lallawassie and is part of the Gullah community. She told him that the things always target their victims beforehand. Once they decide on a victim and are sucking the life-breath out of 'em, the unlucky person falls into a weird fever dream kinda sleep. Boo Hags don't stop after just one visit either."

Her eyes widened. "No? How come?"

"Because they feed off their victims until they're just shells of what they once were." I could tell she was hanging on my every word. "Yeah, if the thought of a creepy creature riding you isn't bad enough, they say the Boo Hag can only ride their victim by removing their own skin before they head out looking for prey."

Ally's face now reminded me of a person unable to turn away from the aftermath of a terrible accident.

"The skin they wear comes from some seriously unlucky people...."

"Unlucky in what way?"

"Well, if you wake up when a Boo Hag's ridin' ya, they take *your* skin and use it like clothes until they wear it out. The now skinless person is left to die a hideously painful death."

"That's gross!" She grimaced before chuckling sharply. "Oh my God, that might explain Mr. Ackley! He totally looks like he's wearing a dead person's skin."

Mr. Ackley, a science teacher stricken with an unfortunate skin condition, was too easy a target for most kids to overlook. He was also stodgy and humorless, with a fixed expression that gave the impression he was perpetually sniffing a hamper full of sweaty gym socks. How much of his disposition, I wondered, resulted from years of teaching kids who saw him only as a punchline?

"Ackley might be related to these things for all we know," I said as the first letter of his name gave me an idea. "If he is, all Boo Hags have one big flaw: they need to collect their energy from their victims before dawn to get back into their stolen skin, or they have to exist for eternity without it."

"So, Mr. Ackley's the local Boo Hag, huh?"

"Nah, his first name is William."

Ally looked at me quizzically. "What's that got to do with anything?"

I flashed a quick smile. "Something really important you should know, something that could save your life."

Ally smirked. "Save my life, huh? In what way?"

"Abe's great aunt told him that Boo Hags have been forced to find new hunting grounds here because Lallawassie's population has become too small to sustain them. She also said that, with whatever weird logic creatures like them have, their method is to search out victims alphabetically. Leggatts is new territory for 'em, so they'll still be on early letters like A and B."

Smirking, Ally eyed me suspiciously, but I continued as if I hadn't noticed. "Abe's aunt said these things prefer girls as victims, more specifically girls who have light brown or blonde hair." Even though my eyes were fixed ahead of me as we walked, I could tell Ally wasn't buying any of it.

"Oh yeah?"

"Yeah."

She gave me a playful push. "They're pretty specific."

"They have to be," I explained. "Remember, they have to be back in their lair before dawn, or they won't ever get their skin back." I then swung around to face Ally, walking backward just a few feet in front of her.

"And don't forget, since they've only recently started roaming over here, they're interested only in people, preferably girls, whose names start with an A or B."

Swinging her head back, she exaggeratedly rolled her eyes. "Like Ally, huh?"

Turning back around, I fell behind her as she ran with my theme.

"I know you're not a girl, but you realize you'd be a target too, don't you?" She glanced back at me briefly. "Your name starts with an A, you have light brown hair, and I don't know, in the dark, a Boo Hag might mistake you for a girl."

While she spoke, I fell back a bit further, darting behind a thicket of saw palmettos.

Ally stopped when I didn't answer, scanning the empty path and the woods on each side. "Very funny, Ash."

I swept out from behind an oak tree, arms flailing above my head. Whooping and hollering, I yelled, "Boo hag want pretty blonde girl!"

Bursting into gleeful laughter, Ally threw her hands up in mock horror and ran as if her life depended on it, disappearing around a sharp turn in the pathway with me in hot pursuit. As I rounded the bend at full speed, the smile across my face was instantly erased. Stark reality had taken enchantment by the throat. Ally was standing frozen like a mannequin. Immediately in front of her stood two people I hadn't thought about once since school had ended: Otto and Trey. Dropping the fishing poles and tackle boxes they were carrying, Otto put his hands on Ally's shoulders.

"Whoah, whoah, what's going on here?" he asked in a surprised but exaggerated manner.

Before she could answer, Trey descended on me, grabbing my shoulders in a vice-like grip. As my friend Carlo might've said, this was a real clusterfuck.

— 196

"What's going on here, dirtbag? Are you following her?"

There was no way they hadn't heard Ally's lighthearted laughter or noticed that, far from fleeing, she was having fun, but they needed to improvise a script to fit their specific reality. Turning his attention to me, Otto left Ally, walked beside Trey, and poked my chest hard.

"Keep your scumbag hands off her, ya hear?"

Meanwhile, Trey stared me down like a German shepherd on the end of a straining leash. "This dirtbag needs to be taught not to scare girls."

"Or do what he was gonna do if we weren't here." Otto looked at Ally. His expression was a mix of a conquering hero and a horny guy trying to score points. "He was probably trying to rape ya."

Standing in a daze, Ally said nothing as Otto turned back to me. "We showed up just in time. He's like a wild animal...or a nigger."

"Same thing," Trey muttered, still staring me down.

"Lynchin's against the law, but teaching you a lesson ain't," Otto concluded.

I couldn't have disagreed more, but fists began raining down on me before I could react. One punch hit me square on the sternum, knocking the wind out of me, followed by hard blows to the ribs. With fists flying, I swung back wildly. I could feel my fist making contact with Otto's side while a swinging left hit Trey's arm, but it was a desperate, hopeless stand. Another fist slammed into my ear, sending me reeling onto one knee. Stars burst before my eyes. A pounding blow struck the back of my head; then, a fist hit my left eye and nose. As I collapsed, my face hit the crushed oyster shell pathway. Buckled up in pain, I lay there only semiconscious.

Blood streamed from my nose and trickled from a gash on my brow into my eye. I could just make out one of the guys talking to Ally through the ringing in my ear.

"C'mon, we'll walk you home and make sure no other greaseballs bother ya."

After a short pause, I could hear their feet crunching along the path and the same voice saying, "And don't worry, he won't be giving you any trouble again."

From my position on the ground, I saw three sets of feet moving away, followed by hands scooping up fishing poles and tackle boxes. I lay there for a couple of minutes to catch my breath and get my bearings. My head and ribs throbbed. Slowly I sat up, trying to digest what had happened. Then, getting to my feet, I used my shirt to dab the blood above my eye and slow the blood dripping from my nose. Limping my way down the path to where Ally and I had parked our mopeds behind a thick group of palmettos, I was surprised to see hers was still parked next to mine. It didn't take long to realize that she couldn't lead her "rescuers" to the mopeds because they would have revealed we had come there together.

With difficulty, I got on and started riding. I made for Carlo's as if guided by an invisible string. Still dizzy, feeling the post-adrenaline crash spreading through me, I managed to steady myself while dismounting my moped in front of his house. I ran my hands through my hair in a feeble attempt to tidy up and was surprised to feel a sizable goose egg on the side of my head. When I knocked on the front door, Carlo's dad met me. A bit of a belly notwithstanding, he was a solidly built, no-nonsense kind of guy with the driest of dry sense of humor.

"Looks like you got into a fight with a brick wall...and lost."

I managed a feeble smile. "Yeah, something like that."

He ushered me in, putting a consoling hand on my back. "Well, come on in, partner. Why don't you head to the washroom and clean yourself up?" As I did that, he yelled upstairs, "Hey Carlo, your buddy Ash is here and could use some help."

As I hunched over the sink in the bathroom off the foyer, Carlo appeared at the door. My back was to him, but we acknowledged each other in the mirror. He shook his head.

"God damn, man, what happened?"

"Otto and Trey," I replied.

He offered no words of support or sympathy. He didn't need to. We existed on the outskirts of school society, like travelers in a foreign land abiding by rules and laws we didn't understand. Carlo handed me a wet washcloth, followed a few minutes later by a fresh T-shirt and a plastic baggie with ice. This silent empathy was more than enough. Once comfortably ensconced in front of the TV set in his living room, I finally explained how I'd fought like a bear in dramatic and minute detail. Carlo nodded, muttering things like, "Two of 'em, huh?... If there'd only been one,... Maybe the whole thing was some kind of setup," and "I can guarantee they'll think twice before trying that shit again."

I wasn't sure what he meant by the last comment—unless he meant they would have thought twice about it if he'd been there. Carried away on the tide of his thoughts, he stared absently. We both knew the feelings that took hold when confronted with such blunt hostility. The level of magnification varied from the barely perceptible—a snicker in a school hallway, a comment about the length of our hair, being labeled a "fag," and the odd spitball in class—to the recent, increasingly alarming escalation into physical attacks.

While we sat commiserating, Carlo's dad quietly walked up behind the chair I was sitting in and thrust a bottle around to me—a bottle of beer.

"This is man to man." He gave me a reassuring smile. "Just don't tell your folks, okay?"

Taking the beer, I smiled, nodding appreciatively. "Okay."

Knowing that the effects of the injuries from the beating I'd sustained were doubled by having had them administered right in front of Ally, Carlo tried his best to get my mind off not only the physical aspect but the emotional one too. Studying the *TV Guide*, he exclaimed, "All right! *Ruckus* is on, and it just started!"

Ruckus was one of Carlo's favorite movies, and we'd watched it at least three times. Instead of distracting me, though, it brought me right back into the thick of the confrontation. The movie begins with its protagonist, portrayed by future A-Teamer Dirk Benedict, being bullied and fighting off several rednecks in a small town. Dirk fared better in his altercation than I had, which made me feel even more inadequate. His character immediately catches the eye of costar Linda Blair, which reminded me bitterly of my far-from-macho performance in front of Ally. That she left with both of my tormentors was yet another hard-to-swallow indignity. Good old Carlo, though. His heart was in the right place. Holding the baggie of ice against my face, I looked over at him and realized it had never occurred to me to head anywhere else after the attack—a sign that he was a great friend, indeed my best friend.

On the other hand, Ally remained a frustrating conundrum. She hadn't said anything to Otto and Trey, not one word. Then she'd left with them as if they had rescued her—as if everything they said about me was true. Knowing all this, I wondered why it was her and not me I was concerned with at that moment. Girls were as mysterious as the ocean's darkest depths, and my toes had only just dipped into the foam of a wave breaking on the beach. This violent confrontation reinforced that I didn't understand much about the world around me; in fact, I knew very little at all. Within a single afternoon, I had experienced the sharply focused counterpoint that always seemed to follow me. Just as my antagonists at school had muted the sparkling glimmers of hope and joy that came from taking Steaming Broth to the stage, they also snatched away the treasure I held with Ally, taking the little confidence I'd had with them—to remind me that I should only cheer up so much before I would meet a dark but just as richly color-saturated disappointment.

11

The movie and beer served only as superficial distractions, so when the credits rolled, I thanked Carlo and his dad and headed home. I usually took as many back roads and paths as possible when traveling around the island, but I found myself being even more cautious than usual, going entirely out of my way to avoid any main routes. I'd had enough confrontation for one day. Even though I opened the kitchen door as quietly as possible, my hopes of sneaking off to my room crumbled when my mom stopped me and put her hands on my shoulders.

"Look at me, Ash."

Grudgingly I did.

"Ohh, Ashey, what happened to you?"

"Nothing really," I lied. "I was playing two-on-two football with Carlo, Scott, and Paul, caught a pass, turned around, and smacked right into a tree."

Two-on-two football was a regular diversion. We played on several low-traffic streets, adapting the rules so that it was touch football only on the street proper but tackle in the dirt on either side. My mom had seen me repeatedly walk through the door with scratches and bruises, so I hoped my excuse wasn't too far-fetched.

She tilted my head upwards to scrutinize it in the overhead light. "It looks like you got into a fight."

I shrugged off her ministrations. "It's no big deal. I just have to be more aware of my surroundings."

That part certainly was not a lie.

"Please, be careful. You boys play far too roughly sometimes."

My mom called from behind me as I tried to exit the kitchen. "Oh, that girl Ally called."

"She did?" I tried to keep my voice calm but knew I sounded a bit urgent.

"Yes, she said she'd call again in an hour." Mom glanced at the wall clock. "And that was just about an hour ago."

Just then, the phone began ringing. Turning around, I grabbed it just as my mom reached for it herself.

"Hello?"

"Ash?" It was Ally, her voice quiet and concerned. "Are you okay?"

I couldn't speak directly with my mom in the room, so I did my best to update her. "Well, I've felt better, but I'm alive. I was playing football with some friends, and I ran into a tree."

"Someone's there, and you can't talk, huh?"

"Something like that, but I'm really okay."

"Oh, Ash, I'm sooo sorry. I just didn't know what to do. It was such a shock that Otto and Trey were just suddenly there."

"I thought so. Kinda embarrassing, really."

"I'm so sorry they did that to you." After a brief silence, she continued, "I know it doesn't help, but I did let them know you weren't trying to do anything. That I was sure, you just thought I was someone else. You know, someone you knew."

"Well, that's true. I mean, I know you," I sarcastically replied.

"Look, I totally understand your being angry with me, but the whole thing was such a shock. I've been so worried about you."

The concern in her voice softened the anger and frustration building within me, but I was annoyed to sense tears welling up in my eyes. With my mom nearby, I had to consciously fight them off. "Funny you should say that because that's what I was feeling for you."

My mom glanced over her shoulder, giving me a wide-eyed provocative look. I shook my head, signaling we weren't talking about what she thought. Then I diverted my eyes as Ally continued. "Please know I love you, and I'm really sorry how everything happened today." Just as I was about to speak, she pressed on, "We're just going to have to be even more careful than we've already been. Like if we're going to ride together somewhere, we'll need to ride even farther apart, so it doesn't look like we're together."

And there it was, finally out in the open. What she said should have been my cue to end our secret relationship, but I couldn't. I loved her, too. Or, more specifically, I loved the person she showed me when we were alone. An image flashed before my mind's eye, and without analyzing it, I blurted, "Don't you believe in everyday miracles?"

"What? Like what, walking on water or parting the Red Sea?"

"No, like you think you've washed a spider down the sink when you're brushing your teeth, and you feel bad when you see him sliding down the drain in what for him is like Niagara Falls, and then, as you turn off the water and are about to shut out the light, you look down and see that same spider climbing out of the drain?"

Ally's wonderfully infectious laughter returned. "What are you talking about, boy?"

"Well, I'm the spider, and I'm not that easy to get rid of."

Rolling her eyes, my mom gave me an incredulous smirk.

"Spiders creep me out. You're no spider, but I really want you to know I'm glad you're okay, and thanks for standing up for me."

A street corner astrologist might've read Ally's reaction to my spider analogy as a bad omen for our future together, but I wasn't privy to such things. And I wasn't sure what she meant about me standing up for her as she had never been in any danger. In those frantic few moments that kept replaying in my mind, I had only been trying, quite futilely, to defend myself.

─── Ally and I were sitting on a picnic table a few yards away from the Oyster Hall boat launch at the end of Cogginsville Road. Nearby, a couple of older black men in a dusty pickup truck were carefully backing a trailer down the ramp to launch their small aluminum fishing boat into the water. The launch seemed the only public location where Ally didn't mind meeting me—no doubt because it was located right in the heart of the "black side" of the island, making the chances of encountering anyone either of us might know minuscule. She gently touched my face, which sported a small cut and bruise from where it had met a fist a couple of days earlier.

"You are okay, aren't you?"

Lightly jerking my head back, I stared across Mitchell Inlet, then back at Ally.

"Yeah, I'm all right." I looked down, wanting to say more.

"And what else?"

"I don't know. I wasn't too effective standing up for anyone, and..."

"And what?" she gently prodded.

"And I hate that we have to be so secret about everything. I really thought we were just keeping it a secret from your dad,...but it's like everyone."

Now it was Ally's turn to look away.

"I totally care about you, but..." She crossed her arms over her chest, and gripped her shoulders. "But my whole life would change, and not for the better, if anyone knew we did things together."

She couldn't even say it.

"You mean if they found out we were a couple?"

"Don't even say that!" she shot back aggressively. "If *anyone* knew, my life would be over, nobody would talk to me, and all my friends would turn on me."

Jumping off the table, she turned to face me. "If we were even seen walking together, I would lose everything I have...that I've worked for at school."

"Jesus, sorry I'm such a fucking burden. Wouldn't want to upset your friends. Those friends who'd turn on you just because we're friends too." I managed to give her the first direct eye contact I'd been able to that day. "And in case you forgot, we were seen walking together, and from what I can see, you're still doing great."

Tracing her fingertips across my cheek, she gently shook her head as a faint smile softened her face. "Don't swear so much."

I again stared out over the water. "So far, the only person suffering from us being seen together has been me."

"And I'm so sorry that happened. I hope you know I am."

I took the hand touching my face and held it in mine. "Well, I love you, so just where do I fit in this whole big secret life?"

"I don't know yet," she answered in a near whisper.

Without any satisfactory answers, we silently settled on a temporary truce. Knowing we weren't yet able or willing to take the discussion any further at that moment, we hugged instead.

Jumping off the table, I draped my arm across Ally's shoulders as she wrapped an arm around my waist. She rested her head against me, speaking in a light and far away voice. "Why don't we head over to your island since we're already so close?"

I motioned to the waves lapping far up onto the boat launch. "I'd love to, but it's high tide."

She looked longingly across the water, our island presently out of reach. Since we were limited in our options on what to do, I offered the only idea that came to mind.

"We could head back to my house for lunch and either show off our moves on the trampoline or in the hammock...." Catching myself, I awkwardly backtracked, "I mean, chill out on the hammock."

Hugging me tightly, Ally looked up and smiled with a playful twinkle in her eye. In her best Scarlet O'Hara accent, she said, "I do declare, Ashley Howe, you have such quaint notions." Then pulling herself tightly against me, she addressed my little faux pas, awakening many things within me. "I'd be particularly interested to see your hammock moves."

Riding the pressing tide fresh off the inlet, the hands of the wind pressed us together. Reveling in the wildness that seemed to pour from the water and wind, as if a message from our island, we kissed—empowered by the strength of a place we silently longed to be where barriers had paused, ceasing to exist. For a moment we were part of a separate earth.

Then the sound of clapping accompanied by a ringing male voice brought us back to where we'd been standing. For an agonizing second, my stomach felt sick until the source was revealed. "Well, all right!" came the voice of the wiry bald man sitting at the front of the just-launched fishing boat floating a few yards in front of us.

Positioned by the outboard motor, his grey-haired and bearded companion said, "Y'all catching more than we are," in a dry, hoarse voice. "Take it slow now, y'hear."

Their motor roared to life, and with a quick, friendly wave, they shot off across the water. Ally and I returned the wave and resumed kissing. In the distance, we heard the departing commentary, "Whooo Weee!"

Ally and I decided before we left Oyster Hall that it would be nice to have lunch on the deck at my house and hang out for the rest of the afternoon. I would have preferred showing her off at the new café that opened right on the water in Sheltered Harbour, but she wouldn't be up for that. On the plus side, she had started to enjoy a lot of the heavier music I listened to, and the idea of Ally, sandwiches, lemonade, and Black Sabbath struck me as an extremely appealing prospect. I also consoled myself with the certainty that the café wouldn't be playing anything heavier than "Cheeseburger in Paradise" anyway.

With the humid wind blowing in my face, I dreamed of snuggling up next to Ally in the hammock—until I glanced in my rear-view mirror and saw that Ally had stopped 50 yards behind me. I pulled off onto the side of the road and watched her talking to her friend Phoebe at the end of a long driveway. Considering all the friends Ally had, I guess it was inevitable we'd bump into one at some point. Still, as houses were so few and far between on that road, I had always considered it one of the least likely places we'd encounter anybody. That's why I'd made it part of our regular route.

My heart sank as I saw Ally dismount her moped and slowly push it up Phoebe's driveway, deep in lighthearted conversation, their laughing voices blowing into my face on the breeze. Even though this was what Ally said she would do if we ever ran into anyone she knew, it was more disheartening and deflating than I expected. The way she acted like I wasn't there, didn't even exist, was like a slap across the face. I could scarcely believe the girl in my rear-view mirror was the same one I had been kissing a half-hour earlier. Turning the throttle, I pulled back onto the road, suddenly noticing I was no longer all that hungry.

When I got home, I headed straight for my room, sat in front of my turntable, put my headphones on, and turned up the volume. A few days earlier, Carlo and I had made it to Savannah. Between his mom's errands, we stopped at Roadie's, our favorite guitar store. After first plugging in and trying out all our favorite Fender and Rickenbacker basses, we attacked the Ludwig and Tama drum sets under the wary but indulgent eye of the long-suffering owner. After fully supping on sound, I finally laid out some cash, buying a set of flatwound strings to alternate with the roundwounds I used. Afterward, we headed to Oglethorpe Mall. While Carlo's mom went to buy him new socks and underwear, we entered our beloved Record Bar. There I finally snagged myself a copy of an album I had built up an unreasonable expectation for—Krokus' *One Vice at a Time*. In due course, I was elated to discover that it exceeded the high bar I'd set.

Carlo and I spent many hours discussing the cryptic meaning of the album's opening track, "Long Stick Goes Boom," the best AC/DC song AC/DC didn't write.

With arms thrusting out before him to drive home his point, Carlo assured me decisively that "long stick is a slang word for a tank gun." I countered that the title was more likely a metaphor for letting loose and partying, and as Mrs. Honse had discovered, I knew my way around a metaphor. Even though we studied the lyric sheet as though we were codebreakers cracking the Zimmermann Telegram, the words flew merrily over our oblivious, naïve, long-haired heads. It was yet another example that youth means carrying a fair amount of innocence close to your person, just like the cigarettes we had in our pockets.

Ally called within the hour, full of her usual apologies. "Phoebe called to me when I was passing her house, and when I stopped, she wanted to show me some new clothes she'd just bought and just to gossip. You know, girl stuff."

"Having two guys get the better of me is one thing, but I never considered shorts and halter tops beating me, too," I said in a dejected voice, trying to engender some sympathy.

"That's not it at all. You know that, right?"

"Yeah, sorta."

"It was just an awkward situation."

"Yeah, it was that."

"And you wouldn't want to look at clothes for an hour, would you?"

She had me there, and I muttered, "No." I just didn't like that her girl time had won out over my time with the person who was supposed to be my girl.

Turning the conversation back to us, she said, "Well, how 'bout I come over to your place tomorrow for our missed lunch?"

I allowed her to roll over me like an incoming tide. "Sounds good. I just hope you don't bump into another friend who wants to show you her new bikini." Before she could answer, I added, "Unless you want to do that here."

"Dirty boy," she giggled, trying to sound offended.

"Naw, just a boy missing his girl."

Sounding truly touched, her voice melted over me like soft butter on a hot muffin. "That's so sweet, Ashey. You're the sexiest and sweetest bad boy a girl could wish for."

With that, I was once again deep in her thrall. She did come over the next day, and we did have lunch. My mom even left us alone until we found our way onto the hammock, lounging in each other's arms. Then her head appeared over us, upside down from our perspective. "Come on, you kids, don't be so lazy! It's a beautiful day; why don't you go for a walk?"

Although Mom had an ulterior motive for her suggestion, the idea wasn't a bad one as it would allow us some time to practice our kissing technique, a form of study I could get behind. Ally was a vision. Her hair was loose, cascading halfway down her back. That late in the summer, she was deeply tanned, highlighted and offset by the white shorts and tank top she wore. Adding to her beauty were the sun freckles that had flowered on her face.

We walked around the sleepy streets near my house. The chances of being seen there by anyone Ally might know were slim, as very few houses had been built yet in the relatively recent residential neighborhood. Most of the streets ended in cul-de-sacs or branched off to meander before rejoining the main road that made a huge loop of about a mile. Only one entrance led into and out of the neighborhood, and laughing and joking, we went into autopilot. Once we'd completed the entire mile circuit, including all the little cul-de-sacs, I absentmindedly turned off onto a path I often used as a shortcut between the street I lived on and Nighthawk. This busy thoroughfare ran between the island's southern end and Merganser, the main road into Sheltered Harbour. I began deeply embellishing a visit I had made to the Declaration lighthouse with my one-time friend Mike, in which I'd lost my footing while we were making one of the first circuits of the exterior of the light on the thin steel tie bars far above the forest floor.

"We weren't paying attention at all, and Mike thought it would be a great idea to have a smoke—"

"I told you smoking can kill you," Ally laughed, giving me a playful push.

"Yeah, well, it was close! So, there we are, a hundred feet up, clear around the other side of the lighthouse from the window we'd climbed through, and I casually take the cigarette Mike's handing me. Then, resting my chest against one of the crossbars, with both my hands free, I start fishing around my pocket for the lighter."

"That doesn't sound like a good idea."

"It wasn't!" I told her. "I finally dig it out, and I'm acting all casual like I'm on someone's porch just hanging out, trying to light the smoke with one hand while holding the cigarette in my mouth with the other, when this huge gust of wind comes up from out of nowhere and takes me by surprise. Before I can react, my feet have slipped off the bar I'm standing on, and I'm falling!"

"Oh my God, Ash!" Ally gushed, as I had hoped she would. "Then what happened?"

Thrusting my hands above my head like I was desperately reaching, I told her, "I managed, somehow, to grab the bar that one second earlier I'd been standing on." I shook my head. "Almost in slow motion, I could see my cigarette and lighter falling all the way to the ground far below me and, I don't know if it was adrenaline or what, but I managed to swing my feet back up and slowly pull myself up to grab the crossbar."

She swung her arms around me, pulling me towards her, giving me a kiss that confirmed all our practice had launched us out of AAA and into the major leagues.

"If you fell, I wouldn't have you right now to kiss."

"Yeah, I'd only be able to haunt you as a ghost."

"You would, wouldn't you—"

Her words trailed off into a distracted whisper, and her tanned face suddenly lightened several shades. I hadn't been paying attention to exactly where we'd been heading and realized too late, like a car unable to avoid an accident, that we were approaching the busy intersection of Sweetgum and Nighthawk. When my eyes followed Ally's shocked gaze, I saw on a collision course, no more than 50 yards away, was Ally's friend Andrea walking with her boyfriend Brett, a guy on the track team. They hadn't yet noticed us as they were deep in conversation, just as Ally and I had been. Taking advantage of this, she said, "We're *not* together. I'll catch up with you later." Then she ran off, feigning she was out for a jog, sandals be damned, acting surprised as she approached the couple.

"Oh my God! How are you guys?"

They both greeted her, but I didn't go unnoticed by Brett.

"Uh-oh," he said sarcastically, loud enough so I could hear. "Don't look now, Ally, but I think your boyfriend's following you."

He meant it as a joke, having no idea that Ally and I were seeing each other, but it was Ally's reaction that sent me reeling. Glancing at me for a split second, she turned back to Brett, laughing in a demeaning manner that felt like a fist hitting me far harder than Otto or Trey ever had. A second, bitter blow followed this. "As if...*gross!*"

Pretending I hadn't noticed them, I turned and headed home, feeling humiliated and dazed. When I got there, Ally's moped in the driveway reminded me she would have to return to get it. My parents weren't home, so I leaned against the front of the shed and lit up a cigarette. Twenty or so minutes later, I saw Ally walking up my street, hands buried in her pockets, head down, looking embarrassed and sad, her face red. She looked like she might have been crying. I didn't feel the need to hide my smoking, so I lit up another one instead. Eyes fixed on the ground, she stopped a few feet in front of me.

The breeze blew her long hair in her face, concealing most of it. She looked up for a second, giving me a fleeting glance. She sniffed. "Before you say anything, I'm sorry." Her voice dropped to a near whisper. "You know I didn't mean what I said. I just had to make it seem like we weren't together."

"Well, it was a great performance." I exhaled a massive drag. "You could've just kept quiet, you know. Why'd you have to throw in an insult? I get plenty of those already. I never expected to hear one from you."

Without raising her head, she looked up at me again, then back at the ground. "I'm sooo sorry, Ash."

"Not only is our relationship a total secret, but you have to go out of your way to humiliate me so your precious friends don't know you actually like me...supposedly *love* me. It's fucked up, Ally."

"I know it is... I don't know what to do." Her eyes met mine, and I could tell with certainty that she'd been crying. "And I do love you, Ash. You're the only boy I've ever loved."

"And you're the only girl I've ever loved."

Pulling her hands out of her pockets, she moved forward, lightly wrapping her fingers tentatively around my free hand. "All I know is that school starts next week, and I'm gonna have a really hard time acting like I don't know you."

Still feeling humiliated, I said, "I don't think it'll be hard for you. You seem to have the whole acting a certain way thing down pretty well already from what I've seen."

Ignoring my observation, she sniffed and then smiled faintly. "We'll figure it out."

Just as I was going to ask her exactly how we would do that, she unexpectedly said, "Let me try that." She took my cigarette, raised it to her lips, where she hesitated momentarily, then inhaled lightly. Immediately exhaling with a loud cough, she squinted hard, and her face turned red. Silently embracing her moment of awkwardness, I waited for it to reach its natural conclusion until, getting herself together, she took another puff without inhaling and looked deeply into my eyes.

"Would a girl who hates smoking share a cigarette with a boy if she found him gross?"

"I don't know, would she?"

Throwing the cigarette on the ground, she wrapped her hands around my waist, pulling me tight against her and kissing me with more tongue than I was expecting—perhaps to erase my short-term memory. When she pulled back, she was looking up at me.

"Well, I know a girl wouldn't do that if she did."

The kiss effectively replaced further discussion without us having settled anything about our covert relationship or the upcoming year. I'd had a phenomenal summer full of magnificent highs and rather deep lows, dark counterpoints that arose to remind me that most of the world wasn't as forgiving or magical as Declaration Island. I often took that rare place for granted, but now I shuddered at the thought of how I would have absorbed the obstacles thrown in my path if the island wasn't there waiting to accept me, recharging my soul.

▬▬▬ One week in, the new school year proved to be as frustrating as I'd thought it would be: Ally acted as if we didn't know each other, only giving me furtive smiles so long as nobody was around who could expose her as a traitor. On the first Friday back, as Carlo and I made our way out of another gym class, we had attended only as spectators, I was overwhelmed with the thought that it was the very building that had served as the launching pad for Steaming Broth just three short months earlier. This thought quickly grew into a full-blown daydream, so I was only half-listening as I agreed with Carlo to meet up later that day. Although we had different classes for the final period, we usually walked back to the Upper School together.

"Where ya goin'?" Carlo asked.

Realizing I had started in the opposite direction to his, I gave a quick wave. "I'm just gonna go around this way, but I'll catch you after school."

Securing the headphones of my Walkman over my ears as we part-ed ways, I pressed "play" and absorbed the prescient words filling my ears and mind. Those words, coming as they did from the recent Gillan album *Glory Road,* made it feel as if Ian Gillan was in a confi-dential dialogue meant just for me as he sang about being trapped and bound in an institution.

The spell Summer had cast, still fresh in my mind, dulled the vigi-lance I usually practiced when choosing the safest routes around the campus, and I made a significant error. Instead of going around the front of the gymnasium as Carlo did, I distractedly headed around the back. Unfortunately, by doing this, I had to pass the weight room, where Trey, Otto, Brice, and a couple of other guys from the foot-ball team emerged from the doorway. Following close behind them was a group of girls, including my secret girlfriend, flanked by her friends Phoebe and Andrea, who were using the building as a short-cut to get to their next class. I shut the Walkman off, lowered my head, and hoped to go somehow unnoticed and reach the front doors of the school, which just then might as well have been a hundred miles away.

Trey spoke first. "Lookee here, guys, if it ain't the school perv." Head back, chin out, he walked up to me and thumped his chest off my arm.

"Whoo-wee, you stink. Whatcha doin', lookin' for girls to harass?"

Otto blocked my path. "Hey Ally, want us to kick his ass again fer ya?"

Trey pushed Otto out of the way and poked the Abominog beastie on the front of my T-shirt. "That a picture of your mama?"

Bone-shaking guffaws erupted from the football contingent, joined by Andrea and Phoebe, whose pointed snickering cut with the preci-sion of a razor. Ally wasn't laughing but smiling, making it abundant-ly clear that she wasn't about to jeopardize herself for my benefit. Run-ning out of insults, the tormentors discarded me with as much thought as they might have given to flushing a toilet. In a variation of our sim-ilar encounter a few months earlier, Trey shoved me over Brice, who had perched on his hands and knees behind me. Instead of getting up right away, I lay there looking at the red laughing faces above me, listening to the girl's laughter blending into theirs, congealing into one.

Arms crossed, Trey shook his head. "You're clumsy as hell."

Face contorted to make room for a smile so enormous that it caused him to squint, Brice pinched his thumb and forefinger together and brought them to his lips. "Too much of that, I think," he said, breaking into another deep, exaggerated belly laugh.

As the group exchanged high fives over my sprawled body, I stared beyond them at white clouds lazily floating by in the blue, blue sky. They walked off towards the school for the next period, their voices and laughter slowly fading. Sitting up, I watched them depart and saw Ally glance back, giving me a quick, sympathetic look before disappearing into school. God damn everybody and everything. There seemed no escape from the ever-tightening circle of those who had deliberately chosen to be my enemies—using me to vent whatever frustrations they harbored. Heaping insult on injury, my girlfriend was now literally a part of that circle, smiling with her friends. *Her friends.* They all laughed at me like I was a punchline to a joke that never grew old. Maybe that was the truth, perhaps I wasn't a person at all, but an object to be mocked, stepped on, spit at, and punched whenever the urge called and for whatever various reasons that urge was aroused. Clearly, to them, my role was solely to absorb abuse.

Standing, I decided, without a second thought to skip the final period. I had ridden my bike to school that day because my moped was temporarily out of commission with a flat tire. That bike had taken me to many places without ever letting me down. With that knowledge and one specific place in mind, I pedaled with a monomaniacal zeal that blinkered me to anything else in the world. I was going to my place, a place where I could find quiet understanding and true solace: the Declaration Island lighthouse.

12

Lacking the speed of a moped and inadequately responding to the urgency that burned in me, my bike could move only at the rate my limited human abilities could provide. However, it carried me as if it knew how I felt, the route so ingrained that the tires seemed slotted into a track leading directly to my sanctuary. Eyes wide open, I headed out of Sheltered Harbour toward the Adventure Inn. Numbness radiated from deep within me, stirred by the echoes of piercing laughter drilling through my brain, feeding nausea that swelled in my stomach. A police car whizzed past me, heading the other way into town, and I allowed myself the faintest smile. One advantage of growing up on a budding resort island was that the police couldn't differentiate between a kid vacationing or one skipping class. The recent humiliation kept repeating in my mind, giving me a sensation of fighting for air in an ever-shrinking box: each breath shallower than the last, as though the tormentors had robbed me of the right to my most fundamental needs.

The roads I had to ride to the beach felt like veins and arteries supplying lifeblood to a creature bent on devouring me. This feeling intensified once I arrived at the Inn, where I had to walk my bike through the soft sand, which only increased a growing sense of claustrophobia as if my whole personality was sinking in the dry powder—as if I could disappear into the earth and nobody would miss me for even an instant. This hopeless desperation started to ease only when I was again standing on the pedals; hands gripped like vises on the handlebars, legs transformed into pistons pumping away from everything bent on erasing me. The salty wind blew across my face, and I noted with relief that my breathing became deeper in an inverse ratio to the ever-expanding distance I put between the school and me. Somewhere in the transition between the white and black side of the island, I began to feel a familiar sensation: invisible strings had attached themselves to me, pulling me towards Declaration. If my fuel had been desperation, fear, and anger at the start of my journey, it switched to a reserve tank of wonder and freedom as I drew closer to that magical place.

Unplanned as my trek was, I realized I'd need water, so I pulled into the Starvin' Marvin mini-mart right off the highway, relieved to find a crushed dollar bill at the bottom of my pocket. With that problem solved, I navigated the last hundred yards of the highway before hanging a sharp right onto Barnwell. Releasing my grip on the handlebars, I sat erect, opening the water bottle to take a leisurely sip. I saw Mr. Garrison stand up from a chair on his porch a short distance ahead. He stared down the road at my approach as I watched him, wondering what had attracted his attention. He was yelling through his open front door and waving his arms excitedly. I could just make out his hoarse voice which seemed to have an edge of real urgency. As I passed his driveway, I thought to give him a quick wave to show I was friendly. This thought withered in a heartbeat.

His eyes burning like two fanned coals, his face contorted into a composition of creased lines that spoke of absolute blind anger. He yelled, "Think that's funny, huh cracker boy?"

His words caught me off guard, causing me to drop my free hand back onto the handlebar and stare at him in astonishment.

"That's right, you don't like being called somethin' neither," he shouted, stepping off his porch. Just then, three muscular young men, one wearing a white dago tee, the other two shirtless, burst from the open door and started running towards me for no reason I could understand. Mouths open, sucking in air, arms pumping like pistons up and down, eyes focused on me like heat-seeking missiles. I felt like a fox during the hunt with hounds hot on his trail.

I could hear Mr. Garrison yelling in the shrinking distance, "Just like yo friends, huh. Get him, boys, and *whup his ass!*"

Clearly, he thought I was someone else, but having become used to such assumptions, I hunched down with one hand firmly clutching the handlebar while the other fumbled awkwardly to grab it while also holding the water bottle.

Breaking ahead of the other two, the guy in the dago tee was running like his life depended on it. "Gonna get you, boyyy!" he screamed.

Peering over my shoulder at the posse, I saw I'd put a fair amount of distance between us, but they were locked onto me and clearly had no intention of just giving up. All three looked like they could run for days. My heart might've already been racing, but panic set in when I realized I was coming to the end of Barnwell and wouldn't be able to continue riding my bike on the narrow root-littered path ahead. The situation was desperate, and my only hope was to get as much of a head start over my pursuers as possible.

I stood up on the pedals, pumping them with every ounce of my waning strength. Barnwell ended in two private driveways and, off to the side, the almost invisible sandy path I needed, which I beelined for furiously. Without slowing, I flung myself off the bike, watching it careen into a clump of Carolina buckthorn bushes. Then, gripping my water bottle, I ran onto the pathway without looking back, hurdling over knotted roots that now seemed explicitly designed to trip me, aiding in my capture.

"Your bike's ours, *boyyy*," came one of the voices through the trees after me.

"I'm gonna teach you a lesson you ain't gonna forget," came a closer voice, that of my new, completely out-of-the-blue tormentor.

I left the path, tearing blindly into the woods, hands fanning out before me, frantically slapping aside the thick cable-like weeds, fronds, and branches as I desperately tried to shake the unseen pursuers crashing through the undergrowth behind me. Pine needles, sharp-edged pampas grass, jagged branches, and unusually thick, thorny weeds sliced and nicked me as I ran. With legs burning from exertion, I risked a glance behind me when my foot snagged on a rotting bough, sending me flying forward. Flinging my arms out, I slid along the damp leafy forest floor, water bottle tumbling out of my hand. All I could hear was my panting and my heartbeat pounding in my ears. As I started to rise, it hit me that I could no longer hear anyone. Raising myself onto my elbows, I came face to face with a St. John's Wort bush in full, vibrant yellow bloom. The flowers seemed to communicate that I was now safe.

On all fours, I crept over to retrieve the water bottle, downing half of it before slowly standing. Holding completely still, I waited until convinced the posse had given up and then carefully worked my way back to the path to continue my original journey. Although Mr. Garrison had obviously mistaken me for someone else, the knowledge didn't mitigate the trauma of having just been chased by three guys who wanted to "whup my ass." The intensity of their anger toward me was bewildering, especially considering the countless occasions I had passed that house without arousing anything more menacing than Mr. Garrison's stare. Yet, rather than inhibiting my resolve, the experience hardened it. After going through so much and coming so far, I never considered turning back. Instead, I decided on the spot that once my visit to the lighthouse was over, I'd head up to the Oyster Hall boat launch and use the payphone to call my parents to come to pick me up. No way was I going to go back the way I'd come.

Fishing in my pocket, I pulled out a cigarette pack and found with great relief that it held three unbroken cigarettes. As I raised one to my mouth, I wasn't surprised to see my hand was shaking. Lighting the cigarette, I inhaled deeply and slowly picked my way down the trail, made more difficult because of the weeds that had grown twice as big as they had been since the last time Carlo and I had passed that way. Some of them were as thick as saplings, causing me to stumble more than once to be pricked by thorns that found any exposed skin with a precision that seemed purposeful. Every few steps, I'd stop to look over my shoulder, listening intently to make sure my pursuers weren't lying in wait to ambush me.

With great relief, I broke from the dark Spanish moss–festooned woods onto the beach of Mitchell Inlet, where the blinding afternoon sunshine and a stiff, warm breeze overwhelmed me. The multiple tiny cuts that covered my hands and arms bore witness to the narrow escape I'd just endured, but the sandy causeway was clear, seeming to hover enticingly on top of the water. That welcoming ribbon of sand struck me like a red carpet of welcome laid out by Declaration Island itself. I removed my shoes more as a reflex than a conscious decision, tying the laces together and slinging them over my shoulder. The swaying trees became more vivid with each step, thousands of silent friends beckoning in welcome, and my pace quickened. The oppressive humidity that crowded me on my ride across Leggatts now took on a different aspect completely, an agent binding me into the very framework of the approaching island.

I was simply another thread, like the island's trees and moss and horses, woven into the fabric of the place. Nothing was hidden; everything was always clean and open, free of artifice. I knew all the paths, every trail, each one leading to a magical place: Mash Creek, Buck Point, the old hunt club, skeleton beach, Bull Point, groves, marshes, lagoons, and meadows. All roads, though, it seemed, radiated out from and led to the lighthouse, the heart of the island. A place feared by so many for so many reasons, but not by me. I had managed to see through the hearsay and lies, successfully navigating the traps and pitfalls that had halted so many others before they'd seen the true heart of the island revealed. Confidence reestablished, I disappeared into the woods, willfully surrendering.

Inhaling deeply, I gave in to a smile for the first time that day. When I exhaled, the tension I'd unconsciously carried evaporated. That clinging tension that accompanied me in my day-to-day life became conspicuous only when it departed in the warm solitude of Declaration. So, with a bit of surprise, I felt the customary butterflies rise in my stomach in the peculiar way they always did at a particular point on my trek, whether or not I was paying attention to where I was. The reason became apparent when I rounded a final turn, and the lighthouse loomed large over me. That day, because of what I needed, it was a massive guardian standing without pretense, exuding integrity, presenting an aura of unimpeachable strength. The rusting walls of the tower seemed to patiently hold a secret, sensing my presence, preparing itself for a time when it would speak and reveal something special. Something extraordinary, worth the wait. A metaphorical grandparent with a pace more measured than mine, watching over me with lessons to share of a design I could not yet hope to piece together into a whole.

The avalanche of relief I'd felt once I reached the island blinded me to how physically tired I was. The dramatic spikes of emotion, accentuated by all the adrenaline that had pulsed through me, had taken their toll on my body—particularly my legs. So instead of immediately ascending the light, I slumped heavily against the sprawling ancient live oak, slowly sliding down its trunk until I sat, arms resting on bent knees. I found a great comfort pressed against that tree, imagining I was a part of it. Then I smiled, thinking how that tree seemed another facet of the rusted structure before me, as if the lighthouse had roots hidden deep beneath me, intertwining and joining with those of the tree. My legs felt so heavy I imagined them sinking into the soil to take root as well, finding all the other roots of the island.

At that moment, with the sun's warm rays filtering through the boughs and moss, the image of being just another element of the island was incredibly comforting. Taking another languid breath, I absorbed the living sounds surrounding and interacting with me. The trees seemed to speak using the wind as a mouthpiece, telling me in their way, "It's all right now, you're with us, you're part of our light, there's always a place for you here in the shade of the trees with the birds and deer and horses." A sense of calm settled over me, a feeling that the trees, like the lighthouse, were guardians protecting me.

The sun's rays played hide and seek with swaying Spanish moss-covered branches that surrounded and fluttered over me as I gave in even further, whispering, "I'm here with you, island." On my face, I sensed the dappled light as I scanned the waves rolling across the sweetgrass field and watched cedar waxwings and mockingbirds flit about the edge of the forest, appearing, then disappearing from the green wall of leaves. Slowly standing, I continued to survey the surroundings; the red and orange brick of the oil house had even taken on a warm, somehow friendly hue, given life by the sunlight playing off its walls, creating ever-changing shapes of dancing yellows. Soft breezes ruffled the moss, making it appear that the forest had hung its laundry out to dry.

Feeling refreshed, I ascended the spiraling staircase of the lighthouse, then hoisted myself up into the Blue Room. A deep calm settled over me in that haven, the epicenter of everything I needed that day. It was my room, and when I'd stood there with Ally, a throne room. The wind lightly picked its way through the windowless frame that had once centered the long-vanished light that shot its beam out over the ocean, just above its sister light lined up beneath it. That room now protected me as it had ships long ago. I wandered onto the narrow gallery and sat, feet dangling over the edge, mesmerized by how they looked as if they could almost touch the false floor of treetops.

Carried in on the wind came the hissing and crashing of the ocean, fanning out as far as I could see, seamlessly joining with the sea of trees beneath me. That green sea, comprising the vast forests of Declaration, covered any hint of the ground below, sheltering like a thick protective blanket all the creatures incapable of flight. Soaring just above the reach of the lighthouse was one of the ospreys I knew so well, heading north. She had a clear view of her domain, and I wished I could see mine with the same clarity.

A warm, steady breeze swirled comfortingly about me as if the island laid an afghan across my shoulders. Above, clouds mingled with the sun, creating shadowy patterns that shifted back and forth from red to black through my closed eyelids. The wind introduced the weighted perfume of magnolia blossoms, alternating with the acrid sharp, then whisper-subtle contrasting scents of pine, salt, and sand. Intoxicated with the waxing, waning patterns, the calming aromas, I brought a hand to my mouth, stifling a yawn. The scented, warm air brought on drowsiness I couldn't fight, so I crawled back to the Blue Room and curled up next to the open door in a limbo where consciousness held the gentlest hand against sleep. The redness of the sun that pressed through closed eyelids, the cry of distant gulls, and the cicadas persistent rising and falling consoled me and assured me I was watched over and safe. I was soon submerged in a deep slumber.

"Just for a while," I thought as I slowly drifted off. "Just a little while."

I was conscious of rolling onto my back from a fetal position and crossing my arms after feeling a cool wind sweep over me, but it wasn't until I opened my eyes that my world was thrown off its axis. Without initially registering what it meant, I realized the room was dark, but more than that, an unexpected sound struck me: the haunting twilight call of the chuck-will's-widow. Disoriented and muzzy from sleep, I pushed myself into a sitting position, rubbing my eyes and sensing all at once that the world around me was coursing with unseen power, a sense of dangerous magic. For a moment, I couldn't get my bearings or even remember where I was, but I felt a panic building within me as it became clear. I was still in the Blue Room, but it now comprised dark charcoal greys, cold, muted blues, and pits of black.

I could no longer hear gulls in the distance or the cicadas that were the very personification of daylight. Instead, bombarding me from every direction came the lonely chirping drone of crickets joining with the lugubrious croaking of toads and the call and response song of nocturnal tree frogs, chorusing in their thousands. The persistence of sounds flooding my ears left me with no doubt that they had been underway for quite some time. Fumbling across the floor, I couldn't help but bitterly curse the irony that this one-time lamp room that used to emit blinding light was now as black as a vat of oil, far darker than it was outside. The wind swirled like searching fingers through the door and window as if aware of my fear, trying to locate me to alert the spirits that inhabited the island of my exact location.

Amplified by the close walls ricocheting it back at me, my voice shouted, "Oh, my God!" From the panic that fueled those words, I heard the fear that had seized me, driving home the desperate situation I faced. Frantically scratching my hands along the floor planks in the darkness, I located the small trapdoor, which I awkwardly lowered myself through, swinging my legs wildly into the watch room. In my frenzied state, I failed to find the windowsill beneath me to set my feet against and instead slipped, tumbling hard onto the floor, landing on my backside. Sounds that had been comforting when heard from the safety of my house became unfamiliar and disorienting, encircling me in an ever-tightening grip, increasing in intensity by the second. All of them were too loud, too lonely, too strange.

Another thought hit me like a blow to the chest, bringing a wave of sheer terror that traveled from the pit of my stomach to my extremities. Throat dry and choked with fear, I screamed, "The tide...Oh my God, the tide!"

Nothing around me was familiar anymore. Every nerve, every sense in my body rushed the same panicked message to my brain—*run!*

Alternately blinking hard, then furiously rubbing my eyes in a vain attempt to see into the darkness, I was hindered by a growing, smothering horror. The wind whistling through the empty window frames carried in foreign night sounds, each setting off an individual alarm warning of a new, unseen dread. Driven on the current of unyielding fear, I could not form even a single rational thought.

Then I heard a voice yelling, "Let me outta here!"

It seemed to come from over my shoulder, but as I spun around, I instantly realized it had come from my mouth. Feeling like a captive in a strange unknown world, I broke into a headlong run down the inky staircase, which felt like a conscious decision to throw myself into the gaping maw of a giant beast—but short of jumping, I had no other options. Escape was the instinctual desire pulsing its throbbing chorus in my head. Any feeble, foolish thought I had entertained that afternoon about being a part of the island had vanished with the daylight. Groping clumsily, my right hand located the railing in the pressing blackness emanating a miasma that seemed devised specifically to slow me, to apprehend and hold me—but for what?

I gulped in air with short, ragged breaths, nearly hyperventilating as I stumbled down the stairs, frantically clawing the railing to guide myself but also to keep from falling. Swinging my head toward one of the narrow windows, I noticed steely blue moonbeams flooding through the now ominous black forms of trees, making them seem to move and contort as if reacting to my presence, regarding me as if I were an invading virus that must be found and eradicated. These fragments swirled through my unhinged mind as I burst out through the entrance, forgetting the three steps that were there. Feeling my body hurling through space, I instinctively threw my hands out to break my fall, but it was too late. With a muted thud, my left knee rebounded off the lowest iron step while almost simultaneously, my face and elbow ricocheted off the sandy, pine needle–strewn forest floor.

Even in my predicament, gripped by dread on all fours in front of the hulking shape of the lighthouse, I recognized that I was within a few yards of where I had recently mocked Paul for buying the story of the Blue Lady's curse. In one unbroken motion, I scrambled to my feet, turning in a circle to get my bearings. All around me, the yawning shadows of night swallowed what had always been recognizable and comforting. With sharp pain shooting through my knee, I continued trying to focus my eyes in the darkness, half running, half limping toward what I hoped was the path to the causeway. Above me, a hazy, waxing gibbous moon threw down its maddeningly selective light. For precious moments, when I was lucky enough to find myself under a gap in the trees, it illuminated the woods with an eerie brightness. I felt like I was walking through a negative from my dad's 35mm camera. The thick forest canopy dimmed or blocked the little icy blue and grey light that managed to make it to the ground. In my delirious state, it transformed the moss-draped branches into accusing arms in ragged sleeves.

The night song of a brown thrasher rose above the evening din as I stumbled past one of the sucking black voids the moonlight couldn't penetrate. Hidden further within came the sound of a whip-poor-will singing his name. These birdcalls stood out only for a heartbeat before submerging in bewildering dissonance. The night songs that had filtered through my bedroom window, soothing me as I drifted off to sleep, became something else altogether here, seeming to compete for supremacy in the wild, dangerous landscape. I could scarcely believe this was the same planet, much less the same island I thought I knew so well. My head swooned, causing my vision to spin as I again was hit with the sickening certainty that I had become a magnet attracting the roused awareness of the black world around me. The trees and creatures had become nerve endings reporting my feeble progress to some greater unseen thing.

Just as I passed the sagging, dark form of the keeper's house, one of the porch planks creaked loudly, causing my already limited vision to weaken, making me feel like I would pass out. I refused to look because no sound should have come from there, and if I did look, what would I see? Hunched over to hold my injured knee, I hurried as fast as I could toward the old asphalt road, squinting to discern it from the several paths crisscrossing the area. A mad racket completely engulfed me, the crickets, frogs, and birds seeming to scream, "Here he is! He's here!"

From the void came a snorting grunt that stopped me as effectively as a hand, making me feel my heart would seize. This noise was followed by what sounded like a human sob.

Knowing I needed to keep as calm as possible but also to convince myself, I spoke aloud, "It's just a wild boar."

I wanted to believe this— there were wild pigs on the island—but my voice startled me. It had trembled. Far from feeling reassured, I now felt certain I was being followed. Pursued for the second time that day, but this time by what? Circling away from the lighthouse, I felt consumed by the roaring night. Sweat was pouring freely down my face, and my shirt was soaked. Suddenly, the weird whining noise I'd heard moments earlier stopped me dead in my tracks. After what felt like minutes, I finally exhaled a huge sigh of relief when I realized it was a barred owl. I had heard its call a hundred times from the safety of my family's back porch, but it took on a completely different dimension in those dark woods.

My house. My parents.

The thought of them gripped me hard. That morning, I'd told my mom I was going to Carlo's after school, but surely by now, she would have called and found out I hadn't been there. Maybe state troopers were marching down the path to rescue me at that very moment. Holding onto that powerful thought while trying to discern where the trail was, I saw a milky mist rolling low over the ground. A shock wave rippled through me, and I gasped. Before I had time to decide on a course of action, it was upon me, engulfing my feet until I couldn't see them. With the arrival of the mist came a new sound—something like music. I rubbed my eyes, straining to see through the silvery black shadows, but all I could make out was that the mist was emitting dim light. Or was it the moon playing off it? I couldn't be sure, but the sound was there. I tried not to focus on it, but it was so clear, steadily growing louder. The way it coalesced reminded me of fiddling with a stereo dial to pick up a distant radio signal.

Then I realized it didn't sound like music anymore but two voices talking. Or was it just one voice carrying on a conversation with itself? Before I had a moped or bike, I would often hold two sides of a discussion on my walk home from school. But the thought of someone walking through those woods by choice and talking to themselves was hardly encouraging. For a few fleeting seconds, I imagined them to be two croaking toads, but my mind quickly turned from a slight reprieve to one of icy, paralyzing dread.

It was a voice.

A girl's voice. Singsong carried on the wind. Before I could make out what she was saying, I caught movement out of the corner of my eye. Ahead, maybe 30 yards, something approached on a merging path that led to the persimmon grove. It seemed to be holding a light as its body appeared oddly luminescent. Scraping up the meager courage I could muster, I stopped and squinted, trying to make out what it was. The path glowed silver in the moonlight, and the Spanish moss hanging from overhead boughs fluttered gently as the figure passed. Hunching over, I placed my hands on my hips, straining to see who it was.

Putting the most hopeful spin on what I was witnessing, I whispered, "Is that Abe?"

Although I had never seen him there, he did know the paths of Declaration as well as I did. Maybe he'd heard I'd gone missing and had set out to look for me. With beautiful hope fueling my lungs, words bellowed from my mouth. "Hey, Abe, that you?"

A barred owl's baritone song, "Who cooks for you? Who cooks for you all?" was the only reply I received. Then, to my utter horror, the shape—which I could now tell was wearing a dress and wasn't holding a light but was itself faintly glowing—shriveled, sucked into the darkness of the woods like a balloon deflating. Her light vanished, leaving only the mist rolling to me like dry ice. After a second, my frightened brain registered that the vapor was glowing. Acting like an incoming ocean tide, a strange, undulating, knee-high mist overtook me.

I refer to it as mist, but it appeared like an unseen hand was pouring plasma glowing from within with a faint blue luminescence. The weight of all the legends I'd heard describing the Blue Lady and the blue fog that was her calling card hit me with force. My frightened brain kept returning to the same conclusion—I'd seen the ghost that haunted the island and was now a witness to the mist that accompanied her. Not only that, but I had the distinct impression that the vapor enveloping me was an extension of the consciousness of the apparition I'd just seen. I felt like a fly trapped in a web; my every movement sensed and reported to the creature I'd glimpsed.

Puncturing the night, like a train braking on slick tracks, came a bloodcurdling sound: "AHHHHooooh!"

It took only a heartbeat to realize that the howl had come from me, but the chill it sent through my body defied the warm, humid air, and I stumbled backward, bumping into a solid object. In one desperate motion, fully expecting a ghostly face to meet mine, I spun around and lashed out, knuckles impacting coarse tree bark. Spinning again, I ran down another path. From behind me, far down the moonlit avenue, a plaintive whimpering sigh rolled toward me over the ground. Immediately after it, came a ghastly, yearning cry that roused other nocturnal creatures I could not see but only hear; their frantic crashing and bounding through the undergrowth set my mind reeling.

Gripping my chin in trembling fingers, I whispered aloud, "It's the Blue Lady.... She's real, and she's coming for me!"

As I hobbled down the new path, a sound of patting footfall came from behind me, but by the time I looked over my shoulder, it had retreated into the abyss. Then, in a flash, I realized hearing that sound confirmed another aspect of the haunting to be real. With my injured knee temporarily forgotten, I broke into a mad dash down the narrow path. Weeds relentlessly lashed my legs and arms while small branches snapped sharply across my face. All of them seemed designed to slow me down, to trip me as the moonlight breaking through the trees became a spotlight, following me across the shapeless landscape, letting everything around me know that I wasn't part of the island, that I didn't belong there.

Vast stands of gnarled oak trees leered, despising the trespasser who had dared to invade the cursed realm where they grew, lived, and died. The boiling light amplified every weakness, every flaw I had ever felt. My lungs burned from more than exertion: all around me, the humid, heavy air taunted and teased me, whispering words like "coward" and "freak." Tears streaked down my face, horrible free-flowing tears that burned my cheeks, but I didn't dare bring my hands up to wipe them away as that would confirm to my new tormentors that I was nothing more than an interloper, an intruder who deserved punishment.

Panic smothers rational thought, but I was unable to recognize this. Running with fear as fuel, I felt my heart pounding. My foot caught on a fallen bough, and I somersaulted awkwardly through the air, my shoulder taking the brunt of the impact when I landed. Sprawled on my back, I blinked up at the blackness, feeling my heart jump into my throat at the sight of two wide, glowing eyes staring down at me. Instantly, they disappeared, followed by a noisy rustling and crunching through the undergrowth. I was just able to discern the outlines of several white-tailed deer scattering, as startled by my grotesque floor routine as I had been. Exhaling in relief and shaking my head, I sat up and listened to the fading sounds of the deer retreating but also a rustling of leaves that seemed much closer, suggesting that stragglers of the herd still moved about in the nearby gloom....or—

My mind filled with the vision of a demented Blue Lady speeding through the woods, using my fear as a rope to pull herself ever nearer. Dread painted the picture in vivid detail.

"Jesus, let me *outta* here!" I croaked hoarsely.

The pain throbbing through my knee and shoulder might have combined to deter me, but the thought of a ghost close behind was all the motivation needed to get me back on my feet to run. A warm rivulet of blood snaked down my arm through a tear in my shirt. Pressing my fingers against the cut, I tried to gauge how bad it was but discarded this concern when I suddenly found myself submerged up to my waist in water. I'd run into one of the many lagoons that dotted the island. The dark brackish water rippled out like waves of mercury in the moonlight. Then I remembered the many alligators and water moccasins I'd seen skimming the surface in daylight. In one unbroken motion, I turned, flinging my body onto the bank, digging fingers into the soil to pull myself out of the water.

Reason had deserted me, taking my sense of direction with it, so I bolted wildly down the first pathway I could discern. I wasn't prepared for the shock, the almost physical blow I felt when I finally broke from cover. Jagged black tree limbs stretched before me, raking the moonlit sky. I stood in stunned silence; then I fell to my knees as realization hit me with the force of a slap across the face: I was on the skeleton beach. In my terrified flight, I had gone the wrong way, running in the exact opposite direction I should have been. I felt the arms of hopelessness embrace me tightly. When I dared to look back over my shoulder, I knew I could not go back into the woods, which now appeared as an immense black wall fronted by a barrier of sharp branches that seemed to dare me to try.

Instead, I trotted off down the beach, despite knowing it would take me twice as long to reach the causeway along the meandering shoreline, going around the southernmost edge of the island. At least the moon was bright, and I knew where I was going. Panic returned when I saw how far up the shore the waves were lapping. To make it, I would need to run again. The memory of the Blue Lady and the constant crashing, hissing waves were all the encouragement I needed. Consciously keeping my head turned away from the dark foreboding woods on my right, I ran as the waves inexorably crawled farther and farther up the beach.

My heart sank when I finally reached the spot where I knew the causeway should be visible. The tide had covered it. I ran into the dark water, feeling a mixture of helplessness and desperation boil within me. But wait! The tide was only a few inches above my feet! With my lifeline still passable, I set out as fast as I could, trying to carefully navigate the narrow land bridge, only stepping off the causeway a few times into deeper water. Those missteps were terrifying, my feet sinking into the sucking mud as lapping water slapped up to my hips. As soon as I could make out the shore of Leggatts, I broke from the submerging causeway and swam to the beach.

With Leggatts beneath me, I stood before again falling to my knees, this time in relief instead of despair. As I plotted the next leg of my journey to the payphone at the Oyster Hall boat launch, I looked out over the inlet at the black outline of Declaration Island. Shivering, I felt my heart first sink, then break. The place I'd considered a refuge, a place I had loved, was now just like most everywhere else, another thing to be feared. Every story I had ever heard about it was clearly and inarguably true. Hopelessness engulfed me, as did shame. I had been taken in again, had hope and beauty dangled enticingly in front of me, only to be pulled away when I thought acceptance was assured —like school, like Mike, like Ally.

My aching feet and legs competed with the throbbing from my shoulder and knee. Then physical pain was overwhelmed by a horrible, gnawing sensation of fear rising from the pit of my stomach yet again. A small group of people were barbequing at the boat launch. The thought that Mr. Garrison and his three aggressive young men might be there forced me back into the woods behind a clump of pampas grass. I crouched there for almost two hours, waiting for them to leave, scratching at the chiggers and mosquitos that attacked me mercilessly. When, after loud, laughing farewells I thought would never end, their cars finally slowly pulled away, I nervously made my way to the payphone, which, luckily for me, abutted the side of the woods I was on. Hunched over, nervously looking about me like the hunted animal I felt, I was relieved to have change from the water I'd bought earlier. When I called home, it rang only once before my mom's frantic voice answered. "Hello?"

"Mom, it's me, I...."

"Where are you? Oh, Ash, we've been so worried. We've been calling all your friends we could think of."

"I...I'm at the Oyster Hall boat launch. I'm okay. It's stupid. I went to the lighthouse and fell asleep. I'm really sorry about all this, but can you please come and get me? I'll explain everything when you get here."

"I can't believe you're all the way over there! We were just about to call the police. It's after midnight, Ash." She sounded relieved and exasperated in equal measure.

All I could do was repeat myself, "I'm really sorry, Mom, I really am. Please pick me up, I've been mauled alive by chiggers, and my bike was taken." Not for the first time that day, my voice surprised me. It sounded ragged, tired, and frightened, and even though that made sense, it didn't lessen my reaction to it.

I heard her repeat everything to my dad, who excitedly answered, "Tell him we're on our way right now and to hold tight."

Hearing mom's voice in that dark place was as reassuring as seeing her face when she would wake me from nightmares when I was younger, so when she hung up, it brought me back instantly to just how alone I was. Fearing that someone else might come down to the boat launch, I crept back behind the pampas grass. Hiding from people but not the ravenous chiggers and mosquitos, which immediately resumed their relentless attack on my legs and arms. About twenty-five minutes later, I saw headlights flickering off the "Do Not Block Boat Ramp" sign and made out a car speeding towards me. Cogginsville Road had no streetlights, so it was impossible to tell what kind of car it was. I shrank deeply into the blades of the pampas grass and then slightly withdrew when I recalled that rattlesnakes often used the plant as shelter. When the car rolled past my hiding place, I saw it was my dad's Oldsmobile, and I broke cover, scrambling towards it just as the passenger door opened and my mom stepped out. Seeing me, she called, "Ashey!" and spread her arms wide, which I ran into, feeling an almost delirious sense of relief.

"Thanks for getting me, Mom," I said, my voice muffled as I nestled my face against her shoulder. I was surprised to feel tears rolling down my face as everything I'd dealt with that day came flooding out in a massive wave.

"God, we're glad you're okay," my dad said as he joined us. When I let go of my mom, he embraced me in a warm, protective hug.

"What happened to your bike?"

"I was chased earlier by some very angry guys. I think they thought I was someone else, but they took it when I had to run through the woods."

That was my entire explanation. I gave no details about what had happened at school except to tell them I'd had a bad day and thought the peace and solitude of the lighthouse would help me. On the drive home, I found myself repeatedly apologizing as a defense mechanism to combat the constantly returning memory of what had happened on Declaration. The last thing I wanted to admit was what I had seen over there. Explaining that I had been chased off an island by a ghost wasn't going to happen. If I did tell them, they surely would've said that fear had merely fed my already overactive imagination.

"We don't want you to go over there anymore. It's too isolated. If you got hurt, you wouldn't be able to get help," my dad told me. "We need you to promise us you won't go there anymore."

"It's dangerous, and who knows what kind of people might go there," my mom added. "If someone wanted to harm you, nobody would be around to help."

She had no idea.

"Promise us, Ash," my dad repeated.

"I promise."

I felt those words passionately at that moment. A ghost haunted the island, and as if mocking the prank my friends and I had played on Paul, it had proven its existence. I now knew that all the stories about the island were true, not just legends or folklore. The ghost at the heart of the island had lured me in, made me feel accepted, and then turned on me. I felt sick.

When we arrived back home, I repeated my apologies.

"Ally's father wasn't very helpful," my mom told me. "When we called there to see if you were with her, he acted like he didn't know who I was talking about, and when I described you, he shouted that she didn't know you and hung up."

Earlier, when my parents told me they'd called all my friends, it hadn't occurred to me that they would call Ally.

"He doesn't want me hanging out with her, I guess because I have long hair," I answered. Then turning, I walked to my room and shut the door. Images of Ally and her dad added to the bleakness permeating my soul. Instead of falling back on my usual antidote of putting on headphones to lose myself in music, I lay on my bed, drowning in the feelings of betrayal, anger, and sadness I felt for everything I had lost. Like Ally's friends and dad, Jemcraw and Mr. Garrison, my island was against me. It thought of me as an interloper—a freak. I guess I was a freak. I lay there, letting tears flow freely down my red, swollen face, not even noticing my mom entering the room and setting a plate on the dresser. I only registered she was there when she sat beside me on the bed and began caressing my forehead with a damp washcloth.

"I made you a grilled cheese, sweetheart. You must be starving."

I stared beyond her at my tormentors, who seemed to come through the walls and ceiling, surrounding me in an ever-tightening circle.

"Why are you crying, Ashey? Please tell me what's going on."

Shaking my head, I could only whisper, "Nothing. Just a bad day. A real bad day."

She continued wiping my forehead, then set aside the washcloth and ran her fingers lightly through my hair. "I'm here to listen, to help you if you'll let me in on what's going on."

"Really, Mom, it's nothing I can explain. I guess I'm just tired. I thought I was going to be trapped on the island for the night."

Even though I was completely unable to share what I was dealing with, simply having her there was a comfort, her voice soothing and caring. She kissed my forehead and said, "Your dad and I are always here for you. Any time you want to talk, we're here." With that, she left, as did any nascent thought of opening up to her or Dad.

I finally drifted off into an exhausted sleep as spiraling images flooded my mind: a circle of laughing faces, a red-faced fisherman's son throwing a punch, and a glowing figure running away from me into the shadows. Along with the visions was the thought that I had fled one island that seemed outwardly hostile to me for another that I had naïvely assumed to be a place of sanctuary and healing. The disillusionment was a more brutal slap to the face than anything Brice had ever inflicted. Declaration was part of the same unstoppable leviathan that would almost certainly consume me, like a single krill into the maw of a blue whale—consumed and forgotten.

13

A tapping sound broke into my deep, troubled sleep. Opening my eyes, I blearily saw my mom peeking her head around the door. "Ally's on the phone for you."

She came into the room, shaking her head. "You must have been exhausted. You slept in your clothes. Let me have them to wash after you get off the phone."

Glancing down, I was surprised to see I was still in my tattered, dirty clothes from the night before.

"And let your dad put some mercurochrome on that cut so it doesn't get infected." As I sat up, she added, "And I'll sew up that tear. I know how important your T-shirts are to you."

Standing up, I felt lightheaded, and stars momentarily filled my vision. As I sluggishly made my way to the phone, I realized that my odyssey of the day before had worn me out physically and mentally. "Hello."

"Oh my God, Ash, I didn't know if you were going to be home or not. Last night my dad burst into my room and was yellin' at me." She affected her father's deep voice, "'Why would the mama of that long-haired boy you were with be callin' over here lookin' for him anyway?' I told him I didn't know, and he told me, 'Well, he's missin', prolly got himself into some kind of trouble like those kinds always do. Prolly bit off more than he could chew.'" Ally was talking fast and stopped to take a deep breath before continuing.

"Are you okay? What happened? Where were you?" She sounded sincerely concerned.

Like an unlucky prizefighter who'd gone too many rounds and taken too many headshots, I had trouble keeping up with her questions. "Yeah, I'm all right, but your dad was kinda right. I skipped last class yesterday after...well...that thing you saw happen." I hesitated, not knowing how to explain my state of mind to a girl who seemed to care about me only when we were alone or on the phone. "I needed to get away, so I went to the lighthouse, and weird stuff happened on the way there, and by the time I got there, I ended up falling asleep at the top and...."

"And what?" she prodded.

I hesitated again, unsure how to say what I was going to say, so I just said it. "When I woke up, it was night."

"Wait, you were there at night?" Her tone was astonished.

"I freaked out."

"Yeah!" she interjected.

"And I started running so I wouldn't get caught by high tide."

"Oh my God, I wasn't thinking about that."

"I was running down a path and, and..."

"And what, Ash?"

"This is gonna sound crazy...but I saw her...the Blue Lady. She was walking towards me with her arms outstretched, and she was like, glowing."

"Whoa, wait, you saw the Blue Lady? Oh my God, what'd you do?"

"I ran away from her. I mean, I did run away, but..." I suddenly thought about the night before, and it struck me differently in the light of day. "I guess she kind of ran away from me too, but only because I freaked out, I think. There was this really sad crying sound, and I took off down the wrong path and ended up at the beach."

Ally didn't say anything right away, and just as I was going to ask if she was still there, she said something that made my head spin for the second time that day. "She was happy you were there and then was sad when you ran off. She must have wanted you to see her."

The comment was like a light brightening a room that had been frightening, simply because it was dark. After another short silence, she said, "I think you're special, Ash." Her voice became slow and measured. "She knows you love that place like she does."

I found myself lost in her words. I knew she was speaking of my encounter with the Blue Lady but also of the time we'd spent together on the island. Almost seeming to talk to herself, she said, "It's incredible and beautiful...." Her voice trailed off, and then she found the word she was looking for. "It's magic."

Magic was the perfect word for how the island seemed to tap into our wishes and respond to them. Her insight took root and blossomed instantaneously, causing me to let out a halting little laugh, the kind of laugh with a mind of its own, composed of joy yet capable of unleashing happy tears. But before I could react, a switch I hadn't detected clicked into place, and Ally's tone became more serious.

"I need to meet up with you to talk today, okay?"

I was surprised when she said she didn't want to come to my house. She wanted to meet at the Oyster Hall boat launch, but considering my experience there the night before and that a flat tire and a stolen bike left me only my feet for transportation, I said I couldn't. After suggesting several ideas Ally discarded, I remembered that the pool where Tab lived was quite close to her house. I told her that Tab wouldn't be around, and it was always empty except for the occasional tourist. That wasn't necessarily the truth, as Tab was there every weekend, but I figured a quick phone call to him could secure us some uninterrupted private time. She silently weighed the pros and cons before finally agreeing it would work.

After showering and having Dad tend to the cut on my shoulder, which turned out not to be nearly as bad as I thought, I sat down at the breakfast nook. Although Mom was still angry that I had frightened her and Dad the day before, she was so happy I was safe that she'd made an extra special breakfast of blueberry pancakes, bacon, toast with grape jelly, and grits slathered with butter. She even placed a small white vase in front of my plate with a single yellow-orange marigold she'd grown in our yard.

Kissing the top of my head, she murmured, "So happy you're okay, Ashey."

Hunger might have eluded me the night before—the grilled cheese remained untouched—but appetite returned with a vengeance that morning. Rapidly shoveling food into my mouth with little thought given to breathing, I asked my mom if she could drop me off at Tab's, telling her I could walk home afterward.

"First, don't talk with your mouth full," she said, shaking her head while I rolled my eyes. "Second, even though you upset us yesterday not telling us where you were going, yes, I can drop you off at Tab's, but if you're going to do anything else, keep in touch and let us know."

Between another overstuffed mouthful, I mumbled an "okay" that came out more as, "oh-kray," before adding, "I promise I will."

"So happy you're okay," she repeated, staring at me with a big mom smile. In return, I grinned slightly and diverted my eyes, feeling like a three-year-old with his proud mother watching him play in the park.

However, I found it appropriate that I was wearing my Black Sabbath *Heaven and Hell* T-shirt because a looped soundtrack of that album's title track had been playing in my head all morning. Ronnie James Dio passionately singing that what we assume to be reality is often just a mirage and that confusion often counters moments of perceived clarity. His words encapsulated the highest of highs and earth-gouging lows I'd experienced that summer, with the added spectacle of coming face to face with the supernatural, the unexplained, the unbelievable.

The Blue Lady was a dramatic example of where the dividing line between the accepted and what many would call the impossible merged. Meanwhile, Ally was a magnificent conundrum all her own, one I wouldn't have missed out on for anything. She straddled a precarious line, somehow managing, often simultaneously, to be impossibly magnetizing, deliriously beguiling, and frustratingly selfish, often bordering on outright infuriating.

When I called Tab, I learned that he'd had a memorable summer of his own. He now had a girlfriend too. She went to the same off-island academy my one-time friend Mike attended. He'd met her at the arcade in Sheltered Harbour, where he was a fixture, and besides discovering that she loved video games, she also shared his passion for the role-playing game Dungeons & Dragons. The happiness I felt was dampened only by the thought that it would have been great if we could have spent part of the summer hanging out at his pool, two buddies with their girlfriends.

However, luckily for me, because of his new girlfriend, he wouldn't be home or at the pool when I was going to be there. I no longer cared about keeping my relationship with Ally a secret, so I filled him in on everything that had been going on. His voice conveyed genuine surprise and maybe just a hint of hurt that I'd kept it a secret from him until then. But when I explained the complexities involved, he enthusiastically responded in typical Tab fashion, "You're an international man of mystery and intrigue...well, at least an island-wide man of mystery and intrigue."

The day was cloudy, and as my mom drove me to the pool, we experienced one brief but intense downpour that stopped just as we pulled up.

Stepping out of the station wagon, she called after me, "Give me a call, and I'll pick you up if it's raining."

I answered, only half listening to what she said, "Okay, but I'm sure I'll be all right."

Those migratory butterflies that used my stomach as a stopping-off point were back. Something about Ally's voice made me sense she wanted to see me for more than working on the kissing technique we had honed to near perfection. Walking up the curving gravel pathway, I could see she was already sitting on a deck chair under the overhang by the changing rooms. The pool was empty because of the rain. The gate squeaked loudly, announcing my arrival, but she looked up only momentarily and smiled wanly. Pulling up another chair, I set it across from her.

Before I even sat down, she shook her head. "Oh, that shirt."

"It's my fave, and it's good luck." I tried to catch her eyes which were fixed on her sandals. "I was wearing it when I met you."

"I remember," she said, and I detected some underlying distraction. With her hands fidgeting in her lap, she finally looked up at me. Her eyes looked sad. "You know, you don't *always* have to wear that kind of shirt. I mean, you could wear other things sometimes."

The comment surprised me as she had always said she loved me for exactly who I was.

"I do wear other things," I told her brightly. "There's also Blue Öyster Cult, Uriah Heep, the Scorpions, Triumph...."

"I mean *all* of those. I mean, why can't you wear just like a Polo shirt sometimes?"

"I did that once," I told her. "Nathan, you know Nathan, he said the same thing once, and I cut out the little horse and jockey logo..."

"No! Wear it without cutting anything off of it or being a smartass."

"Whoa, sorry, I didn't realize we were meeting up so you could give me fashion tips. Should I cut my hair too?"

"Well, why not?" Her answer stunned me. "I mean, then we could be a normal couple."

Rolling my eyes, I couldn't help but let out a snide laugh. "A *normal* couple? Why? What's the fun in being normal?"

She shot out of her chair, her face creased with anger. "Plenty of things. I'm normal, you know! My friends are normal." Placing her hands on her hips, she leaned towards me: "And if *you* were normal, we could do things like other people do."

"Oh yeah, like go out to the movie theater or the arcade, huh? With my new super friends Brett and Andrea, maybe?"

Folding her arms, she angrily turned her head. "Shut up, Ash. It's not like you've ever even tried to make friends with my friends."

"Really? Are you serious? When I first started going to school here, I sure did try to make friends with the people you call friends. They either ignored or made fun of me. You know, just like yesterday when your chums, your superior friends, made themselves feel better by fucking with me. Yeah, super cool friends there who can only make themselves feel better by ganging up on a dude just minding his own business. By just blindly going along with what your friends think, you're not really better than any of them, are you?" I didn't want to be so blunt, but anger was putting words in my mouth that I'd been relatively successful at keeping from my mind.

"Stop talking so superior like you're better than everyone. You're *so* dramatic. Like your friends' opinions are any better, think about it. Stop being a crybaby."

I stood up and grabbed her arms. "I'm dramatic and a crybaby, huh? I can't even get support from Principal Broadbent or Dean Knight. Once when Carlo and I were being hassled by your friends Otto, Trey, and Brice, Knight walked by and said he hoped to see all of us at the pep rally. Like open your eyes, the drama is real."

"If you don't like how you're treated, just *change!*"

I flopped back onto my chair, thrusting my hands in my pockets just as it started to rain again. "Yeah, I could change, but I thought you liked who I was...who I am. I could say everything to you that you've said to me. Why don't you change? Why don't you just admit to everyone that we love each other, that we're a couple?"

The lines of anger that had crossed her face dissipated just as quickly as the rain had returned. She kneeled next to me, looking up. "You think you have all the answers, don't you?"

I shook my head sincerely. "I know I don't have those,...but maybe I've discovered a few clues."

For the first time since I met up with Ally that day, her expression changed to that look of hers that first attracted me; a look of amusement mixed with mild disapproval, her lower lip puckered into a little pout. "Okay, Remington Steele."

Then her face softened. "I don't mean that."

"What, that I'm Remington Steele? I'm just as crafty and suave," I answered, trying to get her to smile again.

"About you changing." She took my hands in hers. "I don't mean that at all. I love you for exactly who you are. You shouldn't change, and I know you'll find answers. You're a strong person, stronger than you think you are. You've shown that. I just don't like the thought of you getting hurt with what you find." Her eyes locked onto mine as she put her hands on my leg. It was a look that told me something big was coming. "I just can't do this anymore."

I knew she was breaking up with me, but it didn't feel like a bullet. It couldn't. Our relationship, our love, had been in darkness far too long, which had taken a toll on both of us. Forget everything you've heard about kids having endless energy—we were exhausted.

I brushed my fingers across her cheek. "I don't like it, Ally,...but I guess I understand. And don't worry about me. Isn't there some poem about the road less traveled? Well, it was on that road where I met you. I just have to keep following it to wherever it takes me." Her eyes blinked several times like she was fighting back tears.

I laid my hand on the side of her head. "I'm gonna be all right...mostly because of you. You were the first answer I ever got that I knew was really true." Grabbing her hands in mine, I smiled. "I wish there were more truths like you."

"I'm not a truth, Ash, and I'm way far from perfect."

"But that's just it, Ally. You did something amazing by becoming my friend, my girlfriend. You were brave, and you were strong. Who needs perfect?"

She rested her head on my knee and gazed at the rain pelting the pool water, and we stared at it, mesmerized by the rhythm as I gently ran my fingers through her hair. She then spoke as if lost in a dream, "If we could be like those Marsh Tackies we saw when you first took me to your island.... Well, we could be happy together forever."

"There's a whole world of people out there, though," I reminded her, breaking the spell. "But you're the first person who helped change how I see things. I really don't care anymore if people see me as weird or ugly or different from their idea of what normal should be."

Ally wore an expression that told me she was cradling our conversation, where we were, even the weather, and the way her face looked took me in another direction entirely.

"You're like fragile china."

Her expression became quizzical as she turned her head up to look at me. "China?"

"The most delicate china in the world. You're thin and beautiful, and light comes through you, light that most people are never lucky enough even to see, and just by you letting that light in, you reveal aspects of yourself that make you even more beautiful than you ever could have imagined. More beautiful than you already are."

Her eyes held mine for a moment, then returned to the rain. "I don't think I'm beautiful or a china cup, but what you're saying is so sweet. No one has ever tried to say to me what you're telling me right now." An inscrutable expression flashed across her face, and she looked past me. She shook her head and laughed dismissively. "I think the sweetest thing Richard ever said to me was, 'You look hotter than shit.'"

Richard was the guy on the football team she'd dated just before me. Following her lead, I shook my head too. "A real Shakespeare, old Richard, huh?"

We both chuckled, but I had more I needed to say and steered the conversation back to that less traveled road.

"I'm just trying to say that what you have inside of you has helped me see myself a lot clearer. The world around me a lot clearer. I mean, we're opposites and have our own ideas on how everything should be, but we decided to take a chance, and even though I was really nervous at times—because, damn, you're a pretty girl—I was always excited when I knew I was going to see you. I mean, even just hearing your voice, I'd sometimes pinch myself to make sure I wasn't dreaming and then smile when I was convinced I wasn't. When we took that risk to be together, it wasn't for nothing; we changed, we made each other more than we were before."

Ally watched me closely as I spoke, even bashfully smiling when I mentioned how pretty she was. But I consciously kept myself from being drawn too deeply into her eyes to keep mine from releasing tears.

"I like how you put that." She looked back at the water. "It's like I'm thinking something, and you put it into words. I wouldn't change anything we experienced together for the world."

"I guess we both learned something," I agreed. "But I had less to lose. You're too damn cute to have to sit by yourself in school."

Ally looked up at me again, her face as serious as I had ever seen. "You're sweet to say what you're saying, but I'm a wimp. I learned I can only go so far with some things." Then her expression changed, lit up by a new thought. "Remember how I said you were special on the phone earlier today?"

"Uh-huh," I answered, wondering where she was going.

"Well, you deserve someone just as special as you. Someone who isn't afraid to walk with you, who wants to show you off to the world."

I wanted that person to be her, but our actions were directed by strong forces both outside and within us. We'd fought for our identities, and I'd be lying if I pretended I didn't cling to mine just as hard as Ally clung to hers.

Then as if wired to the same switch, we both stood and embraced tightly. We clung to each other with an intensity that comes only from love, and I tried to reassure her. "At least the time we had together isn't going anywhere, girl. It will always be there, and we can visit it whenever we want to."

Hugging me even tighter with her face buried in my shoulder, she said in a muffled voice cracked with emotion, "I hope to see you there sometime."

Eyes glassy and far away, she squinted, pulled back, then grabbed me again and kissed me. Then she withdrew her arms, which fell to her sides as she straightened, smiled, quickly rubbed her eyes, and put on a new face. Turning, she walked away into the rain, through the squeaky gate, and disappeared from view.

I didn't blame her then, and I don't blame her now. The will of the tides has a force that affects all creatures unevenly. I had seen the tides divide the islands, forcing me to choose one side or the other. Yet, just below the waves rolling inexorably in, were other creatures who found no resistance, merely a freedom to cross with ease to another place they desired to be. I hoped to one day find a way to navigate my world with the same freedom.

Walking through the gate myself, I felt soothed by the rain. It was one of those brief late summer cloudbursts that seemed to contain in its brevity all the promise, emotion, and exhilaration that had marked the short time Ally and I had been together. Our relationship had been born out of circumstances that, for me, mirrored the storm I was walking through—both storms would again settle into silence, but only after their charged displays had altered their surroundings. The rain softening the ground that often felt so hard and unforgiving, drawing the eye to spaces otherwise kept in darkness through the glistening drops that caught the sunlight breaking through, restoring and refreshing the appearances of everything that otherwise often tricks one into believing that all things are immovable and permanent. That storm, that beautiful storm, seemed to mirror Ally and me, and I wanted to experience every nuance of it before it, too, passed forever.

14

It's nearly impossible to recognize war when, as a defense mechanism, we unconsciously diminish even the battles. The invisible scale of justice balanced the breakup with Ally by allowing for an uneventful two weeks at school. Even though Carlo and I injected several well-timed sarcastic comments into classroom lectures, I couldn't help but notice that my disruptions almost felt residual—a relic of an evolutionary path leading to extinction. While somewhat surprising, this change in attitude had some obvious causes. Despite enduring a sizable share of indignities, I gained some much-needed confidence through Steaming Broth's performance and my whirlwind relationship with Ally, even if I had failed to save it. I imagined some teachers would have been more than happy to conjure up a string of failed relationships if those might help keep me in line. When it got right down to it, I had to face the fact that I was deflated after Ally and I had separated, and that slide had tamed some of my more obnoxious outbursts. I wasn't unreasonably sad or depressed; I was just flat. Finding light where I could, I was thankful I hadn't had any run-ins with the small but aggressive phalanx of football players who'd decided I was an engaging extracurricular activity.

The second weekend after school restarted, I was back at one of a shrinking number of places I was truly at ease. After my banishment from Declaration, the only sanctuary outside my house was Tab's pool. Admittedly, it was a greatly circumscribed location compared to the whole enchanted island I had once felt such a kinship with, but I was happy to settle for what I could get, even though it was where Ally broke up with me—surrounded by my gang on deck chairs or lying on one of the pool chaise lounges. All of us attired in just swimsuits or cutoff jeans. Black Sabbath's latest album, *Mob Rules,* was blasting out of my boombox speakers at full volume. Not for the first time, the words of a song—"Country Girl"—narrated my feelings, describing the two faces of a dream girl: the beautiful, understanding one that draws you in and the deceitful, selfish one hiding just beneath a façade.

I had become so lost in my thoughts that I didn't initially hear Scott trying to get my attention, but he persisted. "Apollo, we need to know if you've taken that first bong hit on the moon yet... Hey Ash!"

I gave him an absent look and smiled, realizing I had been far away. "Oh, sorry man, this tune's just got me thinkin' about something."

In the way that teenagers often avoid touchy subjects, I hadn't told anyone that I'd broken up with Ally yet, not even my parents.

"What? Has it inspired you to become a farmer?" Scott suggested, just suppressing a laugh. "You know...a lot of people who live in the country are farmers."

I stared at him before chuckling distractedly, giving in to his particular brand of humor. "No, I don't have any dreams about buying a plow.... Ally and I broke up a few days ago, and I guess I was thinking about her."

"That's a clusterfuck," Carlo said by way of sympathy, then stood up to light a cigarette.

His expression serious, Tab said sincerely, "I'm really sorry to hear that, Ash." I could tell he hoped for some dialogue to open up, but I acted like I didn't notice.

Shaking his head, Scott gazed out over the pool before looking back at me. "Well, I'm proud of you, man. You guys dated for the whole summer."

He leaned forward in his chair, a smile slowly stretching across his slightly sunburned face, made even redder and more striking because of his fair skin and sun-bleached hair. "You saw, she came, and you conquered." Then, gripping the armrests, he seemed to reconsider.

"No, no wait, you saw, you conquered, then *you* came!" Red face now redder, he leaned back in his chair, breaking into one of his unbridled belly laughs. Although not encouraging in the classic sense, the comment was as soul-baring as one could expect from a guy who always felt he had to consider his reputation and credibility.

To varying degrees, the same could be said for all of us, except Tab, who was always willing to talk about sensitive subjects in a mostly mature manner. But I wasn't ready to take advantage of Tab's open-mindedness or advice at that time. Distracted again by the music, I returned my thoughts to Ally as Ronnie James Dio's song neared its conclusion, imploring me never to fall in love with a country girl.

"Amen!" I loudly proclaimed. "Don't fall in love with any country girls, my brothers." Looking over at Tab, I asked, "You're not dating a country girl, are ya?"

Pursing his lips, he arched his eyebrows and momentarily considered the question. "No, more like a town girl."

"Unanticipated! All right, my man," Scott half-shouted, springing out of his chair to give Tab an awkward high five—Tab not being a big high fivin' kind of guy. Then turning, Scott grabbed a cigarette off the table, put it between his lips, distractedly patted the pockets of his cutoff jeans, looking for a lighter, then unexpectedly jumped into the pool. When he emerged, his cigarette was still in place, broken and plastered on his chin.

Walking to the edge of the pool, I thrust the lighter at him. "Looking for this?"

With a snorting chuckle, he looked at us with a satisfied smile. "I meant to do that."

Tab, reclining on a chaise lounge with a towel wrapped across his shoulders, glanced at the boombox as a middle-aged couple reached the pool gate. They hesitated, looked at each other, subtly shook their heads, and turned around to make a quick retreat.

"So, you guys gonna be entering the talent show again this year?"

"If we're paid enough," Scott joked.

Carlo stood up and, without hesitation, said, "Yeah, I'll only play if I get that elevated revolving drum riser." Then executing a perfect cannonball, he jumped into the pool, dousing an unsuspecting Scott, who splashed water in his face when he emerged.

Acting out the ever-present tension that existed between the two, Scott shook his head indignantly. "Leave some water in the fucking pool."

Shooting Scott a look of pure menace, Carlo delivered one of his typically graphic retorts, "I *want* the water out so I can fill it with your blood."

To diffuse another duel between the two, I told Tab, "The guys are right; I'll only play this year if I have a $15,000 Persian rug to stand on. Greg Lake's got the right idea."

Despite our joking to the contrary, Steaming Broth had resumed regular practices in recent weeks but with new discipline and enthusiasm. Inspired by the reception we received at our inaugural appearance, we had expanded our memories of it into a verbal book of hours and, enhanced with gilding, illuminated with ever more elaborate descriptions. Indeed, the magnificent book of our performance had become as engrossing as an illustrated first edition of Dante's *Divine Comedy* would be to a literary scholar, and we used our reverently recited, sacred passages as the impetus that would hoist us into the rarefied air of winning the talent show of 1983 outright.

With glorious victory occupying an exalted position in our minds, we had decided in a moment of synchronicity (clearly the spirit of Brothman speaking, we all agreed) on performing, or rather "Brothifying," Nazareth's bold statement of intent "Expect No Mercy," which had metamorphosed into the Broth's battle cry. We even floated the idea of adding vocals to our already potent brew. Of course, we all knew we couldn't match the bourbon and cigarette growl of Nazareth's front man Dan McCafferty. But the possibility of having either Scott and me singing together, or Carlo and me, or even all three of us, seemed appropriately reverential while also providing an invisible safety net. We decided that whoever wasn't the lead vocalist could sing backup. It was the way of the Broth. If we were to fall on our faces, we would do it as one, Brothman slowly disappearing beneath the quicksand, fist held triumphantly skyward to the last.

Motivated by our comments, Tab put forth an idea that proved he was the unofficial fourth member of the band. "I was thinking that this year, instead of just a typical backdrop with your band's name, I could make a huge Brothman costume and walk on stage wearing it while you guys are playing!"

"Hell yeah," "Fuck yeah," and "I think it's a jolly fine idea," delivered in an upper-crusty English accent courtesy of Carlo, were our enthusiastic responses. If the world had been that pool, we would well and truly have been the leading captains at the helms of a mighty dreadnought fleet, steering our confident course on calm, forgiving seas.

Although we experienced a little laughter in school, there was no relaxing or recharging, at least for Carlo and me. The invisible strings I became aware of on a Sunday before the following school day now felt more like a thick rope tied to an impossibly heavy anchor. I wished I could use that weight to stop the turning of the minutes and hours that would inevitably lead me back through the doors of school and into the realm of my tormentors. But wishing wouldn't stop the new day from coming. In what felt like the blink of an eye, I was squinting at the bright sunshine passing through my Pinoleum blinds, exploiting even the tiniest gaps between them to announce that Monday had again arrived.

While I showered and dressed—a time my thoughts often unexpectedly drifted to and confronted events I otherwise neatly tucked away —I found myself face to face with everything that had transpired over the last few months. I had been going about my life since Ally broke up with me as if the preceding three months had never happened, like I hadn't been on a roller-coaster ride with her, like a ghost hadn't run me off my island. But life, full of its share of unforeseen twists and turns, was set to spin me around in some surprising ways.

——— The initial sense of foreboding that descended on me upon awakening that Monday returned with force as school came into view. Those one-story lime green stucco walls instantly sent a wave of faint nausea out from the pit of my stomach. My Vespa, its tire repaired, sped me along the narrow road, past the playing fields and lagoon, towards the back of the gymnasium, where I could see Carlo and Scott parking and getting off their mopeds. Scott was wearing a bright orange Polo shirt with the collar upturned and his hair, oh so slightly tousled, his concessions to the downfall of the establishment. Carlo was sporting his Harley Davidson T-shirt, while for me, it was Girlschool, a rare breed, an all-female heavy metal band. That I didn't own an album from them mattered not one bit, as the poses of the badass women on the T-shirt had sold me. Now that I was a single guy again, I didn't feel the need to neglect it at the bottom of my drawer. "See Ally, these chicks aren't afraid of wearing leather and gauntlets for the world to see."

This rumination on female empowerment sprang from Carlo's comment that moment, proving we were telepathically linked, as all best friends are. "Man, more chicks should wear gauntlets."

"Absolutely, my man, instead of pink bracelets or whatever, freshly sharpened spikes let you know that you have a chick who isn't gonna ask if she can put on the Go-Go's." I then shuddered. "Or Rick Springfield."

Carlo and Scott nodded in silent, sage agreement.

"Just don't piss 'em off or check out another chick around 'em," Scott said as seriously as he could. "I mean, they're already pre-armed."

"I'll keep that in mind when I'm dating one of 'em," I concluded as we all put on Walkmans and made our way toward the front doors of the Upper School. A cassette of Tygers of Pan Tang's just-released album *The Cage* flooded my ears with an unexpectedly streamlined, accessible sound. As I caught sight of Ally, looking as spectacularly cute as ever, I fast-forwarded to my present favorite song, "Tides," and turned it up. It had been in heavy rotation at my house, much to Scott's and Carlo's chagrin. It was a moody power ballad of sorts, but the words summed up everything I had felt and still did for Ally. It made me feel oddly mature, even in my Girlschool T-shirt. The tide and waves of the song suggested the passing of time and the way cherished memories of someone you loved can briefly erase whatever intruded to end it.

Effortlessly, I transported to the beach on Declaration Island, just me, Ally, and a few Marsh Tackies. The song embodied the longing, the intense emotion she roused in me. As I lost myself in my fantasy, Ally briefly caught my eye and gave me a slight hint of a smile. I smiled back, slowly letting my eyes drift to the other kids huddled around the entrance. Talk about a study in contrasts: From Ally's soft skin, long braided hair, and even tan, my vision fell on Brice. He was laughing loudly, mouth wide open, letting all the flies out. Over the summer, his face had blossomed with an even more severe case of nodulocystic acne than I thought was possible. His visage had become, quite literally, one large inflamed, red mass. It looked excruciating.

Like most teenagers, I had occasional battles with acne, which had been particularly distressing when I was going out with Ally. Brice's case, though, was in another league altogether. I couldn't quite figure it out, but I felt a bit bad for him, and considering everything he'd put me through, I don't think that was an insignificant thing. That said, looking at him that morning, I couldn't help but think of a low-budget horror movie called *The Incredible Melting Man* I'd recently watched and imagined Brice as the title character, people running in terror at his approach. Although to be honest, the image made the coming school day a bit more tolerable.

Not for the first time, I sat through nearly every class on autopilot, my Walkman providing fleeting moments of escape between bells. Only Mr. Box received my undivided attention, the pencil I held taking actual notes instead of drawing a reasonable approximation of Motörhead's logo Snaggletooth: a beast with spikes on its head and a pair of long, curving boar's teeth. Mr. Box pulled Carlo and me aside as we shuffled toward the door at the end of class.

"All right, gentlemen, you've been doing really well with my extra credit questions, but I have one that I think might stump ya."

"Shoot," I said, smiling.

"Lay it on us," Carlo added.

"Okay, I know we're all fans of B.Ö.C., but what name do they sometimes use when playing small club gigs to this day?"

Furrowing my brow, I shrugged my shoulders at Carlo, who wore a scowl usually reserved for only the most severe concentration, such as when he attempted a more complex drum beat or fill during band practice.

"It was also their original name."

This clue was all we needed, and we said in perfect unison, "Soft White Underbelly!"

Gripping one of my shoulders in one hand and one of Carlo's in the other, Mr. Box tossed his head back in an open-mouthed laugh.

"Either I'm slipping, or you guys are just getting too good." Stroking his beard, he continued, "Well, you got me today; now you can just focus on your homework instead of Blue Öyster Cult's history. Tell you what, why don't you fellas give *me* a question tomorrow? If I can't guess it right away, you win, and it'll count as extra credit on the next test."

Impersonating a stereotypical villain, Carlo rubbed his hands together and let out a short, maniacal laugh.

"As my friend suggests, nothing would please us more," I answered in my best Peter Lorre impersonation, inspired by staying up too late the night before watching *Arsenic and Old Lace* on the WTBS late movie. Then, looking at Carlo conspiratorially, I added another Lorre line from that same movie, "You know, you were right about that fellow. He wasn't very bright."

With another hearty laugh, Mr. Box again stroked his beard as if searching his memory. Then snapping his fingers, he laughed again. *"Arsenic and Old Lace,* isn't it?"

I nodded, appreciating the positive attention.

"Groovy! Can't say I pegged you as an old movie fan, Ash. You guys are full of surprises."

It was a rare, satisfying thing to hear a compliment from a teacher. Absorbing the positive ripple effect of Mr. Box's encouragement, I made it through the rest of the day feeling more upbeat than I had in quite a while. Maybe, though, I should have expected the other shoe to drop. Since we usually rode together at the end of the day, "brothers not of kin but brothers of the wind," Carlo asked me if I was ready to go after the final bell. However, I was locked deeply in a daydreaming mood, which made me forget prosaic things, so I suggested he head out without me. I still had to put my books in my locker and stop by Ms. Zeitz's classroom to see if that was where I'd left a pen that I enjoyed drawing with. To be honest, when I was in one of my daydreamy moods, I didn't feel particularly sociable and instead looked forward to just going where my thoughts wanted to lead me.

I went to the far end of the gym building, where I'd parked my moped. My daydream was of the lighthouse on Declaration, and I was an osprey gliding free in a blue, blue sky high above her. It was the second time that day that I had thought of the island without feeling a chill run down my spine. Below me, the island spread out, green, quiet, and beautiful. By quarter after three, only two other mopeds besides mine were still there as I rounded the corner of the gym. Sunlight glistened strongly off the long, thin, muddy lagoon that ran parallel to the back of the building, causing me to squint as I approached my Vespa. A nagging, familiar voice shattered the peaceful rumination I'd been enjoying. Once again, I found myself a meteorite caught in the gravitational pull of a planet named Brice, falling helplessly towards his imposing will.

"Hey, Pot-Ash, where ya going without so much as a 'goodbye,' faggot?"

He used that word often, reminding me of the weird confrontation he had engineered for Carlo and me the previous year. Summoning all the courage I could pull from where I had lost myself, I blurted something impulsively without thinking of repercussions. "That's funny coming from you since it was you and your buddies who were so stoked to see two guys kiss."

As I spun around, I met an unmistakably red, inflamed face, yet I continued. "Why don't you get one of your buddies and give it a try, instead of...."

I might've been charging ahead on the momentum of my initial proclamation, but my voice started to crack before trailing off entirely when I saw Otto appear from around the corner, apparently just a few paces behind his buddy.

Brice smiled, glancing at Otto before his eyes locked on me like a hawk.

"Y'hear all that? The little man's gotta dirty mind."

Then his eyes broke from me, quickly taking in the lagoon before returning, flashing with excitement. Without turning, he patted Otto's shoulder with the back of his hand in a signaling gesture. "Maybe we should give him a bath."

Although I didn't want to prolong this confrontation, I found myself quite unconsciously rolling my eyes at another of his inadvertent homoerotic pronouncements. A bath? Really? For a guy who called anyone different "fags" or "dykes," he and his buddies certainly found themselves saying some pretty ridiculous things.

Otto picked up Brice's theme: "He needs to be soaked and scrubbed down good."

Leaning forward to just a few inches from my face, he placed his hands on his hips and scrutinized me before straightening up and adding, "He definitely needs a lesson in bathing."

I was so surprised with what Brice and Otto were saying that I hadn't really considered what they were describing, and a tiny, muffled chuckle rose from my throat. This slight was the final straw. Spitting on the ground, Brice nodded towards Otto, and they advanced towards me shoulder to shoulder. My brain conjured a bit of Mr. Thompson's history lesson from a week earlier—the image of Nazis trundling into France unhindered.

Brice shouted, "Let's dunk the fag!" He grabbed my arms, spinning me around. Otto took hold of my ankles, and there I was, being swung back and forth in an exaggerated fashion like a hammock on a lazy summer's day.

"A one," Brice shouted, excitement threading his voice.

"A two," came Otto's predictable response, sounding as excited as Brice.

"A three," Brice continued. Now an image of baseball broadcaster Harry Caray popped into my head, doing his countdown before singing "Take Me Out to the Ballgame."

"A four," the two sang in unison. Suddenly, I was airborne, flying over the dark brackish water. I felt like I hung there suspended for a moment. Brice and Otto stood at the lagoon's edge, arms still outstretched, mouths open in slow-motion laughter, with the school framed behind them, all its windows blank. Then came the rush of air into my ears, the smacking of warm water on my back, followed by darkness rushing over me, sucking me into an inky brine. I felt myself sinking deeper, floating through layers of blackness where time seemed to lose its grip, where mere seconds or months could have passed. Pushing with my arms, I began to rise. Peeling back the sheets of darkness one at a time, I detected the membrane-like quality of the water as it brightened in stages before I broke the surface. My eyes were wide open, fixed on the blue of the sky, the piercing yellow rays of the sun warming the water—and me as well.

Brice and Otto were laughing, saying words I could not fully comprehend. For whatever reason, it didn't seem to matter. Something odd had happened. A smile spread across my face as I pushed the hair from my forehead and moved to the lagoon's grassy edge. My response was not what they expected and seemed to take the fun out of what they'd done. They looked at each other, shrugged with more than a hint of frustration, turned, and walked away. I could just make out a dejected Brice huffing, "It figures he'd like that."

Gifts can come from the most unexpected of situations. When I was tossed into the water and made my way back to the surface, it was like coming into the light for the very first time. This feeling accompanied a simple yet whole joy, unbridled by thoughts of pain or hate. An inexorable sense pushed me through deep darkness, a tunnel of sleep, moving me toward pure light. When I broke the surface and inhaled, I felt I was taking my first breath. Each step I took walking out of the lagoon felt like a regression, a reset of body and mind reverting to an earlier stage of my existence. When I set foot on the soil, I was equal parts wet and oblivious, like a newborn. Ally's voice and words overrode everything else in my mind: "She was happy you were there and then was sad when you ran off...she must have wanted you to see her...you're special, Ash...she knows you love that place like she does...it's magic."

She had said those words to me the day we broke up, and even though they resonated, I had stored them away without analyzing them. I had feared the Blue Lady as I feared Brice and Otto, but now the similarity had become clear: I feared her because she was an unknown and for no other reason. I had treated her much as Brice and Otto had treated me.

With that realization, I finally understood they both feared me, as I represented something they could not assimilate into their narrow reality. Our legs can carry us only so fast and take us so far. Why I had not applied this logic in attempting to understand the motivations of a ghost suddenly seemed ridiculous to me. She was undoubtedly a ghost—but her reaching out to me was utterly human.

We, humans, are all so vast yet fleeting that it seems absurd to ever doubt the importance of finding and holding the positive threads that dance around us. These threads are hidden even in the hard lessons offered by implacable minds, bound by the forces of the strong tides they must navigate. Death, something my mind had never considered, was essential. Death to me had just been a cool word to add to a song— Black Sabbath's "Die Young," Motörhead's "Stone Dead Forever"—or to get someone's attention: "I'm going to kill you," or "You're a dead man." My grandfather on my dad's side had died earlier that year. I was sad, but distantly, as if I was personally immune to death myself, conflating it with the mystery of how some people got chickenpox and others somehow avoided it. When two of my rock star heroes, Bon Scott and Randy Rhoads, died a couple of years apart, I thought of the unusual circumstances of their deaths only as further proof of their unwavering attitude and general badass natures. I had never considered an afterlife or that ghosts could be real, and if they were, that they might share in human emotions they'd been all too aware of when alive. Why would I? Although the belief went unspoken, my friends and I were certain we were immortal.

These thoughts flooded my head, washing all else clean. With water still dripping from my body, I glistened in the hot sun as I mounted my moped and rode home, the chill from my dunking making every nerve aware and alive. Somehow, I had been renewed as I emerged through the layers of water, so everything around me seemed adorned in shimmering mystery. Like a gift finally unwrapped, I held the good and bad in my life close to my heart. For without one, the other would have had no impact.

Finally, only one thought occupied my mind, pushing everything else aside: I would have to journey back to Declaration Island and the lighthouse at night. Alone. The Blue Lady's arms had extended in welcome to me, not malice. I just hoped she would react the same way when I returned. I would return, as I knew I must, that coming Friday night.

15

So effectively had I insulated the memory of that night on Declaration from my waking thoughts that I didn't even tell Carlo about what I'd seen until lunch the following Tuesday in the cafeteria. I also revealed my plan to return there to confront my fears about the Blue Lady. He listened intently, lips pursed, brow slightly furrowed. I told him it was essential for my parents to think I was spending the night at his house that Friday. At least once a month, one of us would stay at the other's house, but I needed Carlo's complicity just in case he stopped by my house before then and the subject came up. When I finished, in a single action, he smacked his hands on the lunch table and thrust himself backward in his chair, producing a loud screeching sound. Several girls sitting nearby, Ally included, glanced in our direction. A couple of them rolled their eyes and shook their heads before continuing their conversations. Ally just looked. I momentarily caught her eyes but averted mine back to Carlo before she had time to look away. I wasn't up for attempting to read her feelings. I loved what we'd had and didn't want to tarnish it.

Meanwhile, Carlo's expression had turned somber and intense. His hands shot out in front of him in sincere supplication. "I want to go with you! You don't know what you might come face to face with, and you might need backup." He punched his fist into his open palm.

I shook my head. "It's cool you want to go, but this is something I have to do alone."

Against my better judgment, I glanced at Ally, who was still looking at me, before focusing back on Carlo. "Like, I think I'm supposed to do it alone. I don't think the Blue Lady would appear if we went there together, and then all we'd have to show for spending the night at the lighthouse would be chigger and mosquito bites."

"I don't know. If it turns out she isn't friendly, it would help to have backup to get outta there. I mean, you almost got lost running away from her last time... Remember?"

His points were valid, but I felt it as intensely as my love for Ally that this journey was essential to do solo. To show the Blue Lady that I had made a mistake and was there alone to prove I was sorry, that I had been wrong.

"Really, man, you're my best friend, but I gotta do this alone. I just know that's how it's gotta be."

"Well, it sounds like a clusterfuck waiting to happen, but I guess I understand what you're sayin'."

After pulling himself back towards the table, Carlo picked up his roast beef and cheese sandwich, pressed it together tightly between his palms (a trademark of his), and took a huge bite. Then, in chewing-hindered speech, he acquiesced: "Okay, I'll cover for ya if I have to."

Moments later, he added, "I still think it would be a good idea to have someone else there in case the Blue Lady, or whatever it is, shows up and turns out to be really scary and unfriendly,...but I get it."

Carlo had said "Blue Lady" loud enough to catch Ally's attention. Feeling her eyes upon us, I quickly tried to cover: "Yeah, we really got Mr. Box on that *Blue* Öyster Cult question." I emphasized the word *blue* to make her think she'd misheard.

"It was too easy," Carlo laughed, clearly not picking up on what I was doing. I remembered then that we were supposed to have a question for Mr. Box that day in the class right after lunch. I reminded Carlo, and we brainstormed and decided to ask him a similar question to the one he asked us about a band's previous name. With the surname Box, we didn't need to think too hard. Mick Box was the only original member left in Uriah Heep by 1982, so we would ask Mr. Box what the band's original name had been. As it turned out, Mr. Box had no idea they were known as Spice before becoming Uriah Heep, so that question guaranteed us extra credit on our next geography test.

⬛ Once committed to returning to the lighthouse, I focused on that objective to the near exclusion of all else. After school on Wednesday, I made a special trip to the general store in Sheltered Harbour to pick up some provisions. "The Mission," as I'd come to think of it, had become such a priority that I was surprised to realize after leaving the store that I hadn't given any thought to Jemcraw or the young employee stocking the shelves. That alone was a small victory.

Even though I was alone when I arrived home, I closed my bedroom door before spreading my purchases on the bed. I matched what lay in front of me with the checklist in my head: water, a can of a new type of mosquito repellant from Off! called *Deep Woods,* beef jerky, a bag of pork skins, a few candy bars, and a couple of RC Colas in case I needed the energy to stay awake, in that way only sugar and caffeine could provide. I also stashed a couple of packs of cigarettes, a lighter, flashlight, a pocketknife, and an afghan my mom made for me when I was ten or so. And I had made sure my moped's gas tank was full. I would repeat this procedure once more on Friday morning. When the packing was complete, I felt confident I'd covered all the bases.

When I showed up at breakfast Friday with what looked like a backpack stuffed with school items and a change of clothes for an overnight at Carlo's, little did my mom know that right under her nose was all the gear for a forbidden expedition. I hoisted the backpack across my shoulders and bent to cram the final piece of bacon off my plate into my mouth. When I turned to go, I was surprised to see my mom blocking the kitchen door.

"Are you going to stop home after school, or are you heading to Carlo's right away?"

For a second, I felt convinced she'd had a motherly intuition, something she had displayed on more than one occasion when I thought I was acting as calm and collected as master of space Captain James T. Kirk.

"Yeah, we were thinkin' of stopping at the arcade first before it closes and then hang out with Tab for a bit before heading back to Carlo's to watch movies the rest of the night."

"Hopefully not *all* night."

She didn't suspect a thing.

"No, not all night, just part of it. They're showing some of our favorite horror movies."

She shook her head and cautioned, "I hope they're not R-rated, and you guys don't scare yourselves."

"No, it's like old-time horror films. You know, stuff like *Frankenstein* and *The Mummy*." Almost as an afterthought, I added, "and maybe *Phantasm*." That was R-rated but was such a favorite of mine that I said it even though I wasn't going to be watching movies.

"Well, that *is* an R movie, isn't it?"

A threat to my plan had arisen from nowhere as a look of concern crossed her face. "Maybe I should ring up Mrs. Spinetta and have her check in on what you guys are watching from time to time."

I shook my head and smiled, knowing how I responded was vital.

"Just joking about *Phantasm*, Mom. They're only showing old horror films on WTOC tonight." This detail is where my planning came in handy. "Take a look at the *TV Guide;* they list all the movies they're gonna be showing in their mini-marathon."

Her demeanor instantly changed as she hugged me, kissing the top of my head. "Well, have a fun time, and give us a call tomorrow to let us know when you're going to be home."

Try as I might to forget it, an otherwise innocuous comment from my mom kept echoing through my mind: "I hope...you guys don't scare yourselves." If my assumptions were way off and the Blue Lady turned out to be the opposite of what I hoped, I faced the real possibility that I might be more scared than I had ever been in my life, and unlike a movie, I wouldn't be able to shut off what I was experiencing. A strong familial bond asserted itself as I stood at the threshold of our kitchen door, with my mom representing safety, reason, and love.

Right then, the contrast between that world and the one I had committed to giving myself over to caused a seed of uncertainty to grow into a swooning wave of fear. Suddenly, I wanted nothing more than to cancel my plans. Still, I managed to push my anxiety aside by focusing instead on the prosaic list of items I was bringing with me. By repeatedly enumerating the provisions and details of the Mission, I felt my sense of resolve return. To my mind, I'd checked every box, but once I entered that forest on Declaration, if something did go wrong, I could rely only on myself. Excuses couldn't help me, just as backing down would only chain me. In a real sense, I knew that facing darkness might be the only way I'd genuinely see the light.

I could sense heaviness in the air as I rode to school, the clouds assembling overhead mirroring the apprehension that was building within me. The day was already very muggy, and if the appearance of the sky was any indication, rain seemed a real possibility. I could have kicked myself for not watching the morning news to see the weather report. I felt like the Blue Lady had made the first move. Of course, she was the reason for the adventure I was perched on the precipice of, but I was also awakening to all we shared. Not fitting certain people's view of the world had marginalized us, and her status as something reviled and feared was something I understood intimately. The Blue Lady's reaction of fear had been reflected in my knee-jerk reaction to run when she appeared. At that moment, she became as afraid of me as I was of her. At least, that's how it seemed as I replayed the events over in my mind. The mournful cry I had heard was the very sound of loneliness, a distillation of rejection, frustration, and sadness. How many people over how many years had used her as a scapegoat for their ignorance, narrow-mindedness, and hatred? The mantle of heat and humidity that draped my body could not stop me from shivering with a new wave of awareness. I clung desperately to the idea that we were both presently stuck in our own unique but not dissimilar predicaments—a common ground I hoped she didn't mind sharing.

Superstitions are woven into the lives of even the most level-headed people, even more so in places like Leggatts, where darkness falls like an impenetrable black curtain and the lonely night songs of the whip-poor-will and chuck-wills-widow cut through the thick salty air like a warning that the world is temporarily not ruled by reason or the living, erasing the order that holds sway in daylight. The little rituals that seemed to bring luck in the past—like crossing one's fingers—would be repeated in the future with the belief that the hoped-for results would also repeat. Yet, a vast segment of humanity refuses, at least openly, to admit to a belief in ghosts. For all the reasons I had been drawn to the lighthouse on the specific day that she appeared to me, I now knew beyond a shadow of a doubt that the Blue Lady, Charlotte Pauley, was as real as she had been when she was alive. As real as my mom and dad, Ally, or Carlo.

I was amazed that people who would never publicly admit to believing in the supernatural were nonetheless affected by the stories repeated down the years about the Lady in Blue. The solitude and quiet that ruled Declaration proved the effectiveness of these stories. The corrupted atmosphere that permeated the island—like a village from the Middle Ages visited by the specter of the Black Death—and was whispered about on dark nights in tin-roofed farm shacks and splendid mansions overlooking green fairways meant that the island could give itself back to nature. Those otherwise hostile citizens provided the unintended benefit of a sanctuary for people who needed to disappear within its borders, people like Carlo and me. Maybe it was also a place where Charlotte Pauley could not escape—or perhaps chose not to.

The place I couldn't escape was school looming before me, steadily growing larger. The invisible rope it cast out tightly constricted my body and mind until I sensed the hold relenting, ever so slightly, as I discerned the figures of Carlo and Scott chatting by their mopeds. Only Carlo knew of my mission, and as I rode up, he gave me a secret nod. I felt we were enacting a scene from a James Bond movie, one secret agent acknowledging the other.

After I pulled up next to Scott, I was startled to see him mere inches from my face before I'd even had time to remove my helmet.

"Do my eyes look red to you?" They were as red as a shiny red fire truck.

"Uh, yeah. Like really red."

Squeezing several drops of Visine into each eye, he then closed them and shook his head vigorously back and forth.

"Better?"

"Yeah, much better," I lied. Visine never worked as well as Scott thought it did to clear his pot eyes, but I always felt that if he thought it was working, it would give him the confidence to get through the day. Opening his eyes wide while pressing his fingers beneath them, he lightly pulled down, closely scrutinizing their reflection in his rear-view mirror.

"Yeah, yeah, they do look clear now," he said, seeing what he wanted to see.

Scott's conviction made me think how often I had done the same thing: seeing what I wanted to see when the evidence in front of my nose suggested it was something else altogether.

Noticing my bemused expression, Carlo looked at me quizzically. "What's up?"

Giving a just discernible shake of my head, I said, "Hard to explain, but if I find the answer, I'll let ya know tomorrow." Then, realizing that Scott was an expert at picking up on coded conversations, I quickly added, "Just thinkin' we should catch a buzz before the flicks tonight,...and if it's really good, not remembering will be our proof we were successful."

Playing along, Carlo assumed a bewildered, slack-jawed expression and, in his best Tommy Chong impression, said, "Movie? I wasn't in any movie last night, man." Then his eyes widened as he looked first at me and then at Scott. "Was I?"

Scott shook his head and let out a loud, dopey guffaw that let us know we'd effectively covered our tracks.

With that, we put on our Walkmans, pushed "Play," and headed into school. I was so thoroughly absorbed and distracted by the details of my fast-approaching mission that the day passed like scenes from a dream—fragmented voices and images of the school day cut in and out of various scenarios I'd manufactured, my imagination spinning them into increasingly complex patterns. As the final bell drew nearer, the tension that had been my psychological white noise throughout the day increased exponentially. At one point during English class, as I stared blankly at the teacher, I nearly convinced myself that, because of the foolishness of my planned undertaking, I should just go to Carlo's to watch movies into the wee hours. At that moment, Scott's red eyes flashed before me, symbolic of all the times I had blinkered myself and downplayed a situation in favor of pretending everything wasn't so bad. The truth was, things weren't going all that well, and I needed to confront this particular situation head-on. Not only for who I was but for who I wanted to become.

Carlo shook his head as we walked to our mopeds after the final bell.

"I was thinkin' about it, and you should just come over to my place tonight. What you're gonna do is too risky." His concern was genuine. "I mean, we could still go over there like next weekend, and then if you were to run into someone like those two assholes we encountered that one time, you'd have backup."

I wasn't surprised that he would try again to get me to change my mind, but the last part of his comment particularly hit me. Thoughts of the night ahead had so consumed me that I hadn't considered the dangers of the living—the two crab-nappers, or others like them, and the posse of three angry black guys who, for reasons I still couldn't fathom, wanted to kick my ass.

"To be honest, I hadn't been thinking of people." I looked at him sincerely. "But we just had bikes that time. With my moped, I'll be able to get away from anyone who might chase me."

Reaching the end of the gym, we stood in front of the lagoon Brice and Trey had tossed me into just a few days earlier. I stared at the sunlight briefly breaking through the cloud cover, reflecting off its tiny windswept waves.

"Not if they have a car," Carlo said, suddenly a pragmatist.

Looking him right in the eyes, I gave what I hoped looked like a confident smile. "I gotta do it today, or I'll probably never do it."

Thrusting his hand out quite seriously, Carlo said, "Good luck then, my friend."

Our solidarity manifested in how he took my hand, gripping it like a vice. He cared, which proved that he was my best friend, not that I needed any further validation.

"Thanks. I'll be all right, though, and maybe I'll stop over tomorrow to tell you firsthand what did...or didn't happen."

"Sounds good." He put on his helmet. "I'll ride with ya till we hit Merganser. Ready?"

I was about to say "yeah" but decided to go through my backpack. "I just want to check my supplies one more time. You go on ahead. I'll see ya tomorrow."

His tough-guy pretense dropped momentarily as he quickly looked to his left and right before giving me the kind of hug I'd only ever had from my dad. "Take care."

"That's just what I'm gonna do, brother."

Watching him ride off, I put my helmet on before flopping my backpack onto the ground. Opening it, I made a final inventory, satisfying myself that I hadn't forgotten anything. Grabbing a bottle of water for my ride, I put it in the side pocket of my track jacket, then hoisted my backpack on. I started, slowly picking up speed as I passed the lagoon. As the end of school property came within sight, the bottle tumbled from its precarious perch in my pocket and rolled towards the football field that paralleled me. Far from empty, the field was at that very moment filling up with football players for the after-school practice. My timing never ceased to both amaze and annoy me. Of all the places in the world for my water bottle to drop, it had to be at that exact spot, at that most inopportune moment. I considered riding on, but as I wasn't carrying all that much water, I stopped, pulled the moped up on its kickstand, and walked the few feet the bottle had traveled. As I bent down to retrieve it, a large, cleated foot appeared, kicking it several yards away until it bounced off the chain-link fence that enclosed the playing fields. As I looked up, a sickening yet familiar feeling of dread washed over me. Boykin, an aide in my gym class, trotted past me and grabbed the bottle while I found myself surrounded. As soon as I stood upright, someone shoved me to the ground.

Quickly scanning the faces of his buddies encircling me, Boykin thrust the bottle in my face. "What ya lookin' for, this?"

Feeding off the energy of an audience, he laughed loudly. "Well, I'm thirsty. How 'bout you guys?"

The predicament escalated so fast my head was spinning. The voices around me slowed down and echoed, entering my dazed mind as the dissonance of tubas tuning up. Boykin opened the bottle, filled his mouth with water, swished it around, and spit it out in a thin stream onto my face. Then, while tubas blared, a knee slammed into the back of my neck, a blow partially deflected by my helmet. The unexpected impact sent me sprawling forward, my hands shooting out instinctively. I managed to push myself onto my knees, and as I glanced above me, Boykin ricocheted the bottle off my face. Laughter, now sounding like rocks rattling in a bucket, reverberated through my head. Then a voice came from further behind me. It was Coach White's.

"All right, c'mon fellas, what's the hullabaloo all about?"

"Nothing, coach, we're just helping a guy who dropped his water," a voice answered.

The circle around me partially opened as Coach White approached, hands on hips, and shook his head.

"Don't tell me we got a new tryout here."

Snickering and muffled laughter broke out from the group.

"Sorry, fella, tryouts are already over."

Once he saw who the reluctant center of attention was, his eyes brightened and scanned his players. "Maybe the gymnastics team would be more your speed."

Laughter erupted again, this time much louder.

Roaring like a drill sergeant, Coach White loudly clapped his hands. "Now, let's get onto the field, boys, and into your squads."

As the group began walking toward the field, I was momentarily hidden, with four guys in front of me and three behind me forming a fence blocking me from view. I knew something was coming and tried to speak, but only achieved the open-mouthed silence of a nightmare. An elbow slammed into my ribs, knocking me back onto my knees. It happened so fast and casually that I found it impossible to tell if the assailant was Boykin or someone else. The pain was the same, no matter the source: nothing seen, just business as usual.

Looking back after the incident, Coach White bellowed, "Not too graceful on your feet there, Howe." The group that, moments before, had surrounded me stopped next to him. Glancing at them surreptitiously, in an unconcerned, lighthearted voice, Coach White added,

"Scratch the gymnastics team," to a round of hearty laughter.

After everyone was on the field, he casually strolled back and gave me a quick once-over as I rose to my feet. "Being a team player's what it's all about, Howe. Things are easier when you get that into your head."

Feeling dazed and humiliated, I walked unsteadily back to my still running moped, positioned myself on the seat, and rubbed my neck and ribs.

"Clear the field unless you're on the team," the coach yelled from the other side of the chain-link fence. He looked directly at me even though I wasn't on the field. I gave an exaggerated salute that caused him to shake his head. He turned, muttering something I couldn't make out.

I maneuvered onto the one-lane road leading away from school and stopped after a few yards to clear my head. Within the blink of an eye, the ranks of the anti-Ash club had grown exponentially—and, more bothersome, that day's instigators hadn't ever been on my radar. My popularity seemed to be rising with all the buoyancy of a fishing sinker.

A voice startled me. "You all right there, Ash?"

Looking over my shoulder, I saw the custodian, James. He was walking up, carrying a bag full of garbage he'd emptied from a receptacle at the far end of the field, which meant he'd seen everything that had just transpired. I could tell he had recently paid a visit to the storage room for a couple of belts. His eyes betrayed a hint of red, and his eyelids drooped slightly.

Setting the bag down, he patted my shoulder. "Those boys are just a buncha assholes. Don't let 'em get to ya, ya hear?"

I smiled, grasping his hand. "Thanks, yeah, I know. I guess I just gotta be more aware of my surroundings."

"You almost gotta have eyes in the back of your head." He looked off into the distance, suddenly lost in private thought. Then with a half wink and a little smile, he said, "You take care how ya go."

That is exactly what I intended to do.

The pain and anger pumping through my heart didn't lessen until I turned onto Cogginsville Road. The physical pain kept reminding me of another possible confrontation that, under normal circumstances, I would have buried in a shallow grave in my mind. "The Mission" made me look at everything I experienced in bright relief, a condition that eradicated the safety net of shadows.

Although the overcast had briefly parted, revealing a glorious blue sky, all too soon, churning clouds returned, far thicker than before. Yet that brief glimpse of blue had given me the strength I needed to refocus on my objective. I reasoned that I would be dry in the lighthouse if it rained, as it looked like it would. However, thanks to a comment from Carlo, I now had to consider a potential threat of the flesh and blood variety along with possible supernatural adversaries. Keeping my eye on the deteriorating weather, I clung to the notion that rain would greatly diminish the chances of dealing with any unwanted human company.

The sand beneath me a blur, I was zipping along the low-tide beach when I saw a figure approaching me on a bike. I squinted, trying to make out if it was someone I knew.

As the distance closed, I could tell it was a black kid who started waving his arm in a wide arc. For a few stretched seconds, apprehension washed over me because of my recent run-in with three black guys. However, this anxiety completely evaporated once I realized it was Abe. He was shirtless, wearing cut-off jeans and a big smile.

"Hey, I was hoping that was you. I could see long hair comin' out from under that helmet." He looked my moped up and down. "When'd you get that badass ride?"

"A coupla months ago—" I stopped as I realized Abe was riding my twelve-speed.

Seeing what I was looking at, he nodded. "Yup, it's your bike. I been riding up and down here on and off for a few weeks, hoping to bump into ya."

"I had a weird run-in—"

He interrupted me. "Man, you was lucky Garrison's grandsons didn't catch you. They'd a whupped your ass."

"Yeah, I know." I smiled faintly. "They told me so."

Retrieving a pack of cigarettes from my jacket pocket, I put one between my lips and offered Abe one. He looked around cautiously to ensure nobody was around, then took it as I handed him the lighter.

"So, what was it all about? I was just riding by when they came after me."

Puffing on his cigarette to ensure it was lit, he returned the lighter to me and smiled.

"Just after I saw you and your friend—" He hesitated. "Carl?"

"Carlo."

"Yeah, Carlo. Well, right after I saw you guys that day along here, I was walkin' on Barnwell headin' home when this pickup truck come up fast along side me with six white dudes in it—two up front and four in back, when the guy in the passenger side yelled 'nigger' at me."

I must have looked surprised because Abe nodded his head by way of response.

"I was just mindin' my own business, and the way they come up on me and the guy yelling at me surprised me, and I fell, skinnin' my knee and hand."

He looked at his hand, reliving the moment, then shook his head. "When I looked up, one of the rednecks spit in my face."

Caught up in his story, I whispered aloud, "What the fuck?"

"Before I could even take that bullshit in, another asshole jumps out the back and kicks me in the ass before I could get up, layin' me out. Then he grabs up my bucket and throws it in the truck, and they take off laughing."

"So why'd Garrison's grandsons want to kick my ass? 'Cause I was white, and they wanted to even the score?"

"Naw, he thought you mighta been one of the rednecks that ambushed me." Abe then considered what I'd just said. "But maybe that was part of it, too. Anyway, I saw your bike in Garrison's yard, and he told me what happened. I told him you're a good guy."

"Thanks."

"Yeah, well, old Mr. Garrison, he heard about them boys yellin' at me—we all pretty close down here—and he wanted to send a message, y'know? Sorry 'bout that."

I nodded. "Yeah, I understand. I'm just really glad I got away."

Abe let out his infectious scratchy laugh, and I couldn't help but join him.

"Well, thanks for going so outta your way to get my bike back to me." Then, without thinking twice, I said, "It's yours. I got this thing now, and that bike needs a new cowboy."

"Oh man, I can't take this beautiful thing; it's yours."

"It's yours now," I said with finality. "Even if I wanted to take it, I don't have anywhere to put it," I joked, motioning to my backpack.

"How 'bout we say I'll look out for it for ya, and if ya ever want it back, you'll know where it's at?"

I shook my head. "Let's just say it's yours."

Looking at the bike again, I felt a wave of happiness wash over me as I remembered all the fun times I'd had on it. "It's a great bike, and that thing's taken me everywhere. Now you can explore with it."

Abe's hand shot out and grabbed mine, shaking it zestfully. "You the coolest."

"There's no way you just realized that now," I joked.

"Ooohhh, and the cockiest." He shook his head while letting out another high-pitched laugh. Then he asked, "Where you headed to anyway, boy?"

I hadn't thought of my objective for the few minutes I'd been chatting with Abe, but now it came back like a heavy yoke across my shoulders. Then another door magically opened, and I saw that everything around me was part of the same objective and that talking to Abe had steadied my mind a bit. Knowing this didn't make me reveal my hand, though. I felt that there was something fragile about my undertaking that would be betrayed if I said anything about it before it was completed. So, I lied, "Ahh, nothin' really, just headin' over to Declaration to think a bit."

Abe saw an opening and smiled broadly. "Don't sprain anything." Before I could reply, he patted my shoulder. "Just foolin'."

Then his expression turned serious. "You got trouble or somethin'?"

Tossing my cigarette onto the sand and crushing it with my foot, I shook my head. "There's just somethin' I need to do." Seeing the curious look on his face and not wanting him to follow, I tried to reassure him, "It's a long, strange story, and next time I see you, I promise I'll tell you all about it." I gazed out over the inlet to the northeast, where I could just make out the southern end of Declaration. "Let's just say it's facing something and not backing down."

Abe seemed to understand I was struggling with something and let it go. "Well, whatever it is, watch out for yerself." Following my gaze across the inlet, he said, "But if you believe you can do it, you can."

How could he have known I was facing a situation where I needed to believe in myself? Yet, somehow, something in my demeanor must have betrayed me.

"You take care now, Ash...and thanks for the kick-ass bike!"

He flashed a big smile, flicked his cigarette behind him, and rode towards the boat launch. Turning the throttle, I was soon speeding along at an even 40 miles per hour, watching my destination grow larger by the second. Butterflies had returned to my stomach, but unlike those I could trace to a tangible source, this variety emerged from the unknown—an unknown I had caught a glimpse of, and that had scared me to my very core. The feelings I was wrestling with didn't feel a million miles removed from what I perceived on any given school day or when I walked into Jemcraw's store. Even so, I had to forcefully mute the desire to take an easier route. In this case, that would've meant turning around and riding to Carlo's, but before I could convince myself that's what I should do, and sooner than I had hoped, I was crossing the causeway.

If I had the power within me to slow down time, I would have called on it then to examine every step, each action, methodically, thoroughly preparing myself for what needed to be done because as the island loomed before me, it looked anything but welcoming. Overhead the heavy sky churned, mirroring the unsettled state of my mind. The clouds seemed to join the tops of the trees, shaking the branches violently. It was far from the gentle, welcome swaying I was accustomed to, and put the final touches on what looked like the backdrop of a large stage constructed of a dark border, flats, and curtains. I suppose I had been rehearsing a more significant role than those I usually played, but this one involved a final act that was still unwritten.

In the days leading up to my return, I kept replaying my last momentous visit to the island frame by frame. Thinking about it was one thing, but finally setting foot back on the island for the first time since seeing a ghost caused anxiety to rise like a storm tide within me until I felt sure raw panic would grip me at any moment. Holding the handlebars of my moped, I stood staring at the forest until I surprised myself by yelling, "Okay!" and releasing the pressure that had been building in my mind. The simple sound of my voice jolted me out of the enveloping fear. With great effort, I moved forward, implying confidence I certainly didn't feel and headed straight for the imposing wall of trees, which for the first time appeared as if constructed to keep intruders out. I pushed my Vespa deep within a thicket of saw palmettos set further back than the customary tree I usually parked against, maybe to unconsciously conceal myself from whatever I might later confront.

Since my crossing, a misty drizzle had been fitfully falling, the overcast making the woods surrounding me appear far more forlorn and ominous than on similar days when I had visited with friends. Even the cicadas sounded languid and muted. Taking my helmet off, I shook my hair, ran my comb through it, took a deep breath, then started towards the old lighthouse. Not for the first time, but never so intensely, I got the impression there were spirits in those woods lurking just beyond my vision that conversed in ancient tongues that had nothing to do with humans.

To keep fear in check, I thought of practical things, like deciding to stash my backpack behind the oil house before journeying on to skeleton beach. I felt that being outside, just a speck on the vast openness of the beach would keep me from feeling trapped. In a very real sense, though, once twilight arrived, high tide would submerge the causeway, and I would be entirely on my own for the night. Yet, despite that realization, walking through a place I needed to be part of eased my apprehension. Quiet solitude, overflowing in such abundance on Declaration, helped me shake the smoldering anger and pain I was unable to put into words with those who loved me. I realized again how important it was to have that release in the natural splendor of that wild island and how very much I'd missed it.

Though the rain had subsided, fat drops shaken off wind-tousled branches pelted me all along the walk until I broke from the forest canopy, arriving at the lighthouse compound. Now changed again, the lighthouse appeared to faintly glimmer as if dappled in perspiration, a motionless runner after a race. I stared up at her for a moment, thinking how she seemed to reflect my pensiveness. Then, breaking from the trance, I removed my backpack and opened it to retrieve a handful of pork skins I stuffed into my mouth before absentmindedly transferring a pouch of beef jerky and a bottle of water into my jacket pockets. Once I had stowed the supplies as planned behind the stout oil house, I headed for the beach engulfed in a misty drizzle, spontaneously slowing as I passed the very spot I had seen Charlotte Pauley.

Yes, Charlotte Pauley, not the Blue Lady, the Lady in Blue, or a wrathful inhuman creature. I felt much better at that moment, remembering that she had once been a person like me and, like me, shared a love for this enchanted place.

When I emerged from the forest's shadows, a grey-riled sea greeted me with an equally unsettled sky; no Marsh Tackies or seagulls were in sight. Big waves crashed and sizzled strongly on the shore, creeping ever higher, pushed by a steady southwest wind. Sitting high up near the dunes on a bone-white bough, I sat nibbling a chunk of jerky, suddenly struck by the realization that even with all the walking I'd done, I felt no thirst. A pride in how far I had already come seemed to fill that need. I also tried to convince myself that it would be a gift to have the opportunity to walk this quiet, enchanted land in the blackness of night, taking in with hopefully untainted senses whatever mysteries lay concealed there.

A strong breeze blowing off the ocean acted as a humidity-clearing broom, sweeping aside the stubborn drizzle, if only for the moment. Stretching out on the damp sand, I closed my eyes and rested my head against the trunk, giving myself a mental pep talk by focusing every bit of my being on seeing "The Mission" through. Maybe "The Goal" was a better term. A goal to face up to something and not back down, no matter how daunting it might initially appear.

With trepidation, I opened a mental box where I'd stored a collection of spiteful laughter, angry red faces, cruel judgments, never-ending humiliation, and an ever-shrinking horizon. It reminded me why I was there, turning negativity into an unlikely source of fuel to see me through. I needed to follow through with my plan, or I'd almost certainly be swept up in the narrow yet mighty stream that was my community's rituals and behavior.

I now understood I needed to look deeper, through the veneer of the narrative, engaging the fight response over flight—fighting only the conditioning of fear I'd been sold as the truth, even though the urge might be to run no matter which island I found myself on. By tempering that urge and my habitual tendency to lock away painful experiences, I allowed a tantalizing new frontier to magically appear, beckoning me with a light as bright as the sun. The strategy of "bury and forget" that I'd settled for had only secured blinkers on my head, blocking the light from me that was just as much mine as anyone else's. Seeing more clearly didn't erase all scars, some of which would continue to surface decades later, no longer raw but tangible. Their reappearance reminding my older self that not all imprints can—or probably should—be erased from the soul. Those scars transformed instead into symbols of learning and harm allayed.

Twilight began making itself known just a bit after seven. As the shadows became a spilled bottle of ink that swallowed the details of individual trees, the disc of the sun appeared, a molten gold medallion showing briefly through a break in the cloud cover, only to submerge into the sea, leaving me quite alone. Waves were now lapping only a few short yards away, a clear reminder that I was on Declaration for the duration. Standing, brushing myself off, I looked to the south, trying to catch a glimpse of Leggatts. All I could make out were dim, murky waves moving up the mouth of Mitchell Inlet. Suddenly, the story of the young boy being held by the unforgiving claw of a stone crab and drowning in that channel, his terrified unanswered screams rising above the night songs of crickets and owls, sent a chill running up my spine.

With a willful effort I didn't realize I possessed, I forced my eyes away from the water toward the trees, which now appeared as one dark, seemingly impenetrable mass. The narrow sandy path into the interior looked as daunting as a high wire strung between skyscrapers. But, then, a jolting shock shot through my body as I realized I'd left something vital tucked snugly in my backpack behind the oil house. It was something that I'd never wanted quite so badly before—my flashlight. Desperately cursing this oversight, I stared ahead at that tightrope, disappearing into the darkness as stark as a once luminous city extinguished by a catastrophic blackout.

Putting one tentative, leaden foot in front of the other, I approached a blackness that would have served as an effective deterrent to anyone without an objective. Just before I crossed the invisible line between the openness of the beach and the fairy-tale gloom of the forest, I halted and took a deep breath as I tried with difficulty to suppress the part of my mind that was screaming, "Get out of here! The tide hasn't crested yet — Go home!"

I needed something to inspire me, someone who would fearlessly walk over the imposing threshold without thinking twice. With that, before my eyes materialized a figure whose grit, boldness, and audacity I sorely needed. It wasn't Iron Man, Thor, or Captain America. Instead, there stood a superhero cut from another cloth: Iron Maiden's Paul Di'Anno, adorned in leather, spiked gauntlets on each arm, and defiant disheveled hair. Lip curled into a cocky sneer, he looked me in the face and unleashed a brazen laugh. "The's nothin' in there half as tough as us, mate." Tilting his head to the side, he looked me up and down and nodded in approval. "Let's go kick some ass!" Turning, he strode purposefully toward the unknown. Following his bold lead, I marched into the abyss. Paul's voice loudly sang Iron Maiden's eponymous song, which acted as a vocal machete, clearing our way.

All at once, the alien night sounds and the darkness itself were subdued, the former by Iron Maiden's battle cry, the latter by focusing all my attention on the imaginary glint of Paul's swinging gauntlet spikes. Our pace was confident and steady, my head nodding in perfect time to the song. Only after imaginary Paul and I had plunged deep into the woods did he begin to fade. I squinted, trying to keep him in my sight, but try as I might, he shrank from view. His leather jacket slowly dissolved into the empty black void, and his voice trailed away into nothingness. A momentary sense of abandonment engulfed me until I realized I couldn't have reached that point without the inspiration I'd taken from his conjured presence. Even under the circumstances, I recognized the irony that just as he had with Iron Maiden, he left me as soon as he had served his purpose.

I realized, too, I couldn't have made it that far if I'd been truly alone in my life. It was now up to me, empowered by everyone and everything that had pushed me to where I presently stood, to finish the journey relying only on myself, alone physically but not in spirit. In that way, my mom and dad, Carlo, Tab, Scott, and even Mr. Box, were walking beside me just as Paul had. I started again with a renewed purpose. As if he passed his powers to me, I felt Paul's gauntlets transfer to my arms, his leather jacket fit perfectly on my form, and his voice rang clear as a bell in my head: "You have the power to do this, mate; you always have." After a brief pause, he added in his tough London accent, "Up the Irons, Ash!"

From nearby, a night heron on the hunt unleashed several sharp, barking squawks, jarring me out of my rumination as all around crickets shook off their sleep to sing. Freshly poured over the island, the deep darkness made it difficult to discern familiar landmarks as my eyes adjusted at a far slower pace than my mind wanted. Tuned to what felt like superhuman levels of precision, all the nerves in my body had become snare traps set, ready to immobilize the threat until I could assess it. My ears tried to pinpoint the source of every sound, and my eyes darted frantically, scanning every tree and bush as I quietly stepped around or ducked under fallen and low-hanging boughs.

As I cautiously approached one of many brackish lagoons, I was surprised to see it was still as glass, the half-moon peeking through the scuttling clouds reflecting broken beams gently upon the surface. The sight unlocked a memory of when I was eleven, delirious with a fever. Sitting with me, my mom had been a constant presence, occasionally resting a calming hand on my forehead, delicately, just to let me know she was there. Absorbing the dim silver light shimmering in my eyes, I took a deep breath and noticed my feet felt just a little bit lighter as I plunged anew into the whispering shadows. A whip-poor-will called from mere yards away in a section of pine forest, followed alarmingly by a screech owl whinnying a "who goes there" as I passed his unseen perch high above in a shrouded oak.

I was beginning to sense a distinct pulse in the dark world around me, only the surface of which I was skimming. To truly appreciate it, I needed to find a still point in my mind and cling to it unflinchingly with a genuine faith grounding me. Slowly, I exhaled a deep breath and became still as a statue, trying hard to dispel the tension wound into a tight knot in my gut. Unfortunately, this attempt only briefly subdued the fear that threatened to break through my reason. As I scanned the dusky trail before me, at the furthest reach of my vision, I detected movement where the path turned deeper into the interior. My heart started racing wildly, and I suppressed a gasp. Craning my neck forward, I squinted to discern a family of white-tailed deer foraging the periphery of a nearby field and let out a long sigh of relief.

Carefully navigating the trail, I tried to reassure myself that animals were all around and I didn't need to panic at every sound. While trying to reinforce that affirmation, I was abruptly overwhelmed by a creeping fear that manifested as the sensation of a thousand spiders scampering over my body. Far worse than the banana spiders I knew were out there was the realization that I was standing at the exact spot I had seen—her.

The flight aspect of the fight-or-flight response was giving me the hard sell. My mouth grew parched, my feet glued to the ground, and my heart felt as if it would beat out of my chest. A wall I couldn't see, in every way as effective as a physical wall, had been conjured, keeping me from moving forward. My vision narrowed, becoming dim except for a small circle, like I was looking through a long tube, visualizing myself standing in the depths of the woods through a convex lens of a telescope, the viewer now the one under scrutiny. Searching for a way to break my fixation, I looked up helplessly.

Above me, the sky had finally managed to shake off the clouds it had worn for most of the day. It shimmered sapphire blue in the light of a quarter moon, appearing as the surface of the ocean must from far beneath the waves, as hints of the sunlight that have pierced the depths first become apparent, not yet rays but blue emeralds suspended, laughing at gravity. The world looked as strange and beautiful as the submerged universe I'd just imagined. Every murky avenue I passed, which I knew so well in daylight, was akin to discovering a new aquatic cave, trench, or coral reef. A low white mist had rolled in from the marshes, pouring freely through the forests and fields, spilling down every pathway, the arteries and veins of the island. For whatever reason, its appearance changed my fear into something closer to being enthralled, if uneasy, and it allowed my feet to move again, one in front of the other.

Realizing that I had decided alone to confront Charlotte Pauley in the hope of facing my fear, I fell prey to nagging self-doubt. This uncertainty manifested as an image of a morphing figure standing before me; one moment, it was my dad, and the next, it was Carlo, shaking me while shouting, "What will you do if she appears?"

They were right! What would I do if she appeared before I was ready? How does one prepare for such a thing anyway? In moments, she might be upon me, reaching with pale skeletal hands, desperately clutching my head, staring into my very soul with white, hollow eyes, hoping I was someone she had known. Her diseased sorrow turned to fury, her visage growing until her gaping mouth was all there was —a cave of echoing blackness, consuming me into an inescapable void for all eternity!

Then an alternate scenario, one just as scary, just as hopeless, came to me—maybe I had been foolhardy, a sucker once again. Perhaps she was vengeful, existing only to terrify those ignorant, arrogant, or foolish enough to trespass on ground she claimed as hers alone. Maybe she could sense my every movement and breath before finally capturing me at her discretion, to possess me and bend me with effortless ease toward her madness—a madness impossible to escape. I forced myself to take a deep breath, silently repeating with the desperation of an adrift person clinging to a life preserver from a ship that slipped beneath the waves, that what I was feeling was only the night. My unfamiliarity with the island in darkness was leading my thoughts astray, pulling me into the trap of hearsay and superstition.

A mental tug of war was in progress: on one side was the effortless pull of lurid speculation, while on the other was a quiet yet powerful wonder revealed when I stopped to absorb the strange new face of beauty unfolding all around me. Gradually, by focusing only on my immediate surroundings, I began by degrees to perceive more of what I never had before. Underfoot, sweet-smelling flowers lined the pathway, meandering haphazardly into the forest composed of gray, silver, and blue shadows. I knelt, straining to perceive their delicate outlines, realizing that my vision had fully adjusted to the faint light, a smeared blue luminescence that played off the folded petals. Extending a finger to touch one, I noticed that although the flowers were closed in sleep, they still exuded a faint fragrance being created and stored for the coming day. Continuing this motion, I pressed my palm onto the earth, surprised to find it quite cool without the sun's heat radiating off it. The soil cradled all the forms of life it nourished, sustaining them through its blackness. The earth not separate from the night around me.

The peculiar relationship between the darkness and the unknown, which is just darkness by another name, led me to decipher what I was perceiving. I understood for the first time that everything I loved about the island and had taken for granted in daylight relied on the darkness of night to replenish itself. The night enveloping me seemed to convey that light is not always literal.

After carefully traversing the final hundred yards, I made out the sagging lightkeeper's house and gave it an extra-wide berth, recalling the porch creaking under the pressure of something unseen during my earlier, unplanned night visit. I walked to the center of the sweetgrass field and stood, trying to compose myself for what I was now irretrievably locked into. I was completely open, but in a way, I had never allowed myself to be in the routine of daily life. Looming over me in the near distance, the hulking outline of the black tower drew my eyes upward to the sapphire sky, mirroring the blue luminescence of the flowers. Highlighted in silver, sprawling live oaks and sentinel pines reached over wax myrtles and palms, delineating the periphery of the field. With razor-edge precision, the moon traced the edges of the topmost leaves against a warm panorama of scurrying clouds and stars. Suddenly, I wondered, if the nebulous impressions of isolated sky, forest, and sea impacted my human senses so profoundly, how might the same vistas be perceived by a spirit rising out of the bark of a tree or a pealing lip of paint clinging to a clapboard wall?

Like a candle flame snuffed by a sharp puff of air, this thought was extinguished as thick clouds returned, blanketing the moon and stars and the warm, frail comfort with which I had been communing. The darkness, a veritable liquid, poured over everything I had only just begun to see like unforgiving hands plunging me into the ink-black water of the old brick cistern just a few short yards from where I stood.

What is true darkness? It's certainly not the dark you find after waking from a nightmare, where relief is just the turn of a switch on a bedside lamp. Instead, for the first time in my life, I was experiencing darkness where not even distant headlights from a car or the warm glow spilling through the windows of a house could provide the certainty that nearby a family like my own was going about its nightly routine. On Declaration, when clouds blotted out the moon, nothing remained but a gaping abyss of black beyond black. My hand invisible in front of me.

A conviction of overwhelming intensity arose then: the black surrounding me had become the body of a hungry beast breathing, tracking me in an ever-tightening circle, its concealed eyes ravenously watching, unseen mere inches from my face. The thick humidity clung to my body so heavily it seemed an appendage of the impenetrable black night, nearly convincing me that I'd become trapped in a confined space surrounded by thick walls. Fumbling in my jeans pocket, I grabbed my lighter and furiously tried to get a flame, but it only spit out sparks. Then, finally, a yellow-orange blade of fire sprang to life, giving off woefully inadequate light. The blackness pressing around it nearly sapped all its intensity. The power of imagination embroidered the darkness into that of a moldering coffin buried deep in the earth, and only with extreme difficulty did I make my way around the back of the oil house.

As I dropped to my knees, my hands fell greedily on the backpack, unzipping it with shaking fingers that rifled through it to locate the flashlight. Panic rose when for a few terrible seconds, I feared I had forgotten to pack it. Following a short, frantic search, I grasped it after mistakenly pulling out the can of bug repellant. When I impatiently snapped it on, the illumination was hardly reassuring. So dark was the night it seemed to eat at the edges of the strangely feeble beam as if acid were saturating it.

From that moment on, improvisation would replace the planned portion of "The Mission." I decided to first climb the lighthouse before returning to the exact spot I had seen Charlotte Pauley. It seemed reasonable to survey what I was trying to conquer, although I can't pretend that part of the decision wasn't to delay the possibility of confronting her. My whole world was circumscribed only by what the sickly yellow light revealed. I had to force my legs to move towards the rusting iron monolith, which had taken on the appearance of a conning tower on a partially submerged warship. Yet it was unbelievable how just the tiny beam I held proved that the layers of darkness only lightly draped the surroundings, darkness concealing some aspects but revealing others.

Faintly, at a pace more unhurried than mine, a delicate nocturnal continuum—comprising navy and Prussian blue through achromatic grays of battleship, nickel, and charcoal—coalesced out of chaos. This spectrum partnered with sounds: the breeze brushing the leaves and Spanish moss overhead; the bewitching dusky song of the whip-poor-will; the constant faux lament of crickets; the high-pitched honking of tree frogs counterbalanced by the dizzying spiral trilling of toads; the faint scurrying of raccoons or opossums; even the whirring wings of a Luna moth seemed amplified and broadcast in supernormal detail. Each fragment joined to reveal a dimension I would never have been able to fathom without experiencing it with my senses. I then understood the blowing night air that communicated with all around me, as the forest breathing. This notion made it taste sweeter than I'd ever imagined it could.

The freshness of these crisply defined auditory outlines muted as quickly as they had arisen by the sickening notion that the little finger of light before me would suddenly fall on a pallid face—emaciated, desperate, and outraged. I had to disperse these intruding thoughts like my flashlight penetrated the night, or I'd succumb to dread, followed by an all-encompassing blind panic. Keeping this compulsion at arm's length was like trying by force of will to subdue the need to vomit. I had been so fixated on each step, processing all the sounds and visions vying for attention, that finding myself standing at the very threshold of the lighthouse startled me. For a moment, I stared in awe because in front of me was something I couldn't recall ever seeing before—the door to the lighthouse was closed. I tentatively grasped the doorknob, mentally counting down from three before slowly pulling it open. Rusty hinges creaked loudly in protest, activating a fear-driven impression that the sound was recoiling from my light. A draft of bottled air, redolent of mildew, escaped from the space before me. Knowing it was now or never, I closed my eyes and took a deep breath, which I held to buy myself a sliver of time. Then, exhaling, I entered.

Plunging headlong into the gloom, I was an astronaut walking in space, moving through a place that, for all intents and purposes, I had never been before. I became aware of mindfulness—my consciousness ascending that spiral staircase in complete accord with my body. It was at once boundless yet humbling, a mixture my teenage brain had never considered. When I came to the first landing, I stopped, indulging myself by lighting a cigarette. My hands were still lightly shaking, but I realized it was from all the adrenaline pumping through me, from fear, of course, but also exhilaration, the heightened alertness steadily rising the higher I climbed. The sensation might have come from the same place as the fear I often felt in daily life, but something was different; it didn't feel impassable. I had started to sense the climb to the top was for more than the advantage of elevation to observe my surroundings. The beacon was working on me inwardly as well.

Just a few steps short of the watch room, I paused to consider how many times I had thought I was capable of seeing things others were incapable of seeing. Impervious only to lies but never treachery. Hubris is never easy to confront, much less remove. Now I was walking on its ruins to witness where I once stood, a gift I spontaneously wished everyone could receive. Standing there, mesmerized by the burning orange tip of the cigarette, I realized that subtly, but crucially, my course had been altered. Never had that old lighthouse stopped serving her purpose: she was directing me to somehow be a part of her.

When my feet passed the threshold of the watch room, an unseen hand turned the moonlight on again, and its hazy light streaked across the speckled white cypress walls. Tossing the flashlight through the overhead trapdoor, I removed my backpack, balanced precariously on the windowsill, and hoisted myself into the Blue Room. Moonlight flooded through the single window that had once framed the fixed beam of light. Its initial function of shining outward long obsolete, the space now seemed a chapel designed solely to receive the light of the moon.

With that oddly comforting thought swirling through my mind, I walked out onto the narrow gallery, set the flashlight down, and rested my palms on the rusted handrail. All at once, goosebumps blossomed across my arms, a warm sensation radiating up them and through my body. Spontaneously, an uncanny impression etched itself in my mind: I was holding the hands of someone who understood and cared for me. That feeling of union was a powerfully emotional sensation. Tears welled up in my eyes as I slowly surveyed the silvery dark forest and sea beneath me. They were tears stirred not by any sadness but by a mysterious and authentic understanding that my beating heart had finally subsumed into a heart far more dispassionate and boundless than the one in my chest. The string of stars before me, the chalkboard, revealed something I thought I had known but realized I hadn't until that moment had come, enticingly incomplete as it would have to be. A fearless spirit was bursting from me, my imagination making it tangible, and the reality caused a warm shiver to run through me.

Just like the cleansing rain that had fallen on and off that day, washing away the dust and grime that had collected over time, everything I sensed had transfigured—tendrils stretching forth supporting new limbs.

During that moment of recognition and appreciation, three things happened simultaneously: clouds swept over the moon, plunging all into deep darkness; a steady rain began to fall; and like a nerve reacting to touch, I perceived behind me a presence that had arrived in the same unexpected manner as during my first nocturnal visit to the island. In all the scenarios I had contemplated in the days leading up to my quest, I had never considered I might encounter her spirit at the top of the lighthouse. My mind held no doubt that it was "her," in much the same way people can sense the sun on their faces when their eyes are closed. Then I heard, faintly at first but rapidly rising in intensity, the incongruous sound of ticking as if an antique wall clock was floating across the shadowy room behind me. Unlike a corporeal clock, this ticking sped up and slowed down as though in pursuit of a rapidly evolving thought.

Somehow, I knew with certainty that this sound—never mentioned in the legends—was there only to get my attention. It had a warm quality about it, something gentle and personal. Instinctively, I started to turn my head but stopped. In that instant, in the way crickets begin to sing at nightfall, and just as inconspicuously, the ticking reconstituted as a faint weeping before giving way to a feminine sigh. My mind painted the dark in vibrant splashes of bright colors, which abruptly ceased when a profound silence ensued. Had my visitor gone? I stood as still as a stone, listening intently behind me when I heard soft breath, an intimation of movement, the lightest of footfalls, and rustling fabric. Looking down at the narrow gallery beneath my feet, I saw blue phosphorescence emanating from the doorway and flowing through the space between my shoes. I knew tacitly that Charlotte Pauley was there looking at me and beyond, the black rainswept world.

The air around me had become thick water, and as I navigated it, I realized I could sense ripples within that water. A delicately directed agitation allowed me to feel her joy, to discern the happy tears on her face because I was there with her. My tears, an acknowledgment I knew she could sense. There could be no mistake this time: I was not from her family or the world of lightkeepers, but that didn't seem to matter. As if harnessed to act as her arms, the wind embraced me, alive with electricity. I started shivering, not because I was cold but from elation. Then I felt warm, too, knowing that the fear that had held me tightly in its grip was gone. That dread had merely been a veneer of darkness, and somewhere exists a mind that knows how many times my heart has beat and how many more it has to go. Within that mind also exists the exact number of steps Charlotte Pauley's spirit will ultimately take, including the few I'd just heard, which led to her standing behind me to share a view that in time would pass too.

I had crossed a powerful but terribly thin frontier and no longer feared being alone atop that abandoned lighthouse, cut off from the outside world on a dark night. Just as I knew the spirit of Charlotte Pauley no longer feared being alone, I could feel her there just as I could feel the wind-directed raindrops hitting and running down my face. Looking up, I watched the blue light flooding from the lamp room grow stronger, silhouetting my body against a canvas composed of darkness and rain. Then a second outline appeared, joining with mine. It was that of a woman, her dress clearly delineated, arms hanging passively at her sides. This form moved in closer to stand directly behind me. Together we were looking out over Declaration. With the miraculous that was the spirit of the Blue Lady joining with me, a novice of magic, we rebuilt our surroundings. Giving way, the Blue Room washed over me on waves of light, roaming freely outward in all directions. Far from somber or melancholy, the blue light spilling around me recalled in sublime detail the summer sky that had witnessed Ally and me kissing for the first time. The conviction arose within me that the light flooding from that lantern room was capable of providing a signal of hope for all fortunate enough to fall within its path.

Overcome with great calm and infinite peace, I stepped back inside the door. I was being offered a chance few ever were. The Blue Lady was there with me, and I had to act right then or sacrifice the opportunity to confront what people like Dean Knight and Principal Broadbent would have insisted was mere superstition and fantasy. An intoxicating feeling of elation seized me but was instantly matched by a wave of terror. All the stories, the folklore I'd absorbed, had formed images in my mind as solid as the lighthouse itself. What if I turned to be met by a deranged, hollow-eyed ghost existing only through the power of her madness and her desire to destroy those too naïve to stay away? With effort, I discarded these thoughts, as all I had felt since sensing her presence was a welcoming peace, and I turned to stare at the glowing room behind me. The sight was almost too much to take in. The entire space was bathed in a powerful but hazy light, its source beyond anything I could have envisioned. Only a couple of feet in front of me was a smiling young black girl about my age, wearing a coarse one-piece frock. Her lips didn't move, but I felt her interacting with my mind. The island's natural beauty drew us there—all of me and the part of her she had chosen to leave there. I found myself swimming in her dark brown eyes that told me so many things: that she had been enslaved and often lost herself in daydreams as I did, in the trees and birds and the sea.

Then her eyes grew tormented, and sad tears began rolling down my cheeks. She turned around to reveal the most horrifying wounds I'd ever seen crisscrossing her back. I knew then that she had been killed as the ultimate punishment for her inability to act as the property another assumed she was. My punishments had stung, but I could never comprehend the depths of her hell. She then turned back towards me and put a hand to her heart as a just discernible smile formed on her lips. She nodded slowly, conveying to my mind that I had been the first to return to see her again, the first friend she'd had in an eternity. At that instant, a drowsiness I couldn't fight overwhelmed me. I felt like I was floating deep within her eyes as the bluish light enveloped me warmly, and I slowly crumpled to the floor, where I curled up, closed my eyes, and surrendered to a sleep that came from deep within. Every ounce of energy seemed to drain from me, and like a twig caught up in the raging current of a rain-swollen river, I floated away on a course I could only obey.

16

I opened my eyes to see dawn light flooding through the window and door of the lantern room, painting everything in warm vermilion, persimmon, and tangerine. Staring at the hexagonal ceiling, I broke into an astonished smile. As extraordinary, even mind-boggling, as it was, I had come face-to-face with a ghost who communicated directly with my mind before I fell into a deep and rejuvenating sleep that had lasted the entire night. Lying there, I felt the cypress wood planks beneath my hand, which cradled my head. Then a dizzying sense of disorientation hit me when I felt something soft and warm covering me. Slowly raising myself on an elbow, I stared in complete bewilderment at the afghan draped across me. Pushing myself into a sitting position against the near wall, I remembered leaving it inside my backpack on the watch room floor the night before. After rubbing my eyes to make sure what I was seeing was real, I ran my hands through my hair and recalled everything that had led to my miraculous meeting with Charlotte Pauley, a woman who had died on Declaration eighty-nine years earlier. Charlotte Pauley! A huge smile reawakened on my face at the thought of it all. Holding the afghan up in awe, unable to contain an overflowing joy, I hollered a sincere "Thank you!" that reverberated throughout the tower.

The previous night came back to me as if a switch had been hit. The spirit I had confronted, had communed with, wasn't Charlotte Pauley—the girl who had stood before me radiating blue light, wearing a beautiful smile and a dress that was little more than rags sewn together was definitely *not* Charlotte Pauley. Her face! I now knew with certainty, the message having been transferred to my mind to be uncovered upon awakening, like a tiny ember growing into a blazing light, that she had been a slave of wealthy planter Pierce Gibbons, a slave viciously murdered at his hands!

That young girl, not Charlotte Pauley, was the ghost of Declaration Island. Something within her spirit compelled her to watch over the forests, marshes, and vast empty beaches, perhaps to prove that understanding, calm, and beauty could triumph over blind hatred, terror, and domination. She watched over all the buildings that remained as well, including the lighthouse built years after her death. The ghost of a child, she was drawn to the long-abandoned lighthouse just as I had been.

So many thoughts were spinning like dervishes, dancing in my mind, that I knew I'd need to wait a bit before standing. In my present state, I could concentrate only on the essence of what had unfolded: I had ventured to the Declaration lighthouse explicitly to face the Blue Lady, which in a broader sense meant confronting my fears. I felt nothing short of giddy to recall that I'd encountered her spirit only to discover her immeasurable gentleness. Stories change to suit the person recounting the tale, altering elements as they see fit. She had no reason to visit me, especially after I'd fled in terror after our introduction. At least, that's what I initially thought, but then I was overwhelmed to realize she did have a reason. We needed our brief encounter to validate ourselves, to empower ourselves. To give ourselves that most extraordinary of things: a second chance. I felt a vitality, tangible, electric, veritably bursting forth from my mind, my heart, the very depths of my soul.

All of it was too much to take in at once, so I stood up, clutching the afghan, swung myself down to the watch room, grabbed my backpack, and nearly levitated down the spiraling stairs. The forest was alive with waking sounds and smells so intense I could almost see the invisible sound waves and molecules scenting the air. Surrounding me in a glorious cacophony that seemed to echo my rejoicing were the competing twittering, trills, and whistles of painted buntings, Carolina wrens, chipping sparrows, blue jays, grackles, blackbirds, and Carolina chickadees. Birds were everywhere, moving from branch to branch; bees hovered among the myriad of flowers spilling throughout the woods, and I knew that somewhere unseen, she was reveling in it all too.

Racing to my hidden moped on legs that felt like they could run forever, I made sure to sidestep the banana spiders that were out tending their vast webs. Everything around me was living in harmony, a balance with which I had no right to interfere. I felt connected to the island in a way I hadn't understood was possible before, allowing my roots to find nutrients that the green all around me had no difficulty uncovering. I was reaching out a hand to steady myself and felt immense joy in assisting the girl's spirit to do the same, partaking generously in the interrelation of everything there. The real Blue Lady had graciously opened the door I walked through with eyes open, discovering acceptance could be mine, confidence too, but also knowing I needed to leave just a bit of my insecurity at the threshold as an offering to be sure I never became any of the things I had feared.

Rainwater that had collected in beads on my Vespa now rolled off freely in streaks as I crossed back over the causeway at speed—carrying a knowledge many wouldn't entertain, much less acknowledge—reveling in the jubilation that the island was a friend once again, one that had offered a secret part of itself to enable me to grow. Why did the bigger world commonly neglect these mystical threads, securely leading those willing to follow them to their beginnings and ends in such a fragile accord of affirmation? Because although mostly invisible, they are as strong as any chain or rope that the imagination can conceive.

Through the kitchen door window, I saw my mom doing dishes, and without a word, I walked up behind her and hugged her. She smiled warmly at me as she looked over her shoulder.

"I don't know what that's for, Ashey, but I like it."

Too often, in the maze of youth, we forget to show love because of our self-absorption. But once in a while, the extraordinary can cause us to break from this pattern.

Turning to me, my mom looked me up and down. "Didn't think I'd be seeing you until this afternoon. How was your movie marathon?" She lightly ran her fingertips over the side of my head. "It doesn't look like you slept too well...or showered."

"I slept really well, actually," I told her truthfully. "I'm gonna take a shower now."

In my room, while rifling through the dresser to find a shirt to wear, I hesitated as I touched my Triumph *Allied Forces* T-shirt. Its arresting design of a gleaming Flying V guitar with a sword comprising the neck and head brought back the memory of kissing Ally high atop the lighthouse. The song "Magic Power" from that album accompanied that perfect kiss, serving magnificently as the soundtrack to the most thrilling moment of my life. Then suddenly, an impulse took hold, and I knew there was something I needed to do as soon as I had washed up and changed.

Yelling from the foyer by the front door, I alerted my mom that I was heading out again and would be back in a few hours.

"Don't you want anything to eat?" she yelled after me.

"I ate at Carlo's," I lied.

Clutching the T-shirt in one hand against the handlebar, I rode with purpose directly to Zippy's Ice Cream Parlor in Sheltered Harbour. The sun was rising steadily in a sky as blue as I had ever seen; every cloud from the night before brushed away. Zippy's opened at 11:00, and by the time I was pulling my moped up on its kickstand in the parking lot, it was already 11:30. Through the wide bay window, I saw that Ally was alone behind the counter, looking ridiculously cute in her apron and red striped soda jerk hat. As the tinkling bell on the door announced my arrival, I was glad to see she was alone, not having considered what I would do if her friend Phoebe were working with her. Unlike Jemcraw's, I didn't mind my presence being announced, especially when Ally looked towards me, it brought such a pretty smile to her face.

"Oh my God, Ash, what are you doing here?"

I walked up to the counter, holding the shirt behind my back. "Something amazing happened last night at the lighthouse."

Her expression was one of total surprise. "The lighthouse?"

"Yeah, a lot of really important things seem to happen to me there," I said without further explanation. Then, thrusting my hand toward her, I held out the T-shirt.

"The most important thing was with you, and, well, I want you to have this." To make my intention clear, I added, "It's just a gift; there's nothing else attached to it."

She took it from me, holding it at arm's length in both hands. As she looked at it, her eyes narrowed before slowly widening, her expression telling me she was traveling far away from the counter of an ice cream parlor—somewhere far wilder, untamed.

Her voice rising in pitch, she said, "Triumph Allied Forces. This is the album that song comes from!"

We both knew the song; there wasn't a need to say more.

"Yup." I made a little placating gesture with my hand. "I just want you to have it as a reminder of a great day."

At that moment, Phoebe emerged from the back room. To save Ally from an awkward moment, I shook my head. "Ya know, none of these flavors are what I was lookin' for." Turning, I returned to the door, referencing that Triumph song I would forever associate with our time at the lighthouse. "I need somethin' more young, wild, and free. You know, somethin' with a little more magic power in it."

With that, I glanced back momentarily over my shoulder. Ally flashed me a furtive smile while Phoebe rolled her eyes, humorlessly chuckling as she turned away.

When I'd told Ally that something amazing had happened the night before at the lighthouse, not only was it true, but it was still happening. I felt as if a light was emanating from me, and I wore a smile that accompanied me all the way to my next stop.

As I pulled up, Carlo was outside trimming the edge of his driveway with a weedwhacker. Alerted by the hum of my two-stroke motor, he tossed the tool aside and trotted excitedly toward me. He grabbed my hand in both of his with a firm grip and shook it vigorously. The sincerity of that gesture matched the look he wore, a mixture of relief and approval. Words spilled impatiently from him.

"Hey man, I was just thinkin' about ya, hopin' you survived spending the night with the Blue Lady...or whatever else you might've come across." His eyes instantly widened as he seemed taken by another thought. "You didn't have to deal with any creepy people, did ya?"

Shaking my head, I muttered, "Nah," and shut the motor off. With Carlo following just a couple steps behind me, I pushed the moped up the driveway, parking it next to his, then took my helmet off and placed it on the seat.

"But I had doubts I'd make it through the night. I'll tell ya that." In a sudden flash of awareness, I knew what I had to say had as much to do with him as it did with me. Once we'd entered his house, he motioned to head out onto the back porch as he sidestepped into the kitchen and flung the refrigerator door open. Falling into an Adirondack chair, I stared out over the marshes of Mungen Cove, immediately falling into a reverie, replaying the previous night's events in my mind. I was startled when Carlo handed me an ice-cold Coca-Cola and pulled up a chair next to mine. Knowing I could skip any preliminaries, I gazed out again over the water and quietly uttered two words I knew would require no explanation. "She appeared."

Carlo threw his arms out before him. *"What?*... Seriously?... What happened?"

"Well, just like here, I imagine, it rained on and off all night, and after having to really psych myself up...." I leaned forward and looked intently at Carlo. "I had to, like, conjure Paul Di'Anno,...you know to lead the way and to say what I needed to hear to get my ass into the forest." Carlo being Carlo, the Paul Di'Anno comment required no further elaboration.

"When I got to the lighthouse, though, I had no one else but myself to rely on." I shook my head. "It's darker over there at night than anything you can imagine...I mean *pitch black.*" I put emphasis on those last two words to drive home just how separated I had been from the ordinary world, the one presided over by a semblance of security.

Carlo gave a slight nod, staring at me, hanging on to every word.

"If getting through the forest was a challenge, climbing the lighthouse kinda felt like jumping out of a plane and then realizing you forgot a parachute. When I got to the top of the stairs and hauled myself up to the Blue Room, I walked out onto the gallery, and as I was standing there, all at once, I heard this weird ticking, like an old clock, but before I could take in that it couldn't be a clock, it changed into the sounds of someone walking up and standing right behind me. Right then, this blue light flooded out from the room, and then...." I found myself pausing, scarcely able to absorb the words coming from my mouth.

"Then what?" Carlo prodded impatiently.

"I don't know how it worked, but it was like the sheets of rain and the darkness became a solid mass, almost like a mirror, and as I stared at it...*her* outline appeared next to mine, framed in the light, reflected at me."

"You mean the Blue Lady?"

I nodded, searching for words. "Yeah, but the Blue Lady isn't Charlotte Pauley—"

"Whad'ya mean it isn't Charlotte Pauley?" Carlo interrupted.

"The ghost is this girl...a black girl who was killed by the slaveholder who grew cotton over there before the Civil War, Pierce Gibbons. Remember I told you about that dude."

Carlo shook his head in wonder, waiting for me to say more, but confusion crossed his face. "So ya musta looked right at her to see who she was, huh?"

"I wasn't gonna turn around at first—"

Carlo nodded.

"But how many chances do you get to meet a ghost? I mean, I didn't want the opportunity to pass me by and wonder forever what was there just behind me." Her image flashed into my mind just as clearly as the night before. "So, like I said, it was this black girl. She had these intense brown eyes, and she smiled at me. She was barefoot and was wearing like a work dress."

Carlo's expression was intense, his eyes wide. "You're blowing my mind, dude!"

"Well, that ain't all of it. The blue light that was filling the room was coming from *her!* I mean, the Blue Room was really the blue room, man! But the weirdest thing, the coolest thing, was that we understood each other without saying anything. She made me realize that it was important I'd taken the risk to see her, and just by facing my fear of going out there, I felt stronger. You know, 'cause I pushed myself knowing that I might've been wrong, but I followed an instinct that told me I had to do it."

Unblinking, Carlo listened, taking in every word.

"But I wasn't wrong, and I didn't turn back, and for one of the first times, well with Ally too, I risked it, and far from regretting something I hoped to have, well, I had it, y'know?"

Seeming to express an inner voice more than responding to me, Carlo simply said, "Yeah, I do." Then, he nodded with finality, breaking from his momentary trance. "I really do."

━━━━ On Tuesday, only three days later, I was hit again by an unseen arrow that had the strange effect of hurting and healing in equal measure. Carlo and I entered gym class, which remained a place where we could typically look forward to an hour of decompression from the pressures of the day, often hidden around the next corner. When Ms. Burns announced we'd be playing basketball, Carlo and I decided on the spur of the moment to dress out and have a go at it. A consequence of our haste in heading into the locker room was that we hadn't seen everyone assembling on the court, but I felt the instant urge to throw up at what greeted us.

Of all the possible choices Ms. Burns could have selected for her aides that day, it was none other than Brice and Trey! An unbelievable twist that made me feel as if the Cosmic Joker had set aside his other victims to revel exclusively in my discomfort. I overheard Ms. Burns telling a student that the regular aide, Boykin, was out sick. Our previous confrontation notwithstanding, his presence and demeanor were more akin to the recurring itch caused by a mosquito than the more explosive aggression of the other two. They were in an altogether different league. Their boldness and intensity had steadily ratcheted up since the prior school year, conditioning me to fear like one of Ivan Pavlov's dogs.

I glanced at Carlo and shook my head. "Look who's helping today." Carlo's eyes narrowed to slits. "Yeah, I see."

His intense focus wasn't the reaction I expected, but I was so distracted by my discomfort and wish that I hadn't dressed out that I asked no further questions.

If things weren't bad enough already, we learned we weren't even going to play basketball but were instead to spend the class in small groups working on the game's mechanics: free throws, lay-ups, jump shots, and dribbling. Ms. Burns randomly chose Carlo and me to start practicing lay-ups in the group headed by Brice. To make matters worse, Ally was in the adjacent group overseen by Trey, practicing free throws at one of the mobile nets set up at half-court. Thinking how much I really wanted to avoid being embarrassed in front of her again, I glanced over and was surprised to see her smiling face watching me closely with no attempt at concealing it. Was I seeing things? I couldn't shake the feeling that her unguarded smile was intentional.

Shaking his head with each of my attempts, Brice was a fount of encouragement: "Wow, that really sucked, Ash....Why are you even trying?... You play like a girl, maybe you should try out for the girl's team." Then he added the coup de grâce with a self-satisfied smile, "Never mind, we know what a perv you are around them, don't we?"

Encouraging another group at the far end of the court with their jump shots, Ms. Burns remained oblivious to us. Several students had gathered on the bleachers between the nets Brice and Trey were assigned to, taking a breather before moving on to the next circuit station. To my chagrin, these included Ally and her friend Regan. Recognizing another ripe opportunity to embarrass me in front of an audience, Brice gestured in a circular motion toward me. "Am I the only one who thinks that something stinks in this general area?"

Waiting indifferently for his next group to assemble, Trey swung around, letting loose a wheezy cackle in tandem with several kids on the bleachers, including Regan, whose ringing laughter provided a familiar accompaniment. I felt my face flush with shame, and I couldn't look at Ally. Then something just happened. Too many fateful things had breached the earlier barrier that had circumscribed all my actions. Whatever the catalyst, I snapped. Looking Brice right in his eyes, I shook my head and laughed loudly and mockingly.

"You're one to talk. Have you looked at your own face lately? You scorch retinas and shatter mirrors with it! You're a walking, talking pizza with extra pepperoni that someone just puked on."

Timid, scattered snickering broke out in the bleachers along with the small group Trey was supervising nearby. Like the wick of a cartoon cannon just lit, I was moving towards the *ka-boom!*

"Your head's an enormous red zit that's gonna explode like Mount Vesuvius and encase all the unlucky locals nearby who won't be discovered for like a thousand years, still frozen with the same expressions of agony on their faces they had when they drowned in your pus." If nothing else, nobody could claim I'd never picked up anything in history class.

The faint smiles of surprise and tentative giggling now erupted into robust open-mouthed laughter, the loudest coming from Trey of all people. I felt that I was back on stage with Steaming Broth. A stage that had been only a few feet away from where I was then standing, and just like with The Broth's performance, I fed off the palpable energy building around me.

"The smell you're talking about is coming from right under your red pustulating nose. It's called *your face...* your rancid pizza face that you need to do something about...*like now!*"

Laughter was all-encompassing as I slowly scanned the faces around me. I felt as if I'd been hypnotized and had just woken from a spell. Accentuated by his deep dimples, Carlo's expression was of an overgrown baby enraptured by a spinning mobile, while Regan, the weights that held her face in place momentarily forgotten, was positively beaming. However, the biggest prize was when my eyes landed on Ally. She was standing, leaning forward with her hands dangling freely at her sides with a face the color of a ripe peach, framing the prettiest unchecked smile I'd ever seen.

Looking left and right in a daze, Brice feebly said, "Whatever."

"Not *whatever*, man; your face is a stinking, rotting pizza. Don't you get it? You're smelling *yourself!*"

To his tanned and inflamed red face was added another shade of red. He was blushing.

Then, the moment that seemed like it couldn't get any better somehow did.

Ally reached down and grabbed the bottom of her gym shirt, pulling it off to reveal another shirt underneath. The words on it read, "Triumph *Allied Forces.*" Holding the gym shirt high over her head, she tossed it behind her onto the bleachers next to Regan, whose mouth was wide open in astonishment. I felt exactly like her expression.

Before I could process the sensory bombardment my brain was under, Ally broke from her group and walked toward me. Past Trey, past Brice, she came, walking right up to me, at which point she pulled me against her, pressed her lips against mine, and imparted a kiss that rivaled, maybe even surpassed, the first kiss we shared high atop the lighthouse. In front of everybody, we were kissing, making it known in no uncertain terms and leaving no room for doubt that we had been a couple. Magic is what it was. Magic I never knew could transcend the boundaries of Declaration Island. A high-pitched, screeching sound pierced the air as Ms. Burns whistled and strode purposefully toward us from the other side of the court.

"What's going on over here? Kissing is not one of the activities we're working on today."

Punctuated with animated murmurs and bewildered laughter, the entire class huddled around Ally and me while Ms. Burns shook her head, chastising Brice and Trey.

"You two are supposed to be my eyes and ears where I can't be."

Disoriented by how fast the situation he thought he was controlling had changed, Brice thrust his hands forward, sputtering fragmentary words before she cut him off.

"That's all right, Brice. You and Trey just get your groups back in order." Hands firmly planted on her hips, she looked first at Ally, then at me. "And you two... I don't even really know what to do or say."

She scrutinized Ally. "Miss, you're the last person I would've ever expected a problem from."

Ally looked down, sporting a bashful smile, while I crossed my arms, striking a casual, "Yeah, whatever" pose. My face wore a smirk created by confidence borne only out of the rarest circumstances when the spirits, chance, or just pure luck intervene, and the world smiles upon you, allowing joy, if only for a glorious moment, to reign supreme. Separating us, Ms. Burns told Ally to follow her back to the other end of the court to practice jump shots while I should sit on the bleachers to "cool off."

I'd forgotten about Carlo and everything else until he jovially smacked my back, plopping down beside me with a huge smile. "Man, that was one of the most unexpected comebacks I've ever seen."

I couldn't help but notice that his whole demeanor had changed. He radiated the impression of someone unguarded, even carefree, as casual as if we were hanging out at Tab's pool, and he grinned mischievously and leaned back, resting elbows on the next tier of bleachers.

"Or maybe I should say rebound in keeping with the whole basketball focus of the day."

Still in a daze, not wholly convinced I wasn't dreaming, I could only shake my head. "I'm not really sure what happened." How could I be? Following such a dramatic acceleration and jarring stop, I had to contend with the resulting whiplash. Trying to comprehend how Ally had gone from keeping our one-time relationship a tightly guarded life-and-death secret to kissing me in front of the whole gym class had my head spinning.

As it turned out, the wait to discover the source of Ally's devil-may-care attitude was short-lived. By the time Carlo and I exited the locker room, concluding the most incredible gym class I'd ever attended, she was nowhere in sight. Carlo nudged my arm, alerting me to something impossible not to notice as we returned to our lockers in the Upper School. All the kids we passed were infected by a hysteria manifest by barely concealed laughter, surreptitious finger-pointing, and myriad expressions of morbid curiosity. I was well accustomed to such behavior but not this astonishing variety. Far from negative, the reactions were of disbelief and admiration at my unexpected victory over Brice. The feeling was far better than being singled out as an object to be mocked, and I was catching a contact high from it. I momentarily imagined Carlo and me as Black Sabbath's Geezer Butler and Bill Ward making our way through an airport terminal as starstruck fans gazed upon us in awe.

The animated voices grew to a crescendo as I felt a tap on my shoulder. Swinging around defensively, as was my default setting, I was met by a smiling but rather serious-looking Ally. With people gawking, transfixed on our every movement, she handed me an elaborately folded note, making eye contact only for a split second. Her voice was muted and small.

"I need to tell you something, and this is the best way for me to do it."

Holding the note up to my face, I basked in the faint smell of perfume it exuded, sending a warm tingle of excitement through me. Possibly noticing the buoyancy of my bearing, Ally put her hand gently on mine and shook her head. "Don't read it now. Wait until I've walked away."

She hesitated before glancing at me again. "Then we can talk later."

Her expression was inscrutable as she turned away, disappearing into the chattering, fidgeting crowd. Slumping down next to Carlo in Mr. Box's class, I hastily unfolded the letter. All mystery instantly vanished as Ally's actions found a context.

Ash, please don't be mad at how I'm telling you this. It's the only way I could. I knew there was a boy out there like you, and I'm so happy I found him. I will always remember the time we had together, and I need you to know that I'm so sorry for all the problems and pain I put you through. Okay, here goes. I just found out yesterday that my dad accepted a job offer from his brother in St. Augustine. We're going to be moving there the first week of October. Everything has happened so fast, I can't take it all in. I just want you to know that I love you and will miss you terribly. Maybe we will see each other again after I move. Who knows! I mean, Florida isn't in another galaxy. I just want you to know

that I'll never forget everything we did together, especially on *our* beautiful island. You know how to kiss, boy!
(She drew a smiley face here.)

Love you, Ally
(She drew several hearts here.)

It was clear Ally had written it the night before while the shock and surprise of being uprooted were still sinking in. It explained her freedom and daring in gym class, as the gravity of the school's hierarchy no longer exerted any pull. However, I also realized her upcoming departure was the only reason she'd revealed her hand. I couldn't help but wonder what choices she'd make once she transferred to her new school. Would the previous pattern repeat itself, or would she walk with the spring in her step I'd seen on Declaration? I also knew that even though mobility had dramatically increased with the introduction of a Vespa, Florida might as well have been in another galaxy. Although my heart felt empty, I was surprised to find myself smiling.

After school, I sat on my moped for a half-hour, hoping Ally would appear, but she never did. Leaning against the stucco wall of the gym, Carlo patiently indulged me as Scott and Tab, in turn, stopped by to tell me how "The Gym Kiss," as everyone now referred to it, was the talk of the school. "You really are the double-oh-seven of Leggatts," was Tab's amiable comment. From a goofy, red-faced, laughing Scott, it was simply, "Dude!" accompanied by a high five. I wasn't surprised to also learn that in the mere span of Mr. Box's class, the school's damage control patrol had gone into overdrive to protect the status quo. The word was that Ally had lost a bet, gently nudging the wheel back into its well-worn rut, allowing school life to continue much as before.

Carlo's impatience won out, and we rode away, once more Hells Angels who didn't take anything from anyone, any time, ever. In some small way, this attitude was a little more real after the day's events— events that had changed me permanently, even though I wasn't aware of it then. As I glanced at my brother of the wind, who sported a bit of a scowl (the whole biker construct), he gave me an almost imperceptible nod. My eyes then drifted up to the sun pouring its rays down on us. I felt as good as I could ever remember, even with so many things left dangling in the air. That questions still needed answering was fine. Inhaling deeply the wind blowing on my face, I held it for a moment before letting it all go—letting go of things I didn't even know I was capable of until that very moment had come.

    ▬▬ We become so consumed with our issues that it's amazing what we miss in those close to us. Of course, I knew that the ostracism we dealt with daily had affected Carlo, but I never thought of it more than fleetingly. After all, he was a big dude, a strong guy. I assumed the barbs that stuck in me ricocheted easily off him. But just a day after my confrontation with Brice, Carlo was thrust into an unexpected skirmish of his own. After school, he'd gone into Sheltered Harbour to pay his dad a visit at his office and afterward had stopped in at Jemcraw's to grab a Coke and candy bar. As Carlo rounded the building, heading for his moped, who should quite literally bump into him but his arch-nemesis Trey. A guy, who for reasons only he could answer, had tried to engineer a humiliation the previous school year that would have been next to impossible to live down had it not been for the fortuitous appearance of Dean Knight and James. The incident had disturbed Carlo, festering in his mind long after I'd filed it away as just another indignity.

"Who d'we have here?" Trey said, puffing his chest out while sizing up Carlo. "Better watch what ya eat, or you'll become an even bigger girl than ya already are." With that, he shoved Carlo, causing him to spill Coke on his shirt.

"Aww, looks like ya got a stain on yer blouse."

Carlo's eyes narrowed when he later recounted the story to me, focusing on his unseen adversary. As his arms flailed wildly, endangering anyone within reach, his face contorted in a bravura performance that would have made Stanislavsky proud. Then, in one fluid motion, releasing a pressure that had built up in his mind since the earlier humiliation, Carlo threw the soda can on the ground and shoved Trey backward. Stunned by this gesture, Trey threw a punch that Carlo partially blocked with his forearm while releasing a powerful jab with his other hand that landed squarely on Trey's nose. Blood exploded from his nostrils in a thick spray as he reeled backward on his heels, tripping over a concrete parking block before thudding unceremoniously onto his ass.

Advancing, Carlo looked down on his now vanquished boogeyman. "Not so tough without your posse, huh?"

Sitting up, Trey cupped his nose with both hands, feebly trying to stop the thick stream of blood pouring down his face onto his shirt as Carlo grabbed his discarded can, stood over his dazed victim, and poured what remained over his head.

"Here's a Coke—how about a smile?" he said, tossing the now-empty can off Trey's belly.

Without looking back, Carlo got on his moped, lit a cigarette, set it firmly in the corner of his mouth, and rode off, no doubt feeling a bit like a moped-riding variation of a character from the movie *Conan the Barbarian*. Whenever I recall this incident, I envision Carlo riding off like a victorious Conan after beheading his nemesis Thulsa Doom. As a result, Scott and I referred to him as "Carlo the Barbarian" for months afterward.

When they harassed us, I don't think Brice, Trey, or Otto ever considered that one of us was just as big as they were. Maybe the long hair threw them off, but the good-hearted Carlo could take only so much. If you repeatedly poke a bear, prepare to face the consequences. Trey had to face a world of questions at school the following day when he arrived sporting a red, broken nose, along with two black eyes, which added a touch of contrast. As it turned out, besides being a fine drummer, Carlo had proven to be something of an artisan with his fists. No doubt the real story would have made Trey a laughingstock of the locker room, so he never implicated Carlo in his injuries.

Although our positions in the school hierarchy didn't alter significantly, the comments we'd had to endure decreased dramatically, if never vanishing completely. They had all but subsided when junior year rolled around, and our one-time antagonists graduated.

One thing that did completely stop was the physical attacks. Trey acquired a grudging respect for Carlo, nodding to him when they passed in the hallway and even becoming an impromptu roadie at that year's talent show, carrying Steaming Broth's amps and guitars on stage for us, belting out a hearty and sincere, "not a problem," when thanked. In Trey's eyes, I discovered Carlo had proven himself to be a man by standing up to him.

As with Brice, Trey's dad owned a shrimp boat, and it was only later that I pieced together scenes I had witnessed when Trey and his dad were setting out or returning on that boat in Sheltered Harbour. His father, whose skin was so dark from working his boat it resembled dyed leather, always harangued and berated Trey mercilessly, who responded like an animal receiving an electrical shock to the verbal and physical prods. With time, I realized Trey had learned to respect and defer to those who ruled with an iron fist. It was black and white, as simple as the motivation of a John Wayne character in one of his movies. It seemed likely that the bond between Trey and Brice had been strengthened by the abuse they both were subjected to by their fathers.

So, our actions reduced the monoliths that had taken center stage in my mind and Carlo's to figureheads, shrunk from the mythological to the prosaic. The pecking order of abuses revealed the equivalent of the Emerald City's wizard as nothing more than people hiding behind façades to shore up their insecurities. The triumphs we fought for were validating. But the battles had inflicted damage, the scars of which, at least for me, lay buried in a mental minefield, making themselves known only years later when I overacted to an otherwise innocuous word or a look from a stranger. Feelings of self-doubt from the high school harassment ran deep. When I later went to college, a place where I blossomed scholastically, merely walking the hallways or entering a classroom could often trigger anxiety and insecurity.

In the final analysis, Carlo and I were simply guys. We were not yet men, but we were becoming rough-sketch versions of them whether we were ready or not. With the hazards and dangers removed and the comfort of the years intervening, the "safe" nights and days that float on in perpetuity like the brackish lagoons on Declaration, creating ever-widening, ever-thickening circles, have allowed me to appreciate more profoundly the bravado, the absurd fun, and—how true it is—the idiocy of our daily actions. Yet, through fate, folly, and sheer goddamn luck, we remain.

▬▬▬ Any further discussion I had hoped to have with Ally didn't happen immediately. She was absent for the next couple of days at school, then avoided me at every turn on Friday. Her spontaneous act in gym class had brought her a lot of unwanted attention, and I can't say I blamed her for keeping a low profile, although it did feed into the growing gossip that the whole scene had been nothing more than a set-up. The following Saturday morning, I heard knocking at the front door that set Geezer and Eddie barking like the world was ending. As my mom and dad were at the pharmacy, I rolled out of bed wearing only my PJ bottoms and shuffled groggily down the hall with Geezer and Eddie running in excited circles, urging me towards the door.

Much to my surprise, standing there with a big smile on her pretty face, wearing that French braid I loved so much, was Ally. We stood on each side of the threshold as both dogs leaped up and down, pressing their paws on us and pushing off in turn, tails wagging so furiously they nearly became airborne. Framed by the doorway, as she'd been the first time she'd come over, she seemed a messenger of the sun, radiating warmth and light. It took me a second or two to realize she was wearing the T-shirt I'd given her at Zippy's. It's a shirt I've never been able to separate from the kiss in gym class or that moment.

Grabbing up my hands, she held them lightly, our arms extending down between us. Her voice was as sunny as the day awakening around me: "I *love* your outfit, sleepyhead." Not for the first time, but more precious because of the circumstance, her presence seemed to freeze time, enfolding me.

"I'm young, wild, and free, Ashley Howe, and you helped me see how totally fun it can be—especially when you love someone." Her face flushed lightly at this proclamation as if it had taken her a bit by surprise. "I'm gonna keep this shirt forever, and when I wear it, a little part of you will be there with me."

Her tone turned serious, and for a moment, I felt like we'd flashed forward into a future where we'd become two mature adults about to have a mature conversation.

"I'm sorry I wasn't at school for a couple of days after...you know... and then didn't talk to you yesterday." She looked down as if searching for the words she wanted. "I wanted to talk to you right away, but so many things were going through my head, and it's been so overwhelming that I guess I didn't know how to deal with anything else."

She furtively looked up at me.

"I figured that," I said.

"It's because I was feeling how much I loved you all over again,... and I think you might've been too."

"I was."

Wrapping my hands around her arms, I could see her eyes had become glassy, looking a bit like mine, I imagined. "But I never stopped feeling that way, Ally."

"Well, I mean, I'm leaving really soon, and we broke up, and I didn't want to start feeling so close again." Then, hesitating, she looked up again. "I just couldn't stand by when you stood up to Brice. I mean, I was so proud of you, and I just suddenly didn't care about where we were. I just wanted to kiss you and to let everyone know how wonderful I think you are."

Was it possible I was lying on the beach of Declaration with Ally? Because just then, it felt as if a wave had broken over us. Without a word, we kissed, then hugged each other hard. Ally's voice was somehow strong but fragile.

"I thought it would be easier to just avoid you until I left,...but I had to see you one more time, boy. You know, up close and personal."

"I'm really glad you did, girl." I found myself contending with a second wave that staggered me. "Magic like you doesn't come around that often, but when it does, you can't forget it.... I know I'll never forget you."

Pulling me close, she whispered, "I'll never forget you either."

Embracing tightly, we kissed again for what I knew would be the last time. The day before she left, we waved to each other from across the school parking lot. Since we had no say in her leaving, it seemed the way it needed to be.

She moved, just as she said, at the beginning of October, and although I thought I might see her again, I never have. My turn came just a couple of years later when my dad informed me we'd be moving to Chicago to allow him to take the head pharmacist position at a brand new Perry Drugs, which had just entered the Midwest market in 1981. The transition from a barrier island to Chicago was a culture shock that made the differences between Leggatts and Declaration stand out in an even greater relief as opposed to lessening it.

Even though our paths never crossed again, I can sometimes open a door, any door, and it opens onto the gallery of the Blue Room. There, spreading out as far as my eyes can see, is a view of treetops and the sea with salty air blowing strongly on my face. Next to me, centering the green and blue and sun with her pretty smile, is Ally. A smile time cannot touch or erase—bigger, freer than anything she ever allowed herself at school. For me, a moment unlocked, a door to anywhere, but most importantly, a door to belonging, to secrets revealed and mysteries explored by the action of one single step. Uncertainty itself is always a door to be opened.

It's never easy to detect the invisible, even when we think our eyes and ears are open. Assumptions close the door until all that's left is a sliver of light but too much room for prejudice to enter, filling in what cannot be seen. We just need to imagine the threshold, for there, the invisible waits until a step is made, a word is spoken, or a stone is kicked, revealing the edges of new worlds once concealed. For me, those worlds have included the best of friends, a girl, and a ghost. No doubt, one curse of memory is that it causes us too often to absolve ourselves from our complicity of guilt. Each moment is part of a perpetually uneven frontier. Human nature induces us to straighten the image until we can live with it. I entered into both the story of the Blue Lady and my relationship with Ally without clinging too stubbornly to reality, at least as others would define it. All of us possess a hierarchy of moments. Two that reside near the summit for me are kissing a girl high above the world and, within a chronological blink of an eye, bathing in the light of a ghost. I've found it crucial to remember that the air that flows from the lungs of creatures supports the nature around us, moving without prejudice as we should too, never losing sight that although equally ephemeral as people, we're equally capable of understanding that the core of our spirit is innocence.

Once I moved away from Leggatts into the strange northern lands, development continued to spread with increasing speed across the once sleepy island, evolving into a destination that would have been hard for anyone from 1982 to imagine. Over time, the wheels of this "progress" gained traction and speed, steering the island's destiny irrevocably towards a tourist-fed economy, attracting and dazzling investors and developers who razed pine forests, cabbage palm, and moss-draped live oak. On came vast resorts, hotels, villas, houses, malls, golf courses, wider roads, more stoplights, and all the added infrastructure, crime, and battles big and small. Development equated with progress as the new breed engaged in plans and investments with a zeal Leggatts had never seen before. The price of a few more inches of sand to call "their own." This new King Cotton made wealthy men and women that much richer with every freshly felled tree and each displaced deer, snapping turtle, and bird.

Greed, the delirium of fever that fed on the green of Leggatts, wasn't going to stop just because developers had run out of room to build. The virus spread to a new host, jumping Mitchell Inlet to the small island off Leggatts northern coast. Five years after my family's move north, with relentless inevitability, the disease made its way to the doorstep of the old lighthouse, where for so many years, the Blue Lady had kept a quiet vigil over her peaceful realm. The poetry of drowning boys and mysterious blue ladies meant nothing to developers when dollar bills replaced the leaves in the trees they surveyed. I often wonder if the Lady In Blue still sometimes stands where she stood with me all those years ago and, if so, what she perceives as she looks out over electric lights that dim the stars and hears motors and voices competing with the crickets and cicadas.

The lighthouse is still there, incongruous but content, added to the National Register of Historic Places, retaining her grace and dignity among the greens and fairways, houses, and roads that blanket the island. Moving through urban sprawl to the drone of motors, I've recognized the irony in the bull rush of an ever-growing humanity who flock to diminishing natural landscapes to recharge from the industrialized world they've created and cultivated. Yet, within that ever-shrinking Earth and overcrowding that desensitizes the individual, tarnishing the sparkle that freed my younger eyes, I retain two memories that refuse to diminish—one of a corporeal girl and the other, the spirit of one. Both taught me so much about what it means to be human. My mind then fills with thoughts of unseen currents, fish, horseshoe and blue crabs, alive and moving under the light chop of waves that fill in the reach between two bodies of water. If nothing else, my memory, like the water between islands, finds no resistance, just freedom to cross with ease to another place. A place now relegated to the mind.

In archaeology, there is a term "bulb of percussion" that is defined as "a cone-shaped bulge on a fractured surface of flint that is made by a blow applied at an angle," and this serves as a metaphor for our lives. All the bulbs of percussion are the choices we make, some more sure-handed than others, that alter and reshape us in surprising ways. Magic rises from our freshly revealed edges, like a beacon illuminating a pocket of night, as sudden changes remove flecks of the naïveté and innocence that armored our young selves. There should never be a wish to reseal those fractures—instead, embracing a surrendering, absorbing the new and gleaming surfaces that reveal and revel in new worlds of clearing blue and grey light. The often accidental blows we make blurring the allure of a simpler, reckless abandon, to become buoys tending the memory that part of youth will always remain, with a strength equal to that imparted from a mother to her child. Resounding, the percussions perpetually signal what we were and continue to become.

Beginning with the Blue Lady, in an ever-growing proportion since my boyhood days, I have sensed many other spirits too. The struggle for inner calm and joy connects my spirit to those of so many people I love, both alive and dead. The line that divides is often invisible, as are every one of the incredible things that make us who we are—revealed by the tide, a ribbon of sand appearing to let us know that the separation can be spanned.

After all, we are created from the impossible and should always consider it reasonable to expect the impossible.

For saintly patience, suggestions, and an unwavering faith in the story, my profound thanks go to my wife, Julie.

For reading early drafts and giving me invaluable feedback, I thank Judith Vanucci, Amy and Geoff Speiden, Susan Greenholdt, and Carole Hanger, who I also thank for being the best mom a guy could finally get to know at 46 years old. Richard Rankin for making his book *A New South Hunt Club* available to me. Michael Bartlett for offering his guidance and expertise.

Ruth Hull Chatlien for her masterful and enriching editing.

Jay Amberg for tightening and polishing.

Sarah Koz, for seeing the ghost attempting to materialize out of a work in progress—I believe the spirits directed me to your orbit.

To my friends: Eric Fronczak, without whom there would be no Carlo; Tad Leckman, without whom there would be no Tab; and the late Len Pantaleo, without whom there would be no Scott.

With love to my late parents, Joe and Nancy Shannon, for everything.

To all the musicians who pulled me up by the T-shirt to remind me that life is worth living—Uriah Heep, Black Sabbath, Judas Priest, Iron Maiden, Motörhead, and too many others to enumerate. You all helped save me from despair and added to the magic that is there if only we listen.

And to the genesis of the tale—a chilly, rainy night at the Hilton Head Rear Range Lighthouse, when a blue ectoplasmic mist reinforced something I already knew—the impossible is everywhere, but once in a while, it pops in to say, "How about this?"

Lastly, but certainly not least, a massive thank you to my successful Kickstarter campaign backers: Amy and Geoff Speiden, Carole Hanger, Cindy and Tim Arnold, Sheila Keating, Sharon Keating, Janina Ciezadlo, Margaret and Gene Zelek, Kari and Rob Fortelka, Alissa Messana, Ann Marie Hayes, John Keating, Paul and Monique O'Toole, Eric Fronczak, Denise Andrews, Dale Lorens, Anita Schaab, Marilyn Walsh, Hugh Keating, Sarah Bacus and Norm Resnick, Rick and Diana Heinz, Vera and Tom Shively, Sara Clarkson, Maureen Keating-Wolosick, Rosemary Kane, Charles and Geraldine Greenholdt, Leslie Rolison, John Speiden, Peggy Albachiara, Marlene Donovan, Mary and Bruce Robertson, and Kathy Wilburn.

A Ribbon of Sand is Mike Shannon's first novel. He spent several years of his youth in the South Carolina Low Country; the culture and natural wonders are woven into his soul. His fascination with folklore and the supernatural stretches back to those boyhood days—and he's had paranormal experiences signposting his life's journey.

Before turning his attention to fiction writing, Mike had poetry published in various literary journals in America and the U.K. He has also had articles in several publications, including a major piece in the English music magazine *Shindig*. Finding music as essential as air, he listens to everything from Black Sabbath to Bartók. Mike has a Bachelors degree in anthropology from Loyola University, Chicago, and presently lives in Westmont, Illinois with his wife Julie and cats Scrimm and Magers.

Made in the USA
Monee, IL
13 November 2023

46393094R00177